EVERYTHING WILL BE ALL RIGHT

FINDING THEIR WAY HOME BOOK 2

CONSTANCE EMMETT

For Agnes, my grandmother— In the undiscovered country, standing in a Belfast street

FIRESTORM—MAY 1941

BELFAST NORTHERN IRELAND

*T*he sirens woke them at one o'clock in the morning. Seventeen-year-old Robert Henderson threw the bedclothes off, trapping the sleeping cat. His father barked from the doorway, "Close them curtains." The cat scrambled out from under and dashed between his feet.

The searchlights rotated through the window and transformed the little room where Robert had slept his entire life into an unfamiliar stage set. Briefly, the light picked out the large wall map of the North Atlantic bristling with the colored pins Robert attached following news reports of sea battles—white for Canadian, red for British, blue for American, yellow for rest of world, and black for German.

Frantically pulling the window closed and the blackout curtains to, Robert whipped around and knocked two ship models off the shelf and onto the crystal wireless set he'd just finished building. Listening to them clatter, he muttered, "Ach," picked up his waiting pile of clothes and school bag, jammed his feet into trainers and rushed into the hall.

"Florrie!" called his father as he clumped downstairs in his untied leather-soled oxfords, the torchlight bobbing. Entangled with the panicked cat at the bottom, he shouted, "Bloody cat!"

Juggling a handbag and too many clothes, his mother shep-herded Robert ahead of her to the top of the stairs.

After the bombing raid in April, the three Hendersons built tidy piles of clothes each night before bed, with shoes to be stepped into without bending and tying. Florrie's younger sister, Meg Preston, had advised her family to form this habit, based on her Women's Volunteer Service experience of having to leave the house at a moment's notice.

Carrying his folded school uniform and book bag, Robert took the stairs two at a time down to his waiting father. He had taken Aunt Meg's advice a step further and after a nightly bath, donned clean pants, vest and socks beneath a dark blue school tracksuit worn to bed each night. If the worst happened, he did not want to be found undressed in the street.

Picking her way carefully down the stairs, his mother shouted over the loud drone of airplanes, "We said we'd go down shelter last time, didn't we? Ralph!"

Standing at the bottom of the stairs and signaling them on, his father yelled, "Too late. They're here. Quick! Quick!" He gestured with urgency and the family ducked under the stairs and onto the mattress placed there for comfort during the raids.

His mother tossed her handbag and clothes to the back of the little space, wartime storage for their photos in albums and frames, and important documents. She squeezed in next to her seated son and her husband followed.

Robert watched the cat race from the kitchen to the parlor and back, skittering on the hardwood floor.

As fast as the drone of the planes intensified, sounding like a swarm of giant bees hovering over them, the booms and crashes of dropping bombs overwhelmed all sound. The ceilings and walls of the small house on Great Northern Street vibrated, hurting Robert's ears. Felt through the floor and mattress, the house shook at its foundation. The hall light flickered and died.

He felt his mother's arm go around his back and, glancing

left, watched her other arm curl around her husband's shoulders. Robert pulled away from her embrace.

At the first close blast, Robert curled forward to touch his forehead to his raised knees. Squeezing his eyes shut, he cupped his palms tightly over his ears and repeated the Lord's Prayer—waiting and praying for the end.

His mother pulled his huddled form to her and wrapped her arms around his head.

The house stopped shaking. Robert pushed out of Florrie's arms and sat up, listening. The crashes, booms and intense drone moved off, faded, and, finally, stopped. The rain of plaster dust lessened, becoming a thick mist swirling in the air.

Nobody spoke until the continuous all clear siren finished, a wait of two minutes, a lifetime's wait.

Ralph crawled out first. "Stay here. I want to check the upstairs."

"Ralph!"

"I'm all right, Florrie." As he walked back down the hall, the light of his torch twirled, picking out items on the coat rack, and the framed and embroidered "Peace be to this house, Luke 10:5" on the wall above the umbrella stand.

Robert listened to his father's hesitant tread moving up the stairs.

The hall light came on again just as the telephone rang. Robert and his mother looked at one another. "I'll go," said Robert.

She swung her arm out like a railway crossing barrier in front of his chest. "No."

Crawling out awkwardly, her broad backside blocked his view as she struggled to get to her feet. She walked to the kitchen, one hand holding the wall. He watched her hesitate before peeking inside, then entering.

Robert clambered out and was on his feet in the one smooth motion of youth. He walked into the kitchen and glanced at the old pendulum clock ticking on the fireplace mantel. It was not even half one in the morning.

Holding the heavy Bakelite receiver, Florrie said, "Aye, we're fine, I think, thank God. Ralph's checking the house now. Bout ye? Oh, aye? *They* were above us? How do you know? What? Have you heard from Meg or David? Hello? Lizzie, are you there? Hello? Hello? Lizzie? Operator?" After listening for a moment, then pushing at the handset cradle buttons impatiently, she said, "The line's gone dead—Lizzie and Tom are worried about their boys." Looking down quickly, she tightened the belt of her pink chenille bathrobe.

Ralph came into the room. "Upstairs looks all right, but we'll have to check the outside in the daylight. The searchlights are still going. I thought I heard the ack-acks." He sat down at the table.

"At least we *had* searchlights and ack-acks this time," said Florrie. She turned, filled the kettle at the old Belfast sink and placed it on the hob. "Lizzie thinks the RAF were here this time. She and Tom worried their sons were flying overhead in their Hurricanes, fighting the Germans."

"I thought Aunt Lizzie didn't know where they were stationed even," said Robert.

Florrie shrugged. "I don't know, but it must be very worrying for your aunt and uncle having their sons up in airplanes." Pointing at him, she said, "Don't *you* think of joining the RAF!"

The cat jumped onto Robert's lap, startling him. She settled and began purring. "Beatrice! Poor wee thing." Her claws began to knead gently into his tracksuit.

"Oh, aye? She nearly broke my neck for me." Ralph leaned over and petted her tortoiseshell head, gently stroking down the fur that stood up. "There, there, wee puss."

Florrie began to wipe the table clean. "Ach. There's this muck over everything again to clean." She threw the cloth down and sat down, her hand balled in a fist and held to her mouth. Tears ran down her face, making rivulets in the patina of dust on her cheeks.

"Me eyes burn, this grit's everywhere and it smells awful, like, like rotten eggs. I can't stand any more of this, I really can't." She gave over to crying into her open hands.

"I'll help c-clean, Mum, don't c-cry."

She pulled her hands away to say, "What if next time they drop a bomb on us? We're not safe here!"

His mother sobbed. Standing, Ralph bent down, put his arms around her and kissed her dust-covered hair, plaited down her back for bed. "Aye, that's right, lass, you have a good cry. But the Germans are interested in the dockyards and the ships, not us. Don't worry, love. And we'll work together like last time. We'll start upstairs. I'll mop the ceilings and walls, you dust the furniture and Robert will Hoover behind us, then we'll come downstairs and do the same. We'll wash all the bedding as a right little team. It'll take no time. Now, I'll make sandwiches and the tea. You rest yourself, love." Opening the cupboard, he took out a bottle of whiskey and poured three small glasses. Without comment, he placed one in front of his wife and one at his son's place. "First, get that into you and don't argue."

"He's too young to drink this."

"He's not. Sip it now, Robert—don't gulp it. It's what needed. I'm shaking like a leaf—I don't know about you two." Contrary to his own advice, Ralph downed his whiskey, poured another, and took the loaf out of the breadbox.

Wiping her eyes with a handkerchief, Florrie said, "How many more times before we're all killed? We had them fellas with their wee bombs in the '20s, but they never bothered us here. But now we've got the Luftwaffe over our heads...what's to become of us, Ralph? Should we leave the city?"

A chill rippled along Robert's spine. He took a sip and felt warmth and calm spread into his chest as he watched his father slice bread. From the shiny top of his bald head to the tips of his highly polished brown oxfords, Ralph Henderson was a beacon of calm and safety when something threatened his family.

"Ach, we'll be fine. The RAF will sort them, you'll see. Don't fret, lass."

The cat's purr grew louder as the house settled into quiet.

"It's amazing the electrics are back on," Robert said, "but I'll sort lamps and candles, in case."

Looking at him, Ralph said, "Go on, then. Good lad."

Belfast still smelled of the burning fires when the wind blew from the east and north, but the yellow miasma smelling and tasting of rotten eggs had dissipated. Robert ran home from the tram call on the Lisburn Road, a few blocks from the house. He wished it could have been a longer run, one without flapping bags to carry—a loose, free, long-distance run. He loved that sort of run along the Lagan River or along the Cave Hill ridge down into the city, the runs he took with the cross-country team at school. Shutting the front door, he stood in the hall catching his breath and listening to the sound of women speaking quietly. *Mum. Aunt Lizzie. Aunt Meg.* He hung his book and gym bags over the bannister and walked into the kitchen.

His mother and two aunts sat around the table, the tea things crowding the middle. Meg, the palest and thinnest sister even in normal times, looked drawn and tired, the purple circles under her eyes prominent. His mother was flushed, her dark hair tied up and covered in the wrap she wore when cleaning. Even though he saw Lizzie nearly every day, she looked older and thinner, a shrunken version of his buxom mother.

"Hiya."

Meg looked up at him and smiled. "Hiya, Curly. Grand to see you. I think you've grown since we last met—have you?"

"Here, have some tea, love," said his mother, pouring a cup, "and some sandwiches. Lizzie brought cake."

He sat down, used to the fuss made over him.

"Don't get your hopes up, mind. Not much of a cake with no butter and a thimble of sugar. I was saying I think wee Tom and Will flew Hurricanes over us the other night, protecting us from a worse bombing," said Lizzie, smiling and nodding.

"Hmmm?" he answered, pulling the knot in his striped tie loose.

Florrie said, "He has grown, just recently. Boys don't stop for years, do they? But Ralph is tall, and I am, so...would you just look at the jacket sleeves crawling up his arms?"

Flushing under the women's scrutiny, he pulled his arms off the table.

His mother looked at him a moment longer before continuing, "You were very late getting home. Is term over?"

Robert cursed himself for blushing. Ignoring her first comment, he answered, "I sat my last maths exam, my last exam period. At morning chapel they told us the summer term would continue, but by the end of the day, they called us back and cancelled the rest of term for the upper sixth. They'll post a letter to you and Da." He blew on his tea before sipping. "I'm lucky I could sit my last exam. I cleared out my cupboard, so I'm graduated."

His mother reached out to touch him, but he shied away a half-inch, enough that she noticed. She continued to look at him, her eyes narrowed.

"S-sorry I was late, Mum." His color deepened thinking about why he was late. After school was dismissed, he'd gone to the Royal Navy recruiting office in Belfast City Hall. After briefly waiting on a line consisting of two other bombing-inspired enlistees, he'd spoken to a recruiter who'd assured him he would be eligible to enlist with proof that he was seventeen years old with a passing school certificate.

The recruiter had lit a cigarette and said, "With no conscription in Northern Ireland and most men in this bloody country standing around with their hands in their pockets, even after these raids, we need every man we can find to protect King and country."

Robert had left the office realizing that when his school certificate arrived, he really could enlist, an action he'd spent many hours thinking about. As though in a trance, he'd walked out through the portico of the massive Victorian building to brilliant green grounds.

To reach his tram call across the square, he had to pass through a gauntlet of boys his age, lounging on the lawn and hurling vulgar epithets at the passersby. Turning their attention to Robert, several made kissing noises, while another offered to share a part of his anatomy, and the rest laughed. He'd hurried away, face burning.

Meg's hearty "Congratulations!" brought him back to the present.

"Our wee Tom and Will took the A levels in maths and physics, *and* passed the RAF exams," said Lizzie, chin up.

"And what is it you think he's done? He's only just taken A levels in maths and physics, and he's taken his general exams in history and Latin, too," said his mother too loudly, her flush deepening. "He's too young to join up and I hope he never does!"

Feeling a drop of his mother's rage, Robert watched Lizzie and thought, *Whenever I was forced to spend time in my aunt and uncle's house, wee feckin' Tom and Will pinched and punched me, sat on me till I couldn't breathe, and like those ones today, called me a faggot. Only, they made fun of my stutter while they were at it. "R-r-robert's a f-f-faggot!" I'd stagger out of their lair after those sessions like a tormented animal, but I never complained. RAF heroes are they now? I just may show them, alright.*

As Lizzie summoned her response, chest rising, Meg quickly interrupted, "Listen, I've got to get back. We've to return the canteen truck to the depot this afternoon. Tomorrow morning we'll buy the train tickets. Pray the trains are running. So, what do you say? Will you come? How many tickets am I buying?"

Pulling her annoyed gaze from Lizzie's and glancing quickly at Robert, his mother turned to Meg and said, "I have to talk to Ralph, but I'd like to go, take Robert to safety, if just for a wee while. I'm sure Ralph will agree, but I don't know he'll come. He just this minute got a steady job again." Florrie shook her head. "The daft man wouldn't leave the cat, to boot."

"The cat could come with you," said Meg. "We wouldn't mind."

Lizzie fidgeted, folding and refolding her napkin. "I, I want to stay, in case the boys get leave and come home. I wouldn't want to miss them. It wouldn't be nice."

"I'm sure the boys would wish you and Tom safely out of Belfast," said Meg.

Lizzie, her eyes darting from Meg to Florrie said, "Anyway, Tom wouldn't leave the business, of that I'm sure. He's in demand now the electrics are down so often. Not that the city has paid him since these raids began."

"Go? Go where?" asked Robert.

"To Portstewart, to Lillian's aunt's cottages, you remember the place," said Meg.

"Oh, aye. It's grand up there. To stay?" asked Robert.

"For the foreseeable, yes. It's not safe here," said Meg.

His mother asked, "Who's going then?"

"Lillian, Beryl, her son Albert, and Mildred Greer. We're packing all the food we can manage and hope we don't get caught by the ration men!" Meg laughed. To Robert, she said, "Albert will be good company for you. We're bringing the two dogs—Albert's wee Bobby and Gordie, the beautiful Irish Setter Martin found on the day...the day he died. David's out clearing rubble for long stretches, so he can't care for a dog properly, asked us to take him."

"Oh, yes. Florrie told us about Mildred Greer's mother being killed. Terrible. And she's living with you, now, is she?" asked Lizzie. "And the father?"

Teacup halfway to her mouth, Meg's brow furrowed. "Mildred's father? Long dead."

"No. Albert's...you mentioned Beryl, but. What's the surname?"

"MacKinley. Albert's father was at the shipyard during the Easter Tuesday raid. He's not been found."

"My good Lord," said Lizzie, shaking her head.

"Anyway, the Greer house was flattened along with Beryl's next door—the Watson's, the house where Lillian and Beryl grew up—their mother had already moved up to Portstewart to live with her sister, thank heavens. Lillian's aunt is the one who owns the vacation cottages, Mrs. Kerr, she is. She's also the postmistress and runs a wee store with it. Lillian and Mildred hope to keep the typewriting business going in Portstewart."

Lizzie nodded and said, "Watson, yes. I remember both Lillian's mother and Mrs. Greer well, from church. Mildred's my age, a wee bit older maybe?" She broke off a small piece of cake and ate it.

"About."

"But what about David? Will he go back to Dublin? We've seen little of him since he came home," said Florrie, frowning.

Shaking her head, Meg said, "No, I've not been able to talk him into coming to Portstewart. His friend Martin died and —*because* Martin died, David wants to stay here and continue clearing rubble, try to find survivors, alive." Her brow creased.

"That was a terrible thing, eh?" asked Lizzie.

"What happened?" asked Robert.

Meg slumped slightly, "It was up on the Antrim Road. All the houses had been badly damaged—most demolished. Martin was digging in the rubble, with your Uncle David and many other men. Martin fell into some sort of hole. We tried to get him out, the soldiers tried too, but he was killed." Meg straightened her back. "So now you know why we're leaving. I hope you and your mum will come, your da, too."

"Robert, run over to Lizzie's. Your father's helping Tom fix some damage to the house. Ask him about going while Meg is here," said Florrie.

"Alright." Robert stood up, gulped the rest of the tea and pushed a sandwich end into his mouth.

"I'll leave with you, Robert. I must get back to number 34," said Meg, standing. The belt cinched around the waist of her dark green Women's Voluntary Service overall revealed how thin she'd become. "Ring me later, Florrie, if the line's back on…I tried ringing New York earlier to let Annie know we were alive, but the line was down." She looked at Robert. "Will you run over to ours if the line's down later? Let us know how many tickets to buy?"

His mouth full, he nodded vigorously and mumbled, "Mmmph."

"You tried to ring *New York*? But trunk calls are so dear… Annie's barely written us since they left ten years ago," said Florrie, looking at Lizzie under her eyelashes, who murmured her agreement.

Meg pursed her lips before answering, "Nor to me, but I thought our sister might be worried after news of the blitz. It must be in their newspapers. Jinny would have let Annie know we were alive, you know she would've."

Florrie looked down. Lizzie folded her arms and sniffed.

Meg looked quickly at Robert. "I must be off, so. Lizzie, I hope you reconsider. Hundreds, thousands have walked out of the city, some in their nightclothes so desperate to flee—Lily and I see them. We don't know how many more of these raids we'll have—two in as many days and getting worse. We mightn't survive the next one."

ESCAPE— MAY 1941

PORTSTEWART, NORTHERN IRELAND

*L*eaning on a shovel, defeated by a section of scrubby grass, Meg spun around at the man's greeting. Smiling, she said, "Frank MacDermott! I'm told we're neighbors, but where've you been since we arrived? It's been two weeks!" She pulled off a work glove and they shook hands.

Dressed in baggie trousers cinched tight by a thick belt, a soft, collarless shirt under a patched jacket, the wiry man had grown thin in his sixties. His blue eyes bright in a sunburned face under a flat cap, the maternal uncle of Mary O'Neill—lover and betrayer of the young Meg—said, "Just home from fishing the Lower Bann. Bagged duck and hare while there, too. Are you here for good?" His sonorous voice belied his weedy appearance.

"We don't know. Lillian and I decided to leave before the bombs got us—bringing our sisters and nephews, and our friend Mildred Greer. Maybe you know, but Mrs. Kerr is Lillian's aunt and Mrs. Watson her mum. Lucky for us Mrs. Kerr let us this cabin. We're cozy, like sardines, and with two dogs in the mix, but safe. I'd like to try and put in a garden, since the rationing's getting worse...sorry, I'm blathering. But you're living in a cottage here, is that right?"

Frank pushed his cap back to reveal a pale forehead leading to grey curls. "Aye, the Carstairs house was shelled a few times —too close for my taste. Mrs. Kerr and Mrs. Watson needed help and everyone was nervy about invasion, so the ladies hired me and let me the wee cottage up the hill from yours. You *were* lucky —the rest of the cottages were already let to others who'd fled Belfast. Anyway, I could help you dig and plant a garden. It looks like there once was a garden 'round the back of yours. It gets the most sun on the place, whenever it deigns to come out. I'd dig it." Frank scanned the misty edge of the property, the views of sea and mountain beyond lost in fog.

"This fog has been in place since we arrived. Does it never lift? But if you would show us what to do, we'll dig it. Lillian and her sister Beryl have gone up to Londonderry to try to find jobs today, but there's three of us women here now and we have two strong boys to help."

"Grand. I'll get me shovels and pitchforks. Give me five minutes. I have good dung for ye, but I'll have to ask a pal for more. Can you pay him? It'll be dirt cheap." Frank grinned.

Laughing, Meg said, "I'll take all the help I can get. We're city people, so."

"You're alright. I can help with the rationing, too, you know, if you're willing to...bend a wee bit. I help Mrs. Kerr and Mrs. Watson, fine Protestant ladies like yourself...it's the way for us all to get on, and it helps with me rent here. Mostly it's me chickens, or me fishing, or trading with farmers, nothing like the black marketeers in them government films at the cinema."

"Aye, we're willing to bend. We're four women, two dogs and the two boys eat a lot." She rolled her eyes.

"Is that lovely Irish Setter yours? He's a beauty. I like the look of the wee black and ginger terrier, although he's threatened to nip me ankle, but that's what wee dogs are like." He laughed.

"Were they bothering you in your yard? I'm sorry."

"They're fine. They can't worry the chickens much—the girls have a nice high house with perches and a closed fence all around, so. Alright, so, we'll chat about what I can get and what it costs another time." He looked at her for a moment. "You look just the same."

"Oh, go on with ye. But you do."

His blue eyes twinkled. "The palaver on ye!" But his eyes lost their twinkle as he asked, "Remember the night we held off the IRA, come to burn the house and kill Mr. Carstairs, the poor man already murdered and buried in yon Protestant churchyard? Mother of God."

"Aye, I do, and I remember his murder in Belfast, caught in the crossfire between police and IRA, so they said. 1922...a terrible year." She sighed. "But *you* held them off here. I often think of it, wonder how we weren't shot dead and say a prayer, thanking you for my life. Mary enjoyed every moment of it, but I was never so terrified...not until last month."

"No need to worry about IRA here, not like those ones that night." Lowering his voice, he added, "We've our own local branch and I spoke to the lads in '22, to the top man. We've never had trouble since. I hope we never do, but I know who to talk to, should all that start up again, being a good Catholic and inclined to the cause." Frank was silent a moment before saying, "Listen, I'll get this off me chest so there's nothing hanging like, you know, in the air between us," he took a deep breath, "about Mary, she's never here now. She stays down in Dublin."

Meg's face colored. "It's what she wanted."

"Ach, Mary never knew what she wanted, and never wanted what she had. But them shares Carstairs left her? Most in woolen and clothing factories, now they're making uniforms and parachutes. She's doing well for herself, enjoying herself in Dublin."

"Maybe," said Meg, quietly.

Frank watched Meg for a moment before saying, "Aye, Mary's happiness never lasted long afore she banjaxed it herself. God help her."

~

Three hours later Albert and Robert were still digging under Frank's baleful eye and spirited instructions. Taking a breather, Meg watched a mud-flecked Florrie concentrating on turning the dug area over with a pitchfork. In another section of the large rectangle being dug, Mildred alternated between digging, turning the soil and wiping her face with her white apron, now dirt streaked. A stocky figure in a floral dress, Mildred's forehead was creased with concentration. Meg smiled as she watched her crinkly grey hair shake with her efforts, one oxford-clad shoe on the shovel top, one firmly on the ground.

Looking past them, Meg leant on her shovel handle and watched the fog lift from the sea.

"Look!" She pointed. As though a curtain had been lifted, the sea reappeared, as did hundreds of boats, small and large, like toys in a vast bathtub.

The two boys ran to the edge of the yard, the dogs bounding behind. The adults joined them and propped their tired arms on the fence top.

"Have you never seen them before?" asked Frank.

"We hear horns and bells, especially at night. But the fog has been so thick since we arrived...," said Mildred, wiping her flushed face with a clean patch of the apron.

"They've been out there a long time now. Londonderry is the refueling port for the convoys crossing and back from Canada and America. Look there, boys, them big ones sailing east with all the wee ones around it? They're merchant ships in convoy, with navy corvettes, Royal Navy or Canadian. They've made it across. And underneath them all, God knows how many U-boats lurking, following."

Mildred hugged herself, her short arms barely reaching across her plump chest.

Florrie said, "Heavens, Mister, em, you've given me the shivers."

"They daren't torpedo them here, the Royal Navy mans the

guns along the shore, and on patrol ships, they've got the depth charges for the U-boats, too. That's a sound to hear, I'll tell ye."

Frank gestured to the boys and said, "All right, lads, back to work. Let's give the ladies a wee rest."

~

After parting the gap in the barbed wire, Albert held it open for Robert, and walked through after him.

Robert pointed to the skull-and-cross-boned signs warning of mines. "I thought you said we were going to a pond. Are we really allowed to swim here?"

Pointing down to the bowl of surf trapped by a keyhole-shaped rock formation, Albert said, "It's the sea, but it's called Herring Pond by the locals, since it's nearly closed off from the rest of the shore. See? It looks like a pond. The army and navy put barbed wire along the entire length of shoreline, but they turn a blind eye to us having a swim here."

Two men in rubber suits sat adjusting air tanks on the other side of the pond. "What are those fellas doing?"

"Practicing their diving. Herring Pond is a draw for divers since it's deep and clear. You can see down to the bottom. Do you swim much?"

Robert leant forward and peered down. "At school—we learnt strokes in a pool."

"When the tides are right, it's very safe here."

Looking unsure, Robert asked, "Are they right now?"

"Oh, yes. I'm an excellent swimmer, so don't worry."

Robert looked away, smirking. *It's official then, is it? He's excellent at everything. The bicycle ride here was filled with the wonders of Albert.*

Pulling his striped polo shirt over his head, Albert said, "Come in, Robert, it will feel good after all that digging and dunging." He took his trousers off and stood in old red swimming trunks, faded in most places to a mottled dark pink. Grinning at Robert, he smoothed back his red-blond hair.

God, he's a long drink of water, but he's muscled, I'll say that for him. Must be all that excellent swimming, eh?

"Alright. I've to put my t-trunks on."

"Rightee-o. Here I go!" Looking over the edge of the rocks that captured a bit of the Atlantic, Albert jumped.

Robert could see him swimming underwater to the middle, where he erupted straight up in the air, his torso and head dripping. "Whoo!"

The divers laughed and one shouted, "Aye, cold enough to freeze thon bollocks off."

Treading water and waving at him, Albert yelled, "Jump in, Robert!"

Before Robert pulled his trousers off, he looked around and, finding no women or girls about, quickly pulled his kex off, too. One foot and leg went into the swim trunks smoothly, the other foot caught in the inner netting, but he managed to keep his balance while pulling the foot through and the trunks up.

One diver yelled, "Hey up! Hang on, boy, your big dark lad is going to shrivel on ye!"

Tying the string of the trunks' waistband tight around him, Robert muttered, "They're k-killing themselves laughing—wish they would."

Although Albert had jumped off the rocks without hesitation, the edge of the cliff gave Robert pause. He walked over to the ladder anchored in cement that led down into the water.

"Only lassies use them stairs, and we know well you're no lass!" The divers now were red-faced and wheezing.

Albert swam over to the bottom of the ladder. "Jump when you get down farther. You can't walk in, it's too cold."

Robert froze.

"It will grow back, we swear!" The fat jokester slapped his thick thighs encased in rubber while his skinny friend doubled over with mirth.

Albert pulled himself up onto the underwater steps. He was close enough to speak in a lower voice. "Those two won't quit till you're in—come down halfway, then jump." Having delivered his advice, he retreated and swam back to the middle of the pond.

Robert climbed onto the ladder and began his descent, but once his feet hit the surf, he stopped. Stuck halfway and facing the rocks, he clung to the ladder as waves of frigid seawater doused him from feet to backside in swells.

In panic and agony, he let go of the ladder rails. Falling backwards, his back slapped hard on the water. Submerged, the icy realm and the sting of the flop were stunning. He opened his eyes and looked up to the clear blue sky. After a moment, Albert filled the view, diving to yank him up to the surface.

Up on the surface he gasped. Albert held onto to him. "Can you tread water?"

"Aye. Ow! My arm."

Albert let go of him. As he'd been taught, Robert moved his arms and legs and to his surprise, he remained afloat.

From across the pond, "Here! That'll sting later. Worse than a belly flop but easier on the lad." More laughter.

Albert turned around and said, "Please, Mister, would you give us a chance?" Something in Albert's voice must have contained the perfect mix of authority and respect, because the fat jokester diver waved and yelled, "Aye, you're alright."

Turning back to Robert, Albert said, "We can go back up, if you like."

"After all that? You must be joking me. Anyway, the water feels good now. I'll stay a wee while. At least until those devils either drown or leave."

Smiling, Albert said, "Good on ye. But keep moving or you'll freeze."

∼

They'd ridden their bicycles down to the harbor from Herring Pond and left them propped against the pub's whitewashed wall. Half-pints in hand, they wandered back outside and sat at a wooden table on the water's edge.

"Thanks again for getting those two to finally shut it."

"School is good for certain things and one is learning how to tell people to shut it so they do—including bullies and even teachers."

"And that works at The Hall? You must be rich to afford that place."

Albert laughed and said, "Sometimes. Not at all rich. Scholarship dayboy and complete swot, at your service. Swim team, rowing team, drama society, science club. Blue and gold, rah, rah, rah——I do it all. Shameless. Since I'm a dayboy and a scholarship boy, son of a shipyard man, that puts me on the bottom rung for the rich rugby players at school. Puts me in my place." He arched a blond eyebrow and laughed again. "Somebody has to…what about you?"

"Castlereagh College. I just got my leaving cert—I think I have, I mean. I've not gotten the results yet, but I'm fairly certain."

"Castlereagh! Are *you* rich?"

"Rich! No. My da's boss is an alum and he put in a good word after I qualified for the entrance exam. I only received a partial scholarship, but enough so I could attend, because my father could afford the rest. But I know what you mean about being a dayboy and a scholarship boy."

"What's your father do?"

"He *was* a candy salesman. Did well for himself, not to mention the candy he brought home for us, but along came the war. No sweets available, no candy salesmen. He works a stall with some pals at St. George Market now, selling whatever they can get their hands on. Bread one day, hats the next. It's fun to visit him there—one of his friends works the Ulster fry-up van. Not much of a fry-up these days—he can only make farl and baps—no sausage, no bacon, no tomatoes, sometimes eggs. Anyway, I'm lucky this was my last term because he's out of money—I wouldn't have been able to go on with school." Robert took a sip of ale. "Your father, he was k-killed in a raid? Meg said."

Albert took a swig and licked his upper lip. "Aye. He was a fitter at Harland and Wolff. We think he was killed during the Easter raid."

Robert watched Albert's tongue flick over the golden stubble on his upper lip.

"He was on shift, but never came home after the raid. He's not been found and so his death has not been confirmed. My mum's waiting for restitution from H&W or the government, but she says it may take years. We lost our house, too. The last two years I won the top H&W scholarship for employees' children—hence The Hall."

"Sorry about your father," said Robert.

Albert shrugged. "Thanks. He was a mild man, never one to call attention to himself. But he may have seemed so in comparison to my mother, who's loud and raring to go. Thankfully I had Lillian and my grandmother to show me there was a middle path in life. I wish I'd known my grandfather better, longer, but he died when I was a kid. He was a fine open ocean swimmer. Lillian and I plan to train for a relay swim with a team, once the war is over. It will take a lot of training. From down there," he pointed to the strand, "across to Inishowen."

Robert looked at the wide expanse of water indicated and shuddered. "Can you really swim that far?"

"We'll see, but we hope to. My grandfather did it. Anyway, the raids were terrible, but I needn't tell you that. My cat disappeared in that raid, too. Good old Red, our ginger tom. We never found him either. Before we came up here, I'd gone back to our street a few times a week to look for him. Our neighbors were all gone, so there was nobody to ask about old Red." He drank some ale. "Maybe he's alive and somebody took him in." Albert cleared his throat. "Mum survived, so did wee Bobby and so did I. Mildred too, of course, but not her mum—nice old lady, Mrs. Greer. Ach, drink up before I cry in my ale. We have time for another before we're due back for tea. How's your back? Your arm?"

"Sore." Grinning at Albert, Robert raised his glass and said, "Cheers!"

"Cheers! What did you get your leaving cert in?"

"Maths, physics—took A-levels in those—and the leaving exams in history and Latin. I only did the one sport, cross-country. I like to run."

"Maths and physics! I'm impressed, and with the history and Latin, too, not to mention the running. Listen, I can be an awful arse, Robert, but put up with me a wee while and you'll see I have a more, a more…"

"Excellent side?"

Albert laughed and said, "Bastard! Aye, I'm owed that one."

"Ah well, I'll give over…you said you wanted to be a scientist—what k-kind?"

"I want to be a biologist. I'm studying biology and chemistry —I'll sit the A-levels in them. I have to study maths and physics, but I'm only alright with them—no A-levels there, I don't think, but I'll swot for them and see. I'll sit A-levels in art history, maybe. I was going for German, but I've stopped studying it for obvious reasons. I love Latin, but I'll sit the leaving exam, not the A-levels. Did you like Latin? I love having the words in my mouth, don't you? *Habemus clara futura!* It makes me happy just to say them—*felix tam clama."*

Robert nearly snorted the ale he'd just sipped. "Ha! But you should stick with German. Somebody needs to understand what the bastards are up to. What will happen next term for you?"

"I'm talking with my mum and Aunt Lillian about finding a school up here. Coleraine College is a possibility. If they get the good jobs they hope to with the Yanks in Londonderry, I'll apply for a scholarship to make up the rest. I don't want to miss too much time off school."

Robert cocked his head. "There are Yanks in Londonderry? Doing what?"

"It's hush-hush, nobody's supposed to know. Helping with the war effort."

"I didn't know. How do you know?"

"Somehow my mum and aunt knew about the jobs on offer and who was offering."

"I knew about the Royal Navy station and refueling depot, but not the Yanks—them being here can only help us." He looked out over the water for a moment. "Are you really only fifteen? You seem older. I'd have thought you were seventeen or eighteen."

Laughing, Albert said, "I'm nearly sixteen. Anyway, it's my size, I think. It's saved me from the school rugby players and most adults have to look up at me so they treat me as though I'm older. I sound older because I have confidence." He grinned. "It's freeing not being treated like a kid." He shrugged and smiled. "Anyway, the H&W scholarship won't come through next term, it's all government contracts for them now so their money is literally not their own. I want to go to university, so the next school has to be something decent, but it can't be expensive, nothing like The Hall. That's alright—I hated the bloody place. What about you? What are you going to do?"

"Not university. There's no money for it and I'm up to here with school. I like understanding how things work—something technical would suit me. But as a matter of fact, I was thinking of joining the navy."

Albert's mouth fell open a little. "The navy! But you'll be sent into the North Atlantic or somewhere else extremely dangerous."

"Probably." Robert pulled his shoulders back. "I'm considering it, seriously, enough so that I talked to a recruiter. Not a word to anyone. Promise?"

"Aye, I promise. But why do you want to join?"

After Robert drained his glass, he said, "If you want to know the truth, I want to get away from my p-parents and out into the world, learn what the navy can teach me. I need a wee bit of t-toughening, too. I've no job, no training, no money of my own, so."

Tracing the rim of the ale mug with a long index finger, Albert said, "Just when I thought we might be great pals, you're leaving. I'm astonished you want to join the navy. Aren't you afraid?"

"I will be, I'm sure. I've never gone anywhere on me own. I won't tell my parents ahead of joining, I don't know about my father, but my mother will go mad—she b-babies me, and it'll be better if it's done and dusted."

"Will you tell me? Ahead of time?"

"I will. I'm not sure about this, mind, not entirely. My round." He collected the two glasses. "In the meantime, would you help me with swimming? I don't want to join the navy only to drown."

Albert smiled. "Of course—will you help me with maths and physics swotting?"

"It sounds like a good summer, after all," said Robert, standing.

"Only if you don't run away to join the navy, so don't."

Robert grinned, turned, and walked toward the pub. He heard Albert's shouted, "Crisps!" and waved to recognize the request.

SOJOURN'S END—AUGUST 1941

PORTSTEWART

"We're off then," said Albert, standing in the kitchen doorway. "My college tour is scheduled for three o'clock—we'll do the messages first."

Lillian turned from the Belfast sink, a dripping plate in hand. She looked Albert up and down, then over at Meg, who nodded. "Hang on a minute." Lillian put the dish in the drainer and after wiping her hands on a tea towel, squeezed past Albert.

"Where is she going?"

"You'll see," said Meg, kneading bread dough at the counter.

Robert joined Albert in the doorway. "We'll miss the train if you keep hanging about."

Behind them, Lillian said, "Coming through." She carried an old tin lockbox and put it on the table. Opening the lid, she counted out notes and coins, and brought out his clothing ration book. "You can't spend your life in school uniforms. We'll have to sort you for winter another time, but today, buy yourself jacket and trousers, mufti, in addition to the school clothes, and good shoes, too. Make sure nothing is tight or only just the right length—the fit should offer a little extra…"

Meg laughed and said, "Time."

Lillian said, "Aye. And buy whatever else you need. Socks and em..." she waved her hand, "underthings."

"But I've to pay for the school uniform *today*—the whole kit, mind—jacket, trousers, tie, shirts, athletic gear—you've seen the list."

"Aye, I know. This should be enough for everything." She handed the ration book and cash to him, turned back to the box, and fished out more coins. Stuffing them into his hand, she added, "Take yourselves for lunch. There used to be very nice places for lunch along the river in Coleraine."

Meg asked, "And what about you, Robert—do you need anything. New shoes?" Dressed in jacket and trousers only slightly too short in the arms and legs, Robert said, "No, Aunt, thank you. I'll make do with these. The shoes fit."

"Are you sure?"

"Aye and thanks. Albert, we should go if we're going."

"Thanks to both of you." Albert kissed Lillian's cheek and the boys ran out the back door and across the garden to the bicycle shed.

At the window above the sink, Lillian watched them run across the yard. "Oh well, if they miss one train, they'll get another. It's early in the day." Lowering her voice, she added, "My sister does not pay enough attention to that boy. Not like yours does to Robert."

"Aye. Florrie pays a lot of attention to Robert. Maybe too much?"

"Where is Florrie?" asked Lillian.

Meg sighed. "In the washing shed. I suspect she took our washing to do, too, even though I've asked her not to, more than once."

Lillian frowned. "Ach, I do wish she wouldn't."

"I know. Where's Beryl?"

"Took a cup of tea back to bed. My sister was out past the curfew, again."

Meg said, "She'll get caught, one of these times. And Mildred?"

"Gone to Lough Foyle with Frank for mussels." Lillian came and leant against the counter next to Meg.

"Lough Foyle with Frank!" Meg laughed.

"Aye. He asked and she said yes. I'm looking forward to the mussels."

"Good, because I want to talk to you while we're alone." Alternating folding and kneading the dough, Meg said, "So, except for this blissful moment, we're never alone. It's driving me mad—if it's not your sister or mine, it's Mildred, or your mother and aunt, or everyone including Frank clogging the rooms. You're only home for any length of time at the weekends, and they're spent working. We've spent three months jammed together except at night when we're paired with our sisters, not together. I'm fond of them all, but there's no relief." Meg gave the dough a particularly vicious thump down onto the wooden breadboard.

"I know and I'm sorry, but this housing arrangement won't last forever, I'll talk to my aunt about letting us a second cottage, but at the moment I don't see what we can do." Lillian folded her arms.

"Nothing. There's absolutely nothing to be done I understand that. I just wanted to say it. I wanted to talk to you about the boys—that's what's worrying me."

"The boys! What about them?" Lillian's voice rose.

Raising one floury finger to her lips, Meg said, "Ssh. Perhaps I am mad already, but they seem to spend all their time alone together. Too much time alone?"

Lillian's brow furrowed. "But they seem busy enough. Are they not working in the garden enough? Or helping Frank?"

"They *are* busy, and they *do* work hard. When they're not working with Frank or in our garden, Robert is helping Albert with maths, or they cycle to Herring Pond to swim and have a pint after—I don't mind that they have a pint at the pub, but don't tell my sister. It's just that they are always together, alone together mostly. Stuck like glue."

"Meg, I can't understand you. We'd hoped they would become friends and they have—very good friends."

"Yes, but...directly after meals they're off to the bottom of the garden, or to the strand, or in their room with the door shut. They're never apart and mostly alone, together. I don't know. I'll just say it—" Meg lowered her voice to whisper. "I think they're in love and I don't know what we should do about it."

"In love!" Lillian's whooped.

"Ssh!"

Laughing, Lillian asked, "You don't mean it?"

Meg continued to look worried.

"You're serious," said Lillian.

"Aye. And I want to know whether you think we should speak to them. I wouldn't want them to get into any trouble, and they could, you know. It's against the law for them and they may not realize it."

Lillian frowned. "Speak to them? How?"

"What do you mean, *how*?" Meg picked up the formed bread dough.

"As in, 'Robert, Albert, we've noticed you're in love?' Like that? I don't think we can do that, Meg, even if you speak to Robert alone and I talk to Albert alone—whether they are in love or not, we can't ask them."

Still holding the dough, Meg asked, "No?"

"No. Either way would be devastation—if they *are* good friends and nothing else, it would ruin the friendship. And if they are in love, is it our business?"

Meg put the dough into a large tan bowl and covered it with a tea towel. "Well...I remember what it was like for me when I was sixteen. It was a devastation, that's exactly what it was."

"Oh, but neither of our lads is like those awful ones...what were the names?"

"Amy Lyon and her boyfriend Bill. Bill...I can't remember his name."

"What she did to you, what they tried to do was criminal. Actually criminal. Horrible."

Continuing to stare out the window, Meg shivered remembering how her childish glee at a romantic assignation with Amy in the shipyard kitchen storeroom turned into the fight of her life. Facing Lillian, she said, "I'm certain Bill would have raped me with her help had I not fought them off long enough for Miss Simpson to save me. But the whole thing, being in love with another girl...even when I was twenty-two, what Mary did to me was so hard, it took me years to recover. I think it's hard to have those feelings when you're basically a kid. It's...overwhelming."

"Aye, I remember how hurt you were by Mary, but we can't protect the boys from life entirely. If our nephews come to us, that's one thing. We can give our guidance or just listen, whatever they seem to need. And that's the other thing, if we did what you propose, it would ruin *our* relationships with them. I'm convinced of that."

Meg sighed. "Aye, I see your point...but what about David? He's Robert's uncle and he's..."

"I can't imagine David is in the mood to give advice to the lovelorn—if they go to him, fine, but it would be just as bad if he brought it up. The boys are probably having a very hard time figuring out how they feel, if they do feel what you say. Remember, they may look like men, but they are boys."

"True. Alright, I won't say anything."

Taking Meg's hand, Lillian said, "Good. Now, do you know what we're going to do later today?"

Meg shook her head. "What?" She pushed her hair off her forehead with a floury wrist, leaving a light grey smudge.

"It's a beautiful day, so as soon as your bread is out of the oven, we're going to take the cycles down to Herring Pond and have a swim or a sit, whatever you like. Then we'll find a place on the waterfront and enjoy lunch. A wee holiday. There's no point working so hard if we never enjoy ourselves."

"So why didn't you invite Frank to join us for the mussels?" asked Beryl.

"We split the haul, which was generous of him, but he's seeing his lady friend tonight," said Mildred.

"Frank has a lady friend?" asked Meg looking around the table, her eyebrows raised.

"Who is she?" asked Lillian, giggling.

"A woman in Portrush. But I don't see what's so funny," said Mildred, lowering her eyes.

"No, there's nothing funny about it," said Lillian, laughing now.

Mildred, frowning, said, "Frank's entitled to some company, some happiness. He's been very good to us so I don't think youse should laugh at his expense. He has to wear work clothes most of the time."

The women fell silent at her rebuke until Florrie said, "Aye, I've seen worse looking men and I imagine he scrubs up."

Mildred blushed. "He does. He looked positively handsome this evening."

Robert pushed at the food on his plate during this exchange but looked across the table at Albert during the uncomfortable silence that followed.

Albert raised an eyebrow and gave him a quick nod.

Beryl lit a cigarette. "Well, ladies, it being Saturday night, I'm off down the Atlantic Hotel bar. Why don't we all go?" She plumped the back of her coif.

"I'd go," said Mildred. "Only, I have nothing nice to wear and my hair..." She touched her steely hair, ridged in silver waves from low on her forehead and combed back into a blunt cut tucked behind her ears.

"Ach, you're fine as you are. Anybody else?"

Florrie shook her head, eyebrows raised.

"I don't know where you get the energy," said Lillian. "But if Meg wants to go, I'm game."

Meg opened her mouth, but before she could get a word out, Robert said, "I've j-joined the Royal Navy. T-today."

The women looked at him.

Albert pushed his chair back from the table and folded his arms.

A forkful of food halfway to her mouth, Florrie whispered, "What did you say?"

"I j-joined the Royal Navy t-today. It's d-done."

"I don't understand you, Robert. *What?*" Her fork clattered onto the plate.

Rushing through the words, he repeated, "I joined the Royal Navy today in Coleraine. They'll send a telegram telling me when and where to report."

"But that's impossible! You're too young! Do they know you're only seventeen years old?"

"They do. I was allowed to j-join at seventeen with p-proof of my age and a school leaving certificate. I had both."

Florrie continued to stare at him, her mouth set. "No. You're not going anywhere."

"I'll have to—I'm in the navy. I p-passed the physical and I signed the enlistment p-papers."

Beryl looked at her son. "You haven't enlisted, too, have you? Please tell me you haven't."

"No, Mum."

Her voice tight, Florrie spat her words. "Dear God. I must ring Ralph—he'll know what to do."

Robert shrugged. "Ring him if you like, b-but there's nothing to be done. I signed the p-papers. I'm in the navy."

Her voice rising, the veins thick in her flushed neck, Florrie asked, "Is this some sort of stupid joke?"

"No, M-mum."

Florrie threw her napkin onto the table, nearly knocked her chair over and rushed out of the kitchen.

Quietly, Lillian asked, "Albert, did you know about this?"

"Yes."

"*Before* you left for Coleraine this morning?"

"I did. Robert asked me not to tell, so I didn't." Albert unfolded his arms and leant forward, resting his elbows on the table.

"Oh, Albert," said Beryl. "How could you?"

Robert said, "It's not his fault I lied to my p-parents. I asked him to k-keep it secret."

Beryl sucked on her cigarette until the ash glowed orange. Everyone sat in silence, listening to the strain in Florrie's voice as she rang the post office. "Hullo, Mrs. Kerr, sorry to bother you at teatime, but would you ring through till Belfast for me? Aye, I'll hold. No, no, everything's all right here." Her voice quavered on the last word.

Meg touched his arm and said, "Robert, go talk to your father."

"Aye."

Albert and the women were left alone at a table, piles of empty mussel shells on plates at each place setting, except Robert's. For a moment, they sat listening to Florrie's jumbled version of the news interrupted by Robert's pleas to speak to his father. Robert's low rumble took over the conversation.

"Well, that's a turn up for the books," muttered Mildred.

Meg said, "I hadn't seen *that* coming," adding the inhalation tic common to the women of her family when upset. "My poor sister. I pray to God he'll be safe." She looked at Lillian.

Beryl exhaled blue smoke and said, "I'm afraid he couldn't have picked a more dangerous branch than the navy." She cocked her head toward the water beyond their garden. "Those poor devils bobbing around out there in the open ocean, like sitting ducks for the bloody German U-boats and the planes."

A stricken Albert asked, "Maybe he'll have shore duty?"

"Maybe," said Beryl.

Mildred got up and said, "I'll fetch whiskey and glasses. We could all use a wee dram I think, especially Florrie."

"She may not drink it, but I will," said Meg.

~

Albert said, "I have a wee surprise to mark the end of your sojourn here. No, not the end, I hope, a pause."

"This sojourn as you call it hasn't ended well for my m-mum, but that was my fault."

"Your Da is not coming up here then?"

"No. We're going home tomorrow—that's what he wanted. M-mum, too. I'm afraid she's quite angry with all the wrong people. Except for me. She's m-mad at me for enlisting and telling her in front of everyone. I'm not sure which was worse in her m-mind."

Albert's face fell. "Maybe I can visit you in Belfast before you report to wherever?"

"I'll let you know as soon as I do, if I'm allowed. I'm sorry, b-but right now, you're one of the wrong people, so Mum w-w-wouldn't...ach!" Robert slapped his chair arm.

"If it helps, my mum and aunt are mad at me too. It's just...I thought we'd have more time. We'll just have to wait until you're allowed leave." Albert poured whiskey into two small glasses.

"Whiskey!"

"The ladies made enough of a dent in the contents tonight, so we can help ourselves to a wee dram or two each. They'll not notice. Cheers."

Robert and Albert sat in the chairs at the end of the garden. Albert pulled his chair closer to Robert's before he took a sip.

The moon rose. For a while they sat in silence and watched the ships move across the strait, silhouetted in the moonlight as they traveled east or west.

"I still can't believe you've joined the navy. It doesn't seem real but promise me you won't drown or… anything."

Robert placed one hand on his heart and, in a deep voice, said, "I promise to try not to."

"You may pass us here one night. How will I know?"

"You'll just have to w-watch for me. I'll wave," said Robert, laughing. He raised his right arm to wave and said, "Ouch!"

"How's your shoulder?"

"It hurts." He rotated his right shoulder gingerly. "You gave it a good yank pulling me up out of the water today!"

"Sorry about the yank, I thought you were in trouble. Sit down here and I'll get the kink out, loosen it up for you."

"Really?"

"It's my fault. It's the least I can do. Sit at my feet."

Robert sat on the ground between Albert's knees. Albert poured a tot of whiskey into Robert's glass and began to massage his shoulders.

"Ow!"

"Relax. Take a good sip. I'll go easier. The right side is very tight."

Robert tilted his head back. "That's grand." Robert felt a frisson run into his shoulders from Albert's strong hands. He opened his eyes and for a wild moment, Robert imagined kissing the lips he'd desired but resisted all summer.

As though asked, Albert bent over and kissed Robert's lips. Wriggling out from under the kiss, Robert stood and turned to face Albert, breathless. Robert took a step toward him, put his hands on Albert's shoulders and pushed him back against the chair. Albert flinched. Robert loosened his grip and slid his hands up to cup Albert's face, before returning the kiss. After some awkward maneuverings—knees down, arms down—they landed together softly on the dewy grass.

An antic period of fumbling with clothing while kissing resolved when Albert rolled on top of Robert, raised up onto his elbows, and laced his fingers in Robert's hair. Robert wrapped his arms around Albert's back, natural shyness gone as they found one another. The intensity of their first caress ran through them, electric and traveling on their skin like blue light, through heart and brain, to the young men's muscles and tendons, crackling with life.

The bells and horns of the ships in the strait were the only sounds beyond their quiet sounds. The house behind them was dark and silent. The planet stopped rotating—the war, their country, town, and home—all at a standstill.

From the other side of the cottage, a loud male voice startled the lovers, "Open up please! ARP Warden!" He rapped on the door repeatedly as Gordie and Bobby set up the alarm.

"Open immediately! ARP Warden! You've a light showing." The knocking turned into a steady banging. "Hello! Hello! Open please! ARP Warden!"

"Shite," whispered Robert, rolling out of Albert's embrace and looking toward the house from the ground.

Albert's belt buckle clinked as he rushed to pull his clothing closed. They knelt behind the chairs and ducked when the warden's dimmed torch shone through the bushes. Albert whispered, "He's at the front door, we've got to get in through the back."

The boys ran across the garden in a crouch and into the utility room behind the kitchen. From there they could hear someone in the house stirring. Lillian's voice called, "Aye, I'll be right there. Coming. Hang on." A dimmed torch light traveled down the hall as though on its own. They heard her mutter, "Does he have to knock the house down? Don't trip me, Bobby!"

Albert giggled behind his hand.

Robert whispered, "T-take your shoes off and go help her with the dogs."

They heard the warden say, "You've a light showing, Miss."

"Where?"

"The front chimney, just there. I have to come in and check."

"Aye," Lillian said.

Albert's stern command rang down the hall. "Gordie, Bobby, come here. Sit."

Footsteps passed back down the hall and into the parlor as Robert continued to crouch in the utility room.

"It's your fire grate." The warden's voice.

"So it is. I thought one of us smothered the embers before bed. We always make sure to, but tonight was a bit... hectic."

"If it happens again, I'll have to fine you, but as it's the first time I've had to call here...I'll leave you with a warning. Now, let's get it smothered."

"What's happened?" asked Albert from the doorway. Robert appeared next to him, yawning.

Lillian turned and said, "No one smothered the embers tonight. Light's showing at the chimney. Can I ask, Mr., em, how did you see that? I think we're at the highest point of the hill, or near enough."

"Bombers could see it well enough, Miss. I was up at the post office, which is a wee bit higher still."

"We'll take more care," said Lillian, looking pointedly at Albert. "I'm aware that bombers can see chimney light." She leant down and shoveled ash onto the embers. "Thank you so much. We've a lot of people staying here at the moment and things get hectic, especially tonight."

"It'll need water to finish the job," said the warden.

She picked up the watering can next to the ancient aspidistra and poured water onto the embers. There was a gentle hiss and plume of smoke.

"Alright. I'll be off now."

"But tell me, what can we do in the cold weather, when it'll be dark so early? We'll need use of this fireplace."

"There's an ironmonger in Portrush who makes tin flue covers to measure. They work well enough but can be smoky if

35

they don't fit perfectly. If you send the lads with accurate dimensions, he can sort it."

As they stood in the hallway to see the man out, Meg joined them. "A light chink?"

"Aye. The chimney. You'll have to take more care with the grate at night, Albert. It's your job to see to it."

"Sorry, Aunt. I'll take more care. And I'll sort it with the ironmonger."

"I'll help," said Robert.

"You'll have to—the fines are hefty."

Meg asked, "What time is it?"

"Just midnight."

"Fancy a cup of tea?"

"I do. I'm parched."

Lillian asked, "Are you hungry, boys?"

The quartet walked into the kitchen. After checking that the blackout curtains were closed tightly, Lillian turned a light on.

Albert said, "I'll just take some milk and maybe..."

Robert said, "Aye, milk. Maybe something to eat. I didn't eat much at tea."

"No, you didn't. I'll make some sandwiches," said Meg, opening the breadbox. "I'm peckish, too."

"We had too much to drink tonight," said Lillian.

"Aye, I've a wee headache," said Meg. She lowered her voice to say, "Poor Florrie cried herself to sleep earlier—talk about a headache."

Robert was stung with guilt, avoiding Meg's eyes when she handed him the milk and sandwiches. She pulled his chin up gently and smiled.

～

The boys lay together on Albert's bed. Moonlight streamed in through the open blackout curtains. Albert whispered, "I'll come down to Belfast to visit before you leave. If your mother's still mad at me, she needn't know I'm there. We can meet somewhere."

Robert said nothing for a moment. "The telegram from the navy will come here. When it arrives, ring us. No, have Meg do it."

"Alright." Albert kissed Robert's cheek. "It's our last night, our only night…" His eyes closed.

He whispered, "I'll go back to my bed, in case my mother decides to wake me early." Hands in Albert's hair, he pulled his head back and kissed him, tasting the whiskey and sweat on his lips, Albert's golden stubble pricking his lips as he lightly rubbed them back and forth. He buried his face in Albert's hair for a moment, inhaling deeply before leaving the bed.

From across the room, Robert gazed at Albert's sleeping face in the moonlight until his eyes fell shut. He was nearly asleep when he heard the whispered, "I love you," from across the room. Unsure that he'd not dreamt it, still he answered, "I love you."

THE NEW WORLD—CHRISTMAS
WEEK 1941

HEADING WEST/SOUTHWEST IN THE
NORTH ATLANTIC TO NEW YORK

*T*he frantic disembodied voice roared down the tube and filled the radio room. "All hands!" Petty Officer Howard hit the switch for the automatic signal. The bells and the Royal Marine bugler's call down the tube pierced every corner of the ship.

Three men jammed together in a closet-sized radio room looked up as the hundreds of sailors serving on HMS *Portland* thundered up the steel ladders, the sound ringing through the metal decks and walls.

Ordinary Telegraphist Robert Henderson pulled one side of his headphones off so he could hear what was happening above them. In his peripheral vision he saw his mate, Gerald Downey, making a frantic sign at him, but Robert's concentration never left the High Frequency/Direction Finding screen—HF/DF, the Huff-Duff—searching for U-boats underneath them. Nor did his hand leave his key, in case the two others were injured, and he was needed to pick up sending and receiving the encrypted transmissions. Sweat ran down from Robert's head, finding the rash under his chin and reigniting an itchy stinging.

"Headphones on proper, Henderson!" growled PO Howard.

The ship lurched sideways as a tremendous explosion hit well forward of the radio room. The sound reverberated down the length of the ship to their room.

Robert squeezed his eyes shut against the roar, just for a split second. Opening them again, he forced himself to concentrate on the Huff-Duff screen and think of nothing else. There were no U-boat blips. It was clear underneath the ship.

"Henderson!"

"Clear. All clear, PO."

"Bloody hell, then. Where the fuck did the torpedo come from? Why aren't they calling for the alarms?"

Some minutes later, a whistle blew down the tube, followed by a shaky voice. "Radio room. Encrypt for Ledbury from Portland. Torpedo forward port. Damage to fuel pump 1. Ship maneuverable. No casualties. U-boat periscope sighted running ahead, N/NE. Maneuvering starboard to drop. Full forward."

"Cut that bloody message in half, Downey, each bit," said the PO. "If the Jerries crack that long a message, we'll have no code left."

Robert imagined Gerald's fingers working his key, transmitting the shortened and encrypted version of the message from his brain, translated to the key, and to the radiomen in HMS *Ledbury* sailing in their convoy.

From above, the voice came down again, ordering those at the controls. "Midships. Full forward."

The ship shuddered as the depth charges were dropped. Robert felt the explosions underwater from his feet to his head, but the percussion landed heavily in his bowels. He waited for further explosions, fire, rolling over, and the final plunge into frigid water. The depth charges continued for some time. Robert's only thought, *Help us, God.*

The tiny radio room was hot, the wall fan providing no relief, merely moving the fug of three sweating and terrified men, men who had little access to bathing beyond a spit and a flick.

Robert said, "Still no sighting. Clear, PO."

The PO spoke again, this time quietly into the tube. "U-boat off radar. Repeat. Off radar. No sighting. Clear. Midships."

"Midships. Aye, aye. No sighting. Clear."

The depth charges stopped, but above them, nobody left their positions, the last order given for silence, they waited.

In the distance, another ship in the convoy, a destroyer or a corvette, laid depth charges, the vibrations carrying through the water to their hull. The radar bleeped softly as it swirled around on the green screen. The distant depth charges stopped.

Gerald took a new encrypted message, scribbled its translation on a piece of paper, then repeated it aloud. "Ledbury. U-boat off radar. No hits. Full forward."

The PO blew into the tube and repeated the message from HMS *Ledbury* to the bridge.

The bridge responded. "Midships. Full forward." The clipped accent of an officer.

The ship moved forward with speed. After an hour, the all-clear claxon sounded and sailors' feet hit the ladders and decks, this time slowly and with weariness, as the men returned to their usual positions, to their quarters or to the mess.

One bell rang and Robert was dismissed from the radio room. Joining a line at the nearest head, his guts roiling, he hoped not to disgrace himself. The sailor ahead turned and offered a cigarette. Robert's hands shook as he cupped the flame. He shivered in his boiler suit and wheat-colored duffel coat.

The man asked, "First torpedo?"

Robert unclenched his teeth to say, "First trip across the Atlantic, first torpedo. I've not been at sea long. And you?"

"Two years, five months. It may not be our last before we dock in New York. Where've you been?"

"Out of Liverpool to Iceland, Norwegian Sea, Barents Sea, and Murmansk."

"Brrr."

"Aye, I try to remember that cold in the sweltering radio room." Robert shifted from foot to foot.

"Here, I'll find another head. You take my place."

"Ta very much!" called Robert to the man's retreating back.

Robert waited to march off the destroyer as part of the second liberty crew. Standing on deck in a stinging blizzard as they entered New York Harbor, the sailors felt the blast of a bitterly cold wind blowing off the convergence of waters. His numb feet hit the wooden dock of the Brooklyn Navy Yard as they were marched to the U.S. Navy barracks, their hosts for the forty-eight-hour furlough.

After dismissal, Gerald asked, "What will you do on liberty?"

"I have family here in Brooklyn—an aunt and uncle, and their children—one cousin is a girl my age and I haven't seen her since we were wee kids. They're on the telephone so I'll ring and see if I can visit. And you?"

"I'll stay here. I hear their navy's food is very good. See the sights tomorrow. But I'll stay here. Solid earth under me bunk, good meal, hot shower—it's all I want." The large and soft Gerald grinned. "Never get enough to eat in the navy."

"Aye, I understand. I'll walk in with you. Find a phone box." Pulling his pea coat collar up, he fell in step with Gerald.

After a few false starts using an American public telephone, Robert found an American sailor who offered to add the correct coin and dial the number for him.

A woman answered. "Hullo! Aunt Annie? This is Robert Henderson, Florrie's boy. Your nephew?"

After a long silence, Annie said, "Robert! I wasn't expecting *you* to call so it took me a wee minute. Where are you?"

"Brooklyn. I'm in the Royal Navy and my ship docked a few hours ago. I have a liberty pass. I was wondering if I could visit sometime today or tomorrow? I know it's out of nowhere, but I'd like to see you, if you're, em…"

Another awkward moment passed, after which Annie said, "Oh, of course, Robert. Come today. We have Sunday lunch at two—it's not even one now and we can wait for you. Where are you?"

"In Brooklyn, at the navy yard. Are you far from here?"

"Far enough. Let's see. Ask someone where you can find it, but you take the train, the subway, the 4th Avenue line to Bay Ridge. Your uncle will collect you at the 77th Street stop." After another a second of silence, she added, "A stop is the same as a call."

Phone receiver tucked into his chin, Robert scribbled furiously on the Christmas card his cousin Betty sent the year before, including their telephone number and address with her greetings and news. "I see…and do you know where I can find the, em, subway here? I mean, where do I start?"

"Oh. I'm not sure…hold a moment."

Robert could hear his Uncle Ned ask, "Who is it I'm happy to collect?"

After a clink and a muffled sound, he heard Annie say, "Florrie's boy, Robert—he's in the Royal Navy. He's here, in Brooklyn." Her voice became more distinct as she said, "Robert, here's your uncle."

"Hello? Hello, Robert?"

"Hello, Uncle Ned. Do you know where I can find the subway near the Brooklyn Navy Yard?"

A moment of silence was followed by, "I'd say it's DeKalb Avenue."

"'Dee' what?"

"D-E-K-A-L-B. Avenue. I think that's the closest to the navy yard. Ask someone there to be sure it's the closest. I'm not sure how long that walk will be, and you may have a long wait for a train on a Sunday afternoon, mind."

"I have your address, but I don't know how to get…"

"We're in Bay Ridge. Take the 4th Avenue line to 77th Street. There's maps down in the subway. I'll come down to meet you in…three-quarters of an hour. If you're there earlier, just wait, I'll be along."

"Alright, see you soon. Hullo?" His uncle had rung off.

Robert sat at their kitchen table opposite his cousin Betty. The metamorphosis of this willowy young woman was completed by the red lipstick and dark hair worn carefully curled onto the shoulders of a fitted jacket, tight against her slim frame, its tartan placket buttoned to the top of a soft, rounded collar, and the arrogance in the tilt of her head. Her eyes, no longer hidden behind the lenses of little round tortoise shells, were large, dark, and intelligent. She'd said little but studied him underneath dark lashes. A smile hovered on her lips, but she didn't share the joke.

By their appearance, Robert never would have matched his aunt and uncle with their home, as tastefully, even formally decorated as it was. Annie's large frame, much broader than his mother's, filled an ordinary print dress back and front, leaving her enormous arms bare. Her silvery grey hair was plaited into a tight bun and she wore none of the makeup her daughter used. Her bespectacled husband wore a white short-sleeved shirt, a cigarette pack in the breast pocket, his pants the sturdy utility cloth of a workman's. Ned's hair was red going white through a blond transition, and what there was left of it was slicked straight back past his mostly bald head with hair oil. Clean-shaven, the man clearly had no interest in appearing anything other than clean and tidy.

Was the fashionable Betty responsible for the decoration of their apartment?

Magnified watery blue eyes blinked behind thick lenses as Ned told a story meant to amuse. Robert realized he hadn't been listening, so he laughed on Ned's cue and turned to see his aunt's reaction, but her expression remained distracted and grim.

Annie brought a platter of steaming sliced beef, carrots, and Brussels sprouts to the table. "Out of my way, Tommy," she told the dog.

Ned said, "Aye, the boys will be driven mad they missed you, Robert. A sailor for a cousin and them not here to enjoy it. It's a wee shame."

"Where are they?" asked Robert.

"On a camping trip with the scouts. Over in New Jersey, up in some mountains."

"I didn't approve, but so it is. Denis has a heart problem and Michael's too wee. They'll freeze!" said Annie.

"Ach, they're in a lodge or a log cabin or some such with a fireplace. They'll be fine. They were desperate to go with their scout troop, would not be denied, but once they know they've missed you, Robert, they'll be kicking themselves," said Ned.

"It's much quieter without them, believe me. They can be pests," said Betty.

Annie stopped her trips to the kitchen counter long enough to say, "There, Robert, help yourself. After you rang, Ned asked how a wee boy like you could be in the Royal Navy, but I reminded him you must be seventeen now, like Betty. Well, you were a wan wee boy, weren't you? Your mother fretted over ye. A good boy, but with a stutter, so you kept quiet, mostly. Not like Lizzie's two."

Blushing, Robert said, "I still stutter sometimes. There, I got that out alright. As for Lizzie's two boys, they were t-terrible b-bullies."

"Aye, but now I see you're a proper man," said Ned, stubbing his cigarette out and moving the ashtray off the table. "And I've never held with bullies." Pointing to the insignia on Robert's right arm—a pair of wings split by a lightning bolt—Ned asked, "What's that mean?"

"Telegraphist, rating of Ordinary Telegraphist. We're called sparkers."

"Is that what you do in the navy? Send telegraphs?" asked Annie.

Scooping a small amount of each vegetable and less beef onto his plate, Robert passed the platter to Ned.

I can't talk about the Huff-Duff or any real code. What do I tell them? "Em, we do the talking for our ship to the other British ships at sea, but we hide the message in code, and the code is kept secret from the Germans. We try to keep it secret, anyhow."

Annie returned to the table with a large steaming bowl of buttered mashed potatoes and a plate of sliced bread, put them down in front of Robert, and with a groan, sat down in the chair closest to the kitchen sink.

"How?" asked Ned.

"So, it depends. It's called encrypting the message, not by Morse Code, you know..." he tapped the table. "Long-short-long means SOS—help, or by flashes of light from a lantern on deck that mimic Morse Code. Whichever it is, it's not in plain language because Morse Code is known by everyone at sea, it's not secret. We had to create a secret way of delivering a message, one that has to be deciphered, translated—its code cracked. The Germans do the same." Noting that everyone had food on their plates, he followed Ned's lead and ate a piece of beef. "That's lovely—I haven't had beef in a long time."

The family fell into silence as they ate, so Robert concentrated on his food. *We nattered away during our meals at home, even breakfast. This silence while eating must come from Ned's family.*

"For dessert, I've a jam roll from Ebinger's," said Annie. From her plate that contained little but beef and potato, she slipped bits to the dog under the table.

Ned pushed back and stood up at the sideboard. "We'll enjoy some of the whiskey you bought, Robert. Thanks. The boys deliver and run errands for the liquor store we went to— they made good money the week before Christmas. Aye, they'll be back at it for New Year's."

"I don't approve, mind. Someone could take advantage of them, rob them, worse," said Annie. She inhaled sharply as if confronted with a mouse in the corner—the tic to signal distress Robert's mother and all her sisters shared—hearing it made him smile.

"Oh, come on. My brothers and me worked when we wore dresses, so we were no more than four. It's good for them." Ned put a generous glass down in front of Robert. "Do you take water?"

"Aye, thanks. Cheers."

"Cheers. So, Robert, how long is your leave?" asked Ned.

"Through Tuesday twelve hundred hours—noon. I thought I'd like to…"

"The boys may be back in time to see you off. I hope so," said Ned. "Aye, they'll kick themselves if they miss you."

"I brought them a wee gift each. The navy yard has a store open for sailors to buy wee gifts, for children, too."

"Oh, that's nice of you, Robert," said Annie.

"Where are you going from here?" asked Ned.

"They never say until we're underway—it's kept secret. I didn't know we were due here until we'd left port."

"'Loose lips sink ships,' eh?" asked Ned.

"Oh, aye? That's a good one," said Robert. "We're not allowed to wear the tapes with our ship's name on our tallies anymore. Everything's kept secret."

"Oh, so your mother didn't know then. I wondered after you rang. I'd got a letter wishing us a Happy Christmas, but the rest was mostly blacked out. Now that America's in the war, I imagine you may cross over more often?" asked Annie.

Robert shrugged. "I had a short liberty with my parents just before we shipped out. A surprise also. Two days, but I hadn't seen them in months and by chance, I was there on my mother's birthday, on the 16th, which was nice for us."

"That's right, Florrie's a December baby too, like Betty. They must have been happy to see you. They must worry," said Annie. "And how are your parents?" She cut a piece of beef in two, put half in her mouth and the rest down under the table.

"They seem well, but they do worry about me. And the rationing has gotten worse over there...it's not as bad as England, but a few things are not to be found and many are scarce. Of course, they're afraid they'll be b-bombed again."

"How long does it take to cross in one of your ships? Quicker than the ocean liner that brought us here, I'll wager," said Ned.

"Em, I don't think I should say, sorry."

"Oh, aye, alright," said Ned, waving his hand.

"Aunt Meg sent them two chickens, big ones, for Mum's birthday. Mum was amazed. The box sent also contained eggs, potatoes, whiskey, all sorts. Mum and Aunt Lizzie cooked a grand birthday dinner for us."

"So, it's difficult to come by all them things?" asked Ned, lighting a cigarette.

"Aye, most, but they've a neighbor in Portstewart, this auld fella, and he knows his way around and finds things rationed or short. He packed everything in a box and his pal on the railroad kept an eye on it. My da collected it at the station in B-Belfast."

I'm babbling. He scratched his neck, realizing that he was beginning to cook sitting in this hot kitchen, wearing a woolen uniform, and drinking whiskey. The large iron radiator behind Betty clanked and burbled, smelling of the steam leaking out of the valve and sizzling on the silver-painted metal.

"That rash you've got, it's from shaving, I'll wager," said Ned. "Are you not allowed to grow a beard in the British navy? I thought sailors were bearded."

Robert flushed furiously, increasing the rash's itch, but he put his hand down onto his lap. "Oh, aye, with permission."

"I had a terrible rash once when I was young. It's from

shaving too quick, too rough, so I've never shaved in a hurry since, nor with a dull blade, mind. But I imagine you can't take your time doing anything on board ship."

Annie said, "You could try witch hazel—it's in the bathroom cabinet—it works a charm on a rash. You know, I'd forgot you had lovely curly dark hair, Robert. Not from any of us, although now that I think of her, Meg's is a wee bit curly."

Robert felt the heat in his blush increase, but Ned made all of them laugh by saying, "Not from your father that's sure— Ralph's always been bald."

"So he has! Da says that he kept his hair just long enough to trick Mum into marrying him. His mum had curly hair he says. I don't remember her. Anyway, I'd enjoy seeing New York tomorrow, if you'd tell me the best spots to visit."

"I can go with you," offered Betty with some languor, "show you around."

"You don't have school, or work?"

"No, we have Christmas school vacation for another week. We could go in the morning and spend the whole day." She looked at her mother, then her father. "You're staying here tonight?"

"I'd planned to stay at the barracks at the navy yard."

"No, lad, stay here, unless you have to report back. I'll lend you a pair of pajamas if you like. You can sleep in one of the boys' beds. They're wee, mind."

Robert laughed. "I sleep in a hammock onboard ship, so whatever it's like will be welcome. Pajamas would be a luxury."

"I'll get dessert," said Annie, standing. To Robert, she added, "On a Sunday, we usually have sandwiches around eight. Later we listen to the radio play of the week or sing along if Betty feels like playing the piano."

Robert said, "I've just thought, Betty, why don't you think of the p-places you like best, and we'll see them t-tomorrow? I'd love a wee dander on solid land."

"OK. We'll go in the morning."

"More whiskey, Robert?" asked Ned.

"I won't say no."

Ned poured generous whiskies for each of them, as Annie brought the plates of jam roll to the table.

"Kettle's on," she said, eying the whiskey poured.

NEW YORK

*S*omething woke Robert from a deep sleep. Utterly confused about where he was, he looked at the radium-painted dial on his navy issue wristwatch: 00530—half five in the morning. His hand reached out to the bedside lamp and after a brief fumble, he turned it on.

Padding to the bathroom barefoot, he locked the door and while using the toilet, found the allure of the large white tub and curtained shower compelling. With a quick decision, he stripped off the borrowed pajamas, turned on the water, and took a short but powerfully hot shower. Toweling himself off, he pulled the pajamas back on and wiped the fogged mirror to examine his angry rash. He decided he'd better let somebody else use the bathroom before he set about shaving carefully, as Ned suggested.

He opened the medicine cabinet, found the witch hazel bottle, and applied it liberally to the rash under his chin and the front of his neck. Three seconds later, he'd stuffed a towel in his mouth to smother his scream at the stinging pain and hurried out of the steamy bathroom.

Tommy, the adorable Cairn terrier, stood between Robert and the bedroom, showing his teeth. His ears flattened, he allowed a small growl, followed by a bark and another growl.

"It's alright, wee man. I'm friend, not foe."

While he hesitated, a fully dressed Annie came up the stairs. "Ach, is he threatening you, Robert? I wondered where he'd got to." She motioned to the dog and said, "Downstairs."

The dog lowered his head, wagged his tail, and ran down the stairs.

Annie touched her chin and asked, "Robert, I meant to ask… Florrie turned fifty this month, is that right?"

"Aye," he said, feeling foolish standing in front of his aunt in pajamas. He glanced down quickly.

"And she's alright? No illness?"

"She seems fine, aye. Like herself."

"And the others? Meg, Lizzie, David?"

"I think they're fine. David still works clearing the bombing rubble, so he must be."

Annie nodded and said, "Breakfast's ready when you are," before going into the bathroom.

Robert closed the bedroom door behind him, pulled off the pajamas and folded them neatly. After pulling on clean boxers, vest and socks from the navy shoulder bag, he made the bed, pulling the cover taught.

He began his daily ten-minute Royal Navy exercise routine with less vigor than usual. While performing the sit-ups, he faced the large crucifixes over each child's bed, Jesus hanging in agony on each. His mother had told him the story of Annie converting to Catholicism to marry Ned and the break it caused between her and their father, the grandfather who'd died when he was little. *I wonder did she ever regret it?*

Robert remained at the kitchen table waiting for Betty. He'd had too many cups of tea, and nearly two hours before, the buttered farl Annie made from last night's mashed potatoes with two real eggs, fried. Annie sat down and peppered him with questions about the living arrangements at 34 St. Ives Gardens, which she and Ned had sold to Meg and Lillian at war's outbreak. Annie moved on to asking about who lived where in Portstewart. While he answered, he checked the clock on the kitchen wall.

At a break in Annie's interrogation, he asked, "Betty is...here?"

Ned chuckled, "Aye, lad. She takes hours to ready herself in the mornings, but she'll be down. Sooner or later. Tell me this, how did you come to be in the navy? Is there conscription in Ireland? There wasn't last time."

"No, and I don't think there will be." Robert shrugged. "I was taken with the idea of it. I joined last summer when we were living in Portstewart. Mum and I returned to my father immediately after I t-told her I'd j-joined. She was upset. I stayed at home until I left for my t-training in England."

"What about your father?"

"Oh, he's chuffed about me serving. He worries, but he's proud of me. My m-mum just worries." *I worry, too.*

At Ned's feet, the dog whined.

"Oh, aye, wee fella, sorry. I walked him at half five, but he's ready for a good walk now. I'm on vacation from my job, but no matter, we stick to his schedule— a quick walk when I first get home from the night shift and then a long one after breakfast, before I go to bed. Well, enjoy your sight seein'." Ned stood and checked his pockets before scuffing into the hall in leather slippers, the dog's nails skittering on the polished wooden floor as he followed. They heard Ned's grunts as he dressed for the cold. The dog's collar jangled, the front door latch clicked and, softly, the door closed.

Annie sighed and said, "The landlord, Mr. Wood, is coming any minute to collect his rents so I'll need to clear the table. We're the supers for the building." She sidled around it, picking up the teacups, newspapers, and ashtray.

"'Supers?'" asked Robert.

"Superintendents. We manage the building for Mr. Wood. I collect the rents and sort out the loonies who live here, manage the plumbers, painters, all the lazy ligs. Ned keeps the furnace going." She made a face. "He digs out the incinerator, too. Not the nicest of jobs for him. Neither is his night job at Con Ed in the city." She sighed before turning to the sink. "To think he had his own business in Belfast."

Robert nodded uncertainly. Just as he felt the first flutter of real impatience waiting for his cousin, she finally appeared in the hallway, dressed to go out. "Ready?" she asked cheerfully, pulling on her gloves.

It was a bitterly cold day, one with near gale force wind that roared down the canyons created by Manhattan's tall buildings. Blown into Betty's choice for lunch, the 42nd Street Horn and Hardart Automat, Robert enjoyed everything about their lunch. From the marble walls containing glass boxes of food portions, to the wealth of choice and the lack of expense. Robert freed many choices with his nickels before settling to eat his vast lunch, while his cousin watched, amused.

After lunch, the cousins hurried to board a bus, appreciating the warmth and the view of a seat on the enclosed upper deck of the Madison Avenue-Fifth Avenue bus traveling uptown. The bus turned uptown on Fifth Avenue and pulled over to the curb. The last of their fellow passengers filed down the staircase, leaving them alone on the upper deck. The driver got down and, with difficulty, lit a cigarette. After he flicked his cigarette onto the sidewalk, they lost sight of him. Abruptly, the bus swerved away from the curb and started off again, zooming south. Betty pointed to something she called "Millionaire's Row" and the vast Central Park on view.

"If you see something you want to visit, we can hop off. In

the next blocks we'll pass The Metropolitan Museum of Art." After the museum, Robert's head swiveled right or left as he followed Betty's pointing finger identifying more grand mansions and hotels, until they pulled alongside a golden statue in what she named The Grand Army Plaza.

Three spotty white boys aged sixteen or so climbed into the upper deck and after some consultation, chose the seats directly behind Betty and Robert.

The back of Robert's neck tingled. He could feel their breath, as though they were leaning forward and too close. They were sniggering.

Betty said, "Coming up on the next blocks, let's see, St. Patrick's Cathedral, Rockefeller Center, and the famous depart-ment store, Saks Fifth Avenue."

At a stoplight, one of the boys got up and sat in the seat next to Robert. Loudly and with an exaggerated lisp, he announced, "Oh, dear, it's the navy. Couldn't you just swoon, boys?" He flipped his hand up to his face and wriggled his shoulder. The other two boys cackled and bumped the back of Robert's seat.

One of the two boys still behind them hit Robert's shoulder as he stood up and moved to the seat in front of them. His pasty face was covered with acne, his pompadour well oiled. To Betty, he asked, "Whatcha doin' wit dis faggot, baby doll?" He reached out to touch her hair, but Robert's hand shot out and stayed the boy's hand with force.

"You leave her be."

The boy remaining behind them tore Robert's tally off his head and made to rush forward to the staircase, but Robert's foot shot out and tripped him. His friends laughed. Robert jumped up and yanked the tally out the boy's grasp.

"You feck off and all, you wee bastards," growled Robert in his best iron Belfast, standing over the sprawled boy.

"Where youse from, anyhow?" asked the one in the seat across from him.

Meanwhile, the boldest one, the one who'd called Robert a faggot, tried to touch Betty again.

Robert pulled his fist back and hit him fast and squarely on the nose, as his father had taught him to do. Blood blossomed, drenching the boy's face and coat collar as he howled and held his nose.

Robert yanked Betty up and out of the seat, stepped on the boy still struggling to get up in the rocking, speeding bus, and pulled her with him to the staircase, his sea legs serving them well.

Downstairs, they chose a seat near the driver. Robert, panting a little, rubbed his throbbing hand on his coat. Looking at his cousin's pale face, he said, "Let's stop somewhere for a drink."

Betty reached up and pulled the cord. The driver pulled the bus up to the curb. The cousins got down off the bus and began to walk down Fifth Avenue. The bus roared away with the boys still onboard.

Looking pale and shaken, she said, "Thank you for saving me from that awful boy, pawing at me like that."

"It was my pleasure." He found that he was shaking a little. He put her arm in his.

"Oh, here's Lord and Taylor's—they have the best windows at Christmas—let's look, just for a minute. The Algonquin Hotel is a few blocks away. We'll have a drink there. A lot of famous New York writers drink there. Who knows? Maybe we'll see one."

Robert noticed that her chin rose in the air a little when she used the phrase, "...famous New York writers..." She'd dressed well for their day out, wearing a toque hat on her curled hair. Looking at her sheer stockings, he thought, *she must be bloody frozen.* At least she'd worn ankle-high lined galoshes over her shoes. His shoes and socks were soaked from walking through the slush in the streets.

"Do they sell men's clothing in this store?"

"Yes."

"Do you mind if we go in so I can buy a few things?"

"No, not at all, but it's not an inexpensive store…"

"I'd pay anything for dry socks." They twirled through the revolving door and landed in the warm, scented main floor of the vast department store. Locating the men's department, Robert asked, "Do you mind meeting me in a few minutes?"

Once alone at the underwear counter, he purchased a set of full-length soft underwear and two pairs of boxers and vests, before moving on to the counters selling thick socks and woolen gloves. What the lower ratings wore at sea never concerned the officers. He could stow these in his kit, break them out and enjoy their warmth under his serge boiler suit, should he have to serve on another freezing route. After purchasing them, he asked for a changing room and gratefully pulled dry socks on. There was nowhere else to stow his wet navy issue socks, so they went into his shoulder bag.

Betty waited at the perfume counter, sniffing and dabbing, but she refused his offer to buy her the Worth fragrance she seemed to enjoy, asking him to smell it daubed on her wrist. "No, Robert. It's too dear, really. When I work at Altman's again, I'll get a discount. I can wait. They'll hire me again for the January sales."

"Alright, I give up. Let's have that drink!

A bald, mustached, and well-dressed man looked Robert up and down with faint disapproval. He stood like a sentinel at the entrance to The Blue Bar at the Algonquin, looking like neither a waiter nor a customer. Eyebrows raised, he asked, "May I help you?"

"May we have a table?" asked Betty haughtily, one eyebrow arched, her chin in the air again.

Robert blushed.

"And may I ask how old you are? I'm afraid I must."

"Eighteen," said Robert, flustered by the lie.

"And me," said Betty.

Smiling, the man said, "In that case, come this way, please. May I take your coat, miss?"

"I'll keep it around me, thanks."

"Sir?"

"Yes, alright."

The man brought them to a banquette table and pulled it out so that Betty could slide in easily. Robert took off his tally, unbuttoned his coat and handed them to the man, whom he assumed was some sort of factotum. The man put his hand out for the Lord and Taylor bag, which Robert relinquished after a small hesitation, but he slung his shoulder bag over the chair back.

Robert sat across from Betty, and leaning forward, said, "I was bracing for another New Yorker having a go at us."

Betty sniffed. "Acts like he owns the place."

The man reappeared immediately. "And what may we serve you today?"

"A daiquiri, please," said Betty. She opened her compact and proceeded to examine her face.

"Sir?"

"Are there American whiskies?"

"Bourbon, Rye and variations of each...I'm fond of a Tennessee whiskey, shall I bring you a glass?"

"Yes, thanks."

Betty took her cigarettes out of her bag and, shaking two halfway out of the pack, offered Robert one.

He took The Blue Bar matches from the table and lit hers, then his. "Thanks. If I rolled my own in here, they'd throw us out."

"I hope you're enjoying being here, despite those boys on the bus. After all, it's been an adventure." Betty's brown eyes were merry. She blew blue smoke out in a thin stream off to one side. Her lipstick left a deep red smudge on the cigarette end.

"It has been that—not that I don't have enough adventure in

the navy. No, honestly, I am enjoying being here, but do you think we could return to Bay Ridge after our drinks? I'm ready for a wee bit of peace and quiet."

"Sure."

Looking around, he said, "This place is blue all right. A few drinks and you'd mistake the walls for the floor or the ceiling."

The man returned with their drinks and a small bowl of mixed nuts, and placing them with care on the table, said, "Enjoy your drinks." He shifted the tray in his hands. "I'm called elsewhere in the hotel now, but I wanted to tell you that whenever you can join us, you're more than welcome. However, just one or two blocks west, in the theater district, there are many bars and restaurants of quality, but less expensive and where you can dance—just a friendly suggestion, because you are welcome here. You are an Irishman, Mr., um?"

"Robert Henderson, Ordinary Seaman Henderson. Yes, I am. A Belfast man. Thank you, sir, and your name is?"

"Fred Campbell. I own this hotel. Stop at the registration desk and meet the hotel cat on your way out—I believe that cats are lucky for sailors. His name is Romeo and he's the toast of New York. May you have a fair wind, Seaman Henderson. Well, now that we're in the war with you, we hope to see you again." He held his hand out and Robert took it for a firm and quick grasp.

"A pleasure to meet you, Miss, um," said Fred Campbell.

"Wright. Elizabeth Wright, of New York."

The hotel owner smiled at them before leaving their table.

Betty and Robert fell back in their seats, laughing.

"He *does* own the place! Haha! Here's to your New York, Betty!"

"Cheers!"

They raised their glasses and sipped.

Betty's brow furrowed as she looked at the groups of customers seated around them. "Oh, dammit. Why didn't I ask him if there were any famous writers in here now?"

"There's a famous cat, I gather, and I'd better pet him on the way out—would be bad luck not to. After that, let's find one of those places he mentioned for a dance before we go back. I'll risk one more side of New York."

"You like to dance?"

"I do. Meg taught me, and we'd dance sometimes in the evening up in Portstewart. I was the only fella who could dance with the four ladies in that house—Albert has two left feet and Frank won't even try."

"I'm glad Aunt Meg is safe. I adore her. She and Aunt Lillian were so good to me when I was little. I send them cards at Christmas."

"You called her *Aunt* Lillian?"

"I did. She was like another aunt to me when we lived together with Aunt Jinny at 34 St. Ives Gardens. I had many aunts, your mother and Aunt Lizzie, too. Anyway, Lillian and Meg took me places, especially Meg. I'm glad to hear they are all well. She usually sends a card at Christmas, but perhaps it's held up somewhere? Do you remember our farewell dinner at our house? We must have been six."

"A little. I remember sitting at the big table with the family all around. There was a baby…"

"My brother Denis."

"It was Denis? I remember him crying. I was the only one who got him to quiet."

"You were. I remember that, too. The next day we left." Betty's smile faded. "I miss having such a large family around me. We've no one but ourselves over here." Quiet for a second, she asked, "Do you go to Mass? I mean is it served on your ship?"

"Do I what? No."

"No, I don't go either, but it's been hell to pay with my mother since I stopped. My father couldn't care less. Do your parents care?"

"But I'm not C-catholic, we're not C-catholic," spluttered

Robert.

"*Not* Catholic?"

"No. None of our family are."

Betty sat up straight. "What do you mean, *none* of them are."

"We're P-Protestants, Betty—the whole family. Your mother converted from Protestantism to marry your father. But you must know! It's what my p-parents told me, but I've heard it spoken of by the others, too. It caused a fall out between your mother and her father, our grandfather." Watching Betty's face turn pale in the blueish light, he asked, "Don't tell me you really didn't know?"

She sat back. "No. I didn't know. She never told me. I mean, it makes sense now that you say it. From my memories, and things my mother's said, the hymns she sings, it makes sense, now that you say it. But she never told me."

"I've put my f-foot in it then. I'm sorry."

"No, it's not your fault, it's hers." She stubbed out her cigarette with force.

"Listen, don't tell your p-parents I let the c-cat out of the bag, will you? They've been so welcoming, I'd be sorry to repay them with a bombshell like this."

Betty shook her head. The two drank in awkward silence for a minute, Robert searching for something to say. "Do you think your parents will go back home one day?"

In a flat voice, she answered. "Go back? No. I don't see that. My father likes it here, the boys too. My mother would go in a second, she misses Belfast terribly, but not without them, obviously."

"What about you?"

"Oh, yes, I will, to visit. I remember Belfast so well. I could find my way around now, from our house to the school, to the greengrocer, to your house. I'd like to travel to many places when the war's over. London and Paris when I have a job and money."

"What will you do when you're out of school?"

Betty perked up. "I'll apply to newspapers for junior positions. I want a career, to be a newspaperwoman. A woman of business, like Meg and Lillian."

"A newspaperwoman...that's exciting. Will you stay in New York?"

"Oh yes. I can't see living anywhere else. I want to live in Manhattan and work for a big paper. What about you? What will you do when the war's over?"

"Something technical, I think. I'm good at maths and I like understanding how things work." Raising his glass, he said, "Here's to meeting again in Belfast."

Betty raised her glass but frowned. "The invasions in Europe... the bombings were so shocking, first England, then Belfast, then Pearl Harbor. Now we're used to it, I suppose. What you do must be very dangerous—we see the convoys in the newsreels."

"Sometimes. Listen, Betty, I am sorry about telling you about the religion. P-please forgive me."

"You only told me the truth. What were you supposed to do? Lie for her? Lie for them? My father never told me either. I wonder why, though, I really do. Now that I think about it, of course they're Protestants. I remember, Meg tried taking me to her church for Christmas and my mother wouldn't let me go."

"I c-can't imagine why they haven't told you. All the family knew and liked your father—they all knew about your mother's c-conversion. My parents held the reception for their wedding in our house and everyone came, your father's family, too, they said, everyone except our grandfather. But I'm sure your p-parents meant well, whatever the reason. Will you ask?"

She met his gaze and laughed. "*Ask*? Are you serious? You don't ask my parents things, believe me. I don't even know how they met or where. There are no photographs of their wedding. I mean I know they were married in St. Malachy's in 1922, but *I* didn't know the reception was at your house." She sipped her drink. "One day, I'll ask my father. My mother doesn't talk about the past, not about anything serious. Oh, the hell with it. Forget it. Drink up and we'll go for that dance."

Robert smiled. "Alright. I must meet the cat and, then could we duck into a bookstore? I've read everything I can stand to in the ship's library. Also, could we bring something back for our tea? I hate sponging, and your mum can't use my ration book like mine can. Is there somewhere we could buy what they like? Would she like that?"

"Yes, she would. I'll call her to tell her what you're planning. You're too nice, Robert."

∿

"Let's walk down to the end of the platform. You'll have a great view from the last car."

Robert followed in Betty's wake through a packed platform until they came to the sparser end of the platform. Once on the train, she elbowed her way to the end of the car and stationed Robert at the last door and window, standing across from him.

Once on the Brooklyn Bridge, he did indeed enjoy the view, looking west at the tallest of Manhattan's buildings.

"Look at that sunset. Beautiful," said Betty, pointing to a display of intense purples, gold and orange behind the tall buildings, the light refracted by the many windows.

"A winter evening sky is the most beautiful. At sea we often see..." Urgently, he said, "Betty, look." He pointed to the destroyer docked below them. The hulking dull grey ship was covered with masses of wires and lines, with impossible numbers of antennae, large and small, some revolving to rove the air waves. The big guns were shrouded, and the shore ensign snapped in the stiff wind off the East River. He whispered, "That's my ship!"

"Oh!" she said. "It's huge! How do you find your way around?"

"It takes a wee while to learn. I still haven't been to all parts of her."

They found two seats together after passengers left at the DeKalb Avenue stop. The rear of Robert's bellbottoms caught on a sharp bit of the glazed caned seat. Furtively, he felt to ascertain the damage to the fabric, but the glare of the woman next to him ended his search. He grasped the nearest white porcelain pole and looked around at his fellow passengers' mask-like faces in the dim interior. The riveted metal beams and the swaying car reminded him of a ship. Betty had called these crowds "the rush hour." Few spoke to one another, most read newspapers or books, or stared stoically ahead. Many slept. Nobody smiled.

They left the subway with the crowd at Bay Ridge Avenue. He trudged along carrying his shopping bags, Betty leading the way in the now dark street.

As they passed a group of giggling schoolgirls, one yelled, "Look, girls, the fleet's in!" One wolf-whistled and the others laughed.

Betty muttered, "Silly little girls," before pulling him into a delicatessen called The Scandinavian.

Bone-lean women wearing woolen hats with earflaps and speaking in accented, singsong English patrolled the back of the deli cases. He trod the saw-dusted wooden floor down the length of the cases, admiring the quantity of food displayed.

"That macaroni and cheese I had for lunch was delicious. Shall I buy macaroni and cheese? It all looks delicious, but what shall I order?"

"Would you like me to order?"

"Aye."

Robert sat on the chair in the apartment foyer to remove his soaked shoes. The strains of a piece of piano music he recognized but could not name floated out from their parlor. *When I'm home for good, I'll listen to good music, go to the concert halls.*

In the kitchen his aunt assessed the food items as she unpacked the bag. "Oh, this is very nice, Betty. Your father likes their almond ring cakes very much, and Swedish meatballs." Annie stuck her head out of the kitchen to say, "Thank you, Robert."

"It was the least I could do after the lovely meals you've fed me."

Annie looked at the shoe in his hand and the sodden socks on his feet. "There's newspaper in the closet there, for Ned's boots. Always covered in coal dust, they are." *Like my father's*, she thought. "Stuff your shoes with paper and put them on the radiator, they'll dry. Have you dry socks?"

"Aye."

Nodding, she walked back into the kitchen.

Robert walked up the stairs to the boys' room in his wet socks, carrying his shoulder bag, the Brentano Bookstore and Lord and Taylor shopping bags. He sat down on the little bed that was his for one more night and, sighing, changed into a pair of dry socks. Relief was instant until the memory of the boys on the bus reemerged—the one boy lisping, the other boy calling him a faggot. *Did they see something in me? Was it just the stories about sailors being at it with one another—not that I've ever seen any sign of that—or was it something about me?*

After dinner, Ned and Robert refilled their glasses. Annie announced that she was returning to the basement to hang the clothes to dry. She'd refused Robert's help with the washing up and the clothes hanging. Nobody else offered. Ned, Robert and Betty moved into the parlor. Tommy sat at Robert's stocking feet, which he rubbed together in appreciation of their dry, warm state.

"There's a radio play on at 9, Robert—the Lux Radio Theater. It should be good," said Betty, settling in at the piano.

"Ann Todd's in the play. You must know her—the British actress?"

She peered at the stacks of sheet music for a few minutes. "Here's one I can play but can't sing, it's too difficult. Do you know Hoagy Carmichael's music?"

Robert shook his head. *Hogie?*

Betty stretched her fingers and began to play as Annie entered the room and sat down in an armchair.

He had never heard it, but it was very pretty. When Betty finished, she turned a few pages and played the most popular song of the war, which Robert did know, of course. Whenever he heard it, the sentimental words about meeting someone again, he thought of Albert, a secret he could never tell anyone. Betty sang alone in a sure alto, and then her tenor father joined her. When Annie began to warble along, Robert's baritone joined.

"I'm sure you think of your mum and da when you hear that song, eh?" asked Annie, smiling. "It's too bad you can't stay for our Hogmanay. We've friends in the building who join us every year. Glaswegians, they are, very jolly."

"Aye, too bad, but we'll have a wee party wherever I am." He smiled and took a sip of whiskey, comforted by the warmth of the room and the presence of this family, his family.

The comfort was fleeting. Feeling suddenly frightened of what awaited him the next day and the day after that, wherever he would be sent, into whatever danger, he controlled the tears that formed in his eyes, but only just. Clearing his throat, he asked Betty, "Would you mind giving me one of those lucky cigarettes of yours?"

"Sure. Here. Take the pack, I have another." She pulled a cigarette out and tossed the Lucky Strikes pack to him.

Betty stood, moved to an armchair across from Robert, and lit a cigarette.

Ned winked at him. "I can't thank you enough for protecting Betty today. Your father would be proud. You are a proper man. You tell him I said so. Did you ever box?"

Annie stood. "Oomph, I'm that stiff. I'll put the kettle on. Who wants tea?"

"I'll have some, Mommy," said Betty. She pulled a strand of tobacco off her lower lip.

Annie turned in the doorway and said, "Hooligans, they were. Accosting people on the Fifth Avenue bus. What's next? Where was the driver?"

"Downstairs, driving," said Betty, rolling her eyes.

As she left the room, they heard her mutter, "Well, they ought to have conductors onboard."

Robert made eye contact with Ned and said, "No, I never boxed, but my da taught me how to handle meself."

"I practiced Savate when I was young. French kick boxing. I should teach the boys. Have you ever seen a match?"

"No, I haven't. How did you learn it?"

"My brother John and I went to the racecourses in France, for our business. This was after the first war, and we saw some matches. I found someone to teach me in Belfast. He was a sailor, as a matter of fact, a merchant seaman. Savate was popular after the 1924 Olympics. My poor brother was gone by then, dead two years earlier." Ned looked into the middle distance.

Betty twiddled the dial on the large mahogany radio cabinet. Robert could see the tubes glowing brighter and brighter, until a resonant American bass voice addressed them quietly, reading the news.

"What number is the Lux Theater, Daddy?"

"NBC is it?

"Got it," she said, turning the dial. "Where is Mommy? She won't want to miss the beginning."

"Shall I fetch her?" asked Robert.

"I will," said Betty and she left the room.

"Here, Robert, can I pour you another?"

"Aye, thank you. It will be a long time before I have whiskey again."

"Tell me this, if people write to you, how do you pick up your mail?" asked Ned.

"When we get to port, our mail's there. The navy's very efficient."

"What time must you be there again? Oh, noon—that's right, you said." Ned was quiet a moment. "Would you like me to go with you, down the navy yard? That way you don't have to worry about which train to take and so on. And if the boys are home in time, they could come with us. I know they'd enjoy meeting you and seeing the navy yard."

A terrible anxiety seized Robert just imagining embarking and casting off. There was no choice, he knew. A sailor who goes adrift is in terrible trouble.

His uncle was looking at him, waiting.

Robert was glad he'd visited and made the connection with these nice people, but they didn't love him, and suddenly he missed his parents. "It would be nice to have c-company to the yard," said Robert weakly, even though he wasn't sure it would.

The dog jumped up on the couch and snuggled next to him. Without thinking, Robert laid his arm around the dog and scratched his chin.

"He likes you," said Ned.

Trying to regain his relaxation, Robert took a large sip of whiskey and tried to sink into the feel of the warm dog, the orange glow of the radio tubes, the deep murmur of the radio announcer, and the company. But anxiety brought him back to what the next day held, and he hoped the night and the morning would pass quickly. Once back with his mates, marching lock-step to the destroyer, routine would replace this anxiety. He'd enter the chute to whatever lay ahead, his fate sealed, at an end with the civilian world, temporarily he hoped, but released from the temptation to run away, and relieved of some of his fear. The job and the routine would take over for much of the journey, the fear of death remote until an attack, when the world crystallized into one pure feeling—terror.

THE OFFICIAL SECRETS ACT—
FEBRUARY 1942

WESTERN APPROACHES, IRELAND—
BLETCHLEY, ENGLAND

*D*estroyer HMS *Keppler* fought the water at high speed
—struggling up each crest and down each trough to
push forward. If by no other means, Robert knew their location
by the speed with which the engines propelled them forward
through a rough sea—they had entered the Western Approaches.
Part sound nautical practice, part superstition, the order was full
speed ahead to survive the treacherous west coast of Ireland and
any lurking U-boats at the end of a perilous Atlantic crossing.

Spreading his legs, Robert braced against the violent pitching
and rolling. Headset on, head bent, he barely blinked studying
the Huff-Duff. *English people give everything silly names, like children do.*

The engines slowed then sped again as the ship tacked starboard. *Are we turning north around Donegal? Please, God.* He
barely breathed, waiting for the worst. His vision riveted, he
waited for the blip in the screen detecting a U-boat underneath—
or worse, a wolf pack of U-boats. The engines reverted to top
speed. Groaning with the strain, the ship continued north-
eastward.

The radioman with his chair back against Robert's passed a
handwritten note over his shoulder. "Londonderry calling.

Welcome home." Robert passed it on to the third man and hands over microphones, the three men packed into the radio room cheered.

Still silencing the microphone, the chief signaler shouted, "We made it! We're around the Malin Head," before whistling over the intercom with the news for the bridge.

The engines slowed and slowed yet again as the first bell rang. Slowing again confirmed for Robert the hope that they'd rounded Malin Head and reached the section of sea filled with Allied ships of all sizes and types in a safe area.

One bell signaled Robert's stand-down time from his one-watch-on-two-watches-off over twenty-four hours.

On his two earlier return cross-Atlantic trips, he'd relished assignment to middle watch because they arrived to greet the dawn along the coast of Northern Ireland. At the sound of the destroyer's *Wup! Wup! Wup!* Robert's chief nodded at him and ripping off his headphones, he grabbed his coat and tally, and took the ladders up to the deck two steps at a time.

Scanning the coast from the starboard railing, he was in time to see the few twinkling lights of wild Donegal in the neutral Republic of Ireland. His tired eyes scanned the gathering light along the coast. It was a game, he knew, indulging a mirage of home when they arrived at the turn on the Causeway Coast. On a moonlit night, he enjoyed the light glinting on dark house windows eastward past Donegal.

Was he ever rewarded with correct identification of the town of Portstewart, let alone Meg's and Lillian's cottage—Albert's home—high on a hill and overlooking the harbor? Probably not —but he told himself he may have seen the cottage in dawn's light, once. He'd waved and waved.

The blackout made a point of reference impossible to fix when moving. Sometimes he saw lights through rips in the blackout in all the Northern Irish coastal towns, but generally the blackout held through the night and as twilight brightened to a winter dawn.

A sparker named Louis—the only other Belfast man on board —stopped to chat. "Shame we can't anchor and go ashore. I haven't seen my parents in two years." Gesturing to the collection of large troop ships escorted by the convoy ahead of them, he said, "But we have to deliver that lot to Liverpool. You'll see Belfast Lough in the morning light and the hills, lucky devil. I'm on watch now. The beard looks good on ye."

Rubbing his eyes, Robert said, "Thanks. I got permission to grow it a few weeks ago. My eyes are burning now, but I'll wait to get some kip till after we sail past Belfast. What's the grub?"

"No pork and beans left, so back to pilchard, but maybe they'll pop open another tin of corned beef...bread's gone green around the edges, tinned carrots. Thank God we'll dock soon and take on fresh supplies. Rumor is we'll have two-day passes —I was hoping for longer. Don't know how you Huff-Duff men stare down them things all night but thank God you do. Well, say cheerio to Belfast for me." The sailor disappeared down the nearest ladder to the lower deck.

Robert decided to get down to the mess, even though he shuddered thinking about the pilchard, a fish that did nothing to lessen his dislike of seafood. He'd return to the deck once the ship tacked starboard rounding the Antrim Coast, on her way past the closest Scottish towns and south past the Belfast Lough and the hills.

I'll post letters to my parents and Albert once we're docked in Liverpool. It hit Robert again how selfish he'd been—and reckless —to join up. The terror of crossing the dangerous waters of the North Atlantic and the Norwegian, and Barents seas had drilled into him just how foolish he'd been.

He prayed that he would live to tell Albert how sorry he was he'd joined the navy, breaking both their hearts. He'd never be able to write that to him, or about his fear of his feelings, their feelings. Not in a letter read by somebody in a cramped office at the admiralty.

"Chief wants to see you, Henderson."

The petty officer stood over Robert, stopping the motion of a forkful of tinned beef to his mouth. He looked down at his plate and then up at the PO.

"Now."

His hand out for the plate, the junior cook said, "I'll keep it warm for you, Bob."

Robert followed the petty officer around the corridor to the chief petty officer's office, squeezed between the sickbay and the entrance to the engine room of the *Keppler*. The engines roar and heat, the smell of hot grease and fuel exhaust formed an invisible wall they had to pass through.

Robert snapped to attention and said, "Henderson, Robert R. reporting."

Sitting at a small desk, the chief looked up from a small stack of paper. He mopped his forehead with a large handkerchief. "At ease. Make ready to leave us in Liverpool, Henderson. You've got new orders. Liberty is cancelled."

Robert assumed the stance: hands clasped behind his back, legs apart, chest out, chin up, and eyes trained on the regulation Royal Navy photo of King George filling the wall behind the chief's desk. Robert asked, "Aye, aye, Chief. Where to?"

The middle-aged man looked up from the piece of paper he held. "You'll be given instructions in Liverpool." Shoving the pile of papers back inside, he carefully wound the string around the clasp, securing the folder.

The chief handed the folder to Robert. Looking down at the folder cover—"Royal Navy, Ordinary Seaman Henderson, Robert R., C/JX.262365 HMS Keppler, DOB 04/04/1924, Blood Group A+, 5'11", eyes brown, hair black, no scars or tattoos, Ordinary Telegraphist. Trained telegraphy and signals, Portsmouth; trained HFDF Liverpool. Enlisted 1941 Coleraine, NI. Next of kin..."—Robert frowned. He looked down at the older man's doughy face and into his bloodshot eyes.

"That's all I know, lad. Off you go. I put the Commander's permission slip to grow the beard," he pointed at Robert's face, "per regulation 3818, is in the folder. Go on and pack your kit. Best of luck."

Robert left the tiny room with the petty officer. "Finish your grub, Henderson, then get some kip. You've got two watches off to sleep and pull your kit together. You're a good Huff-Duff man, sorry to lose you."

Bulging kit bag hoisted onto one shoulder, gas mask and shoulder bag wrapped around him like bandoliers, Robert picked his way down the corridors of the rolling train cars. He'd had to stow his sea chest with the conductor, who promised to fetch it off the train at Bletchley.

Gingerly stepping over sleeping sailors, snoring soldiers and the women of the Royal Navy, chimes of WRNS— *wrens of a feather, sticking together*—he traveled the length of the crowded train. He brushed past feet, kits, and bags, worked to keep his balance, and inhaled the particular pong of British rail—over-flowing toilets, tobacco smoke, body odor, flatulence, the rare whiff of perfume, all undercut with the smell of burnt electrical wire and fuel. A few of the corridor dwellers were awake and nodded at him.

The actual passenger compartments were stuffed with sleeping humans, the lucky ones in seats, and the unlucky at their feet on the floor. Since they'd left Liverpool Lime Street Station at midnight, the train had not made any calls, but roared south, carrying its burden of hundreds of passengers, all in uniform. Searching for a spot on the corridor floor, he arrived at the penultimate car. There were more groups of Wrens in this car, the sleeping ones with their heads on their friends' laps or slumped against their pals' shoulders. The ones serving as pillows were chatting and smoking, and most said hello when he passed.

One called to him, "Sailor, sit here. We can make room for

you. There's nothing better in that last car, believe me." He turned around and she pointed to a spot as she and her neighbor scooted apart.

He smiled at the Wren smiling at him and made his way back. He tried to sit as gracefully as he could, but the train lurched sweeping around a bend and he ended up sitting on his Good Samaritan.

A Wren farther down yelled, "That's one way to get your man, Jo!" The others laughed.

Rearranging himself and his kit, he squeezed into the empty spot. "S-sorry." Knees up and back against the wooden car wall, he shoved the kit bag under his bent knees. Pulling the shoulder bag behind his back, he turned to the Good Samaritan and said, "Thanks so much."

"My pleasure. We sent scouts hours ago on a search and rescue for seats or more floor space, but it's hopeless."

He pushed the tally back off his forehead and extending his hand, said, "Ordinary Seaman Henderson, Robert. Hiya."

The Wren laughed and shook his hand. "Hiya. And you're a Belfast man! I grew up in the shadow of Belfast Castle. Ordinary Wren Bray, Josephine. I'm called Jo. And squashed on the other side, Ordinary Wren Aarons, Holda, called Holly."

In yet another Belfast brogue, Holly complained, "Oh, Jo. Nobody but the navy calls me Holda!"

"Holda? I've never heard the name."

"A long story—"

Robert turned back to Jo. "Aye, I am a Belfast man. South Belfast, Great Northern Street." Robert turned back to Holly. "Hiya."

"Hiya...are you Bob, or...?"

"Robert." They shook hands awkwardly since his trapped right arm and hand had to twist around to reach hers.

Pointing at the folded newspaper on her lap, a fountain pen in her left hand, she said, "Crosswords. We're both fanatics. Do you like the crosswords?"

"I like all puzzles, but I haven't tried crosswords much."

"You should do. Oh! You're a telegraphist! We are too! Look at his insignia!" Pointing to his sleeve and hers, Holly sat forward to relay this information to Jo.

"So, he is! Where have you been stationed?" asked Jo.

"On convoy duty in the North Atlantic, before that up to Iceland, Norway and Murmansk. I'd just got retrained and had a few trips under my belt doing something important and they've pulled me away! Seems a waste. I don't know where I'm going exactly, or why. I mean I don't know what I'll be doing."

"We don't know what our next job is either. Bletchley is our call."

"And mine! Do you really not know more?" he asked.

Jo shook her head. He turned to Holly, who said, "It's all very hush-hush. I expect they'll tell us at some point. Whatever it is, you'll be a damned sight safer than when you were at sea."

"Hush-hush, eh? What were you doing before?" he asked.

"I trained in Portsmouth before shipping up to Liverpool. I've been in the admiralty station for two years. Before that, I was studying mathematics at Queen's. Afore that I was a wee girl at school with Jo."

Jo laughed. "Holly only ran the Western Approaches out of Liverpool. I pushed wee wooden ships around a map with a long stick. Before joining the Wrens, I was studying law at Queen's. I can't imagine what hush-hush project they want me for, but since Holl's an utter chatterbox, I can't imagine what they want her for, either."

"We both speak German, that'll be it."

"I only read and write it to a very modest degree, but Holly is fluent and can chatter away in it. And she's a mathematician."

"Don't hold it against me, but I was born in Germany. My family were one step ahead of the Nazis—we escaped when I was a wee girl. That's what the name Holda is, German. I'll explain. Mum's mad for textiles—mad full stop. That's how we came to Belfast—my mother juggles jobs at Linen Hall Library and Ulster Museum—she's a textile expert. Mum named me Holda for the German patron saint of textiles, which is doubly odd since she was raised in a Jewish family, but that's her all over. My father had no say in the matter. Thankfully, my siblings called me Holly as a baby, so Holly I am."

Holly took her gold wire-rimmed glasses off and covered her eyes with the heels of her small hands.

"Alright?" he asked, softly.

Pulling her hands away, she smiled and said, "Oh, aye—utterly exhausted, but fine. What were you doing before, Robert?"

"Doing? I got my leaving certificate in May '41. I joined in August. I'm still seventeen now."

"Seventeen!" She gestured along the outline of his face. "It's the beard makes you look older."

"But your parents must be so worried about your convoy duty! They'll be relieved to know you're on terra firma," said Jo.

"Not about the convoy duty but they knew I was serving at sea, so yes, they were worried. I rang from Liverpool to tell them I was reassigned to a stone ship. Hope that's true."

"Why did you join?" asked Holly.

Robert surprised himself by laughing. "I've asked myself that question whilst on convoy duty. The answer is, I had no good reason, not good enough to risk being killed. What about you?"

He looked at both in turn.

Holly answered, "I was eighteen when I joined, encouraged by my father." She snapped her fingers. "I'd no choice. I'll go back to university when this is over."

Robert turned and asked, "And you, Jo?"

Jo hesitated before speaking. "Why did I join? My father was killed, and our home destroyed during the blitz—the May bombing. I lost everything in one night, except for what I stood up in and my father's law office in South Belfast. Even the wee dog was killed. My brother left university and joined in '39. So, after a few nights staying with Holly's mother, crying myself sick, I decided to join. Holly had already joined the Wrens, my brother's an officer in the RN—joining the Wrens seemed obvious. I was out of basics and working in Liverpool like a shot."

"I'm that sorry. And...your m-mother?" asked Robert.

"She died when I was a baby." Jo's face, from what he could see in the dim railway lighting, was clouded, her infectious and ready smile erased.

Holly tapped him. "I like to misquote Oscar Wilde at this point in her bleak tale to tell her that it's careless to lose one parent, never mind two."

To Robert's amazement, Jo burst out laughing.

"See? I get her to laugh every time. We met as infants at our wee school, Brookvale, and we've been best friends ever since," said Holly.

"Holly's anything but the demure Belfast lass she sounds, so we became friends for life at age six."

"Oh, aye. Salt of the bloody earth, me."

"She likes to swear—pay her no mind, Robert."

Holly laughed. "I can actually speak English quite correctly thanks to Miss Spenser, the elocution teacher my parents hired to rid us of our German accents. Miss Spenser spent her youth touring in rep and sounded for the all the world like Queen Mary, but I soaked up the Belfast accent like a sponge."

Robert laughed. "You two have cheered me no end. I don't suppose there's anything to eat or drink on this train?"

"Not a thing." Looking at her watch, Jo said, "We should call at Bletchley in, oh, under two hours—too early for breakfast, alas. We made it to the station canteen just before closing and ate something. Literally, some *thing*."

"It was closed when I ran into the station. Disembarking took hours. I nearly missed this train."

"Perhaps they'll take pity on us and feed us when we arrive, whoever they are," said Holly.

Jo said, "Best to get a bit of kip." She pulled her cap off, revealing a head of short, wavy hair, which in the low light looked brown. She ruffled her hair vigorously. Folding her over-coat into a pillow-shaped object, she placed it behind her head and closed her eyes.

~

"Bletchley! Bletchley! Five minutes! Five minutes!"

Starting at the other end of the corridor and repeated the length of it, the announcement woke Robert, who jerked his head forward painfully. Holly's head lay against his right shoulder, her fine blonde hair, bluntly cut at the ends of her ears, fanned across his upper arm. Her glasses were folded and sitting in the overturned cap on her lap, her hands neatly folded over the cap.

Jo began to get up, pushing up along the wall. "Oomph." She stretched. Cupping her mouth, she yelled, "Val. You're the last one in this car. Pass on the message to the next. Bletchley, five minutes."

From the end of the corridor, they heard, "Aye, aye, Captain." Some of the women laughed.

Looking down at Robert, Jo said, "Here, you'll have to wake her. Sleeps like the dead. Anywhere and during anything."

Robert didn't know how to wake her, so he tapped her head, lightly. "Holly. We're here."

"Here." Jo leant across him and, shaking her with vigor, said, "Holly! We must make our way to the exit! Now!"

Holly sat up, put her glasses on, fixed the cap to regulation depth and tilt on her head, and stood up. She tugged her double-breasted jacket down to straighten it.

Robert picked up his kit and the trio picked their way through the crowd lining the corridor to the rear door. The train slowed and stopped with a long lurch and screeching wheels. The platform was dark except for the conductor's dimmed lamp. He waved the dim green light and blew his whistle after the three moved away from the train door.

Robert watched the shaded red light on the back of the train move away. "I hope that fella put my sea chest on the platform. He said he would."

Jo put down her case, flicked her lighter for a second and looked up. "The sign's painted over. I hope we're in the right place." She closed the lighter.

"It's bloody pitch dark—can't see a thing!" said Holly. "Not even my hand in front of my face."

"I'll walk down to the other end and see if the conductor remembered my chest. Wait for me?"

"Here, take my lighter." She flicked it on.

Robert returned carrying the chest. "Thanks." He flicked the lighter off.

"We were told someone would meet us," said Jo.

They heard steps ringing on metal, and seconds later, an Army officer approached, holding a dimmed torch and a clipboard.

"Good morning. I am Lieutenant Traemore. When I call your name, please answer 'here,' if you would. Aarons, em, Holda, WRNS." He enunciated the letters and not the more common-place pronunciation.

"Aye, sir."

He ticked Jo's name after she answered, and then asked, "Henderson, Robert R., RN?"

"Aye, aye, sir," said Robert.

"Come this way, please. It's a short walk."

They trudged behind him over a metal bridge, downstairs and onto a road, their surroundings obliterated by darkness. Following the tiny circle of light from the Lieutenant's torch up a black road, they could not see the large house until they stood on the doorstep, and he shone the torch on the massive doorknob.

"Here we are, Bletchley Park mansion." Opening the main door, Traemore encouraged them to enter the dark foyer quickly, before closing the door again and leading them through a blackout curtain to a lighted area, the main hall of a grand house.

Blinking in the bright light, Robert took in the vast room. Chairs and sofas were haphazardly positioned around a grate with a small fire. A long table ran down the center of the room around which a surprising number of people moved, pouring from urns into mugs and taking buns from baskets.

"Please put your cases down in the far corner and help yourselves to tea and buns. I'm afraid we haven't anything else this time of the morning. The facilities are located at the back. Let's convene at the fireplace in oh, at 0300."

Robert dropped the chest and kit in the corner, then made his way to the back, where a queue already formed at the ladies' and gents'. His queue moved quickly, and he soon joined the queue for tea and buns. He took two, hesitated, and took a third.

Holly sat next to Robert on a sofa with her tea and bun. "They must work 'round the clock here." Leaning close to him, she whispered, "These baps taste like soap."

The officer sat down. When Jo sat down, he said, "Right. You'll be off duty until 0800, when you'll report back here, breakfasted and ready to go, the canteen is off to the left. Oh, we want you dressed too, of course." He smiled. Nobody laughed. You'll often work on four hours of sleep and may have shifts in the wee hours like these chaps do, but as navy personnel, I'm sure you're used to it." He checked his clipboard. "Beginning at 0800, you'll engage in several administrative procedures, after which you'll receive assignment to your work group and your permanent billet. It's my job to welcome you and tell you that you have been chosen to perform work of the utmost importance to the war effort—work that very well may spell the difference between our winning or losing the war. I include some of the very dangerous and difficult service already given in that assessment. Finish your tea and buns please, and I'll walk you to barracks."

Robert drained his mug and stuffed the rest of the bap into his mouth, shoving the other two into his pea coat pocket.

Jo and Holly walked to the luggage in the corner with him.

"See you in the morning," said Jo, ruffling her hair before replacing her cap.

Standing next to her in the light, he saw that she was not much shorter than he was and that her hair was dark blonde, not brown. Her face still held its welcoming smile, even at three o'clock in the morning.

"Sleep well," said Holly, slight and diminutive, head and shoulders shorter than Jo, and a monochrome of light blonde hair, eyebrows, eyelashes, and gold-rimmed glasses.

After collecting their belongings, the lieutenant walked them to a back door and out again into the pitch dark.

"Wait here a moment, Henderson, I'll be back for you."

Standing in the dark, he could only see the small pool of torch light moving, as the lieutenant walked Jo and Holly to the women's barrack. He could hear their voices moving away in the dark and wanted to call out, *Wait for me!*

Robert sat between Jo and Holly at a long table, one of five tables stretching nearly the width of the mansion's library. Pages turned, pens scratched, someone sneezed and a kind soul whispered a blessing. Seated at the front table were five young men dressed in tweeds and jumpers, behind them were two tables full of Wrens, followed by a table of Auxiliary Territorial Service, in their khaki jackets and skirts.

"Two minutes, please," said the Army Major at the head of the room.

Robert barely understood what he was signing, as they'd been given little time to read the Official Secrets Act, 1939. He flipped back a page and tried to concentrate.

---

1. — (1) *If any person for any purpose prejudicial to the safety or interests of the State —*

(a) approaches, [inspects, passes over] or is in the neighbour-
hood of, or enters any prohibited place within the meaning of this
Act; or

(b) makes any sketch, plan, model, or note which is calculated
to be or might be or is intended to be directly or indirectly useful
to an enemy; or

(c) obtains, [collects, records, or publishes,] or communicates
to any other person [any secret official code word, or pass word, or
any sketch, plan, model, article, or note, or other document or
information which is calculated to be or might be or is intended to
be directly or indirectly useful to an enemy;

he shall be guilty of felony …

"Time. Please sign your full names, date and pass to your left. Now, please."

WAAFs in their RAF blues stood at the table ends collecting the signed documents.

Robert looked at Jo, who rolled her eyes. She whispered, "I know, lawyers make a mystery of the simplest of things. All that gobbledegook meant we can't tell anybody anything—ever. That's all ye need know."

The major clapped and said, "Silence, please. I'll call your names and the room numbers for your first interviews. The WAAFs will direct you from the hallway."

The civilian interviewing Robert was a Mr. Sinclair. With a face like an angry raptor, his bushy, springing eyebrows contained more hair than the thin strands of white hair carefully combed over a bald pate. Mr. Sinclair did not explain his function.

"I have your service record, Henderson." He frowned down at the folder and flipped the page over. "Your experience in signals and telegraphy, particularly HF/DF on active duty and under fire, plus your high test scores." He turned the page. "Ah, and you've top physical test scores—you passed all the timed exercises and your eyesight is quite remarkable, apparently." Sinclair looked at Robert for a moment before returning his attention to his service record. "But your record has nothing about studying mathematics at university. Is that correct?" He looked up at Robert, who perched uncomfortably on a wooden chair in front of Sinclair's desk.

"I studied A-level maths and physics at school, not university." Robert straightened his back but the chair yielded no comfort.

"School? Where?"

"Castlereagh College, Belfast."

"I see. And you're only seventeen. So you have a leaving cert? What did you study at the college? Exactly."

Puzzled and exhausted, the man's vaguely disapproving demeanour began to annoy him.

"Yes, sir. I received my leaving cert. I sat and passed leaving exams in Latin and history. I sat A-level maths and physics and passed."

"But you've no modern languages?"

English, you daft bugger. "No. Sir." Robert spread his legs and folded his arms.

Mr. Sinclair's frown deepened. He looked up. "Do you need a barber and a shaving kit, Henderson?" His eyes moved from Robert's curly head of hair before descending to the full moustache and thick beard. The man's mouth crinkled.

"I'm just off my ship, but I'd everything trimmed to regulation full set last week. I have permission of my Commander for the full set. The signed slip's in that folder."

"All right. You're to be billeted at the White Hart Inn. Report to Major Baker's group tomorrow morning at eight. Someone will fetch you in the canteen and bring you over. You are off duty from now." He looked at his watch. "I make it half six." Find your kit and settle in, Henderson."

Robert stood, grateful to be out of the spindly chair. "May I tell my parents where I am? They worry…"

"You may tell them you are stationed onshore only, and by telephone only, not by letter, but you must never discuss what you are doing, do you understand? You must never tell anyone about the work we do here, or even the name of the place or town. You must never tell *anyone anything* unless you work together in the same group here at Bletchley Park. Clear?"

I don't bloody know what I'm doing, do I?

"Yes, thank you, sir."

Carrying his full kit again, Robert was caught in the doldrums of the competing tides of the shift change, as hundreds walked toward the gate with him and hundreds more poured through the main gate against him. He'd been directed to the jitneys lurking at the main gate to ferry workers to their billets. He found his way onto a bus, dark except for the glow of the shaded red tail lights and the dimmed headlights.

"White Hart Inn?" he asked the driver.

"Right-o! I'll call out to you, mate."

A woman's voice from the back called, "Robert!"

Feeling his way along the aisle, he walked to the back.

"It's us—Jo and Holly."

"Hello! Where are you off to? Am I allowed to ask?"

"I think so. There's a seat beside us."

His eyes adjusted and he threw his burdens up into the luggage rack and sat down.

"Vicarage Lane. We're billeted together. Sounds like a lot of chintz and bone china cups. What about you?" asked Holly.

And here's me hoping we'd be together in the same billet. Silly.

"The White Hart Inn."

"Lucky devil, a pub!" said Holly. "If we're lucky, we may be given a thimble of bad sherry on Vicarage Lane."

The driver closed the door and put the bus in gear with a crunch.

"I hope it isn't too noisy. I'm dead on my feet," he said. "But yes, a pint and supper first. I'll drink one for you." He smiled at the women suddenly illuminated by the red glow of the reverse lights.

"What's your shift tomorrow?" Holly asked.

"0800."

"Ours too. We'll look for you in the canteen, unless the landlady gives us breakfast. Or we'll look for you..."

"We'll find you," said Jo.

The gears ground again and the jitney pulled away.

The women's billet stop was early on in the jitney's rounds.

"Mind your language in Vicarage Lane, Holly. 'Night, Jo," called Robert as the women made their way up the aisle. "See you tomorrow!"

"Mind how you go, Robert."

He was glad of the dark bus interior, as he wiped his eyes. Digging himself down into his coat, Robert fell asleep with his face against the glass, his breath fogging the window, as the little bus wound its way down pitch-black lanes and streets.

The driver woke him by calling, "Sailor! Sailor! This is the White Hart, lad."

"Haven't seen you in ages, apart from a glimpse at shift change," said Robert. "Nor Jo. We should plan another pub night at the White Hart when I'm off the four to twelve. We haven't had a pub night in a long time."

Holly pulled herself up onto the short brick wall and sat next to Robert. "You wouldn't mind after our last night in the pub? I had rather too much drink. Truth is, I'd adore another pub night. What shift change? We're all one long, continuous shift now.

Look what I've got," she said, showing him a half bar of chocolate.

"How did you...?"

"One of the Wrens in our group." Her blue eyes merry, dimples creased, she tapped her nose. "Don't ask. Have some."

"I won't ask. Oh, yes I will, which one?" He broke off two small squares and the two sat in silence, enjoying the chocolate. Chocolate was so heavily rationed that Robert was shocked by the molten flavor, the sugar with a hint of salt.

"Never you mind. Listen, after what I told you the other week, while in my cups...about Jo. I thought maybe you were avoiding me."

"Why would I do that? We're friends, aren't we?"

"I hope so, but I thought you'd, I don't know, disapprove."

"You told me how you felt about her, that's all. It wasn't a shock, if that's what you think."

Holly nodded.

Two of the Wrens from their group, called the Bakery after the boss, walked by, grinning and waving. After they passed, they fell to looking back and giggling.

After waving back at them, he asked, "What's the matter with those two?"

Holly laughed. "The Bakery girls are mad for you—didn't you know? Although they miss the sailor suit. They love the beard. Blackbeard, they call you—"

"They talk about *me*? As for the sailor suit, It's freezing in Block F, so the more layers, the better. I just bought this tweed jacket at a church jumble sale, big enough to fit over the jumper, boiler suit and warm layers of unmentionables."

"It's a nice jacket mind, but wear regulation at the next dance and you'll be spoilt for choice."

"That's fine. I like to dance. How is Jo? You haven't said."

"Oh, Jo's got man trouble."

Robert's thick, dark eyebrows shot up. "*Does* she? Who?"

"Let's just say one of the galloping majors...the handsome one. The married one."

"Oh...both are a wee bit old for Jo, aren't they? Which one? Not Major Baker. I don't believe it."

"Ssh!" Holly pantomimed looking all around them before answering, "No, not Baker. She calls him 'Johnny, darling.' She hasn't actually said that to me, of course, but I've gotten the basic facts out of her. Surname is something silly, like Badger-Clock."

"Badger-Clock? What?" Robert laughed.

"No, but something like it. Veddy silly, veddy English."

"He's taking a chance isn't he?"

"She's the one who'll get it in the neck if they're discovered, or worse, she'll get into real trouble. He'll get a wee lecture over a fine malt. I've had to cover for her at Vicarage Lane more than once. But that was the case in Liverpool, too. Plus she's got dark circles under her eyes and sunken cheeks."

"We all do. Terrible food, fourteen-hour days, if you're lucky, six-day weeks, round and round. Still, I'm enjoying being here."

"*Are* you?"

"Oh, aye. First and foremost, I'm in little danger of losing my life. Second, I enjoy the work, however endless and brain cracking it is—there are those breaks in the decrypting that are so exciting. Third, it's how I imagine being at university. I have real chums for the first time in you two. The concerts and plays, lectures, and the sessions when the geniuses chew a problem with us in the room. The library is open to us. I've learnt so much in the 20 months we've been here. Is it like university?"

"Well, here they work us harder, but there's the same level of learning and culture available. Thankfully there are the dances and the crazy plays some of them write and perform. There's more fun here than university, I'd say—and camaraderie. At least for me there is."

"Camaraderie—that's exactly what I meant." Robert hesitated but asked, "What about you? Are you alright, you know, since she's with Major...Johnny?"

"I'm used to it. The thing is, I've always been mad for Jo. She's my oldest friend and my best friend, except for you, but I've moved on."

Robert pulled out a pipe and tobacco pouch and began to fill and tamp the bowl. "The chocolate-wielding Wren?"

Holly sighed. "We're great pals too, more's the pity."

Quietly, he said, "I thought you were in love with Jo." He didn't look at Holly.

"Aye, starting when we were six. Fool that I am I told her when we were fourteen—I was bursting—and you know what she did? She took me in her arms, kissed the top of my head and as my heart pounded, said, 'Holls, I'll always love you, but I dream about kissing boys, not girls. Can you forgive me? Will you still be my best friend? Always?' That's Jo all over—clear, honest, kind. I do love her. How not? She's beautiful, brilliant, fun, thoughtful, and she wastes it all on men."

"Here, now!"

"No offense meant. Not sure what went on at Queen's—there might have been a professor here or there, none of the boys ever succeeded with her, but we were in different worlds there and she was busy at school and working for her father—we didn't see each other often. Once in the navy she chose older men, always officers, married but available, as they were in Liverpool at the Admiralty, as they are here. But it's not like she's a calculating witch—she agonizes over her role in harming marriages. I don't understand her."

He said, "I'd no idea." As Robert smoked his pipe, they fell into silence for a moment. "By the way, how is it you're out of doors now?" He looked at his watch. "It's not even three."

"I'm on with you tonight—they've switched me over. Jo will stay on the nine to four shift. I imagine she needs her nights free for...sorry, that was cheap. Anyway, I wanted to spend a little time outside on this beautiful day." She yawned broadly and without constraint.

Robert laughed. "I'm glad we'll be working together again. Let's walk around the lake. There's an apple tree I've my eye on. It seems I *can* ask now, so what are you doing?"

"They had me sight-reading the German decrypts for a long time. Mostly plain language, but it took a wee while to translate all the abbreviations. It got so that I knew the men producing the crypts just by their language. Weird, that. As hard and tedious as that was, somebody realized I'm a student in mathematics, so they switched me to some decrypting. Much harder, but it can be more fun and now I'm a two-for-one for them—using the keys they give me to pry open the encrypted messages and then translating the German decrypt. By hand it's all much too slow of course, but at the moment, I'm helping confirm what you lot produce on the bombes, which are so fast, but I gather they still don't trust the results? Are you still a *bombe* boy?" She giggled.

Robert grabbed her around the shoulders and gave her a tiny shake before hugging her. "Here now! I am a *man* on the bombes. Everyone else is a Wren on our shift—yours now too. The decrypts come flying off so it's wise they get confirmation of the computation from a human. Anyway, yes, while the Wrens can fix most things on the big machines, often with hair pins, if you can believe it, sometimes they need my brawn. Insulting, that."

Holly giggled again. "Have you learnt decrypting at all?"

"Basic key use on the encrypts, not that I can find the keys by myself, but I'd love to learn how to engineer the big machines. I'm no genius, and it takes one like Turing to design such a thing, but I want to learn and become a technician at least."

They continued walking across the Bletchley Park campus to the lake and the orchard.

"Gosh, it's an ugly house. Horrid. All that money and that's what they built...still, the grounds are lovely—the family spent their money well there," said Holly. "I *have* tried saving Jo from herself, you know."

"I know you care very much for her, Holly." Reaching up, Robert pulled four ripe apples off the tree and handed Holly two. He stuffed two into his jacket pockets.

"Thank you. I imagine these will be very welcome around eleven tonight."

They sat on a bench and watched a colleague feed the ducks. "But you can't save people from themselves, can you?"

"Robert…promise you won't be angry, but something you said in the pub…I must ask, have you a girlfriend?"

He didn't answer for a moment, but puffed thoughtfully on his pipe. "You know I don't."

"A man?"

"I must have had too much to drink, as well. How did you know?"

"Well, when you talk about your friend—Albert, is he?—your voice changes, and your face, from what I can see of it above the beard."

He blushed, but said, "Yes, I imagine it does."

"Are your feelings…reciprocated?"

"They were. We write to one another, but of course, we can't put any of it to paper. The thing is…I'm afraid of it. My feelings, his, the trouble we could find ourselves in with the law. My parents knowing and his mum, his aunt—and he's a wee bit younger."

"There's a lot to fear, but you shouldn't throw away whatever you could have with him for fear, should you? I wouldn't."

Robert said nothing, then laughed loudly.

"What is it? What's funny?"

"You sound like an agony aunt, Holly."

Holly looked at him while he continued laughing, then joined him. "I suppose I do. But you do know what I mean, don't you?"

"Yes, I do. That Fiona does not reciprocate your feelings, at least not at the moment, so I should count myself lucky."

Eyes wide, she asked, "How did you know it's Fiona?"

Pointing his pipe at her, "There! The way you say her name. The way *you* look when you say it. Plus you babbled on about Fiona last time at the pub. Endlessly."

Holly put her hands up in the air. "You got me, guv, bang to rights."

"Alright, alright. We're even. Let's shake hands. Friends for life. And no more secrets, except the ones we keep just between ourselves?"

"That is a relief. An astounding relief. Thank you!"

"Let's go in and have whatever lifeform they've prepared for tea before we're mobbed by the shift change in the lane," said Robert.

They walked slowly toward the mansion. "One thing though. We'll know when Jo's affair is over before she does," said Holly.

"Oh?"

"She'll join us on the night shift, poor lamb."

LIBERTY—MAY 1944

BELFAST—PORTSTEWART

"Can we drive down till the old place up the Stranmillis?" Meg asked after she settled in the back of the taxi with her brother. Exhausted but hopeful, she felt the outline of the medicine bottle prescribed by Dr. Boyd in her handbag.

"Of course. Tomorrow you'll be rested and we can take a wee dander if you like," said David. He gave the cabbie directions to drive down to Sandy Row, back around to the Stranmillis and then onto St. Ives Gardens. Sitting back he said, "Well? How does the old city look?"

Passing Queen's University, she said, "Wonderful, really. Little damage here. Have you cleared most of the rubble in the city?"

"Some nights it does feel like I've cleared most of the rubble in the city, but no. Much is cleared and most flattened, but there's been no rebuilding. There's no money for it. Also, I think it's feared we may be bombed again, so there'd be no point to it."

"Surely not," said Meg.

"Until the war's over, we just don't know." He took her hand in his. "Listen, now be calm, but I told Florrie you were coming today."

"Oh, David! *Why* did you?"

"Sorry, but I had to, Meggie. She'll be out and about like mad today, and she might even stop in, she often does. If I hadn't told her, there'd been hell to pay."

She sighed and said, "Why is she 'out and about like mad' today?"

"Robert's due home on liberty tomorrow. He rang yesterday. Anyway, she's at the shops and may even come to the house to raid our larder. Don't worry, she'll be too busy to go to the hospital with you and they won't visit. She and Ralph will want Robert to themselves. Do you see?"

"I suppose so. You told her about my doctor's appointment?"

"I did. She'd murder me if I kept that from her. Come now, Meg, be reasonable."

"I don't want to be. I want to be a cranky invalid."

He laughed. "You are that. Well, here we are, good old number 34." He jumped out, helped Meg out and paid the driver. "I've Jinny's daybed made up for you and there's a stew on the hob—no meat to speak of but a wee bit of bone."

"You've taken up cookery?"

"I'm a dab hand in the kitchen—so's Niall. I can't imagine what we could produce with plenty of fresh food to cook. We bring what we can down from Ballycastle, but if there's two of us eating it, and sharing with Florrie and Lizzie, it disappears quickly."

"Won't he mind me here for the five days Dr. Boyd tells me I must stay? Will you? It's not what you bargained for...what's that joke about fish and guests?"

"Both go off after three days. I can always fob you off on Lizzie and Tom on the fourth day..." He smiled and put the key in the latch, "No, of course I don't mind and Niall's in Ballycastle. He moved his surgery up there and the students do their rotations at the farm practice. But allow me to remind you that it's your house and it'll be grand to spend time together. I don't get to see much of you. Let's get you inside and settled."

He opened the front door and as Meg walked through, she was shaken by emotion. Looking up the staircase, she remembered the chaos of the day in 1932 when Annie, Betty and baby Denis left this house, their house, and Ireland for good. The house had been rented to Meg, eldest sister Jinny, and Lillian two years prior to that, when Annie, Ned and Betty left the first time for America, and sold to Meg and Lillian at the start of the war. *We left at the worst bombing and now it's David living here.*

She half expected to hear the sound of Lillian's unhesitating typing clacking from the second floor. Walking through to the parlor, tears formed in her eyes, both for the loss of Jinny and for the fact that with her own heart trouble, the circle would be complete as she slept in Jinny's day bed, saving climbing up stairs. Here she was, in the home she loved, her own home, the one they fled with few of their possessions in 1941 after the worst of the bombings. Yet, all she could think was, *I want to go home to Lillian.*

David came into the parlor with her case. "I meant to ask, what have you got in here? Rocks?"

"Mind it, now, be gentle, there are jars of jam Mildred made out of wild blackberries last fall. Two loaves we made, well, Lillian. Some tins. Oh, and a bit of bacon—Frank has a pal with pigs—we can add that to your stew. Other things, but I can't remember what."

"Really? That's wonderful! It pays to have relatives in the country. Did you bring any clothes?"

"I'm not sure what I packed, but I thought we still have clothes upstairs, don't we?"

"Aye, you do."

"Well, that'll be alright then." Meg tried to brighten and said, "Let's unpack the provisions, shall we?"

～

Sitting at the kitchen table, Meg could hear David's deep voice but not the words spoken on the telephone in what had been Lillian's office on the second floor. Her gaze lingered on the fireplace, in front of which she and Jinny had taken turns warming themselves in the rocker now in Portstewart. Annie's copper-bottomed pots and pans still hung on the board over the range, abandoned when they left for America, but shining as though somebody had just polished them. David and Niall had placed two comfortable chairs in front of the fire, she noticed. The low rumble stopped. Meg envied David's quick steps on the stairs.

He came into the kitchen rubbing his hands. "I've rung Niall and Lillian to tell them you must stay five days, doctor's orders. Niall won't be back in time to see you, he doesn't think. He said to tell you to rest and worry about nothing. Lillian was kicking herself that you never installed a second receiver downstairs here, but she'll ring every day to see how you are. How are you?"

He pulled the kettle off the hob and filled it. Turning to her, she saw the concern in his face.

"I'm not sure. Tired. Tea would be nice. Is Lillian worried? Shall I ring her back?"

"I think you should rest yourself and not take stairs. She knows you're fine. You are fine, aren't you? You haven't told me why the doctor wants to see you every day."

"I am, just more tired than I've ever been, I think. And my head is woolly, I can't think. Oh, yes. The doctor said that this medicine he gave me takes time to…that he has to make sure it's the right dose. That's it. So he wants to check my heart every day."

"I see. Well, I'm at loose ends and at your service. Now let's see what wonders you've brought." He put the case on the table and opened it. "It's like Aladdin's cave! You didn't mention eggs, whiskey…" Picking up a sealed earthenware pot, he asked, "What's this?"

"Jugged hare. Frank for the hare, obviously, but also Mildred.

Bless them. Frank finds the whiskey, smokes the trout he's caught, and Mildred runs the chicken coop..."

Through the glass in the back door, Meg saw their sister Florrie, who opened the door and walked in carrying parcels.

"Hello, dear." Florrie bent down and bussed Meg on the cheek. "You look very tired, dear, alright? Hello, David. I've been to the shops, but there's so little...oh my! What are all these wonderful things! Did you bring them, Meggie? I keep telling Ralph we should travel up to Portstewart and go to the shops."

David said, "I'm making tea, Florrie, sit down. You can't find these wonderful things in the shops up there. All homemade, except for the whiskey—a nice bottle of Bushmills, no poteen here."

Florrie sat, clutching her parcels and eying the provisions on the table.

Once she was within the circle of light over the table, Meg was shocked at Florence's appearance. *She's got very stout and grey, and looks as exhausted as I must do.*

Arms akimbo, David said, "Alright, we'll give you a bit of everything for Robert's homecoming. Just don't tell Lizzie."

"Will you? Thank you. Them's lovely spuds."

The kettle whistled and David turned to make the tea. Florence still stared at the items on the table and Meg realized she must be mesmerized by the cornucopia after nearly five years of rationing and increasing shortages.

"I'll be here nearly a week, Florrie. Do you think you and Robert would visit one day?"

"A week? How was the doctor's visit?"

"Five days, anyway, while he checks how I'm doing on the medicine he gave me."

"That's good news, isn't it? He had medicine to give you."

"Aye."

"I'm sure Robert will visit. He's bringing a girlfriend with him. She's a Wren. They're stationed together in England and taking the ferry from Liverpool. I'll have to feed the girl something, at least once. She's a Belfast girl, but we know nothing else about her. We have high hopes."

One eyebrow arched, David looked over Florrie's head at Meg.

Shifting her eyes quickly from his, Meg said, "Oh, but that's grand he's not on board ship anymore. You can stop worrying."

David said, "Alright, so's you can celebrate, we'll add in enough to make it up for the girlfriend. What were you able to get today?"

"Swedes and a bar of soap." Her lip curled.

David burst out laughing. "That'll be a treat boiled up together!"

Florence frowned.

"I'll tell you—give me a swede for our stew and we'll give you generous tots of whiskey to serve Robert and Ralph. And the girlfriend. And you—you look like you could use one." Laughing again, he began to pour the tea into cups.

"Keep the whiskey for yourselves. Ralph and Tom keep their houses well in whiskey, but we don't ask questions, me and Lizzie. No tea for me. I should go. Do you mind if I help myself?"

"I do mind. I'll divvy everything up. I've a box you can carry home."

Meg sipped tea and watched her siblings haggle over the numbers of eggs and potatoes, and ounces of bacon and trout each would take. David and Florrie admitted they couldn't stomach the jugged hare, so that was destined for Lizzie and Tom. Fortunately, Mildred had packed three small jars of jam in Meg's case, so Lizzie could be given one after the others claimed theirs.

She put her cup down quietly, stood without scraping the chair on the wooden floor, and softly stepped from the kitchen to the parlor, where she pulled her shoes off, lay down on top of the day bed and curled into a ball.

It was dark in the room when she was awakened by somebody putting heavy blankets over her.

"Night-night." David's voice.

～

Jo said, "It's awfully nice of you to put me up. I told Robert's mother I could stay in my father's office, it's just up the Stranmillis from here, but she insisted Robert bring me here, sorry…"

"We've plenty of room and you're very welcome," said David.

"I'm sure it's an imposition, but you're terribly kind. The bath was heavenly. My English landlady is careful with the hot water, I can tell you. As in, there isn't any."

Jo sat in front of the fire, drying her hair with a towel, and wearing an old bathrobe of Lillian's. Jo's brown eyes were intelligent and merry, and her wide mouth broke into rubbery smiles often. "Robert's mum served a very nice lunch, but I think she wanted to see the back of me for a wee while, not to say that she wasn't gracious, her husband too, very welcoming. But I understand. They've been worried about him for years, having seen little of him."

"You're right about our sister…so that's why he ran back like a frightened rabbit." Meg laughed. "And what do you do in the navy?"

"Telegraphist."

"Where are you stationed?"

Jo's eyes shifted from Meg's before she spoke quickly. "I'm not supposed to say." Her eyes shifted back. "Robert told me you live in Portstewart, Meg. Is that right?"

"Aye. We ran away from this house after the firestorm bombing." Meg looked up at the ceiling that had rained plaster dust during the bombings. Turning back to Jo, she said, "David stayed here to help clear rubble." Worried, her eyes flicked over to David, whose eyes were cast down. "Robert and his mother came with us to Portstewart, but he joined the navy up in Londonderry, and my sister returned to her husband over the road. The rest of us stayed in Portstewart—my best friend, Lillian, her sister and nephew, and our business associate and good friend, Mildred. Lillian's sister works for the Yanks in Londonderry. Mildred married a local man, but she and Lillian still run the business in the Portstewart area."

"What type of business?" asked Jo.

"Lillian started a typewriting business many years ago now, here. First it was the two of them, Lillian and Mildred, long before the war. They mostly typed for students and faculty at Queen's. I worked at the shipyard and only handled adverts and billing for them—they did the real typewriting. But with the war came fewer typing jobs from Queen's. Lillian and Mildred turned to billing, keeping books, typing for local businesses. Soon after we arrived in Portstewart, the young girls were leaving their office jobs for the Wrens, which was a godsend for us. Lillian worked with her sister for the Yanks for a while, to keep things going, before turning back to her business full time."

"That's grand to keep a business going like that. I know how hard it is—my father worked very hard at his business, at his practice. My late father was a solicitor, and he had a client in Portstewart. That client died, but his ward became a client, too. The client's asked that I conclude a house sale in Portstewart."

"You're an estate agent?" asked David.

"Solicitor, nearly. I must finish my qualifications, but I can do what's needed for the house sale. That's the reason I'm spending my liberty here. I'll go to Portstewart tomorrow and meet with the estate agent."

"What a coincidence! How long will you stay in Portstewart?" asked Meg.

"I'm not sure, but I should be able to finish within a few days. I can finish the paperwork in my father's office here."

"Stay with us in Portstewart, take a wee holiday," said Meg. "Perhaps Robert will join you, escape his mother's clutches."

"Meg, dear, you won't be there," David reminded her gently.

"Lillian will be there. We'll ring her tonight."

Jo squinted a little and said, "That *is* kind, but my billet's arranged, so..." her smile faint.

"Well, you must say hello at the least. Come for a meal. The strand is lovely for long walks. We're forbidden to swim in the sea because of the defenses, but there's Herring Pond and the rivers, and we've bicycles, you can borrow one."

Jo smiled broadly. "It sounds delightful."

"And your liberty? When does it end?" asked David.

"We have a fortnight, minus two days. We've used one to get here and will need one to return—can't risk being adrift."

"Adrift?" asked David.

"Royal Navy for liberty without permission. A serious offense."

"I'll be here for another four days or so, but we'll cross paths again, I hope," said Meg. "We'll ring Lillian and tell her to expect you at some point. I'll write the address down for you."

"I look forward to it. Now, what can I do to help with the tea?" Jo yawned before giggling, "So sorry. Not much sleep."

"Not a thing. We have a stew on the hob," said David.

"Sounds grand and it *smells* absolutely delicious! Give me two ticks to dress."

Jo ran out of the room and up the stairs.

"She's got energy," whispered David.

"I'm jealous of it, but she's a nice girl," said Meg. "David, I'm sorry I brought up..."

"It's alright. I'm used to the pain of thinking about it now, thinking about Martin."

Meg reached for his hand, and he gave hers a squeeze.

They sat in silence for a moment before Meg whispered, "I wonder who the client is, and which house he's buying...But imagine Robert having a girlfriend! What's her surname again?"

In a low voice, David answered, "The name's Bray, like the sea town in Wicklow, south of Dublin, a nice place. I couldn't see it either, you know, him with a young woman, and she doesn't act like they're involved. But tell me this, are we talking about the same thing now?"

"Oh, aye, we are."

David gave her a meaningful look. Meg nodded before whispering, "I've thought so since Robert and Albert lived with us in '41."

"*Have* you? You'll have to tell me that story when we're alone."

ADRIFT—MAY-JUNE 1944

PORTSTEWART

"*Really*? Foxglove?" From her seat on the garden bench, Lillian turned to look at the clump of tall green plants standing at the back of the perennial border, spikes in swollen bud. She pointed. "You mean, those?"

"Yes, foxglove from Wales. Would you believe medicine is made from flowers? Dr. Boyd said the medicine was supplied from Germany before the war. Now Girl Guides are picking foxgloves in Wales so our chemists can make them into this medicine. Apparently, the Welsh ones are best." Meg held up the blue glass bottle. "Isn't that amazing? Dr. Boyd said to be patient, it could take weeks to full effect, but he was pleased enough with me to let me return early. I *am* glad to be home." Meg took Lillian's hand. "I'd dreamt of walking in Belfast before I went, but I was so exhausted by everything—the travel, the *talking*! And I'd forgotten how noisy and smoky Belfast is, with everyone rushing by. I have an appointment in a fortnight."

"I'm going with you. No argument."

"You'll get none. In fact, if we could find enough petrol, we could drive down and back the same day—that's what I'd like, if the doctor lets me."

"I'll work on finding petrol with Frank starting tomorrow." Lillian turned to Meg with twinkling eyes. With a smile, she said, "*So!*"

Meg laughed. "Go on then."

"I've saved telling you about the mystery of the nearly-solicitor-slash-Wren, Jo Bray."

Meg said, "Don't tease."

"Alright, I didn't think too much about it when you rang and told me about Jo and the mystery client."

"Yes, but now…"

Lillian sat up straight and leaned toward Meg. "Jo Bray is here in Portstewart, and I've met her now, too. A nice young woman. She's staying with Mildred and Frank."

"Mildred and Frank! She never said. How does she know them?"

As the twinkle in Lillian's eyes brightened, Meg slapped her thigh and said, "I *knew* it!"

"Oh, yes? Tell if you know so much."

"Mary O'Neill's buying the Carstairs' Estate and Jo Bray's her solicitor for the sale!"

Lillian's face fell. "You're no fun. Who told you?"

"Nobody. But when Jo was talking about her father's client here in Portstewart, I remembered that Frank said Mary's making a great profit from those shares Carstairs left her. Remember? We called her a war profiteer and laughed? Also, I finally remembered why the name Bray meant something to me —Mr. Bray Esq. took care of the estate after Mr. Carstairs was murdered. I remembered that."

"His solicitor, then hers. But that last bit was more than twenty years ago!"

Meg smiled. "I know. I'm quite pleased with myself. I've felt muddle-headed lately but remembered that name."

"Well, you might have taken the wind out of my sails with the story, but Mary buying the place made me think."

"About what?"

Lillian said, "34 St. Ives Gardens. The rent here isn't much, not compared to our mortgage for number 34, but I'm determined we keep it for Albert's university stay. It's only months away and he'll find some roommates to keep the place going. After he graduates, we can sell if you like, or move back."

"That's a lot to consider, but aye, we'll keep it while Albert is at university. David's still paying rent, but I don't know how much longer he'll stay there. He prefers being in Ballycastle with Niall."

"Understandable." Lillian sat back and stretched her legs out.

"What was I going to say? I've forgotten what I was going to say about Mary...oh, yes, you had better warn Mildred."

"About what?"

"Mary's mother and Frank served Mr. Carstairs and Mary like servants. They did all the cooking and cleaning, and the gardening, farming, car repair, and odd jobs—everything. Mary might have it in her head that Mildred and Frank will fill those shoes when she lives here. I wouldn't put it past her, with her nerve." Meg expected Lillian to laugh, but she looked downcast.

Quietly, Lillian said, "Yes, *we* should tell Mildred."

"Alright, *I* will. But listen, I've something else to tell you."

Shading her eyes and looking at Meg, Lillian waited.

"Florrie presented Jo Bray as Robert's girlfriend. Wishful thinking on her part, we think, David and me."

"David, too? So, you were right about Robert and Albert, or at least Robert?"

"Seems so. David thinks Robert is homosexual, always has. We had a long talk."

"Oh, I see. Won't Florence be disappointed?"

Meg frowned. "She liked the idea of a girl in his life, I suppose."

"They're friends, Jo and Robert? What about her? Is she...?"

Meg shrugged.

"He chose the right family to be so, is all I can say." Lillian removed her glasses, closed her eyes, and rubbed the spot between her eyebrows. "Albert, too." She yawned.

"Where is Jo now?" asked Meg.

"She borrowed a bicycle and went off to the estate, but she offered to make us dinner tonight. I told her you'd need to rest, perhaps tomorrow night. Said she'll buy what she can in the shops. I warned her about how disappointed she'll be."

"She's generous with her ration book—she flew around South Belfast buying everything she could find for David's larder before she came up here. A tireless girl and not much bothers her, or so it seems," said Meg.

"What do you mean?" Lillian yawned.

"She struck me as a young woman who's seen worse, and enjoys what she can," said Meg. "Mature for her age. Experienced. Full of confidence. The opposite of me at her age."

Waiting for her reaction, Meg saw that Lillian's eyes had closed. She pulled off her silk scarf and draped it over Lillian's shoulders.

Poised at the edge of the rock surrounding Herring Pond, Lillian faced the looming height of Inishowen, Donegal, part of neutral Ireland in what felt like an endless war. The trio had set up camp chairs, towels and their clothes in a semi-circle facing the open sea.

The two young people chatted behind her. Strangers to one another, they kept their voices light. She heard Albert ask, "How long have you been stationed with Robert? Is there a chance he'll come up here this weekend?"

Jo answered, but the wind took the words away.

Plaiting her hair, Lillian thought of Mercedes Gleitze and her historic thirteen-mile swim from Donegal to Portstewart in 1929.

From behind, a hand tugged her plait. "Ready?" Towering

above her, Albert stood in his faded red trunks, a towel around his shoulders and his toes clutching the very edge of the rock.

"How cold is it?" asked Jo, wearing chic sunglasses but one of the tatty swimming costumes stored in the cottage, this one ancient and woolen, the original color long faded into a light grey.

"Bloody freezing," said Albert, laughing.

"Albert," cautioned his aunt.

"It's all right, Lillian. I'm in the navy. I've heard worse," said Jo.

Albert laughed.

Lillian said, "I wish Meg had come with us. She could have read her book here, not been left alone."

In the last weeks, Lillian often left Meg alone to swim, and she secretly began taking risks. She swam where the local Royal Navy station forbade swimming, but Meg, aware of the prohibition, was equally sure that Lillian would never do such a thing. And for her part, Lillian swore that she trained in Herring Pond, a boring swim, but better than nothing.

In fact, she'd begun training in earnest for the day when she could attempt the thirteen-mile swim. She swam increasingly far toward Donegal from Herring Pond, timing her swims with the out-going tide from the bowl that formed the pond. The out-going tides prompted the departure of all the other bathers, who wished to avoid being swept out to sea and the mines laid for defense.

At the turn of the tide, Lillian used it to launch into open water, where she swam along the coast toward the Foyle River and back—a shallow stretch empty of mines, she thought, she hoped.

In doing so, she broke the wartime prohibition set and enforced by the Royal Navy, HM Coastguard, and British Army, and she broke the first rule her father had taught her: never swim alone.

"Listen, perhaps this is too dangerous," Lillian said. She checked her watch. "The tide's about to turn out."

Albert's blue-grey eyes searched her face. "I swim here this time of day and I haven't had trouble."

Lillian watched Jo, who was reading the Royal Navy warning sign screwed into the rock.

Jo said, "I'm afraid I can't. This is Royal Navy and I'm a Wren. It is too dangerous for me, if caught. I don't mind sitting in the sun while you swim. Alright?"

"Of course. I should have thought."

"I'll swim with you," said Albert, and without another word, he threw the towel off, jumped off the rock cliff, and disappeared beneath the surface. The women waited. Finally, he sprung up as though something lifted him and with a whoop, shook his head, like a wet dog. Waving at her to follow, he bobbed in the salt water like a cork.

The sky added warm colors to its silvery blue palette as the sun began to set, while the mist descended on the loom of Inishowen. Lillian adjusted the greased goggles her father had repurposed from motorcycle goggles, her inheritance from the man who had taught her to swim at age three. With one quick step, Lillian plunged into the frigid water and began stroking in a circle, passing Albert who tread water in the middle. At the next turn, the tide helped push her out of the pond and she swam on, straight for Donegal. At the one-hundredth stroke, out in open water, she stopped and waited for Albert.

Catching up to her, Albert asked, breathless, "You've been swimming a lot, I can tell," said Albert. "But we should go back, it's dangerous out here."

"We won't be able to turn back now, the tide's too strong," said Lillian. "We'll swim across to the nearest landing point and walk back. There." She pointed.

"Look!" Albert made his aunt turn around. Just beyond them and parallel to the coastline, sleek grey fins moved at high speed.

One leapt up and grinning, seemed to encourage the others to take their turns leaping in synchrony. "Dolphins!"

Albert and Lillian began to stroke again away from the entrance to Herring Pond and toward shore at an angle.

Lillian stopped and pulled the goggles up.

The sleek grey fins circled back and swam closer. "Isn't it wonderful?" asked Albert, his face golden and joyful in the setting sun.

Once on the shore, they climbed up the rocks to the top of Herring Pond.

Barefoot, Jo met them as they reached the top.

"I get so little exercise, working all the time, I never could have kept up with you two—just as well I didn't risk it. But surely it's dangerous out there?" She handed Lillian and Albert towels.

Albert, said, "It is dangerous and you're taking a great risk, Aunt."

"Don't fuss, Albert. But I know what you mean, Jo. After a lifetime of exercising, I stopped once I started the business. Too busy sitting at a desk, so I know how quickly you lose wind and strength. And then there's what you've yet to experience—age."

Jo laughed. "I'd better get myself into shape now. I'll just pull my clothes on."

Albert rubbed his chest and arms briskly with the towel as Jo walked back to their little camp. "I'm amazed that she knows Robert, the navy is so large. It seems an amazing coincidence that she's here on business, doesn't it?"

Lillian shrugged. "Coincidence always seems that way to me —amazing."

He turned his back to the last rays, and bending over, toweled his legs with vigor.

Lillian looked down at the back of his wet dark red head with a wave of affection. She looked up. Far behind him, the mist dropped and covered purple Inishowen like a shroud. A violent shiver rippled up her spine, like the chill of fever.

~

In the golden light of Saturday evening, Albert stood in the garden, throwing old tennis balls for the two dogs. Each dutifully ran after the balls and snatched them up. Gordie allowed the ball to roll gently before picking it up. Each time he returned to Albert, he dropped the ball and waited politely. Bobby grabbed the ball on the hop like the best cricketer and without stopping, ran in low, fast circles, his long, ginger eyebrows and black floppy ears blown back by the speed. Nearer and nearer to Albert's legs he circled, a mischievous gleam in his brown eyes, the ball clamped in a smiling canine mouth. Albert pretended to try and grab him, in between clapping and exhorting him on, "Run, Bobby! Run!"

Finally, Albert took a break and sat on the grass, his long legs, encased in old flannel bags, stretched and splayed in a V, the dogs lying panting next to him. While scratching his dog's chin, Albert talked to Bobby, "We landed on our feet living up here, wee man. Didn't we? You have the run of the garden, the strand, and your pal Gordie. Not bad. Not bad at all."

He listened to Jo typing her legal papers in Lillian's office. Even if he hadn't been turned out of there with his books to make way for her, he'd have known it wasn't Lillian or Mildred typing—far too slow, hesitant, and irregular.

His intense revising ending abruptly by Jo's need for the desk, he announced his plan to take the dogs on a long walk along the strand, but his aunt nixed the plan—there wasn't enough time before tea.

As background to the typewriter clatter, Albert heard the women in the house preparing the tea. Silverware jingled together in someone's hand, metal clanked as pots and pans were put on and taken off the hob, glasses clinked. A musical laugh rang out—there was no mistaking Meg's laugh. Someone turned the radio on, and a sentimental tune floated out above the voices as they chatted. Mildred began to sing along.

The golden sky began to fill with purple and orange. Turning, he saw through the open windows and doors that a light had been turned on in the kitchen. He heard the brass rings of the blackout curtains being pulled in other rooms, but for now, he could see through the parlor to the kitchen.

The telephone rang.

Jo called, "Shall I get that?"

"Please," answered Lillian.

"Hullo, em, 425. Yes? Oh, hello, you!" Jo's voice dropped after that, and while he heard her continue to speak, the words were lost until she gave out with a loud, "Oh, no! You're joking! No, I know you're not."

Albert turned back to watch the convoys continue past Portstewart at speed. Usually sets of convoys passed in two directions, east and west in the North Atlantic, and many anchored off the town's coast. At that moment though, it seemed to him that all the ships travelled east, but he guessed that was an illusion. He lay down cupping his head in his hands.

"Albert! Telephone!"

He sat up and turned to her. Framed in the office window, Jo called, "It's Robert, hurry!"

He was on his feet in a flash, covering the ground in four strides, and jumping over Bobby, who joined the rush to the house.

In the office, Jo held the receiver out to Albert before quickly leaving the room, her sensible Wren's oxfords making little noise.

His heart pounding, he took the heavy receiver. "Robert?"

"Hold one moment."

Albert heard an unidentifiable sound before Robert quietly said, "There. Can you hear me?"

"Yes, I can."

"Can you talk?"

Albert closed the door silently. Joy softening his voice, he asked, "Yes, and you?"

"A bit. I can't stay on the line long, but I wanted you to know I'd planned to visit tomorrow, just for the day, but I received a telegram from the navy, cancelling my liberty. They've cancelled everyone's liberty. I just told Jo that she'll have to come back very early tomorrow."

Albert's smile quickly faded. "Oh, I see. I'm sorry you can't come, very sorry."

"And me, but we must go. Jo's to meet me at the ferry terminal tomorrow, so she'll have to be on the earliest train coming down." He dropped his voice. "I wanted to tell you in person, because I can't really say now...I mean, sorry about the cancelled liberty and visit, but I'm more than sorry I ran off and j-joined the navy." His speech speeded up so that in almost one breath he finished with, "It was reckless and stupid. Heartless. Sorry about everything. Will you forgive me?"

"Forgive you? It never crossed my mind to...I just...I worry about you. I'm terrified I won't see you...I mean, *when* will I see you?"

"On my next liberty, I swear. And don't worry. I'm safe in my current station. Do you understand? Safe. Will you write?"

"Of course. Have you not gotten my letters?"

"I've gotten one or two lately. They arrive in bursts. Write to me and I'll write. I should go. They'll all be blacked out, but still..." In a rush, Robert said, "Listen, I love you."

Albert dropped his voice. "I love you. Take very good care."

The line clicked and while he still listened, buzzed.

Mildred snapped the radio off and joined Meg at the kitchen table. Lillian leant against the sink lip, arms folded, and a tea towel thrown over her shoulder.

Jo stood in the kitchen doorway. Albert came up behind her in time to hear, "I'll have to catch the earliest train, if you'd run me down to the train, please, Lillian. I'm so sorry to trouble you, but..."

"I'll run you," said Albert.

Turning quickly, Jo said, "Oh, you made me jump. Are you sure? It will be terribly early, I imagine. I haven't checked the timetable yet."

"I don't mind."

"Thank you, Albert, I appreciate it. Oh, so where was I? I don't know what to do about the house sale. I've just finished the document Mary needs to sign, and the letter to her, but someone must represent her to the Carstairs' solicitor. I've got to be on duty by midnight tomorrow. There's nothing to be done about that."

"I'll mail the letter for you tomorrow—special delivery," said Lillian.

"Would you? That is thoughtful. I'll pay the postage, of course. A business expense."

"Listen Jo, Frank and me, we'll shepherd the rest of the sale with the estate agent. There's a solicitor in town, we type his bills for him. I know him pretty well, so if we need him, we'll ask," said Mildred.

"I was hoping to keep Mary O'Neill as a client. My father's clients were mostly men and mightn't take to a chit of a girl as their solicitor."

"Frank will give Mary a ring, smooth it over with her. You're in the navy, you must go when they tell you. Anyway, can't Mary come up and complete the deal herself?"

"Thank you—you're all so kind. Mary will need a solicitor to represent her to the Carstairs family's solicitor. I wouldn't dream of her signing the sale contract without one, and no decent solicitor would let her. We've completed the survey, the list of contents was done years ago—well, Frank knows that better than anyone. I should ring her tonight. No, now." She looked at Meg and Lillian. "I'll pay for the call, but may I?"

~

"I must look silly, like something out of a play—'tennis anyone?'" he said, stroking with an imaginary tennis racket. "But I don't have clothes that even remotely fit, other than my school uniform, which would be even sillier," said Albert, pulling on the open charcoal grey jacket, purchased at the same church jumble sale as his grey flannel trousers and pressed white shirt. His white trainers the only new thing he wore, socks and Fair Isle pattern jumper Meg had knitted completed his outfit. "Everything's too small and rides down or up in a maddening fashion."

"You think *you* look silly?" Gesturing to his sailor suit, Robert laughed. "I think you look great. How tall are you now?"

Making a face, Albert said, "Six-four. I'm praying I've stopped."

The young men stood along a railing at the far end of the terminal loading dock, facing the ferry Robert would board to Liverpool.

"Much taller than me now, even though I've grown two inches since we met."

"And you, look at you! The beard is very handsome. *You* look fit." Shyly he asked, "You don't have a photo I could have?"

"I'll get one taken. Send you it. It was a nice surprise, you showing up with Jo."

"You didn't mind?"

"Mind? Of course not! I should have asked you to come, but I didn't think of it."

"Nor me, until I drove her to the Portrush station early this morning. Fortunately, I had my wallet and gas mask box."

"Won't they mind at home? Being without a motor all day?"

"Frank has an auld banger now, too. He'll run them wherever they want. It's true my aunt sounded a little..."

"Annoyed?"

"Cranky. Barely six o'clock when I rang from the station, but she was alright when we rang off. I'll be back by teatime. Where will you be?"

"By teatime? In six- or seven-hours' time? Well past the Isle of Man, but one hour out from port, possibly two."

"That's a long trip. What do you two do to pass the time?"

"Jo's a great sleeper, but when she's awake, we talk, we visit the café, the bar. I smoke. Read. I have a wee chess set so I'll study champions' plays—I have a book. There's not much to do in third class. I've heard they have entertainment in the better classes, like films, and a library."

"You're good friends, you and Jo?"

"I'd say we are. I'm good friends with her best friend Holly, too, maybe more so. But yes, Jo and I get on well. It's easy between us. She doesn't have such an easy time with her boyfriends, though."

"Oh, no? I'm sorry to hear that, she's awfully nice. I like her. Accomplished, but not full of herself."

"Not like you then?" Robert mock punched Albert.

Grabbing Robert's arm, Albert said, "No, not at all like me." He laughed.

"What train will you take back to Portrush?"

"It doesn't matter as long as I'm home for tea. It's only half nine now. I thought I'd visit the bookshop at Queen's, walk around the campus before I get the train home. I wish we could have spent time together."

"Oh, aye, that would have been...grand. I hope we spend time on our own, just walking around Belfast—next time. You'll go to university next year?"

"Aye, that's the plan. I've applied, so. I'll hear very soon."

"Surely you're not worried, a boffin like yourself?"

"Boffin?"

It was Robert's turn to blush as he realized he only knew the word through working at Bletchley Park, which of course he could not mention. "It's British for scientist or mathematician."

"Oh. I've never heard it. Boffin, eh?"

They fell into an awkward silence for a moment.

"Listen, I've good news. The aunts say I can live at number 34 St. Ives Gardens when I'm at university. They say your Uncle David is leaving Belfast."

"'The aunts?' Good shorthand for them. Where is David going? Back to Dublin?"

From inside the terminal shed, they heard the tannoy screech and its unintelligible human voice begin.

"We should dash and find Jo, but it was g-grand to see you. G-grand," Robert's voice cracked as tears burned his eyes. Albert enfolded him in his long arms without hesitation. Robert thought he would return the embrace for a second only and then pound Albert on the back in brotherly fashion. To his astonishment, he allowed himself to sink into Albert, where he'd found sanctuary only twice before, and grasped him around his back, crying into Albert's neck.

Albert spoke into his ear. "You'll see. We'll be all right."

Robert uttered a deep choke before stepping back and wiping his face furiously.

Albert held Robert's arms.

Robert looked up into Albert's eyes and saw tears there too.

"Let's find Jo and fetch your kit. C'mon," said Albert, before pulling a pressed handkerchief out of the breast pocket and offering it to Robert. "Keep it, to remember today—me."

"I'll not need reminding. But don't come with me now. Please. Let me go alone, alright?"

Albert nodded and watched Robert walk off briskly. "Write!" he shouted.

Robert raised his hand but did not turn around. He broke into a run.

Albert waited at the railing until he saw Jo and Robert move in the queue up the gangway. At the top, Jo stepped off first onto the deck, but Robert hesitated, turned, and scanned the railing. Albert waved with both arms and a big smile. A frown furrowing his brow, Robert waved back before disappearing into the melee of the loading ferry.

Albert found that he could barely swallow as his eyes filled with tears.

~

Meg and Lillian lay on their backs. It was an unusually warm and foggy night and they'd pushed the blanket and sheet down, the still and heavy air settling down onto their sleepless forms. The foghorn sounded regularly, answered by the deep horns and various bell tones of ships sailing through the strait. They'd rolled apart before turning toward one another again, knees touching.

"It's just us."

"Yes, just us."

"How are you feeling?" Meg asked.

"Exhausted."

"Working too much? What about the swimming? Too much?"

"In the old days, it would be nothing. I did both and never bothered."

"Is that why you're low?"

"Am I? I haven't any cause. None at all. You're feeling better so why am I not jumping for joy?"

"What then?"

"I'm not sure." Lillian rolled onto her back.

"No?"

"It's silly."

"Tell me anyway."

"Well...when I was young I thought I'd become a real athlete."

"You are a real athlete."

"Not like Mercedes Gleitze. I hadn't enough education for other things, but I wanted to be that." Lillian turned her head to look at Meg. "Silly, but in some small way to be..."

"Not silly. Your father said you could do what she'd done. Encouraged you to try."

"Remember, I told you I hadn't the head for it, not then. Now, I might not have the physical stamina, but I might have the head."

"Aren't you training for it?"

Lillian turned her head away again. "The pond swimming isn't real training. I need to get out into open water."

"Isn't swimming off the strand forbidden by the naval station, the Coast Guard?"

"Oh yes. When the war's over, we can train properly, Albert and me."

"You'll need a team, won't you? Shouldn't a boat follow you for safety?"

"There's an Irish open water club I'll consult, but Frank can handle a boat, can't he?"

"I imagine so. If not, he's sure to have some pal who can." Meg raised her head up onto her bent arm. "You don't seem... this doesn't seem to make you happy, the planning of it."

"Remember that word Jo used, 'adrift.' Not the gone without permission meaning, but the other..."

"At sea? All at sea?"

"Yes, at sea. Why do I feel all at sea? I have you and you're on the mend. The business is doing well enough for us to make ends meet. We survived the bombings and so did everyone dear to us. Robert is safe now and Albert is thriving...I should be very happy. But I feel tired much of the time. Sometimes...sometimes I'm frightened for no reason."

Meg was silent a moment, before speaking softly. "Maybe it's because of the bombings. You saw much more of the horror than I did. It must weigh on you. Listen, why not give this training planning up for now?"

"Hmmm."

"Possibly now is not the time?"

"If I thought the war would end soon, or ever, I could step

back and relax. Swim to keep fit and forget the long swim across till war's end. But I feel time passing very quickly, so..."

Meg pulled the sheet up over them and rolled onto her back. "The war seems endless, I know."

"I'm sorry. Compared to your troubles, this is nonsense. Utter nonsense. I should count myself very fortunate that I can swim at all."

"Getting sick like this has been a blow, I'll not deny it, but that shouldn't weigh on everything we do, especially on you. I fear it has and that's why you feel so low and frightened." She turned back to face Lillian. "Lily, I feel the medicine working. As long as the lovely wee Girl Guides in Wales continue picking the flowers, I'll gain my strength. Gain back some energy. You'll see."

RESCUED—AUGUST 1944

BLETCHLEY—PORTSTEWART

olly sat on Robert's bed, her hands clasped on the footboard and her chin resting on her hands. Robert sat on the room's only chair, a spindly affair that creaked with the occupant's slightest movement.

He looked at his watch. "Shouldn't you check on her?"

"No. It's what happens now. But I think she needed a wee moment alone, too." Holly picked up the telegram on the bed.

"Should I get tea?"

"Wait and ask her…"

The friends fell into silence, listening to the rain pelting the windows and roof. Holly sighed. "We can do nothing except commiserate about her brother, and I do grieve—I knew Ronnie all my life. But for the other problem, I'll get to the point—I have a solution," said Holly.

The door opened and Jo entered the room, a handkerchief to her lips.

"You're green, Jo," said Holly. "Here, lie down. I'll move."

"No, I'll sit. I need to sit up. There." Jo picked up the telegram and read it.

"Water?" asked Robert.

"Aye."

Robert busied himself pouring a glass of water from the pitcher on the bureau.

Jo pressed her hand over her mouth for a moment. "'Missing, believed killed.' My dear Ronnie..." Jo bent her head and sobbed.

Holly put her hand on Jo's arm. "Your poor brother. It is terrible."

Jo raised her head, her face puffy and a pale greenish-grey. "I'm all alone now. Alone and pregnant! I'd laugh if it wasn't so tragic, so...predictable."

Robert and Holly shot one another a look before he asked, "What will you do?"

Jo took a long draught of water. She placed the glass on small bedside table and blew her nose. "I'll have to leave the Wrens. Even if I were married, I'd have to leave, but as it is... I don't know about BP, though. Perhaps they'll keep me on until...not that I'm much use right now, but it will pass. I saw the local doctor and that's what he told me. I don't think he believed that I was married, but he was kind. I appreciated that." She stopped and took a long breath. Shakily, she said, "Whenever they turn me out, I'll go home. Once I feel better, I could take up my studies again, perhaps, if I'm more convincing about being married. My mother's wedding ring is in my father's safe, but Queen's may say no to pregnant students."

"But where will you live in Belfast? And don't say your father's office," said Robert.

"I could manage there, not ideal, but until I can make other arrangements..."

Holly said, "My mother would welcome you—you know she would."

"I know she would, but I'm not sure I can face her, not in this condition. She'd think me the fool I am." Jo's voice trembled on the last word, and suddenly, she began to sob. "Oh, God, I'm in such a pickle."

Holly put her arm around Jo's shaking shoulders. She looked up at Robert with a raised eyebrow.

"What can I do?" he asked.

"Listen, Jo. We can only grieve for Ronnie, but for the other thing, there is something we can do," she looked up at Robert, "Marry Jo."

"*What?*" Robert's voice rose.

"Marry her."

Jo raised her head. Tears streamed down her face, and she nearly howled, "No! I won't ruin his life. It's too much to ask."

"For heaven's sake, you won't ruin his life. Tell her, Robert."

"T-tell her…?"

"Tell her why you won't ruin your life if you marry." Holly's face pinched with exasperation. "Honestly, the pair of you. Never mind. She knows, Robert. She knows you're homosexual. Jo, you won't ruin his life because he's not in the market for marriage. It may even help him, with his parents, and so on, I don't know, later in life. You wouldn't hold him to anything, like support or fatherhood, or husbandly…" Holly stopped and flapped her hand.

Sniffing, Jo sat up straight and wiped her face with the handkerchief, her face turning from a greenish-grey to white. Robert's face flushed furiously.

She reached for the water glass and sipped. "No. I wouldn't. In fact, I wonder…could I write a marriage contract to protect both of us?" A light pink came to her cheeks. "I could try. What do you say, Robert? We could marry in name only, get me out of this pickle now and help my daughter in the future. I'd make sure you weren't bothered by me or her unless you wanted to know us."

Robert took the water glass from Jo's hand and drained it. "I'd have to tell my parents, wouldn't I? I mean, *what* would I tell them?"

Jo let her hands fall into her lap and said, "Holly's told me that Albert's your…what you tell Albert will differ from what you tell your parents and the rest of your family, possibly with the exception of Meg."

Jo looked at Holly. Holly shrugged and said, "Sorry, Robert, about Albert—I can't keep secrets. I should've told you."

"Well, you had better keep mine, and his, from now on," said Jo. "Anyway, I figured the Meg and Lillian part of the equation out myself."

Holly said, "I swear."

"Alright, alright. Robert, you need time to think this over, and we have time. I'm only two months gone. But will you have a talk to Albert?"

"I will, at some point. He's intelligent and strong, he's been through a lot, but still, he's only eighteen. I'd like to help you, but I think I'll ask for Meg's advice first. I'll ring her today before shift. I hope you understand. Understand too, that I've not talked to Meg about m-myself."

"I see. I do understand, and I will understand if you decide against it. Now are you happy, Holly? Putting all of this in motion?"

"Of course. We can't send you out into the cold, alone and pregnant, unmarried, with no family. You didn't expect us to do that, did you?"

"It's not so dramatic as all that. I will be far from destitute, thanks to my father. The wee bairn and I will survive, but aye, I suppose married parents would help her in life."

Holly asked, "What makes you sure it's a girl?"

"I hope it's true—I'm off men entirely. Present company excepted. And excepting my dear father and brother." She looked at her watch. "Do you know, I'm absolutely famished. I must eat something." Jo tried to smile, but it fell into a chin wobble.

"I'll run down and tell Annette we're three, again."

Robert left the two women sitting side by side on the bed. Holly read the telegram again. Quietly, she asked, "Are these always...certain? Is it possible that he's not...that he's missing but alive?"

Jo shook her head. "I don't know. I think it is certain, though. His ship must have seen action for them to send me this telegram. I don't think I can let myself hope, to be honest."

The women fell into a silence that Jo broke. "What makes you sure he'll agree? I'm not so sure he should, or that I should. I mean apart from anything else, it'll mean living a lie for both of us. I can't play his wife for his parents for instance. It would be hideous."

"Ach, you'll do it a wee while and separate at some early point, people do. We'll think of something. Listen, Robert's the best of souls and a brave man. He's crisscrossed the North Atlantic, the U-boats nipping at his bum. He'll agree. I feel it in my wee bones." After a moment, Holly asked, "You aren't planning on telling Johnny?"

"God no, but Johnny may be told about my condition and my exit. If he causes any fuss, I'll handle him."

"Did you never think of marrying? I mean a real marriage."

"I don't want a husband, I don't think."

"But what if you change your mind one day?"

"I'll be a solicitor. I'll find a way."

"What about the other...direction. Did you contemplate it?"

"Of course, but I could not screw the courage. It's that simple. Girls take their lives in their hands going that route. Back alleys and..." She shivered. "I'm less afraid of one than the other, in my ignorance of both."

"I think you're the opposite, Jo. Very brave."

"In this predicament, I've little choice. But I quite like the idea of having a child, so. I wish my father and brother were alive so we wouldn't be entirely on our own, the two of us."

"You won't be," said Holly, patting Jo's hand.

"Robert! I'm so glad you called! After hearing the news of D-Day, we worried that your liberty cancellation was due to being shipped to Normandy. Not that I said so to your mother."

"I...I'm fine. Can't say more, Aunt Meg," said Robert. "Safe." Robert switched the telephone receiver to his right ear. "Will you ask Albert to ring me?"

Meg said, "Alright, we'll ring Albert's house at school and leave the number you gave. I'm sure he'll ring you right back."

"Any time before three, I'm on shift at four. In fact, I must leave for work in a few minutes," answered Robert.

"Alright, I've made a note of that, too. Listen, you'll tell Jo that if we can help, she shouldn't hesitate to ring us?"

"I'll tell her. I don't know what I'll tell my parents. S-should I t-tell them?"

"That's tricky. I can't advise you to lie to your mother...I think the right thing will come to you in time. Until then, until it comes to you, say nothing, that's my advice. Say nothing until you're sure, because once you cross that line..."

"Yes, I see that. But you don't think this is...loony? My offering to marry her?"

"I didn't say *that*." Meg laughed, "On the other hand, you'd help her out of a fix and if you're sure about yourself, your own feelings, that you'll never want to marry...anyway, you could always divorce in future, I suppose. I hope you know her well enough...that she won't hold you to anything you don't want?"

"I can't see her doing me harm, no."

"When is this marriage to be?"

"We haven't gotten that far. I'll let you know. I must go but thank you for talking it through with me."

"When we were young, Lillian and me, we never had anyone in our families to talk to about ourselves. I hope this helped you. It helped me when Jinny accepted me and then David and I were finally honest about ourselves, but it took us far too many years for that honesty—that he loved a man named Martin and I loved Lillian."

"I didn't know about David. I mean I thought so, hoped so. I was nervous before talking to you, but now I feel relieved. I must ring off and dash over to my shift. Best to you and..."

"Wait, I've just thought—you should talk to David. He'll give you the best advice, being your uncle and...all.

"Aye, I will. Must dash...all the best."

"One second and I'll fetch his number. Have you a pencil? Hello? Hello?" The line buzzed.

After ringing off, Meg glanced at the clock. Lillian had left for a swim more than two hours before and Meg was eager to tell her Robert's story. Meg hoped this false marriage would not entangle them in an endless lie to be kept, but she feared it would.

Swimming alone again from Herring Pond and along the coastline, Lillian began to count one hundred strokes toward Inishowen.

Fifty strokes later—she could only guess—she was in trouble. She'd lost the count some time ago, her fingers numb with cold, her mind wooly. A dolphin pod swam past, their fins a glistening steel blue in the bright silver light of the Northern Irish sky. Lillian tried following them, but they were so fast she fell far behind instantly.

Treading water again, she turned around and around, but she could not tell where she was exactly—that's when the nausea from the wave chop hit. Was she too close to the mouth of the River Foyle and the numerous boats and ships plying the lanes? Blindly, she sought to correct her course. The hulks of ships and boats clogging the channel were obvious, even through the mist descending, so she turned to the opposite direction.

Her vision clouded by the fogged glass goggles, she saw a man, stroking to catch her now, swimming fast. He drew even with her. Relief buoyed her. He did not stop, and she followed his lead, matched his stroke, prayed he was taking her ashore. Wasn't it her father? Her brain felt as clouded as her vision, for she knew this could not be her father. Her father was dead. Yet there he was. She was not alone—she was not going to die. It suddenly seemed very important not to die, but she wasn't sure how long she could keep to her father's pace. He never wavered, keeping his face above the water. Expressionless, eyes wide open. She willed him to slow, but he swam like a machine.

Lillian was sleepy now, longing to stop and drift. Perhaps if she rolled over and floated, her father would stop with her. She rolled and floated. The intense cold of the water entered her bones. A terrible despair filled her. Longing to see the sky, she opened her eyes, but could not keep them open. It was then that she felt his touch. She found the support of his arms in the water, as she had as a child. Still, she was dropping, down and down— she must be dropping, mustn't she? Why did it feel like being lifted up? Lillian surrendered and slept.

She heard burbling sounds echoing, like being underwater. She tried to thrash but could barely move. Something grabbed her shoulder and she tried to fight it off, but she was too weak. The burbling sounds coalesced into a human voice.

"Lillian, Lillian, open your eyes now."

Opening her eyes was the hardest thing. She let herself drift again, but the grabbing and shaking interfered with her desire to sleep, kept her from going under.

She heard herself slur, "Whasis?"

"Lillian, it's me, Meg. Open your eyes."

Something in the force of the persistent hand and voice made her open her eyes.

Hovering above her was Meg's worried face, her eyes wide with fear. Lillian fought to stay awake, but she drifted away, hearing Meg's voice, "Oh, Lily."

~

A hand shook her shoulder again, more roughly this time. "Oh." She opened her eyes, and her sister's face snapped into focus. Beryl was speaking but Lillian could not understand the words. She sounded as though she spoke down into a well. "I can't imagine what you thought you were doing, but you're lucky to be alive. Lucky you've not been packed off to a loony bin, too," Beryl hissed. "They may arrest you, you know. I've told the Coastguard, the police, and the doctors that you must have been sucked out the Herring Pond by the tide. I can't imagine you getting into trouble in water, but you must have been sucked out...mustn't you?" She sat down. "Do you hear me? The police will be here to ask questions. The Royal Navy, too, I shouldn't wonder. A boat of Wrens saved you, so I imagine they've had to write a report of some sort. The Coastguards stayed out for hours searching in case another swimmer was with you. The Lifeboats were called out too, poor devils. Do you realize what you've done? Here, sit up and drink some of this broth." A warm cup was shoved into her hands. "Hold it steady!"

"Wrens?" Her hands shook as she slurped hot broth. "Ah, sh'lovely."

"Well? What were you doing? They told us you were in the shipping lane for heaven's sake. You'd swum past convoys at anchor. You might have been killed twelve times over. The mines, maybe even U-boats. Anyway, our navy might have shot you for a spy. Was someone with you? Some poor drowned devil? Half drowned you were. Are you daft?"

"Alone. I was alone." *Aye, I'm daft.*

Beryl shook her head. "What would Da have said? He taught us to be safe in the water above all things, and never swimming alone was first. I can barely look Albert in the eye, he's so upset —lost his dad, now this...thank God Mum and Aunt Agnes didn't live to see this, that's all I can say!"

"Shorry. Sorry."

Beryl rummaged in her purse, pulled out a handkerchief and noisily blew her red nose. "Ach, now I'll have to do me face again." Beryl pulled her compact out again and with a deep frown, began to fill in the cracks and crevices.

Lillian had been sure that she could not feel any worse, but now she did. The mug began to shake dangerously in her hands. Beryl took it out of Lillian's hands and placed it on the bed table.

"Always so sensible you were, Lily—steady—what's happened to you? Is it that time of life?" Beryl handed her the mug again. "Drink this whilst it's hot."

The sisters sat in silence while Lillian slurped. Beryl snapped the compact closed, stood and straightened the bedclothes. "I've got to go back to work."

"Albert?"

"At school. I thought it best he returns to normal."

"Aye. Only, where are we?"

"Coleraine, Causeway Hospital."

Shakily offering the mug, Lillian asked, "Take this? I'm so tired."

"Alright, sleep. I'll be back in a day or two—I'm not sure. The nurses know how to reach me in Londonderry. Remember Lillian, you're very sorry for breaking the rule against swimming off the coast but it was an accident with the tide at Herring Pond. You are not daft and you're not a bloody Jerry spy. Remember."

Waking with a start, Lillian felt relief. She turned her head to find Albert sitting and reading in the visitor's chair. His profile made serious as much by concentration as by his long, straight nose— like the noses on the marble heads of famous Romans in the books he studied— like Lillian's nose. His strong and prominent jaw line was like hers too, only his was covered with golden stubble. He wore his straight, reddish-blond hair—golden, really— brushed back off his forehead, and long enough to cover the back of his collar. As though he'd heard her thoughts, he raked his hair back with his left hand in a habitual gesture, and as it always did, the fine strands parted and fell back into angels' wings on either side.

"Bertie," she croaked.

He turned and instantly a broad smile relieved the serious aspect of his face.

"When did you get here? What time is it?" Lillian asked.

Checking his wristwatch, he said, "It's half three. I walked here after my tutorial. And don't fret, I asked permission of the housemaster. You look better, Aunt Lillian. The other day you were quite blue."

Lillian struggled to sit up.

Albert moved to the foot of the bed and turned the crank. "Better?"

After the head of the bed rose, she said, "Yes."

"Here, drink some water. You sound parched." He stood and held the glass for her.

"Ah, that's better."

He sat on the side of her bed. "Aunt Lillian...I've been thinking about what I want to say to you, so let me get it out in one go, all right?" Letting some air out, he continued. "Two days ago, we thought we'd lose you and I want you to know that I need you to be around. You know what mum is like...if it weren't for you and Meg, it would have been much harder on me since mum went wild."

Tears darkening his blonde eyelashes, he stopped speaking.

"Albert—"

"It's not just that you and Meg were there, meeting my teachers at school, taking me to the dentist, and for haircuts, to the pictures...you even took in the wee dog for us."

He cast his eyes down and blushed deeply, nearly as crimson as his school jacket. "It's that I was given hope by what you were to one another, and how you were...together. How you took care of each other, and me."

Lillian grabbed his freckled wrist, the jacket cuff nearly halfway up his forearm.

Wiping his eyes quickly, he pleaded, "Promise?"

"I promise I'll try to live to be a hundred."

"No more swims to Donegal? No more swims on your own, ever? No more swims off the coast until we have the all-clear?"

"My father would be ashamed of me, doing something so foolish. I'll only swim when someone can swim with me. I'd like it if you would. And I'll not swim off the coast until the war ends." They sat in silence holding hands for a moment. "I am sorry I worried you, truly."

"That's alright then," said Albert, standing.

Lillian blushed. "And will you promise me something, Albert? You're old enough now and I haven't the right to ask, but please don't join up like Robert did. It broke his mother's heart. It would break my heart, and your mother's. Don't be too hard on your mum, Albert. She's a nice wee flat in Londonderry and she's got a man her own age now, an Ulsterman, not a Yank."

"No, I won't join up, I promise I won't, and I'll be kind to mum. I understand Robert's reasons for joining, he told me, but it's not for me. He's told me not to enlist, as well. I've joined the officer-training course at school— I had to do that or never have a minute's peace, but I'll be fine. We'll not have conscription here."

"Has Robert written you?"

Albert's blush deepened. "Yes, but half's blacked out. I write him. He rang me."

"Oh? That's nice." Closing her eyes again, she said, "I must look awful, like something dead, washed up..."

～

"Miss Watson, hello. I am Dr. McKay." A large man in his late forties moved toward her, hand stretched out. She took it for a dry and firm grasp.

He pulled the curtain closed around her bed. "I wanted to talk to you. First, we are very pleased with your recovery. You are a very strong woman. You're forty-four? Well, you must be very fit to swim so far and survive such turbulent water. But I wonder, have you begun the change of life?"

Blushing, she said, "No."

"You still have regular menses? Periods?"

"Yes."

He nodded. "I have good news and possibly distressing news, although I don't want you to worry. We will discharge you tomorrow morning, as long as no fever develops tonight."

Lillian licked her lips. "And the distressing news?"

"We've managed to keep the Royal Navy at bay, but I'm afraid they will want to question you. You rather wasted Coastguard and the Lifeboats' time searching for swimmers who might have been with you, not to mention the Royal Navy prohibition of swimming off the coast. Now, please don't make too much of this, it's routine procedure. A local constable will be with whomever they send—some young officer, I imagine."

"Will I be charged?"

"Oh, I don't think so, but they must reassure themselves that you are not some sort of spy—a Mata Hari." He laughed, showing bright, even teeth.

His smile faded. "Don't swim alone again, Miss Watson, however strong a swimmer you are. That's the first rule, is it not? You nearly drowned and would have certainly, had it not been for the coastal warden who spotted you and alerted the Wrens who rescued you. You're not a foolish woman, are you?" He patted her hand and was quiet a moment, his fingers on her pulse. "I was told that you served with the Women's Voluntary Service? There's still a war on—best to keep busy. Now if you'll just sit forward, I'll listen to your lungs."

He listened, tapped up and down her back, and commanded deep breaths, held breath and normal breaths. He moved the warmed stethoscope head to the top of her left breast.

Pulling her hospital gown together at the back, he said, "Very good. Make an appointment with my surgery, for ten days' time, but if you develop a fever or cough, ring immediately. Best of luck." He left her bedside, leaving a trail of the scent of freshly ironed linen.

As the tears sprang to her eyes again, Lillian scrunched down in the bed and pulled the starched sheet up to her chin.

Pushing the buzzer for the nurse, she heard it ring at the station desk.

A nurse swept to her bedside as though on wheels. Middle-aged and with enormous bosoms, she asked with annoyance, "Yes?" She pulled her watch fob up off one bosom to look at the time.

"I'd like some tea, please."

"Tea?"

"Yes, tea. And toast."

"Toast? Breakfast will be served at five."

"I've had nothing to eat for days, and I'd like tea, and toast. Please."

The nurse's eyebrows shot up, but she went away without another word.

Lillian folded her arms and waited for the tea. She muttered aloud, "And another thing, I'm sick of this bloody hospital and I'm sick of being in a funk. Lucky to be alive and healthy, and there's Meg and Albert to think of…enough of this nonsense. But if one more person tells me there's a war on…"

"What's that, Miss?" A young nurse stood at the foot of the bed, holding a tray of tea and toast.

"Nothing, sorry."

THE FURIES—AUGUST 1944

PORTSTEWART—BLETCHLEY

*R*igid in posture and facing the sea, the two women sat at opposite ends of the garden bench. Meg, fists at her sides, eyes forward, asked, "I want to know what you thought you were doing?"

Arms tightly crossed over her chest, Lillian hesitated. "I…"

"Breaking the law by swimming out into open water, full of mines!"

"I, I don't know."

"You don't know why you did it or you don't know why you lied to me about it?" Meg turned to glare at Lillian.

"I didn't want you to worry."

Meg's voice rose. "Is that meant to be a joke? Is that why you nearly drowned yourself? So I wouldn't worry?

"Meg, don't upset yourself so."

"Don't. Don't you dare." Meg raised one index finger then used it to point downhill toward the sea. "You're the person who stood on that strand and told me that lies make you sick to your stomach, remember?"

Lillian nodded. "I didn't mean to lie, not really."

"Not really?"

"No."

"What *has* happened to you?"

"I don't..."

"Because if you've lost your mind and want to end it all, I deserve to know, and so does..."

Lillian interrupted, "Can I just say?" Lowering her voice, she repeated, "Can I just say? I know. I know I'm a fool and arrogant with it, to think I could swim a thirteen-mile stretch so difficult only one person has managed it on her own, and that was *before* it was mined. Not even my father could do it alone. I'm an ordinary swimmer, a good amateur, but that's all. When Mercedes Gleitze swam to Portstewart from Donegal she was twenty-nine, not forty-four." Lillian stopped and looked at Meg. "I don't know if you can understand what I was thinking, but I thought, if I don't train now, I'll only be older later. It's now or never. But I swear I'll never do anything so foolish again—I'm very sorry. We're lucky to be alive, you and me. All those dead bodies in Belfast..." her voice shook. Lillian was silent a moment as her shaking hand touched her face. "My father may have been right about my potential when I was a girl, or he may have been blinded by my love of swimming, swimming well *for* him. I'll never know. It's over now. When I swim, it will be with a swim club, even if it's just Albert, but not off the coast until the navy allows, and never alone again. I swear."

Meg sighed heavily before speaking softly. "You're not a failure, if that's what you think. You started a business in the Depression and kept it going through this endless war, without much help from me. You've cared for me, loved me...helped with the war effort, in dangerous and very unpleasant circumstances. You've cared for Albert and helped pay his school fees and much more—took the place of his mother when she went mad over the Yanks and left. Not a failure. He loves you and your sister loves you. I love you—that must count for something."

"That counts for everything. Forgive me?"

133

"Yoo-hoo!" From the other side of the house, Mildred's familiar call rang out.

Lillian asked, "Does she know?"

"Of *course* she knows. How do you think I found out?" Meg stopped speaking, took a deep breath, and spoke quickly. "After you were gone too long, I asked Frank to drive along the strand and find you. She stayed with me and eventually he rang from the Coastguard station to tell us they'd pulled you out of the water alive. Frank fetched us and drove us to hospital. An ambulance took you."

"Yoo-hoo?" Mildred's call drew closer.

"Meanwhile, I'd thought you'd gone for a safe swim in boring old Herring Pond!" Meg whispered before raising her voice to call, "In the garden, Mildred."

Mildred bustled into the garden carrying a parcel. Gently, she touched Lillian's shoulder and said, "Here you are! You look fine, Lily. Thin, but. Alright?"

"Aye. I'm an eejit, but I'm fine."

"Ach, no. If you're fine, everything's fine, right, Meg?" She glanced over at Meg, who sat at the other end of the bench glowering into middle space. "I'm making tea at the minute, must dash back. Here, Meggie, the chicken for your brother." She handed over the rotund shape wrapped in brown paper and tied with string.

"Wait, Mildred, I'll get my purse," said Meg, beginning to stand.

"No, no, it can wait."

To Mildred's receding back, Lillian said, "Tell Frank I'll make up the petrol used."

Without stopping, Mildred waved and called, "Aye, he knows."

Lillian turned to Meg. "Your brother?"

"In all the upset, I forgot that the day you went missing I'd asked David and Niall to come for a meal, tomorrow. They'll be here in the afternoon and stay to tea. I'd like to see my brother."

"Of course." Lillian took a deep breath. "There's one more thing, though. The doctor warned me that the navy and police would question me. Sorry."

"I shouldn't wonder. You put them to a lot of trouble, *and* you broke the law. There *is* a war on."

"So everyone feels the need to remind me, including the doctor...told me to keep busy and rejoin the WVS. Anyway, he didn't think I'd be charged, but they need to make sure I wasn't a spy. He made a joke about Mata Hari. Me! A German spy!"

Meg shrugged. "Perhaps they want you to apologize."

"Perhaps. I've apologized to you, but will you forgive me?"

"I will, but not just at the minute—you'll have to let me be a wee while." She stood. "I'll be in the kitchen. I need time on my own." She picked up the bundle and faced Lillian. "Do you think this has to do with all the loss? You lost your father years ago, but just this year, your mother and aunt. But also, the death you saw in Belfast, the bodies piled in carts...do you think that's affected you? I mean, you have nightmares, often."

A chill wind blew down the hill behind them, lifting the loose end of Meg's scarf over her chin. Lillian pulled up the collar of the Aran Isle pattern jumper Meg had knitted for her. "I don't know, but I'm sorry—about all of it."

Pulling her scarf down, Meg said, "I know," before turning to walk into the house.

"Meg, wait."

She turned back.

"Didn't you have something you wanted to do more than anything, but didn't? Is there something you'd like to do now?"

Meg's eyes widened. "Oh, yes. More than anything I wanted to stay in school, but our father took us out of school and put us to work the minute our mother was in the ground. I worked for the shipyard from age eleven to middle age—an entire life! And then the Germans bombed us and *then* I got sick. I'd laugh if it wasn't so desperate."

"I am so sorry. But what about now?"

"Now? Now, I feel much better and I'm happy to spend my time reading and making bread. I love to sit and knit while listening to the wireless, and I like working my way 'round the garden a wee bit at a time. My cookery's plain but I enjoy that, too. And on a lovely day, I like to take a dander on the strand with the wee dogs, and you, when you think to join us. I want no more rushing around again, ever. I *really* don't want a job ever again, or to work toward something grand, like you do. You've always been more ambitious than me. I'm content to read and enjoy books. I love making useful things with me own hands. I'm doing what *I* want to do, for the first time in my life. I'm not earning, but I expect I've done my share."

Lillian said, "Aye, you have that—more than your share."

"So, it's too late for school, but I am doing now what I always wanted to do. I learn from some of the books I read." Meg nodded before turning to walk to the back door of their cottage.

Folding her arms, Lillian sat still for a few minutes as wind down the hill met a chilly air stream coming up off the water. She got up and walked through the back door and utility room—crowded with stuffed pantry shelves, coats, hats, boots, shoes, walking sticks, bathing costumes, and the gigantic green washing machine—to her office.

Sitting behind the desk, she pulled a pile of papers out of the inbox. Unseeing, she began to sort through the files and letters. Music from the radio in the kitchen drifted down the hall and into the office.

She'd finally focused on a list of bills paid, a column of numbers in the business's ledger. Adding the column under her breath like a prayer, her pencil tip following along, she felt almost calm, when the peal of the phone bell set her heart racing. Fumbling the receiver, she said, "Hullo, hullo. Lillian Watson speaking."

A gravelly male voice spoke, his accent such a thick Scots she had to strain to understand. "Miss Watson, Chief Petty Officer Harris calling from the Royal Navy station, Portstewart. I'm calling to inform you of the interview arranged for you with Lieutenant Reynolds, the secretary to our adjutant, and an officer of the Coastguard, Captain Pierce. A member of the local constabulary will attend as well. Have you pen and paper at hand?"

"Em, yes."

In rapid fire, he told her the time she should arrive and the address, adding that it was required a male relative in his majority accompany her—husband, father, brother, son, son-in-law, uncle, nephew, brother-in-law, cousin. If that was not possible, her doctor, pastor, or solicitor must accompany her. He asked her to agree that she understood before he rang off.

Stunned, she slammed the receiver down and sat forward, her elbows on the desk. She brought her fingers to her temples and rubbed in circles. She muttered, "Of *course* I understand what a male relative is! Does he think I'm an imbecile?"

Lillian sat up straight, turned and looked out the window, the clear light reflected in her dark blue eyes. Pulling the brass address book toward her, she touched the lever to flip the book open, and the W name page lever with the little brass pencil. Under Women's Voluntary Service, she found several telephone numbers and a cable address for the main office in Belfast. Her finger skimmed to the bottom of the page and the telephone number for WVS in Coleraine, County Organizer Mrs. Estelle Cosgrove. She raised the receiver and asked the operator for the number, tapping the little brass pencil on the wooden desktop as the call rang through.

The next afternoon, Meg and Lillian provided tea in the garden. Sitting on the grass, Albert helped himself to a third sandwich, the dogs bookending him and staring at his food. Lillian told the story of the impending interview.

David said, "I can be the male relative in his majority. Say I'm your cousin."

"I can't, David, but thanks. People in this wee town have known my family since Beryl and I were children—since my mum and Aunt Agnes were children, and their parents before them—so they know all about us. No brothers, no living brother-in-law, no living uncle, no male cousins, only Cousin Alice. I'd ask Albert, but he's not yet twenty-one." She smiled at Albert.

"Ah. What will you do?"

"I have a plan. Part of it involves asking Reverend Horne to accompany me—we're meeting this afternoon. He's known me since we were young and he's a nice man. I think he'll help. And I have another plan in motion, but it's not certain yet."

Lillian looked at her watch and said, "I should leave now. Albert's coming with me." Looking at Meg, she said, "We shouldn't be too long."

Albert jumped up. "I'm the male relative in his minority." He laughed. He linked his arm in Lillian's as they left through the garden gate.

After calling Gordie over to him, David tried to catch his sister's eye. "You're awful quiet, Meggie. What's up?"

"Listen, do you mind if I go for a wee dander?" said Niall, rising from the garden bench quickly.

"No, of course not. Enjoy yourself," said David.

"Am I allowed to walk down on the strand toward the River Bann? I'd like to see the Mussenden Temple. Will I see it from there?"

"Aye, except if the fog rolls in, you won't see much, but it's a lovely walk," said Meg. "There's soldiers in the pillboxes, some-times—they'll ask for your identity card."

Niall patted the breast pocket of his jacket. "In my wallet. What time do you want me back? Six?" he asked, squeezing David's shoulder as he walked behind him.

"Perfect. I'll put the chicken in the oven at half three," said

Meg. "If the weather turns, there's a nice pub right on the harbor front. Lovely warm snug."

Bye, love," said David.

Once Niall left the garden, David chuckled and said, "Niall always knows when to make himself scarce." Petting the dog, David said, "He looks wonderful, Meggie—Martin would be pleased. I felt guilty letting him go with you, like he was part of Martin, but he's so much better off up here than in Belfast waiting for me to come home from work or going back and forth to Niall's." David got no response from his sister, who sat with a face like stone. "Now, what's up? You seem very quiet and low." David tapped a cigarette out of the pack and lit it.

Putting her teacup down into its saucer, Meg said, "I feel well enough. Better than I have in a long time. It's all this upset with Lillian. Telling me lies, putting herself at risk swimming where it's not allowed, nearly drowning herself. Now she's up on charges or something with the Royal Navy. The truth is, I don't know what's up."

David raised his eyebrows. "And you've asked?"

"Aye, and she's answered. I shouldn't say she's hasn't told me, but I'm still angry that she lied to me. We're tiptoeing around one another. What she did seems...daft."

"Perhaps when the interview blows over, you'll be able to talk properly?"

"I love her and after all these years together, we'll sort it, but it's as though she's gone mad."

David asked, "Mad? You mean like the sister?"

"I'd not thought of Beryl, but yes. Not in the same way exactly, not wild, I don't think, not running after GIs. But who knows what's she's up till? Lillian's always been so steady, so truthful and open. Or so I thought."

David whistled. "This *is* a turn up."

"Aye. And I don't know what to do, I'm so angry. We've never let anger go on so long between us. This after she nearly died out there," she said, waving her hand toward the water and Inishowen. "You'd think I'd just be happy she's alive."

"If I may offer some advice to me wee sister?"

"Please."

"Take her on a dander out on the strand where you won't be bothered by others. Tell her everything you've just told me, but without anger in your voice. You didn't inherit the Preston coloring, but you've got the Preston temper on ye, Margaret Preston, that I know. You're slow to the boil, but…" David whistled.

She nodded but was silent. "So, I have a wise brother, do I? I will take your advice. I know exactly where we should go for the talk. When we were young and Lily taught me how to swim, we'd change behind a large rock, our rock. We'll go there."

"Good. After all the blather, forgive her, just forgive her. Alright?"

Meg said, "Ach, but it feels good to be on me high horse."

"Better angry than frightened?"

Meg laughed. "Aye, much better, but I will take your advice, your wise advice. Tomorrow." Checking her watch, Meg said, "Listen, before Albert comes back, I wanted to ask what you think about this marriage of Robert's? He rang you?"

"One more thing—don't lecture her. You've made your point, I'm sure. Alright, so, about the marriage—yes, he rang me—I warned him that if Florrie finds out the marriage is false, the baby not his, and worse, we knew it, God help us all. He understands that well enough. Otherwise, I thought that Jo would be fair to him and if they married, it would help her and the bairn. Niall is all for it, but then Florrie isn't his sister."

"Niall is for this marriage?"

"Aye, so much so, in fact, he'll marry her if Robert doesn't. Really, what would be the harm? Anyway, Niall says since Jo has nobody but Robert and her other friend, what's her name?"

Meg touched her chin and said, "He told me it. A plant name —something starting with haitch. Hazel?"

David exhaled a blue stream of smoke and shrugged. "The

point is, Jo hasn't anyone else to help her on this earth and she'll need help, no matter being a solicitor's daughter. Niall's mother raised him on her own and it was a hard life for her, he can tell you. Anyway, nobody need know who doesn't already."

"So, you remember being able to keep secrets from our sisters, is that it?"

"Never. Ha! They always wheedled things out of me, like pulling a whelk out of its shell with a pin."

Meg laughed. "Aye, and me. But yes, Jo will need help, so I wanted to ask, since you mentioned leaving Belfast for Ballycastle, if number 34 might be available to her to rent? We'll want it for Albert when he's at Queen's, but he'll need a lodger anyway. Those two seem to get along, but if it doesn't work, they can sort it."

"Really? Aye, I've wanted to leave Belfast. Niall says I could give up my job at Queen's and work in his practice, and I'm happier in Ballycastle with him. So yes, I'm happy to give number 34 and the rent over to Jo."

Meg nodded. "Now to the other thing worrying me—Albert and Robert."

"Meggie, love, you really must stop worrying. It's not good for ye. Here's what I think—whatever is between Albert and Robert is not our business, they are old enough lads to understand the dangers—so, it's settled?"

Just as Meg was going to answer, a cold rain poured down, sending them scurrying into the house, leaving the tea things to a watery grave in the garden.

∾

Mrs. Cosgrove, in full WVS uniform and regalia, stepped back from the table and waited as the Royal Navy lieutenant skimmed the letters quickly. He passed them to the subaltern next to him and stood. "Thank you, Mrs. Cosgrove. Miss Watson, my apologies for our treatment of you as anything other than a brave patriot who risked her life to aid the British Army, ATS, Royal Ulster Constabulary, and firemen fighting the destruction of Belfast. Captain Pierce, Sergeant Meadows, are you satisfied?"

"Absolutely," said the Coastguardsman, as he edged toward the door.

"Never doubted Miss Watson, known the family for years," said the uniformed police sergeant, gathering his notebook and pencil.

Once escorted outside of the naval station, Mrs. Cosgrove led them to the waiting canteen truck, a WVS driver holding the door open for them.

"Will you come up the hill for sherry, Mrs. Cosgrove, Reverend?"

Several sherries later, the group left the cottage garden in merry spirits, Lillian walking them back to the canteen truck. "I drove many miles in one of these, just as Meg stocked hundreds of pounds of food and gallons of tea into them. Not happy memories, exactly, but..."

"Important work to be proud of," said Mrs. Cosgrove.

"Certainly," said Reverend Horne.

"And we are," said Lillian.

The driver opened the door for the departing Mrs. Cosgrove and the Reverend.

"Thank you, but I'll walk to the rectory. Lovely to meet you, Mrs. Cosgrove. Lillian, see you on Sunday." He donned his hat with a light pull on the brim, and with a wave, set off at a brisk pace down the steep hill, arms swinging.

Through the open truck window, Mrs. Cosgrove said, "My, you do have a beautiful view up here! Till next week, two o'clock, Tuesday, at the office on Queen Street, you can't miss the WVS banner."

Once back in the garden, Lillian slumped into a camp chair. Mildred and Frank sat on the bench munching sandwiches.

Meg sat at the table holding the refreshments. "No! Gordie, down! Did you see? He nearly got the rest of the sandwiches." Laughing, she said, "Look at Bobby, waiting for something to land on the grass. They're only cress, I can't imagine why they're so interested."

Lillian said, "I could use a proper drink. Frank, I've got yours. Mildred? Meg?"

Frank chuckled.

"I won't say no," said Mildred.

"A sherry, a tiny one," said Meg.

Lillian returned with a tray and put it down on the table. Handing the glasses around, she said, "Frank, just as it comes, Mildred, yours with a splash. And here's your tiny sherry, my dear." She poured herself a drink and sat. "Here's to the WVS!" They raised their glasses and then sipped.

Mildred asked, "How did you get that Mrs. Cosgrove to do so much on your behalf, Lily?"

Lillian yanked the knot in her tie-down. "Well, it didn't come free, I can tell you." She put her drink down and unbuttoned the WVS uniform tunic. "Whew!"

"What do you mean?" asked Mildred.

Lillian picked up her drink again. "From now on, I'm officially back in the WVS."

"Oh, no!" Meg groaned. "Lillian, I just won't do it again."

"And I wouldn't ask you. You've made your wishes clear. No canteen trucks again, but Mildred and I are engaged now in WVS billing and typing, whatever Mrs. Cosgrove needs. It won't cost us much and it helped me today, certainly. Also, I've told Reverend Horne that I'll become more active in church—whatever I can do to help. Don't fret, Meg, I did not involve you in any of it."

"Aye, tit for tat, even with clergy," said Frank.

"Remember I taught all of you in the wee Sunday school? You two, Beryl, Annie, and David? I loved going to church before the Germans dropped a one-ton bomb on my poor mother. I've not been so keen on God since, which is why we married in a registry office. I'd no interest in going to my church, let alone converting to *his* church for the wedding." She nodded at Frank. "But here, you don't mean you agreed to take care of the billing and what-not for *nothing*?"

Grinning, Frank said, "'*His church*?' You mean the one, true church, don't you, me love?" He winked.

Mildred nudged him with her elbow.

Lillian said, "Think of it as war service. There's still a war on, you know." Laughing, she raised her glass again. "So everyone reminds me. But here's the best bit. I'll be loaned a car, an auld army wagon really, and a special petrol ration. So, Frank, we're in business!"

"That's grand, Lillian. I won't syphon off ye, but if ye'll run me over a time or two to Coleraine when ye go? Also, since I learnt to fix every auld army wagon ever built, I'll keep it running like a top. Very reliable they were, simple, those wagons."

"I've never understood what they would have done to you anyway. A fine?" asked Meg.

"No, I suspect the satisfaction of reducing me to tears would have been sufficient, but I denied them the satisfaction. Mrs. Herron was as angry as I when I told her the story of the proposed interrogation, and they daren't say no to all of us in our uniforms, including the pastor. You know, sometimes, it's good to get angry, furious, ragin'—and to stop feeling sorry for yourself, as I have been. Being furious gets the brain cells sparked. Here's to ragin'!"

Looking at one another, Meg and Mildred raised their glasses to Lillian. Mildred said, "To ragin'!" while Frank drained his glass.

Meg did not drink, but holding Lillian's gaze, said, "To Lily."

∼

Jo left Bletchley Park mansion and quickly crossed the open yard of the campus to the bench where Robert and Holly waited.

"Well?"

"That's that. I'm out. 'Dissatisfactory discharge.' The Third Officer sent to sack me was in her glory, acting like I was a contamination. Itching to write dishonorable on my discharge papers, since she clearly thinks that's what I am. But my fallen state doesn't rise to the dishonorable level in the navy's view, which I find interesting."

Robert asked, "But didn't you tell her we'd asked for the calling of the banns?"

"I did, but she seemed unmoved, and regardless of marital status, being pregnant is not allowed in the Wrens."

"What about your hut boss?" asked Robert.

"Irrelevant. It's in the navy's hands, not Bletchley's."

"Are you sure BP won't keep you on?" asked Holly.

"No, but apparently there has to be some confab about it. Words like 'unprecedented' were used. Funny to see the geniuses not have the foggiest idea what to do with a pregnant woman."

"So?"

"So, I don't know." She shrugged. "Are we still on for dinner tonight at the White Hart?"

Robert said, "Aye. We're off shift at eight and Annette has it all arranged. And she'll see to the wedding collation if you want one. But we should see the minister again and confirm the date for the wedding."

Jo asked, "Do you have time to walk over to the church now?"

"I do," said Robert.

"Ha! Practice makes perfect," said Holly, laughing.

"I swear, you're twelve, aren't you? Isn't she?" asked Jo, looking over Holly's head at Robert.

~

Holly leant forward to say, "Don't look now, but Major Johnny just came in. Twelve o'clock."

Jo finished chewing and said, "With or without a woman?"

"With."

"Young or old?"

Holly squinted and pushed her glasses up. "Young. In uniform. WAAF. Definitely not the wife."

"Can't resist a girl in uniform, that one. Pass the bread. Annette bakes the most wonderful bread, doesn't she?"

"Did you talk to her about moving in here?"

"I did and she was most accommodating. Showed me the little cottage at the back of the garden. It's quite livable, with reasonable rent. There's a wee cast iron range for heat and cookery, too. But I asked her to add board, too, for my lunch en famille in the kitchen. Suits me. I'll keep the local doctor in town for the baby visits, and so we'll go forward through the winter."

"I think it's grand you'll stay in Bletchley," said Robert. "We'll keep an eye on ye."

"I don't have anybody but you two who would, so it seemed the best idea. I'm going back to Belfast tomorrow, spend a few days packing up some law books, talking to my tutors at Queen's, visiting the city hall about our destroyed property. Oh, and picking up my mother's wedding ring from the safe. I might even buy something to wear. What'll you wear to our wedding?"

"Not this," he said, pulling on the scarf of his sailor suit. "I have a dress uniform in my sea chest, it has a double-breasted jacket, regular trousers, and a peaked cap. I've worn it twice. I hope it fits—I've grown an inch and gained a stone since I enlisted."

"If it doesn't you could try the tailor near the train station.

Wish I'd grown an inch." Holly laughed. "I'll be in my Wrens' best. Listen, you two, unless you hate the idea, I thought I'd organize the girls to form an arch for when you leave the church, take a few photos, to show the wee bairn one day. Don't think I can swing swords, but we'll think of something to hold up."

"Rolled up decrypts?" asked Robert, laughing.

"Would you? I love the idea. Do you know, this is sort of fun, don't you think, Robert?"

"I'll be nervous until I tell my parents."

"Do you have to tell them?" asked Holly. "I mean, why do you?"

Robert furrowed his brow. "I am confused about what to do, I admit. I've talked to my uncle, my aunt, Albert...n-nobody suggested I t-tell them. N-nobody."

"On the other hand, if you told them, it would get them off your back in the future about wives and kiddies," said Holly. "But if you don't tell them, and there's no need, mind, you wouldn't have to lie to them, I mean, not outright."

"Would you tell your p-parents?" asked Robert, looking down into his red wine glass.

Holly thought for a moment. "No idea. My parents may want me to have a family, but I have the enviable character of an eccentric, and after the war, I'll become an eccentric mathematician. Problem solved. I'll wear loud colors and surround myself with dusty tomes and wee pets. I'll eat chocolates and get fat. Fortunately, I have siblings who can provide grandchildren."

"I don't know what to do," said Robert. He sipped his wine.

"Oh, Robert, for heaven's sake cheer up. It will come to you," said Jo.

"Really? I mean that's what my aunt s-said, those exact..."

Holly leaned forward again. "WAAF on the move...to the loo to freshen her lipstick? Uh-oh, don't look now, but the major's on the move, too. Our way." Clearing her throat, she sat back and waited.

"Jo?" He addressed Jo only, as though her companions didn't

exist. A tall, thin, ramrod straight, army officer with greying wavy hair, Johnny stood between Jo and her dinner companions. "Jo, we must talk. I just heard you've been discharged from the Wrens."

"Hello, Johnny. Yes, alas, I am a Wren no more. But I don't see that there's anything for us to talk about."

He hooked his thumbs in the leather belt of his tailored khaki twill uniform. "I'm not an idiot. I can guess the reason."

"I'm sure you needn't guess, since somebody told somebody, and now everybody knows," said Jo, "but there's still nothing to talk about, not with you."

"Don't make me ask you now, here."

"Let me introduce you to my fiancé, Robert Henderson."

Robert stood and offered his hand, which Johnny ignored.

"And my life-long friend, Holly Aarons."

Holly, pinned to her chair between the standing men, nodded up at him.

Johnny turned and looked Robert up and down, sneering. "What is this? You're never marrying this *sailor*."

"I am."

"The child isn't his—I know it's mine. Tell me I'm wrong." His voice had gone from a deadly whisper to one loud enough to make the diners at the next table turn. "There, you can't tell me it's not mine."

"It's not yours. Now go away, please. You've become loud. You must be drunk."

Robert moved and Johnny whipped around. "Oh, yes? Go on. Striking an officer of another branch is an offense—I'll have you arrested."

"I wasn't going to, but you should leave," said Robert, pulling his thick shoulders back.

Jo pushed her chair back and stood. "Listen to me. If you don't go away this minute, I'll ring your wife from that phone box. After that I'll ring your adjutant and tell him." She turned her head to see the WAAF standing uncertainly at Johnny's table, watching the scene. Jo raised her voice so that all the diners and the WAAF paid attention. "He's married, dearie, and he'll never leave her, if you're interested, which you shouldn't be, since he's vastly too old for you and a dried-up old *turd!*"

The WAAF looked around at her fellow diners before fleeing the room like a frightened doe. Johnny's face darkened as the dining room exploded with laughter.

"You're still here? I'm off to the phone box, then." Throwing her napkin onto the chair, she said, "Please move and let me out."

Johnny turned and quickly strode out of the room.

Jo sat down and said, "Close your mouth, Holly."

"But you were magnificent! I want you to defend me in court, should I ever commit a crime…much more of him and I will."

"God that felt good! I'm shaking, I'm so furious. There's nothing like ragin'!"

"Jo, now I have another problem," said Robert, resuming his seat.

"What is it now, Robert?"

"I'm afraid of you!" Robert smiled and the three friends laughed.

Holly raised her glass and said, "To Jo, ragin'!" The friends clinked their glasses together.

"But tell me this, how do you know his wife's telephone number?" asked Holly.

"I don't, but I do know he's an idiot, so."

"I hate pouring ice water on calling him an idiot, but he's a top linguist," she lowered her voice further, "and code breaker."

"Oh, I know, although really, Holly, you of all people ruining a good joke. Here's a better one—he has beautiful green eyes and I liked sleeping with him—but that joke was on me."

FOUR WINDS—AUTUMN 1944

BLETCHLEY—BELFAST

*H*olly sobbed in Jo's arms. Robert walked back and forth across the tiny room, pulling clothing out of the lower bureau drawers, stopping at the open sea chest to pack his belongings.

"Now, Holly, it will be fine. You'll see. We'll always be the best of friends and you'll see us in Belfast."

"Oh, Jo! This is so bloody unfair. How is he able to do this?" She raised her head from Jo's shoulder, her face tear-stained, and took the handkerchief offered.

Robert said sourly, "He's a major in the army and a shift leader nearly equal to Baker at BP."

Jo said, "It's all right, really, for me. I don't blame Annette for reneging on the cottage. Johnny and his friends are very good customers. But I'm so sorry, Robert. I've really put you in the soup."

Robert said, "As long as they don't send me back to Murmansk, that's all I pray."

Holly blew her nose and spoke calmly. "I could talk to Mrs. Whist. Now you're married, she may welcome you back to Vicarage Lane."

"Now *you* listen—it's best I get on with my life. I'm going back to Belfast and as soon as I can qualify, I must. Staying here to be tormented by Johnny is just not on."

"But who will help you?"

"I know it will be hard, but I'm only temporarily destitute, just until the probate of my father's estate is completed. Lots of people have offered help already. Robert's in a much bigger pickle."

"Oh, yes, of course. Sorry. Any news?" Holly blew her red nose.

"I've been told nothing yet. And there I was feeling a wee bit sorry for the major. Bastard." Folding his Lord and Taylor long underwear, he pushed them down into the sea chest with vigor. "I've been given liberty for a few days, and I plan to see Albert. I've not told my parents I'm coming to Ireland, which I may regret, but."

There was a quiet knock on the door and a telegram was shoved under it.

He bent to grab the envelope and stepped over the chest to stand at the window. Seconds passed.

"Oh, thank God. Thank God! I'm safe. Em, Holly, read it to yourself, please. Sorry, Jo." Handing the telegram to Holly, he turned to Jo, "I'm reposted here, in this country. I'll be safe. I can say too, I'm an Able Seaman now."

Jo said, "Ex-navy or not, I signed the Official Secrets Act and know it's for life, but no worries...yes, thank God you'll be safe. I am relieved. When do you report to the new post?"

"The fourth."

Holly read the telegram silently before handing it back to Robert, who reread it.

To Able Seaman Robert R Henderson
White Hart Pub, Bletchley

> *You are reposted permission Royal Navy J Stoughton Commander GC&CS Stop Report to Thomas Rose Post Office Research Station Dollis Hill London NW 0800 4 October 1944 Stop Temporary billet provided Stop Royal Navy rank promotion to Able Seaman Coder effective immediately Stop Insignia delivered to Dollis Hill Stop*
>
> *R Baker Major Army Int Corps*

"I'm glad we'll *almost* be working together," said Holly, smiling. "I'm so glad you're safe."

Robert pulled an envelope off the bureau top. "I ordered copies of the wedding photos, for each of us, plus a few extras. Here, take two, Jo. Holly, here's yours."

"Lovely, thanks," said Holly, smiling. "I think the girls made a good showing, forming a canopy of oars over your wedding march. Where they got them, I shudder to think."

Checking his watch, he said, "Jo, I'm afraid…"

"Aye, time to go." Standing, she pulled Holly up onto her feet and into her arms. "Now lovey, we'll meet again, and soon, you'll see."

Putting her arm out, she drew Robert into the embrace.

There was a hard, quick rap on the door, accompanied by a second telegram pushed under the door.

Ripping it open, Robert read it quickly. "It's from my father. Mum's in hospital, very ill. He's asking if I can come." He crushed the telegram.

"Do you know what's wrong?" asked Jo.

Robert shook his head. "I must telegram before we board the train. I'll take the cases down. We must hurry." Slamming the sea chest shut, he picked it up.

Holly picked up two cases and said, "I'll send the telegram for you, tell him you're coming. Don't worry."

~

The two young men stood in the kitchen of number 34 St. Ives Gardens holding one another.

Albert said, "Go on now, run over to Belfast City. Your father needs you."

Robert pulled back from Albert to whisper, "You don't mind Jo staying here? I don't know when I'll be able to get back...my father will expect me to stay with him."

"Don't worry. I'll be here in the evenings. Anyway, no, I don't mind Jo here. There's plenty of room. I think we have extra keys for both of you. Meg said there should be extra keys in an old tea chest on the shelf. Ah, here it is." Albert pulled the tea chest off the shelf and emptied the contents on the kitchen table. "Here, let's try this one in the door."

"Wait." Robert put his arms around Albert again and kissed him deeply.

~

"You?"

"Aye, Mum. I'm here with Da."

Her eyes remained closed, long grey hair spread upon the starched white of the pillowcase, her hand searched.

Taking her hand in his, Robert asked, "How are you feeling, Mum?"

Her hand grasped his. "I wanted to live."

"What?"

With effort and a furrow between her closed eyes, she tried to speak louder. "I wanted to...to see you settled. My Robert."

Robert looked at his dad who sat on the other side of the bed, holding her right hand, which lay open in his grasp. Robert watched his mother struggle to speak.

"Settled with someone. You'll be all on your own once we're gone and I feel..."

He waited a moment before asking, "Feel what, Mum?"

"Sorry...so sorry..."

Robert looked over at his father, whose eyes were filling with tears. He stood, still holding her hand in his.

Heart racing, he said, "As a matter of fact, I have a surprise for you. Jo, J-Josephine, you know, she came home with me last t-time." He inhaled and let it out. "We're m-m-m—we wed."

"Oh, that's grand, son," said his father. "Did you hear him, Florrie? He's wed that nice girl, Jo. Isn't that grand?"

"I'm sorry we couldn't wait to m-marry here, with you in the church, b-but there's no getting around it, she's fallen with a b-baby. She thinks it'll be a girl, expected early March."

"Oh, Florrie! Did you hear him? He's going to be a father! We'll have a grandchild. Florrie, love? A wee girl?"

A small smile pulled one corner of her mouth up. She whispered, "Aye, grand." Her brow relaxed. Looking down at her face, Robert could see the effect of the stroke in her lopsided features. He turned his face away for a moment.

When she didn't say more, he sat down again, still holding her hand.

A young nurse came into the room, her starched uniform rustling. She came up to Robert's side of the bed. "May I?" Taking Florrie's wrist in her hand, she said, "I should put her oxygen on again. Let her rest now, alright? Visiting hours are nearly over."

The men stood uncertainly. Tweed flat cap in hand, Ralph, stooping, asked, "When can we come back, Sister, em?"

"Sister McElway. Tomorrow at eleven. Your wife needs rest, Mr. Henderson, that's the very best medicine for her now."

"This is our son, Robert. He's just wed, he's told us."

"Congratulations." She began to tug on sheets and rearrange Florrie slightly, but firmly.

Ralph bent and kissed Florrie's forehead. "Alright, Florrie, we're stepping out for a wee while. This nice sister will care for ye till we're back, love." His hand lingered on her cheek for a moment.

Robert bent and kissed her cheek. "Sleep well, Mum."

~

Robert followed his father down the large staircase and out the main door of the hospital into the late September evening. The older man donned his cap and stood still, unaware of the throngs of people moving around him.

Buttoning up his pea coat, Robert said, "Here, Da, when's the last time you ate?" He put his tally on, angled to the front and one side, and took his father's arm. *He's not taller than me anymore.*

"Eh? Oh, I had something…"

"I haven't eaten much in nearly a day. How about a pint and some grub?"

"Alright, son."

"Let's go to your local. They still serve food? Ale?"

"Aye, they do. Oh, I should fetch the wee dog out to the yard, feed her and the cat. Lizzie said she'd check on them, but I don't know when that was, rightly. She was sitting with me and Florrie in hospital, and it was daylight outside."

Robert looked into his father's watery blue eyes and felt deep sorrow settle in his chest. "Alright. Then we can go 'round."

"Look, thon tram call is crowded—means one's due. Let's try to catch it." He stopped and, turning to Robert, asked, "Hey up…what about your lass? Where is she?"

Robert moved them along to the tram stop. "Jo's staying at Meg's house, just over on St. Ives Gardens. You remember it. W-we brought our luggage there and thought we'd stay there. We'd had a long t-trip. You don't mind, do you? But she doesn't expect me for tea tonight, she knows I wanted to be with mum and you…"

"No, no, you should stay with her tonight. And what about her meal? She has to eat regular now. Mothers need to eat—it's very important."

"She was going down the shops when I left. Lillian's nephew is living there too. You remember wee Albert?"

"Oh, aye, I do, now you mention him. Albert's red headed, but a good-natured wee fella, as I recall. Bright. He lived in that house with his mum after they were bombed out, I remember—packed like sardines they were in them days."

"Aye, that's right. You've a good memory. Albert's a very big lad now and a student at Queen's, so he'll be living in that house."

"Youse can stay with me if you like. There's your old room—not the best for two, but."

"Alright, I'll t-talk to her about it."

"That's the ticket, son, the secret to a good marriage. Let's hurry now."

∾

Robert let himself into number 34, removed his coat, tally and shoes, and ran up the first flight of stairs softly. Jo's door was closed and there was no sound. He padded up the second flight. Albert's door was closed. He switched off the hall light and opened the door, shutting it quietly.

The blackout curtains were open and the moon shone through the window over the bed.

Albert sat up in bed, his face in shadow, his hair silver in the moonlight. "Alright?"

"Aye. Sad, but alright. My poor mum and da." Robert walked around the bed and sat down.

Albert drew Robert to him and whispered, "Would you like me to hold you?" as he lay back.

Robert whispered, "Aye." Robert pulled his jersey off and pressed along the length of his lover.

∾

Twilight's silver light crept into the room. Robert watched the change of light in the room. He turned over and looked at Albert's sleeping form by his side, his young face relaxed and peaceful. Albert's left hand rested on his chest as it rose and fell. *He is beautiful…long and graceful, broad in the chest and shoulders.*

Robert's gaze followed the swirl of golden hair darkening as it grew down Albert's stomach to the dark russet thicket, genitals nestling on muscular thighs. His hand traced the swirl.

"Hello," said Robert, smiling, as Albert opened his eyes.

"Hello. Did you just wake?" Albert smiled and stretched.

"No." Robert's face fell into a frown. He pulled his hand back. "I've been awake for a wee while because I need to tell you something, something I should have last night."

"What's wrong?" asked Albert, turning on his side to face Robert.

"Well…yesterday at the hospital, my mum seemed so bad, so ill b-but fretting about *me*, that I'd be alone in the world after they're g-gone. So," he took a deep breath, released it as a sigh and said, "I told them I'd m-married Jo and that she was having a baby, let them think it was m-my b-baby."

Albert blew air out through pursed lips.

After a moment, Robert said, "S-say s-something."

"I am stunned, I'll not deny it. I'd hoped you wouldn't."

"That's not what you said, you said…"

Albert sat up to lean against the headboard. "I know I told you I would accept whatever you decided to do, it was up to you, but *I* meant the decision to marry Jo, not the decision to tell your parents you were married and the rest." He ran his fingers through his hair.

"I mean, I c-can't tell them about *us*, now c-can I? I d-don't see the d-difference?"

"The difference is that there's life to the lie now. And I'm relegated to who knows where! Oh, wait. I do know. Dear Uncle Albert to the child, or whatever they'll turn me into. The nelly bachelor friend. The thing I never wanted to be."

"B-but I never meant to do that, what you j-just said…"

Albert lowered his voice to an angry hiss and said, "But that's *exactly* what you did. You denied me by telling them, denied what I am to you. I thought the point was to help *her* out, not help yourself by lying and presenting your parents with a daughter-in-law and a grandchild—it's all a lie." He pulled the sheet over his nakedness with a snap. "Not say to the world, 'Albert's just me pal. I'm a normal lad, a wife and baby on the way.'"

Robert's face flushed. "We never disc-cussed me telling my p-parents about you, I don't know what you're t-talking about."

"If you can't see the difference, then I can't explain it to you."

Robert swung his legs over the edge of the bed, turning his back to Albert. "You weren't there, in hospital, seeing her, how she w-worried about me, how ill she is," he said quietly.

Albert said, "Alright. It's done. Now you have to tell Jo."

"Aye. Now I must t-tell Jo. She'll be as angry as you."

Robert sat with his hands hanging between his knees, staring at his naked legs and feet. There was no movement from Albert's side of the bed. Hands pulled up to his knees, Robert shifted to look out the window at the shifting light of daybreak. The increasing light filled the room and fell on his clothing, hurriedly discarded into a disorderly pile on the floor.

The sound of the telephone ringing broke the stony silence between them.

"What time is it?" Albert's voice was thick.

"Nearly half six."

"That'll waken Jo. The telephone's in her room," said Albert. The ringing stopped. Robert turned his head to listen but heard nothing. He picked his bellbottoms out of the pile and pulled them on.

Jo called up the staircase, "Robert, it's your father ringing." They heard the stair creak as she walked up a step and stopped. "Robert?"

Robert buttoned the drop front panel deftly as he'd learned to do in drills and battle station calls. "Coming right down." He opened the door just enough to squeeze through.

Jo stood yawning on the staircase. "It's your father on the line."

"Sorry, Jo," said Robert.

"No, it's fine. I meant to have an early start—loads to do today. I'll get the kettle on."

Bare-chested and barefoot, Robert ran past her and into her bedroom. He located the black Bakelite receiver lying on her pillow and picked it up.

"Da?"

"It's bad news, son. Sorry. Can you meet me at hospital? Mum's..." His voice breaking, he said, "...gone."

Robert inhaled audibly. "R-right away, D-Da."

"No, no, don't rush. Not now. I've called the undertaker and they'll meet us there at ten."

"Aye. How are you?"

"I don't know. Tell lass I'm sorry to waken her. I'll meet you in the main lobby at quarter till, alright?"

His father rang off and Robert put the receiver down gently. He sat down on Jo's rumpled bed.

From the doorway, Albert, dressed in pajamas and robe, asked, "What is it?"

"My mum's d-died. I'm to meet my d-da at hospital at quarter t-t-till...ten."

Albert sat next to him and put his arm around Robert's shoulders. "I'm so sorry."

"I'm s-shaking. Like after one of my n-nightmares."

Albert leaned in and rested his head on Robert's. "I'll switch the geyser on for your bath. Make breakfast. Come downstairs."

"Alright. I'll get some clean clothes and come down." He stopped at the door. "Listen, I want to tell J-jo I passed her off as my wife before I leave for B-Belfast City. Get it over."

"She *is* your wife, but I don't think she'll be hard on you, under the circs."

Robert said, "I'm s-so sorry about t-telling them, Albert, I n-never meant what you said."

"I won't be so hard on you either. Come here."

THE SEASON WHEN TO COME AND WHEN TO GO —AUTUMN 1944

BELFAST—PORTSTEWART

*J*o and Robert stood together at the hall table holding the sherry, whiskey, and ginger ale. The rest of the family, friends and neighbors sat with Ralph in the parlor. The collation—tea, sandwiches and plain cakes provided by Lizzie, David, and Meg—was laid out on a table in the parlor.

Jo looked at the framed photos hanging over the table, pointing. "There's us! It's a funny photo with all the girls and their oars, isn't it? Holly's wonderful. Is this you as a baby?"

"Aye."

"Adorable. And your parents on their wedding day. Your mother looked beautiful. And Ralph, he actually looks the same, bigger then though."

"He does, in a general way. You look nice. I meant to tell you," said Robert.

She turned back to him. "Thanks. I went to Robinson's yesterday and bought the entire outfit. Solicitors must wear a black suit in court, so I'm hoping it fits after the birth. The pearls are my mum's. They will fit for life, and then I'll give them to Rosie. I actually also bought a few things for when I'm large, so I guess I believe it's happening." Jo sipped her sherry. "You look nice in your dress blues—like our wedding day."

Robert poured himself a whiskey. "You've settled on Rosie?"

"I think so...I kept coming back to Rosamund, after my mother, and in that case, I think she'll thank me for calling her Rosie. Rosie Bray. Do you like it? But would you mind if I gave her Henderson-Bray? Rosamund Holly Henderson-Bray."

"Honored and my da will love it, so will Holly love her name in the middle. I do like Rosie, very much. Rosamund Holly Henderson-Bray? That's a mouth full for a wee thing."

"My girl's going places, so she'll handle the hyphenated name. I'm not completely sure about the given name. It's all right, I've time."

"Here, what if it's a boy?"

"Cross that bridge...but not John, definitely. Ronald after Ronnie, or Ernest, for my father? Ronald Robert?"

He smiled. "Listen, thank you for coming today to the church and the cemetery. Also, for coming earlier this week and meeting them all, and...for being so nice."

Jo turned away from those watching her from the parlor. She lowered her voice. "Playing the part? I do owe you. We'll have to discuss continuance, if you know what I mean, but not now. Anyway, your father is a dear and it makes him happy." She turned to look at the guests in the parlor. "I haven't had a chance to talk to Meg."

Robert nodded and followed her.

"Hi, Robert. Before you settle, would you pour me one?" asked his Uncle Tom. "Here, will you look at this fella?" He shouted to the room at large. "He was a puny wee thing and now he looks every inch Royal Navy. You know, I think he's bigger than my boys." Shouting even louder, he asked, "And the beard! And how'd he come by that head of hair? Not from you, Ralph!" Exploding with laughter, he held the empty glass out to Robert.

Pressing her lips into a thin line and snatching the glass out of her husband's hand, Lizzie said, "*I'll* get him the next one."

His father rescued Robert by calling over. "Come sit with your auld Da."

Robert squeezed in between his father and Meg, Jo on her other side, completing a quartet on the sofa. The two women were having a quiet conversation. Putting his arm around his father's rounded shoulders, he offered his whiskey glass, "Would you like this, Da?"

"You drink it, son."

"Are ye alright?"

"Aye, alright, lad." He squeezed Robert's knee. "Where's the wee dog?"

David, who was sitting in a straight-backed chair to Ralph's left, leaned over and said, "I'll look for him, Ralph. Is he outside, do you think?"

"Mebbe, she is. I'd like to know where she is. I know the cat is hiding—he hates strangers. I'll not find Harry till you lot leave. He'll only tolerate Robert."

Standing, David said, "I'll look for her. What's she called again?"

"Girly."

David blanched. "Has she a lead?"

"Aye, by the kitchen door," said Ralph.

David picked up a ham paste sandwich before heading for the kitchen.

Turning to Robert, Ralph said, "He doesn't have to look for her."

"It's alright, Da, he's good with dogs."

Lizzie came back into the room carrying two glasses. "Here, Ralph," she said, handing him the fullest one. "Get that down your neck." She crossed the room to her husband, who took the second glass and looked down at the scant volume before throwing it back. Lizzie kept moving into the kitchen.

Meg stood and walked after her.

Lizzie was standing at the sink crying when Meg entered the

kitchen. Softly, Meg said, "Hiya." Walking over to her older sister, she said, "Sit down, Lizzie," her hand on Lizzie's back.

She sat down on a chair by the window and cried into her handkerchief. Meg pulled a chair up and sat down facing her. She touched Lizzie's knees lightly.

Lizzie said, "Florrie was me best friend. She and Jinny were thick as thieves until Florrie wed. But after, we were. They moved to our street, to this house, and the two of us, we saw each other every day. Every day we had tea, or shopped, or whatnot. Took care of one another during confinement, after a birth. Took care of each other's babies, children, and the husbands. We talked about things only women with husbands, women with children talk about. Worry about. I'd nobody else, even when Annie was still living here, because she was still... Annie. Always with her mother-in-law. Now I've nobody."

Meg sat back a little and pulled her hands off Lizzie's knees.

"Nobody—only Tom and he's, ach. The boys are grown. Once they're out of the service they'll marry and I'll never see them." She sniffed. "This girl Robert married. Will she stay here when he goes back on duty?" She looked at Meg, her eyes red, her face mottled.

"I think so. She's living in my house now."

"Oh, I know, but she could move in here. Look after Ralph and I'll look after the two of them. Do you think I should ask her?"

"Maybe not today."

"No, no, I expect you're right about that. But I'll invite her to tea one day soon—just the two of us. There, I feel much better. Do you think anyone else will come this afternoon?" Lizzie wiped her eyes.

"I don't know." Meg's hands fell limply into her lap.

The kitchen door opened, and Girly ran in, happy and excited, followed by David. "She was asleep at the far end of the garden. I was happy not to have to walk around the neighborhood calling 'Girly!'" Laughing, he unhooked her lead and she trotted into the parlor. "She didn't like the idea of me putting her lead on, but the sandwich did the trick."

Lizzie blew her nose, now bright red.

Looking from one to the other, David said, "It's just the three of us now, in this country, anyway. Does Annie know about Florrie? Have you written?"

"I plan to," said Meg. "I thought of ringing."

Sniffing, Lizzie said, "Ach, she's never written much to me or to Florrie, I can tell you that. I don't know about you two."

David said, "Not to me."

"Nor me," said Meg. "Robert did say that she and Ned were very welcoming when he had liberty in New York. And Betty. He hears from Betty, I do, too, at Christmas. But I'll write Annie. She deserves to know."

Lizzie sniffed and folded her arms.

David asked, "What about Will and Bob?"

Lizzie and Meg looked at him.

"Alright, I'll write them," he said. "Not sure I have the addresses," he muttered.

Lizzie said, "I'll check if more tea's wanted." She stood, wiped her nose briskly and left the room.

Meg nodded and looked out the window.

"What is it?" asked David. He put his hand on Meg's shoulder.

"It's silly, but I feel like I'm ten again."

"In that case, why don't we leave? I'm ready to go. Would Ralph mind?"

"It might get Lizzie to take Tom home and he needs to go home. Let's ask Robert."

Meg went to the doorway and tried to catch Robert's eye, but he was engrossed in conversation with his father, who stared into the middle distance. The smoke from Robert's cigarette curled upwards. The dog lay at their feet. At the other end of the sofa, Lizzie was deep in conversation with Jo—Lizzie doing all the talking.

Through the open doorway to the hall, Meg saw Albert step inside the house uncertainly before looking into the parlor and taking two long steps to stand in front of Ralph. As Robert looked up at him, his smile erased the strain and grief etched on his face. Ralph tried to stand and after the second try, succeeded and shook Albert's offered hand.

"By God, now who's this fella? How's the air up there, big lad?" roared Tom, red-faced and laughing loudly, spittle flying. "Would you look at the size of him! These lads get bigger and bigger! No wee skinnymalinks in this house. Hahaha!"

The other occupants of the parlor, pale-faced Henderson relatives, church friends and neighbors, quickly looked down at their plates of cake.

Lizzie scrambled to her feet and moved swiftly from the sofa to her husband. Meg saw the anger in her pinched face as she hissed in his ear.

"Alright, alright, woman. We'll go," said Tom, standing unsteadily. "Just trying to cheer auld Ralph."

She hissed again, rather too loudly, "He doesn't want cheering. His wife's just died!"

Tom lurched over to his brother-in-law. Albert caught his arm in time to steady him.

Meg and David walked over to the group of men standing in front of the sofa, and as they did so, the friends and neighbors sitting in the parlor took the opportunity to bring their plates into the kitchen and gather their belongings.

Robert stood too, and there were brief goodbyes, as Lizzie picked up her purse and pushed at her husband. "I'll come back to help with the dishes," she told Ralph.

Robert said, "There's no need, Aunt Lizzie, we'll take care of everything—you've done so much today. Thank you."

Pushing at Tom's back, she nodded at Robert. "All the same, I'll be back to help."

Jo stood and said, "Ralph, do you mind if I go too? Sorry, but I'm desperate for a lie down."

Ralph patted her shoulder and said, "Of course not, dear. You need your rest."

"I'll stay here, Da, clean up," said Robert, who began to take his jacket off.

Meg said, "Aye. David and I want to walk back, too. I'm feeling tired myself and you must be too, Ralph."

"It's a hard day, Meggie, I know," said Ralph. "There were all them sisters of yours, years ago—the Preston girls—the five of youse. Jinny the eldest, then my lovely Florrie…" His voice gave way at her name and he hastily pressed a handkerchief to his mouth.

She patted Ralph's arm before turning away, tears on her cheeks.

"So, your sister has decided to take me in hand," said Jo, strolling in between brother and sister up the Malone Road.

"I was afraid of that," said Meg.

"No, it's alright, but on my terms. I *will* need help and she and Ralph can help, but I'll not move in with him. I doubt if she'd consulted him before suggesting it, for one thing."

"I doubt it, too."

"Here's what I'd like to try and see how it works—tell me what you think. From our brief acquaintance, Albert and I seem to get on well, and if living together doesn't grate on our nerves, I'd like to stay in your house and pay half the rent…when the baby comes, it may not work for him, so I'll make other arrangements. So, yes, Lizzie's offer will suit me, but with a slight adjustment. I can run the baby over to Great Northern Street and be at Queen's or my father's office in half a tick during the week. There's a wee nursery at St. Thomas, and they'll take her for part of the day once she's two, I've asked. Do you see? That's Ralph's church, Lizzie's too."

Meg said, "I wouldn't worry too much about the baby bothering Albert—I never heard Annie's baby when they slept on the second floor and I slept on the third.

David said, "Are you saying you'll keep the secret, the…"

"The lie? I suppose I am. I might be able to hire a nurse for part of the day, but Ralph and Lizzie seem ideal to help for some of the weekdays…although I'll need some help at the weekends, too. Ach, I'll figure it out. I'm being unscrupulous, I know, but I didn't tell them we'd wed, Robert did, to make them happy, especially his mother. And it does make his father happy, and his aunt, and you must admit, it's kind of fallen in my lap. What do you think?"

Jo looked at David, who nodded and said, "Aye, and let me tell you a story. Niall's mother Bridie was unwed when she fell with him. She was sixteen and her father had often threatened to take her to one of those orphanages the nuns run if she ever fell pregnant out of wedlock, and she believed him. In those places, the unwed mothers are put to work and the babies taken into the orphanage for adoption. Bridie's father was a tenant on the farm owned by the grandfather of her baby's father, so it was tricky, do you follow?"

"Aye."

"Right, the baby's father was only a lad himself and *his* father a wastrel with a brutal temper. So, she went to the boy's grandfather, the farm owner and a widower who was thought to be kindly, and asked him to wed her, for the sake of a certificate and a name for her baby, promising not to bother him, his son or his grandson, ever. He agreed. There may have been a wee bit of blackmail, but we'll draw a veil over it. Anyway, there was further complication about religion, but they sorted it quickly, married, and after the birth, she left with the baby and I shouldn't wonder, a wee bit of cash to get her started in Belfast. Bridie's husband, Niall's great-grandfather, died shortly thereafter so she could honestly claim she was a widow with a wee bairn."

"That's quite a story," said Meg. "Is it true?"

"Aye, so you see, this sort of thing, the lie you're prepared to live with Jo, has been done before and probably in a hundred different ways."

"Niall's mother sounds absolutely brilliant," said Jo.

"He says she was—I'm afraid I missed her. She died some years ago, sitting in Niall's house on the farm in Ballycastle, her revenge complete."

"Her revenge?" asked Jo.

"Niall bought his great-grandfather's farm and that's where he brought her to live the last years of her life, quite happily I might add. Niall had been in practice for a few years so he'd some savings, not a lot, but the family—Niall's own family, mind —had lost the farm to the bank. Niall's father had aged into a drunken gambler, like his father before him, and Niall could afford what the bank asked for the mortgage. Yes, her revenge. She's buried in the family plot on the farm, near her husband, but at a small distance, and with a Roman cross. A very large one, and the farm owned by a Morrison."

Jo laughed. "Not just brilliant, but Niall and his mum... formidable. What a story! It's given me the strength to go on with my plan then. Niall's mum has shown me that's all it takes, strength and nerve."

Meg looked under her eyelashes at Jo and said, "Sure, you have the strength of thousands, Jo. As for nerve..."

"Meg!" said David.

Jo laughed and linked her arms in theirs as the trio turned the corner to walk up the right-angled Chlorine Gardens and cut through the Botanic Gardens nursery to St. Ives Gardens. "I'll say this, and I'm sure you'll both agree—the world would be an easier place if everybody let others just be."

Clicking her fingers, Lillian called. "Here, Bobby." The dog trotted over. She patted his glistening black head and smoothed back his long ginger eyebrows, to gaze into light brown eyes. "Best wee man in the world…and the handsomest."

Mildred put the tea tray down on the garden table. "Bobby? Aye, he's that alright."

Lillian watched their burnished Irish Setter Gordie snuffling under a shrub at the other end of the garden.

Sitting next to Lillian, Mildred asked, "Did you not want to attend the funeral then?"

"I didn't, to be honest. She has her brother and sister and I'm feeling…"

"Unwell?"

"Not unwell, but tired."

"You've been working a lot after that Royal Navy interview!"

"That's all it may be. It's been a hard month. All my own doing, of course. I suppose I should have gone to the funeral, but I couldn't face it. Meg seemed to understand. For one thing, Lizzie always looked at me like I'd three heads, so it's easier on everyone if I'm not there."

Mildred smoothed the folds of her pleated tweed skirt. "Lillian, I haven't had a chance to say…you're a grand swimmer I know but I don't understand what you were doing out in that nasty sea with the mines and all that. I've known you all your life and yet now I didn't understand how you felt, not entirely— the weight of it, whatever it is. I'm very sorry."

"Listen, I promised Albert I'd try to live to one hundred, and I'll try. I'm the one to apologize. The truth is, I didn't know what I was doing, not really. Your war has been as hard as mine. Meg's doing well on her medicine. I've little excuse."

They drank the tea Mildred had poured out into china cups, each keeping her own company as she stared down at the sea spread below the hilltop garden, light dancing on its surface. Ships of various sizes were anchored at intervals, as others sailed across in both directions.

"I do mean to board an ocean liner one day. See something of the world. If the war ever ends." Lillian patted the back of her heavy chignon of silver-streaked chestnut hair.

Mildred said, "There's something else...I've something to tell you, to ask you. Frank told me to ask you. He said he'd tell her no for you."

"Who?"

"Mary O'Neill is coming up today. She'll be here later and she wanted to visit Meg and you. Frank told her that Meg was in Belfast for the funeral, but she said she wanted to meet you."

"Do you know why?"

Mildred shrugged. "Do you want us to tell her no? We will."

Absentmindedly, Lillian shook her head. "No, that's silly. I mean she'll be living up here, so..."

"I'm surprised you've never met her."

Lillian shook her head, watching Mildred's thick fingers fidget with her skirt, folding the pleats just so. "I've never laid eyes on her, as far as I know. Why is she coming up? Is she moving in already?"

"To look over the progress of the renovations. Frank's due to meet her at the estate, so I don't think she'll bother you for long. She's booked at a hotel near the Old Course." Mildred's eyes were filled with worry. "You should rest now, Lillian."

"I'll take a walk instead—take the dogs and perk myself up. Then I'll get to my desk while I wait for Mary O'Neill."

Upon returning from her walk, Lillian spent time cutting mums and arranging them in vases, picking up magazines and plumping the pillows in the parlor. She set up a tea tray and made some sandwiches, placed the kettle on the hob and added coal to the parlor fire grate.

After she settled at her desk the day turned on its head as a storm blew in from the west, bringing a drop in temperature and a heavy cold rain rattling the windowpanes. The trees bent eastward and swayed in the maelstrom. The desk light flickered.

The dogs barked at the sharp rap on the door. Lillian stopped at the hall mirror, smoothed her hair, straightened her scarf.

She hadn't expected what she found when she opened the door: a small, decidedly plump woman, heavily made-up and looking older than the age Lillian calculated for her.

Helloing cheerily, Mary closed her streaming umbrella and left it on the porch before taking a quick hop over the threshold.

Mary made a fuss of the dogs swarming around her when she entered the cottage and seemed nervous and flustered as Lillian took her wet mac. Pushing and plumping at her Victory roll hairstyle, she said, "You're very tall, Lillian—I didn't know that."

Looking down at the grey roots of Mary's brassy blonde hair, Lillian blushed and said, "Yes, well...I've the kettle on," before gesturing that they make their way into the parlor.

Fidgeting with the belted waist of a tailored, bottle green suit, Mary said, "To be honest, I'd love something stronger. I've brought, em..." Reaching into a copious brown leather handbag, she produced a bottle of whiskey.

After a quick glance at the clock on the mantle behind them, Lillian took the bottle of the fine, aged malt offered.

"I'll get glasses."

Lillian returned to the room with a tray containing two glasses and a small pitcher of water. There were no nuts to offer —there hadn't been nuts in the shops for years—but she served the sandwiches she'd made earlier: real butter and riverbank watercress nestled between rounds of Meg's brown bread loaf.

"This is a lovely room. So cozy, and the view must be breathtaking. Not today, not on a filthy day like today, of course, but..." Mary giggled before putting thumb and curled forefinger over her lips.

Lillian provided no answer to the observation as she poured two whiskies, for which she had to admit she was grateful.

"Water? Please sit down, Mary."

"Just as it comes for me."

Glasses in hand, they sat down in the armchairs flanking the fireplace. Each woman took a sip of whiskey.

"A lovely fire. How do you manage the coal? Oh, don't tell me—my Uncle Frank."

Lillian gave her a small smile. "He's very good to us."

Mary looked around the room again before taking a larger draught of her drink. "Which sister was it?"

"Which sister...? Oh, it was Florence, Florrie. A nice woman."

Mary nodded uncertainly. "I don't remember mention of that one, only the one who was sick, but then I'd never met any of the family. No, I did meet her brother, David, was he?" She paused before saying, "You must want to know why I wanted to visit you. I'm sure you must." She finished her drink in one swallow.

Lillian nodded.

Mary's rouged cheeks had a darker blush now. "I wanted to meet you, as long as I was coming up. I'm close to my uncle, and he and Mildred are your good friends...it didn't seem, well, unreasonable, I suppose, after all these years. Not unreasonable to be cordial at the very least, with you and Meg."

"No, not unreasonable."

"Especially since, well, I've bought the Carstairs place, my guardian's estate. I plan to move back here. So, we'll be neighbors."

"Yes, Mildred's told us." Lillian rose to refill Mary's glass.

Seated again, Lillian was shocked to see a tear rolling down Mary's face. With an inward sigh, she asked, "You want to talk to me about Meg, is that it?"

Sniffing, Mary produced a handkerchief from her bag. "You're very sympathetic." She stopped and sighed audibly. "You must understand, but. I wanted her to forgive me, and I always thought that with enough time she would. Do you think she has forgiven me? I betrayed her, I don't know why and that's the truth. I was very young and foolish, so."

Suddenly, a heavy exhaustion lay on Lillian, but she again stifled a sigh. "She told me she wished you no harm, and she saw your good points."

Mary smiled in return and said, "I am glad. Thank you, Lillian."

With her smile, Lillian caught a glimpse of the pretty young woman Mary had been.

Eyes glittering, Mary asked, "What else did Meg say about me?"

"Do you mind if we don't?"

"Oh, sorry. Of course. Clumsy of me to ask." She drank down her whiskey and rose. "I'll leave you in peace now. Have you ever visited the estate where I was raised? It's lovely. I hope you come down and visit me. Both of you. In fact, I'll throw a party, a housewarming and invite all the neighbors. Will Meg return to Portstewart soon?"

"She's planning on spending time with her family." Lillian stood up too, and said, "Here, don't forget your whiskey."

"Oh no, it's a gift. Please keep it."

"Thank you very much, but there was no need."

"Will you tell Meg I was here?"

Lillian's brow furrowed in confusion as she said, "Yes, of course."

"That's grand. I'll be in touch."

After showing Mary to the door, Lillian returned to the sitting room and refreshed her drink. Bobby helped himself to the chair Mary vacated, curling into a contented ball. Lillian sat back down opposite and stared into the fire.

"Yoo-hoo!" Mildred's voice carried from the front door, followed by the sound of a flapping umbrella. "Yes, hello, Gordie, dear." Mildred hurried in accompanied by Gordie, and said, "Well, she didn't keep you long."

"Sit down and have a drink."

"A drink?" Mildred's eyes flicked to the mantle clock. "Early, but alright, I will."

"She brought us a fine bottle and I found I was grateful for it. Now I'm having another. Save me from having a third."

Mildred gently moved Bobby off the chair and sat down with him on her lap. "I will. At least have your third with us if you must, and not on your own. My fish pie's set for the oven—Frank caught a lovely haddock last night. I've potato apple cake for afters, so join us for tea. It's turned nasty, hasn't it just? I'm fairly chilled." She shivered, pulled the thick cardigan draped on her shoulders closer around her, and patted the dog.

Lillian stood to hand her a glass, added a scoop of coal to the fire, poked it alive, and sat down.

Mildred sipped. "So, what did she want?"

"She wanted Meg's forgiveness. She wants to be friends and invited us to visit her at the estate. Says she'll throw a big house party."

"Forgiveness? A house party? Oh, dear. I hope she's not going to be a pest, a pest dressed as Lady Muckross."

"I got the feeling she will. In fact, has anybody told you about how Frank and her own mother would serve at table, both the lord and master Carstairs and Mary, with their guests? Meg was one."

"Aye, Frank mentioned it and I thought it very odd. After all, Carstairs was her father, his housekeeper her mother—they were her parents. Surely Mary knew he was her father? Frank thinks she did, but they never discussed it. Why didn't they just sit down together? You don't think she'll try that on with me? Serving, I mean."

"Meg does—talk to Meg when Frank's not around."

"The place has a housekeeper's cottage—she'll have to hire a housekeeper. I'm sure there's plenty of choice."

"What will Frank say?"

Mildred shrugged. "He can do as he likes, but I'll not serve her. I have a job. Cheers! Here's to Stranmillis Typewriting, may she stay afloat."

DEMOBBED—SEPTEMBER 1946

LONDON—BELFAST

*T*ommy Rose called his group together and begged for silence in his unmistakable East London accent. "Sorry, chaps, but we're at the end of the road. We won't build another Colossus." Gesturing to the computing machine that spanned the entire room at the back, width and height, he continued, "This one, the eleventh, is our last. We weren't given the job of building any other types of computers, either. The work's gone elsewhere, to capable hands, mind, but not here. I think we had a good run, but all things must end. I'll keep my position here at the GPO and take up electronic switching research again. I want to speak to each of you individually this afternoon about leaving and opportunities open. I'll miss both our work and our working together. The war's over and we must all move on, just as our Wrens had to take their leave ahead of us." He clapped his hands together. "With that, my first interview will be with our very last colleague in uniform. Henderson let's go into my office. Please hang about chaps and when we're done, there'll be a trip to the pub."

As Robert followed Tommy Rose to the office, he felt all eyes on them.

Rose was sandy-haired, spare and sharp in features. "Have a

seat, Henderson." Adjusting his old-fashioned round spectacles, he opened a folder on his desk. "First the good news, the very good news, before the best." He adjusted his round spectacles, looked up and smiled at Robert. "You've been offered a compu-tation position, University of Manchester, Dr. Clarke's lab. He'll need an answer tomorrow week. Now for the best news, your demob orders have come through. The notice says that you can appear at Admiralty House as early as today, if you like, and they'll sort you out. Congratulations and well done on your service to your country."

His infectious smile disappeared. "I've won a cash prize of some sort from the ministry and I'm sharing it with you lads." He pushed an envelope across the desk to Robert. "Open it later, alright? It has the contact information for Clarke in there, too." Sitting back, he smiled again. "Congratulations on all counts, Robert."

"Dr. Rose, I'd like to go home to Belfast, not to Manchester. Are there no opportunities for me there?"

Looking down at Robert's open file, he asked, "You're a married man, aren't you?"

Robert's answer was a deep blush, mostly hidden by his beard, and a vague nod.

"I understand how much you want to go home—I'm married with children myself. I'm sure there are opportunities in Belfast for you, but nothing that I can put you on to—do you see? If you want a career in computation of any sort, you'll find nothing better than Dr. Clarke's lab."

"What about you, sir? You said you would stay at GPO?"

"Yes, I'll go back to engineering switches. I believe the entire telephone system can be built and function electronically. If you'd like to stay, you're very welcome, but that would be selfish of me. You should take the position in Manchester, at least for a few years. You can send for your family once you're settled. All doors will be open to you after that experience. I must remind you, as I must the rest of the lads, you'll always be under The

Official Secrets Act for the work you've done here and at BP, you do understand that? It's for life."

"Yes, sir, that was made clear to us at BP."

"Sorry, Robert, but I must get on and interview everyone today. I'm very sorry to lose you, truly. Best of luck and don't let the deadline for this job pass. Don't let this opportunity pass—it's a once in a lifetime opportunity." He held his hand out. "Oh, why not hang about for our trip to the pub? I won't be long, there's only five others and at less than five minutes each..."

Robert shook his hand and said, "It was grand working here, Dr. Rose. Thanks for everything."

"Robert, one more thing—I wanted to say that you should attend university—I urge you to apply. Another reason the University of Manchester job would be so valuable to you. Do what I did—I was a married man with children, so I worked and attended the University of London in the evenings. You're a born electrical engineer."

"Thank you," said Robert, his voice a croak.

Before he left the lab for the last time, he stood alone in front of the last Colossus built by Dr. Rose and the team, Robert's team. Knowing its power, he took in its size, picked up a damaged photocell lying in a heap on the tool desk, and put it in his pocket.

Albert opened the door of number 34 St. Ives Gardens as Robert pulled his belongings out of the taxicab. Crossing the short path to the curb quickly, Albert said, "Here, let me," and picked up the sea chest.

Robert paid the driver and picked up his RN tote, shoulder bag and leather suitcase. Once inside, he said, "That's it—all my worldly goods. Well and truly demobbed!"

Taking him in his arms, Albert said, "Congratulations and welcome home! I can't believe you're here and for good! Come in, come in, we can carry your cases upstairs later. Let's sit in the garden—I'll pour us some drinks. You look very handsome—new clothes?"

"I had to buy clothes or live my life in a navy boiler suit and secondhand tweed jacket. Oh, but it smells grand in here! What are you cooking?"

"I'll pop the pork roast in at five. Jo and Rosie never get home before six. But I just baked an apple cake. Your favorites."

"They are indeed, but where did you find a pork roast? Haven't had one in years."

"Jo has a butcher for a client. She says he's quite taken with her. How he came across a pork roast she didn't want to know. The Armagh pig farms may be producing again, but somehow he got around the rationing."

After they sat down with their glasses, Robert loosened his tie and said, "Albert, I have something to tell you, and something to ask you. I need your advice. Your honest advice."

Albert sat back in the garden chair. "Go on."

Robert said, "I don't want to spoil our reunion, but the opportunity I've been offered is in Manchester, not here." Taking a sip of whiskey, he continued, "Thanks to my boss...my ex-boss, I've been offered a job in a new lab there, run by Dr. Clarke at University of Manchester, working on similar projects to what we, em—sorry, can't tell you, but I can say they involve electronics. Anyway, my ex-boss strongly urged me to take the job in Manchester and to apply to study electrical engineering while working there."

"England...again. You just got here. Is there no alternative to your leaving here?"

"My boss was clear he thought Manchester a once in a lifetime opportunity. Either I move to Manchester to take that job, or I don't have a job, or worse, I miss a grand opportunity. 'Once in a lifetime,' he said. What do you think?"

"Manchester's what, eight hours travel?"

"At least eight, but still closer than London. It would be difficult to return most weekends, especially if I have course work, too."

The men were silent for a long moment before Robert asked again, "Well, what do you think?"

His face flushed, Albert rubbed the side of his face in silence before answering. "You must take the job in Manchester, Robert. You've really no choice. If it's a once-in-a-lifetime opportunity, then how can you not? You'll come back here when you can, and I'll visit you there when I can."

Relief cleared Robert's face. "It's what I thought, but I don't *want* to live across the sea from you. I'd hoped to come home."

Reaching his hand across the small table, Albert took Robert's in his. "Aye, I'd hoped so too, but this job and the chance of university? We'll find the time to spend together, but we each have our own studies and careers, and we must tend to them while we're young and have opportunities. It's possible, after my doctorate, that I won't find a place in Belfast. I'll have to go where I've been hired—that could be anywhere, including abroad."

Robert said, "I hope to be able to follow you wherever you go when the time comes. Until then, we'll be together as often as we can. University holidays, perhaps some bank holiday weekends." The familiar crease between his eyebrows reappeared. "I'll miss you terribly. I'm always missing you, but I'm always somewhere else, aren't I?"

"You are, but at least you're out of the navy now. Some of your time will be your own. I'm fine here with Jo paying half the rent—we still get on well, very easily. Rosie's a little charmer, even though she's teething, I'm told—wait till you see her! Wait 'til you hear her! She chats up a storm. Will your new salary cover decent digs in Manchester?"

"I've no idea what my salary will be. My navy pay covered my billet in Northwest London, sharing. I won't share digs with others in Manchester, though, so that when you can visit, we can be alone. Oh, but I've had a windfall. My boss was so generous to share a cash bonus with all of us, and I received my demob cash out at the admiralty, so I'll be able to find something to let. I bought these clothes with a little of it. Brand new!"

"They're very nice and it's nice to have a nest egg. I'm still wearing second hand myself." Leaning forward, Albert said, "Listen, I know this is hard—nobody smooths our paths and nobody will—our families helped when we were lads, but now... We have to make our own way, but we're up to it—we can do anything." He took Robert's hand back into his own and felt his reassuring grasp.

Albert took a sip of his drink and asked, "When do you have to be in Manchester?"

"Monday next, first thing." Robert also leaned forward. "I have to spend time with my dad, too."

"I know you do. Problem solved, well, partly—he's coming for tea tomorrow. You'll have to leave Sunday morning then?"

"Aye, Sunday morning."

Albert stood and said, "It gives us a few days. Let's not waste the time we have. Alright?" Holding his hand out, he led Robert inside.

"Where *is* Holly? Do you know?" asked Jo. "She writes fairly often, but all I can see in the letters are her endless descriptions of the abundance and variety of the delicious food wherever she is, which is irritating. She has cocktails and goes dancing, which is even more annoying. Much of the rest is blacked out and that's the most annoying—the war's over. They come with English postage stamps on them, but I *know* she's not in this country."

Robert laughed. "She's not, but the one who blacks the letters out *is*. Pound for pound, that wee thing could eat and drink anybody under a table. No, I don't know. She couldn't tell me more about her reposting in '45 than something like this, 'think of the spot farthest away on earth from Southern England, and that's where I'll be.' But they'll have to demob Holly at some point, no matter how valuable she is to the navy. You don't think she'd stay in?"

"No, I don't think so. No. She'll come back and finish her degree."

Rosie, sitting in her highchair at the table, clapped her pudgy hands and hit her plate. Jo spooned mashed potato and gravy into Rosie's mouth. "Yum, yum, wee Rosie."

"Num, num," Rosie answered.

"She's a little stunner, Jo. Those eyes…green, are they? And look at those wee teeth!" said Robert. "She's a good appetite."

Jo sighed. "Yes, green. Johnny did have the most beautiful, green eyes and she has his remarkable eyes. I'm afraid she has the average number of teeth for eighteen months. Nothing remarkable there, but everything else is extraordinary. Enjoy this interlude while you can." Jo glanced at the clock on the kitchen mantle. "She'll most likely tip into exhaustion in a few minutes, then you'll hear her remarkable vocal cords."

Robert lit a cigarette and sat back, patting his stomach. "Wonderful dinner!"

"Yes, wonderful! We're very lucky living with Albert—he is a marvelous cook and baker. Unfortunately, he has to put up with mine some nights."

"Ach, no. You make very tasty food and we have your butcher to thank for the pork," said Albert, pouring himself a glass of wine.

"How is business, Jo?"

"Terrible, but not a total disaster. I've kept Mary O'Neill as a client—she even offered the housekeeper's cottage for our summer hols this year, but we like to stay in the cottage near the aunties and Uncle Frank, don't we, Rosie dear? Bray Esq. have kept Mary O'Neill's estate business, real and otherwise. I've Jimmy the butcher, he's new to business and has various troubles, and many of my father's older ladies and gents have stayed. Too old to switch they tell me. I've got to find younger clients. Rosie will help."

"And how can Rosie help find younger clients for you?"

"The wee school at the church she'll attend in March is supported by parents edging toward middle age and needing house closings, estate planning and so on. I've met a few already and I'm working on luring them in—trouble is, I'm a woman solicitor, which doesn't sit well with some, many, make that most, men. Oops, time to make a warm bottle for my girl." Jo leapt out of her seat and rushed to the range.

"I put the pot on the hob, Jo," said Albert.

Rosie closed her eyes, turned beet red and let out a long yowl after a moment of breathlessness. "Ma! Ma!"

"Here we go!"

"I've got her," said Albert. Moving behind her, he lifted her up and out of the seat. "Come and sit with Uncle Albert."

Robert asked, "Can she sit with me? What shall she call me?"

"She calls me Ma, not Mama, and Albert something like 'But,' I'm afraid. Shall she call you Pa?"

"What about my dad, what does she call him?"

"I call him Ralph, so at the minute, she calls him Ruff. But she certainly knows who he is."

Robert jiggled the toddler on his lap, his arms tight around her. She stopped screaming and he turned her around to face him. "Now, wee Rosie, what's all this, then?"

She hiccupped and with tears on her fat cheeks, looked up into his face with fascination. Her fingers reached out and pulled on his curly, black beard.

"Ouch! I plan to visit a barber tomorrow. Get shorn for the new job."

"Oh, don't Robert," said Albert. "Just trim everything." Rolling his shirtsleeves up, Albert picked up two of the plates from the table.

"No, you don't. I'll do the dishes," said Robert.

Waiting at the range, Jo asked, "Now that's a trick. How is it you're good with babies?"

"I don't know, but I was always good with babies."

"Would you mind carrying her upstairs and I'll put her down? The bottle's nearly ready."

"Aye. I'll be back for those dishes. Don't you dare touch them, Albert. Come on, wee Rosie. Beddy-byes now." Robert carried Rosie up the stairs, singing to her. "'I'm an Irishman...' dee da dee da dee da. I've forgotten the words to this wee ditty," sang Robert, tickling Rosie and making her giggle. "Yes, wee Rosie, silly Pa, I'm a silly Pa."

Jo laughed. "I recognized it—you've got the tune—you sing well. I haven't heard that ditty in ages. Brigie Brennan, God love her, sang it as she worked in our house. It's a Belfast song about a faloorie man, a mythical creature. She said her boyfriend sang it, not that any of us ever saw *that* mythical creature. Poor Brigie was the skivvy for our terrifying but excellent cook Mrs. Doolin, but Brigie was made to do a lot of the housework, too."

Robert's eyebrows rose. "You had servants?"

"Yes. We'd no mother...oh, that sounded awful. What I meant was my father had to manage with two small children somehow and he could afford to hire help. He started with a nurse for Ronnie and me. I must say my father did a lot for us himself, but it all became a lot for him to juggle with his practice. He'd no sisters nor had my mother, and our grandmothers were gone, so. A family bereft of women to *do* for us. Eventually, the household included a woman who came in to do the heavy cleaning and another for the laundry and mending. The kitchen was always filled with women and men drinking endless cups of tea and eating Mrs. Doolin's baps, which were light as feathers— I loved sitting at the long table with them all, listening. Let's see, there was a man who did the garden every week, a fella who cared regularly for the brand new but finicky boiler and geyser. And our lovely nurse, who stayed until I was sixteen—a Scots woman named MacBride. Ha! When Ronnie and I discovered that MacBride's name was Lorna, we never let her live it down—called her Lorna Doone for months. We *loved* that ridiculous novel! Anyway, she'd a good sense of humor and she was kind. Lorna returned to Glasgow before the war, but we're still in touch. Oh, sorry, Robert, I'll take her. There, I've got you lovely Rosie." As Jo began to change Rosie, she asked, "But how do *you* know that song?"

"A sailor on the destroyer, named Byrne, Jimmy Byrne. His family were Belfast people, from the Ardoyne originally, but the family had lived in Liverpool for a long time, long enough so that the poor devil had been born there and conscripted into the RN. He sang a lot of songs—that was one. Made the rest of us laugh. 'A roaring Irishman.'" He was that all right, poor Jimmy." Robert watched Jo for a moment before asking, "Was Brigie Brennan in the house the night of the bombing?"

"No. She wasn't, thank God. None of them ever slept in except MacBride, and she'd gone years before and was tucked up in her Glaswegian bed, having survived their bombings in March of '41. Brigie and Mrs. Dooley came to the house in the early mornings and left after making our tea. It suited my father not to have them live in, although he never minded MacBride. I dreamt he'd marry her—she was very pretty, not too young, but nothing came of it. I don't think my father ever recovered from my mother's death. A shame, that." She bent and kissed Rosie's cheeks. "No, my father and our dog Winnie were the only ones in the house that night. I was at Queen's studying late with a group of law students. I couldn't get back to Fort William once the bombing started..."

"Thank God for that!"

Jo turned and smiled at Robert. "Thank you, Robert." Turning back to her baby, she added, "I can only hope both of them were asleep and didn't suffer. I pray they didn't."

Robert sat down in the armchair next to the cot. "How are things, really, Jo? Are you managing?"

"Aye, I am, but only because your father and aunt are brilliant. Ralph takes her for walks in the Botanic Gardens, gives her lunch and tea if I'm stuck in court or with a client. Lizzie carries the less fun days, like taking her for the day at home when she's got sniffles or has a bad day teething. They've helped like mad. Based on the lovely MacBride, I tried a nurse when I first went back to work, but she cost the earth and I didn't quite like leaving Rosie with her—there was something about Rosie's little face when I got home—I felt meanness in the woman, a dislike for my child, or perhaps for me. It was a pleasure to see the back of her. We leave Albert alone as much as possible, but he's been marvelous as well. Truly. When I've really been in a pinch, he's helped and hasn't complained about Ralph or Lizzie showing up here to fetch her. Fortunately, this wee lass is a real trooper."

"I'd expect nothing less from her. I'm sorry to have been no help at all."

She laughed. "No, you haven't been, but that was our agreement, wasn't it? Anyway, your relations more than make up for your absence. What about you? What's up?"

"Ah, well, I'm off to Manchester to work at university and take the entrance exams, too. I must leave Sunday morning. It's a grand opportunity, so my ex-boss assures me. I'll miss him and our crew, but London's even farther away. I can't believe that just days of being demobbed, I'm off again, away from Albert, away from Belfast. Away from helping with Rosie."

"Oh, dear, that is a long trip on the ferry! You hate the ferry!"

"Aye, that ferry! At least there aren't any U-boats to worry about, although you read these stories about U-boats still cruising around, refusing to surrender."

Jo laughed, "Yes, my darling girl. Here's you all clean and in your jammies. Pa will give you your bottle." She handed the child to Robert who sat her on his lap. He held the bottle while she contently sucked, her mother in full view. "At least Albert can visit you there and you can visit here. It won't be as bad as our navy liberties."

"No, I don't expect so, but we won't see each other most

weeks. We'll have to wait for bank holiday weekends at the very least, but more likely university vacations. Albert tells me there's only three of those a year. My ex-boss urged me to study electrical engineering, so if accepted, I'll have course work as well as work."

"But that's wonderful, Robert! You'll have plenty of swot time on the ferry crossings." She lowered her voice to add, "I remember how well they thought of you at BP. But Manchester does present another hurdle for you—explaining the decision to Ralph." Towel over her shoulder, Jo took Rosie into her arms again and swaying a little, rubbed and tapped her back.

"Oh?"

"Leaving your 'wife and child,' you know."

"Oh. So it does. Well, I'll tell him what I've told you and hope for the best. He'll have to accept that you're a solicitor here and I'm an engineer there. I'll spend some time with my dad tomorrow before he comes for tea. We could take Rosie for a nice walk. We'll visit Lizzie, too."

"We'd invite her for tea, too, but Tom is simply impossible and there's no guarantee she'd leave him at home, although I'm sure she longs to. I sometimes invite her out to lunch or a cup of tea in my office in the afternoon, or to join us out at the shops with our messages on Saturday. She likes pushing Rosie's pram around to the stores on the Lisburn Road."

"Do you? That is kind."

"It's absolutely the least I can do. She's a lifesaver. There we are! What a good wee girl! Night-night, Rosie, dear." Jo put Rosie down in her cot and pulled the blanket over her, tucking her teddy bear in with her. "Sweet dreams." Jo kissed her child.

Thumb in mouth, Rosie looked at Robert.

Robert waved. "Night-night, Rosie.

"She's usually easy to put down, thankfully," said Jo. She closed the bedroom door quietly behind them and they walked downstairs.

Robert stifled a yawn before asking, "Jo, has it been really all right? Playing the part as you put it?"

"Not sure where telling the truth would have got me. It's all been much harder than I imagined, especially when I was swotting for exams and she was an infant—that was hard. Plus, she gives your da and aunt pleasure. They love her. You can't fight love."

"Aye, I've noticed," said Robert.

"Here's mail for ye, I forgot earlier," said Ralph, pulling envelopes out of his jacket pocket. As Robert took his mail, Ralph walked over to Rosie in her highchair, his face beaming. "Hello again, my girl, here's my Rosie. My Rose." He sat next to her.

"Ruff!" she said and giggled and clapped her hands. "Park now? Doggie?"

"What did I tell you?" asked Jo. "Ruff. What would you like her to call you, Ralph? We can work on it."

"I don't mind. We already went to the park today with the doggie, love. We'll go to the park tomorrow with the doggie. The wee doggie is home, but she'll come with us tomorrow. She's tired and needs a wee rest now."

"You could have brought the dog tonight, Ralph," said Jo. "You always can."

"Thanks. Next time, I may. You've a letter from New York in that pile," said Ralph.

Robert shuffled the envelopes of various sizes. "It's from Betty." He sat down, opened the blue aerogram, and began to read it.

Jo said, "Now Ralph, we've only leftovers tonight, but they're good ones—a roast pork with crackling, and all the trimmings."

"I don't mind. I always think leftovers taste better."

"I told Albert I'd heat everything up as instructed. He should be home soon." said Jo.

Robert interrupted. "Wait till I tell ye—Betty's m-married! A fellow she works with, demobbed from the U.S. Army Air Corps, named Sam, em, S-Sharpham. They married at New York City Hall. Does that mean a registry office? And invited nobody from the family."

"What's that? She didn't invite her own parents?" asked Ralph.

Robert looked up at Ralph. "But I wonder why...let me read on. S-Sam's s-sisters and their husbands attended, but nobody from Betty's. Oh, I see why. She written he's P-Protestant and her family's noses were out of j-joint."

"Here, Annie has a nerve having her nose out of joint, doesn't she? Converting as she did," said Ralph. He sniffed.

"What's this?" asked Jo.

Ralph said, "Betty's mum, my Flo's youngest sister Annie, she converted to marry Ned Wright—a Catholic—in 192...2. A nice fella mind, but still, not a good year and auld Preston was in an uproar, a real one, not his usual sort. Now *he* wasn't invited to their wedding," said Ralph. "It was tit for tat maybe, for Annie. It doesn't sound very jolly, having everyone mad at you when you wed, does it? It wasn't jolly for Annie, I can tell you. Still, we hosted their reception at our home, Florrie and me, and Florrie did a lovely job. We'd both families over, both sides, and it was a much better craic than expected. Very jolly for the rest of us."

"Ah, well, it'll work out," said Robert.

"Is Betty converting back?" asked Ralph, crinkling his mouth.

"She doesn't say. Anyway, B-Betty sends her best to you two and wee Rosie. She enclosed her new address in B-Brooklyn. I'll write her a note."

"I am surprised Annie kept to it, the Catholicism," said Ralph.

Looking over his father's head, he saw Jo pointing at the

whiskey bottle on the sideboard. "Would you like a d-drink, D-Da? Whiskey?"

"Won't say no. How about yourself?"

"I won't say no." Robert rose and poured two drinks at the sideboard. He and Jo exchanged a look behind Ralph's back as she mouthed, "Tell him."

Jo brought a small plate of mashed squash and potatoes to Rosie's highchair. "Robert, would you feed her? It's a golden opportunity for me to have my bath."

Ralph piped up, "I'll feed her. Robert can feed her any time. You take your time—you work too much. Now, wee girl, let Granda have one wee sip and we'll get that good food into ye."

After Jo left the kitchen, Robert said, "I've g-good news, D-Da—a new job, an opportunity my ex-boss brought my way."

"That's grand, son. Doing what? Where?"

"Electronics. I'll be able to study electrical engineering, I hope, as well as work in D-Dr. Clarke's laboratory at university. My b-boss told me I was born to be an electrical engineer and that I should get my d-degree."

"Never! But that's wonderful news. At Queen's?"

"No. In M-Manchester."

Ralph's mouth fell open while the hand holding the small spoon of mashed vegetable hovered near Rosie's face.

Robert gestured to the child.

"Oh, sorry. In we go, Rosie! Why not here? You're a married man with a child—responsibilities—you can't go off to England for work. I know many do, but it's no good for a family, son. You're a very young man—a wee bit young for such responsibilities—it may take a while before you see that. Surely you can work and study engineering here at Queen's?"

"The opportunity offered is in M-Manchester. I'd rather stay home but my b-boss, he strongly advised me not to t-turn it down. There's no job here for me. I'd have to find one and it would never be at the same level, the same opportunity, with ability to work toward an engineering degree. This is a g-golden opportunity."

Ralph fed the baby who tried grabbing the spoon. He frowned. "I suppose you'll send for Jo and Rosie when you're settled over there?"

"No. J-Jo has her career, her p-practice, here. She's worked very hard for it, and I wouldn't ask her...I wouldn't ask her to g-give it up. Plus, she has the freehold of her father's office, which she's using, so that roots her here." *This is the conversation I had with Albert turned inside out, upside down.* "You d-don't mind helping with Rosie, do you, D-Da?"

"No, no. I love helping with the wee thing. But listen, Robert," he lowered his voice, "I've wanted to talk to you about Jo living here with Albert, you know, even when you were in the navy. But I never thought you'd be off again once demobbed. Do you think it's safe? I mean, leaving your wife alone with a fit young man? I can't think what the neighbors say."

Rosie took the next spoonful in but spit it down her chin. "Ach, wee thing. Here." Ralph leaned over and wiped her face with a cloth.

"It's all right, for n-now. There's loads of room here at a g-good price—Lillian and Meg don't charge more than the m-mortgage and fees—and they're friends, Albert and J-Jo. I'm not worried." Feeling a blush to the roots of his hair, Robert took a swig of whiskey.

"I don't think it's right. Your mother wouldn't have liked it. Why don't Jo and Rosie move in with me? I could get someone to help me do a little painting, give them the bigger room."

"She says it's very p-private and comfortable for her and the b-baby. Let it go, D-da."

Ralph's eyebrows shot up. "None of my business, I'm sure."

"Oh, D-Da, d-d-don't..."

Ralph looked toward the loo before lowering his voice again. "And another thing. I noticed when I was in her office, on her new sign and the letterhead, it's Josephine *Bray*, Esq. She hasn't changed her name even. What does this mean, Robert? Don't be fooled by how nice you think Albert is or Jo. I never hear the end of it from Lizzie, I can tell you. Thank God I thought not to tell her that Jo was fallen afore you wed! That's one secret I'll keep to me grave."

"Alright, D-Da. That's enough now. We'll sort it, but J-Jo will live here, until she wants to move. I can't t-tell her what to do. And what is it you want me to do? Give up this g-grand opportunity in M-Manchester? T-tell J-Jo to give up her p-p-practice?" Feeling the heat in his face, Robert had let his voice rise. He slapped the table at this last stuttered word.

"Alright, alright, you'll upset the baby!" said Ralph. He picked up the spoon and turning his back on Robert, attempted to feed Rosie again. Rosie would have none of it though and scrunching her face into a shut-eyed, wrinkled, red ball, she yowled.

"There, look what you've done!"

Robert stood and, picking Rosie up, he sat and held her tight on his lap before turning her around. The maneuver worked again as with fascination, she pulled on his beard, looking into his face. Fat tears rolled down her cheeks, but she stopped screaming.

Ralph laughed and said, "She knows her da. Good as gold for you, she is."

Jo rushed into the room wearing a bathrobe and a towel wound around her head.

Looking at Robert and Rosie, she said, "I heard…"

Ralph said, "Aye, but look how settled she is with her father. Lovely."

"We're fine, J-Jo. Really."

"So I see. She hasn't even turned at my voice. I'll dress quickly, just in case."

They listened as Jo ran up the stairs.

"Alright, lad. You two know best what to do with yourselves.

I'll mind me own business. I'm happy to help with the baby and anything Jo needs. But just one more thing…"

Robert groaned. "Da…"

"No, it's just, come home as much as possible. And, Robert, I'm that proud of your success. Imagine your boss saying you were a born electrical engineer. Your mum would be so pleased. Boys a dear, she would." With that, Ralph patted Robert's shoulder and took a sip of whiskey, his eyes full of tears.

"Thanks, Da. Ouch! Rosie! That hurts!"

A giggling Rosie pulled harder.

Robert closed his eyes and asked his father for help.

THE TOASTS OF NEW YORK—
DECEMBER 1957

*A*ddressing the woman's reflection in the mirror, Annie said, "I'm off now, Mrs. O'Hare—I'm due at my daughter's work to pick up my granddaughters."

Lucky O'Hare, interrupted in applying make-up to her beautiful face, met Annie's eyes in the mirror. "Oh! I thought you were helping with luncheon today."

"Not today. We're going Christmas shopping together and then I'm off the rest of the week. When I asked, you said yes."

Pouting slightly, her beautiful lips shown to full advantage, Lucky said, "That is just too bad. Darn. I was counting on you." She shot Annie a dazzling smile and raised her voice a quarter octave. "Your daughter works at NBC, doesn't she? Perhaps she could put in a good word for us?"

That she remembers.

"She does, in the publicity office for *The Tonight Show*. I'm sorry I can't stay but the caterers are very good. They always do a good job with the clean-up, too."

Annie picked up the padded pink satin bathrobe draped across the O'Hare marital bed and carried it into the overstuffed walk-in closet, where she pushed and pulled at the puffy quilted hangers to make room for the robe. She began to sweat with the effort. *Why don't they have hooks in the bathroom like everyone else?*

Her voice descending to its usual octave, Lucky sighed and said, "Yes, well, I suppose Selma will have to do." Cocking an eyebrow and drawing the Max Factor pencil along it with skill, she said, "Enjoy your Christmas bonus."

After her exertions, Annie straightened the skirt of her dress. "We will and thank you again, Mrs. O'Hare. Are your boys coming home today?"

"Hmmm? Oh, no. We're invited to the Whitmoores' for Christmas and the boys are already there. We're driving out to the island tomorrow." Turning away from the mirror at her vanity she faced Annie. "Will you be a peach and come in next week? We're recording a New Year's Eve special at the Waldorf, dressed to the nines at nine in the morning in Peacock Alley! That's the advertisement tagline. Isn't it cute? We hope to do several shows there in the new year." She stopped to sigh. "Just think…1958. I think it will be a great year, don't you? So let's see, who's coming on the show?"

Whoever they are, they'll be half-cut by ten in the morning. I add the tipple provided to the coffee served and am tipped very well, so yes, I'll work next week.

"Martin, Ernie, the rest of the usuals, and two surprises I can't even tell *you*, just that they're the absolute *toasts* of New York—everyone wants to be on our show when we broadcast from the Waldorf. Dorothy and Dick will be kicking themselves in their little sound booth on 47th or wherever they live. Can't imagine who they'll host that morning—who'll be free in New York? Nobody."

On the rare occasions she was at home on a weekday morning, Annie preferred the Dorothy and Dick radio show to the O'Hares', if truth be told. Forcing a smile, Annie said, "Oh, yes, that will be fine. My sons are…"

Turning quickly around to face the mirror again, Lucky said, "Great! You're a doll! Merry Christmas!"

"Merry Christmas. I'll be here on Tuesday at seven in the morning. Tuesday the 31st." Annie had learned over the years to be very specific so that she wasn't blamed later for Lucky's chronic inattention to the lives of others.

"Don't. Go straight to the Waldorf. We'll expect you there. It's not far from here."

"Here" is far from the subway, and a walk from the station with the wind off the river tearing your clothes off! The trip to the Waldorf will be better for me.

Annie made her way down the hallway toward the back of the apartment. Hesitating at the doorway to the living room, she could see her employer standing at his bar, his broad back to the door. She tiptoed past Reggie O'Hare mixing cocktails for their catered luncheon. As she passed, he poured some of the martini mix into a glass and downed it.

At the utility closet in which the servants hung their belongings, Annie looked in the small mirror she'd hung on the inside of the door. Her hair, worn in a tight chignon, was silver and still very thick, smoothed and moisturized with Alberto VO5. Adjusting her angora toque just so, she secured it with a hatpin. She pulled her overcoat and scarf off the hanger, picked up her handbag, and walked into the kitchen.

The kitchen was empty but Annie could smell cigarette smoke. The back door was open a crack. Pulling it open, she found Selma puffing on a cigarette as she sat on an old chair between the kitchen back door and the service elevator reading the *Daily Racing Form*, her feet up on a small metal garbage can.

"Careful she doesn't catch you..." said Annie.

Curling her lip, the wiry woman said, "As if she'd come back here. Likes ringing the bell like this joint's Tara or somethen'." She sniffed, folded the newspaper and pulled her feet down.

"Mind yourself—she's more than ready to show the sharp side of her tongue this morning—I can feel it rising off her. I'm off now and for the rest of the week. Listen, they're driving out to Long Island tomorrow for Christmas at the Whitless' mansion, so you get your money today. He's in the living room, so I'd go for him before she comes out of the bedroom."

Milky eyes magnified behind inch-thick lenses, Selma asked, "He drinkin' already?"

"He's making them, so. Did she tell you them caterers are coming to do today's lunch? She's expecting you to help." Annie pushed the button to summon the elevator. She could hear the thrumming of the car rising as she struggled to get her arms through the coat sleeves.

Selma rose and held Annie's coat so the sleeves were more accessible. "Nah, I do the heavy work, then I'm off. OK, Annie, I'll get my money out of him and scram down the back elevator, too. The laundry's done and all the cleanin'. Appreciate the heads up. Merry Christmas, now. Have a nice time with your family."

She's ninety pounds if she's an ounce and even older than me, but she does do all the heavy work, then throws her money at a bookie's head. "Thanks. Merry Christmas, Selma." Nodding at the racing form, she added, "Don't spend it all on your nags."

Selma cackled loudly before coughing alarmingly.

Pulling her gloves on, Annie asked, "Is your family coming for Christmas?"

The elevator car arrived. Annie pulled the gate open.

"Sure. Big meal, big fight! Ho, ho, ho!" Selma bent forward with the force of her coughing.

Icy gusts blowing off the roiling East River at her back, Annie walked the blocks toward Rockefeller Center from the O'Hares' apartment building, called The Campanile, the last address on E. 52nd Street. She was understandably nervous about today's plan, having scheduled her granddaughters' baptisms behind their mother's back. Waiting for the red light at the back of St. Patrick's Cathedral, she watched a small priest scurry out of the buff-colored stone rectory, one of two imposing buildings book-ending the back of the cathedral, and hold his black hat down in the blast of wind up Madison Avenue. Looking up at the two ornate spires rising above Fifth Avenue, the chiselled Tuckahoe Marble a soot-stained green-grey, she considered her determination to have the little girls baptized in secret. She shivered. The light changed and she and the few other pedestrians at the corner trusted the straining yellow cabs and green Madison Avenue bus to remain stationary while they crossed.

On the Monday six weeks earlier and after a year of indecision—during which Ned told her repeatedly to mind her own business—she'd walked the same blocks from the O'Hares' apartment to the rectory at St. Patrick's Cathedral. Flushing deeply, she'd introduced herself and told the priest a rambling tale about her granddaughters, now seven and five, and not yet baptized.

"My daughter was raised Catholic, but she's given up her religion. Sorry, Father. Her husband isn't even Catholic, and so of course they weren't married in the church. But I am—would you baptize their two little girls, Father?" She stopped speaking and waited. *He thinks I'm an eejit.* She dared not tell the priest that Betty and her Protestant husband weren't even married anymore, that they were now divorced.

The priest was not a young man and wore every story in the world on his haggard, drooping face. After only a moment's hesitation, he confirmed that Annie was not a parishioner of St. Patrick's. Next, he asked, "If I baptize your granddaughters, Mrs., um, is there any hope they'll take First Holy Communion?"

"I'll do my best, Father."

Hands shaking, he opened a tall, well-thumbed ledger and turned many pages in silence. He then went about scheduling the baptisms for six weeks hence, also on a Monday, and charging Annie a staggering sum for their performance. She'd gulped and written a check.

After a tense and frequently sleepless six weeks, she was on the precipice of enacting the plan. Now, standing in the large holiday crowd waiting at the Fifth Avenue crosswalk in front of the cathedral, Annie thought for the umpteenth time, *Mother of God, if Betty finds out…she's still mad at me for not telling her about my conversion. But how can I leave the wee things heathens? I promised my mother-in-law to carry on in our church. What would Ned's mother think about the state of their little souls? I've waited and hinted to Betty long enough. Margot is seven and wee Gabi five— Margot and Gabi—why in God's name did Betty name them such daft things? Naming the first girl Margaret was fine, after my sister she said…alright, but she could have been called Meg, like our Meg, Peg or Peggy, or Maggie. But Margot? I nearly told her to catch herself on when she told me, but I bit my tongue. And what is Gabrielle? A French-sounding project. And Gabi? Makes the poor wee thing seem like she talks too much—so it is—she is a wee chatter box. I wonder was it the father's idea? Sounds like one of his ideas, not that Sam Sharpham is French at all, but a real American—so he liked to tell us— his family coming over from England in 17something or other to settle near Nyack. Betty was so impressed with everything about him when they were courting…she made her bed.*

The light changed and Annie crossed with the crowd to the western side of Fifth Avenue. She turned downtown, passing several uniformed Salvation Army members, standing over their kettles for donations and ringing bells in front of the giant statue of Atlas holding the globe. The delicious smell of chestnuts roasting in braziers accompanied her as she turned into the channel between Rockefeller Center buildings and navigated around crowds looking down at the skaters, and up at the enormous Christmas tree, ablaze with lighted decorations. Rows of lighted angels holding trumpets led the way. Finally, she reached the giant brass doors of Betty's office building. Welcome warm air rushed at her as she entered the cavernous lobby, while the doors closed behind her with a whoosh. The elevator operator manager was strutting the elevator bank with a mechanical clicker, signalling the operators when to close their doors. Annie raised her chin and pulled herself up straight before entering an elevator and telling the operator her floor.

∼

The bored-looking receptionist seated under the large *The Tonight Show NBC* red and blue sign raised an eyebrow and asked, "Yes? May I help you?"

"Would you ring Elizabeth Sharpham? She's expecting me, her mother."

The girl pasted on a smile and picked up the phone. "Oh, yes. The little girls are adorable." Picking up the phone, she dialled and said, "Hi, Liz, your mother's here."

Annie sank gratefully into one of the upholstered chairs in the waiting area.

One of the glass doors to the inner sanctum opened slowly before she heard, "Grandma! Grandma!" The little girls, the older copper-haired and the younger blonde, ran to Annie, hurling themselves at her.

"Oof, mind me legs, girls," she said, but she drew the giggling children to her and smiled.

"All right, girls. Now, mind Grandma," said Betty, standing behind her daughters.

Annie looked at her daughter in the harsh fluorescent light. *She's looking thin and tired—even though she's dressed so nicely—that suit is hanging off her.*

She waved her daughter closer before saying, "Listen, Betty, I'll take them home with me. You've your office party tonight, don't you? Don't worry about the girls."

"The big party's after tonight's show, but I can't go to a party at one in the morning. But some of the office people are going out at five tonight. So I'll go out for a drink and then come home. Thanks for taking them today, Mommy." Bending closer to her mother, she lowered her voice to add, "And *don't* spend a lot of money on them."

"Mind you eat something with the drink and ride home with the crowd tonight, not in an empty train car. I'll send your da to meet you at the subway—ring us before you get on the train."

"Oh, don't make him, Mommy, I'll be fine. Let him enjoy his vacation, feet up."

"Ach, the wee dog needs his last walk. Your da won't mind. You know how he likes a walk. Anyway, this time of year the trains and streets are full of drunks and God knows."

Annie had planned time for the little girls to enjoy the extravagant Christmas windows the department stores created, in addition to the shopping and their usual lunch, and of course the baptism scheduled at three o'clock.

On the way back to Fifth Avenue, they too stopped to look up at the enormous lighted Christmas tree and down at the skaters on the ice rink below. "Could we skate, Grandma?" asked Gabi.

"Skate! Isn't it dangerous if you don't know how? We'll ask your mommy another day," said Annie.

Margot said, "But we *do* know how. Daddy and Nora taught us. They take us to a pond near their house. They own it. We'll skate when we're up on Christmas."

Annie looked at Margot and thought, *If that's the stuff Betty has to listen to, no wonder she's sour.* "Well, we've a lot to do today. But I'd still want to ask your mother."

Annie steered them to the bus stop on Fifth Avenue. "We'll ride down to 34th Street and then look in the windows along the way back up to Schrafft's, alright? Can you girls walk that far?"

Stopping at the decorated windows at Macy's and Altman's, they waited their turn to reach the front row at the mechanized Christmas worlds behind the glass, both of which had 19th -

century themes. Their hands gripped in Annie's clench, Margot gazed seriously and Gabi pointed and chattered as puppet craftsmen of olden times hit nails into wooden toys, and elfin helpers shinnied up and down poles on a loop to Santa's workshop.

The cold got to them, so Annie steered them back on a bus to the Schrafft's at 46th Street. Once through the revolving door, they entered a large panelled hall. The smells of hot apple pie, coffee and toast greeted them. The glamourous hostess in a long gown whisked them past the ladies' bar and the pastry counter to the large restaurant area, where the sound of women's voices, tinkling glass and silverware provided accompaniment to the rushing waitstaff. The front hostess raised three fingers to the floor hostess, who pointed three fingers at an empty table, where Annie and the girls were deposited.

A seated Annie put her glasses on and studied the menu before ordering their usual lunch: sliced chicken sandwiches on white toast with iceberg lettuce and mayonnaise; a pot of tea for Annie, hot chocolates with whipped cream for the girls.

Their waitress, dressed in a black uniform with white cuffs, hat and apron, sounded fresh off the boat from Ireland. A southerner, she spoke softly and smiled warmly at the little girls, less so at Annie after hearing the Belfast accent, Annie thought. *Who knows what these girls have to deal with here in this country? However bad it may have been there—and this one sounds like she's from Cork, a lovely accent—it's not easy leaving your own country, however you slice it.* Annie always tipped well, especially the Irish girls.

"There now, girls," said Annie, fussing with her gloves and handbag. "Wriggle out of those coats and hats now or you won't know the good of them when we go out. We have to walk uptown again in the cold. We'll stop at Saks Fifth Avenue and Lord and Taylor for the windows, go inside St. Patrick's for a wee while, then Best's. We'll buy your mommy some nice things for Christmas." Looking at the large clock opposite, she said, "I have a surprise planned and we mustn't be late."

"What is it, Grandma?" asked Margot, frowning, her russet eyebrows squeezed together.

"It's a secret between us, just the three of us and Grandpa. But not your mommy or daddy, mind."

Margot's frown deepened.

Gabi clanked her fork down on her spoon and yawned.

"I'll explain when we're inside the cathedral. Now eat up. Butterscotch sundaes with toasted almonds if you do."

Betty brought the excited girls downstairs to her parents' apartment from theirs on Christmas morning. They wore their new woolen bathrobes and leather slippers, thanks to their grandma and the trip to Best & Co.

The girls ran into the living room, where more presents with their names on tags were piled.

Betty called, "No more presents opened until after breakfast!"

Christmas carols crooned from the large old radio in the living room, the burble of Bing Crosby's baritone making its inevitable rounds.

Annie began frying a second round of bacon and eggs and making a fresh pot of tea. It was nine o'clock. The dog lying contentedly at his feet, Ned sat at the end of the table, smoking and reading the newspaper.

Betty stifled a yawn. "They were up before six," she said, pouring tea.

"What time is Sam coming for them?" asked Annie.

"He's picking them up at noon." Pulling a cigarette pack out of a pocket, Betty tapped one out.

Annie looked at Ned, who said, "It's pretty up there in Nyack. I can see why the girls like it. The hills and the river—a nice ride on the bus—I enjoyed it that time his car broke down and I took them up there for the weekend."

Betty frowned, the unlit cigarette in her hand. "Oh yes, the girls love being in that big house with their father and baby brother. They love the fireplace and the woods, the dogs, the cats, not to mention the horses *she* keeps. Sam takes them skating. And they like Nora a lot—they love her. She's pretty, beautiful in fact. Margot doesn't say much, but I can tell she loves being there and Gabi's too little to keep it to herself. She says they'll have a big tree decorated in the house. His family and Nora's family will come over—she has loads of younger brothers and sisters who make a fuss of them. All the things we don't offer."

"Isn't Butch here a dog?" asked Ned, bending down to pat the dog's shaggy gray head. The dog looked up into Ned's face.

"She's not Irish, is she, Nora?" asked Annie. "You don't meet Noras here unless they've come over, do you?"

"Oh no, she's American—her name's Eleanor. Her family has lived up there for more than 250 years, so Margot tells me. I didn't mean the dog, Daddy. I meant all the rest of it. Mostly the baby brother, the beautiful young stepmother who never loses her temper—the happy, jolly father."

"We could get a tree next Christmas," offered Ned. "I don't mind."

Annie laughed. "Sam, jolly? Ha! I'd love to see that. Is she cooking Christmas dinner?"

Shrugging, Betty said, "I imagine they're making Christmas dinner—you know how Sam prides himself a great cook." Her lip curled after she stopped speaking. She slid the cigarette back into the pack.

Annie turned around to say, "Michael and Carol aren't coming today. The baby's sick. But Denis will call, I'm sure."

"It's only eight o'clock out there," said Ned. The two women looked at him. "In Cheecago. He'll not call now, Denis."

"Ach, the bacon in this country is all fat." Annie added the crispy bacon strips to a pad of paper towels. "Nothing's left by the time you cook it."

Betty called, "Girls! Breakfast!" She waited. "I'll get them."

After Betty left, Annie turned and whispered, "I wish she wasn't made so unhappy by him and the new wife, and their child. She's young enough to remarry and if you ask me, she's better off without him."

"I don't think *she* thinks so," said Ned, carefully lighting a cigarette. "No, she still loves Sam and it's soured her."

~

The girls sat on the floor amidst the giftwrap, shredded and tossed around the room as though by wild animals. Annie patiently picked up the paper near her swollen ankles, smoothed it flat and wound the ribbon into balls. Gabi examined her new doll, a Scottish piper in full regalia, including lifting his kilt up. Margot read her new book, *Black Stallion*.

Stubbing out her cigarette, Betty said, "It's nearly eleven. Time to get dressed, girls. Your father will be here at twelve."

The phone rang in the kitchen. Ned said, "It's one of the boys, I'll go."

"Come on, girls. Let's go upstairs," said Betty. "After he picks them up, I'll come back and straighten up the living room, Mommy—make sure none of the actual gifts go down the incinerator. I want us to open our gifts, too."

"Alright," said Annie.

Ned returned, looking a little stricken. "It's for you, Annie. It's your sisters ringing. A three-minute trunk call. Hurry."

"*Who?*" Stunned, Annie uttered the one word.

"Come on now," he said.

Like a sleepwalker, Annie walked to the kitchen. The receiver lay on the sideboard. She sat down and picked it up as though it would explode in her hand. "Hello?"

"Hiya!" Belfast—there was no mistaking the way that word was spoken. "Annie, it's us! Meg and Lizzie. Happy Christmas!"

Looking up, Annie saw her husband, daughter and granddaughters framed in the doorway. Gabi came forward clutching her piper doll. She unabashedly stood at Annie's elbow to listen.

"Em, which one is this?"

"Lizzie, you daft thing. Do you not know *me*?"

Annie heard giggling in the background.

Lizzie continued. "We're all together at Meg's house—your old house on St. Ives Gardens. We're waiting while Robert fetches his daughter and her mother before we serve Christmas dinner. Meg said, 'Let's ring Annie and Ned!' So, we have. 'Bout ye then—alright?"

"Oh, aye. We're fine. Betty's wee girls just opened their gifts."

"That's sweet now, isn't it? What ages are they now?"

"Seven and five."

"So, tell us. Howareye? Is everyone well? Ned? Betty? The boys?"

"Aye, everyone is well, except my wee grandson, Michael's baby, so they can't come today."

"And Denis?"

"Denis lives very far away, in Cheecago. He'll ring us though, they both will. What about your boys?"

"Will's in England, but Tom and his family are coming down from Larne. They live in Larne now. Did you know that?"

"I'm not sure." Annie offered nothing further.

A brief silence followed. Lizzie said, "It'll be quite the crowd. We've set three tables. Well, here's Meggie. Happy Christmas."

Betty came forward to hiss, "Let me speak to Meg."

Putting one finger up, Annie said, "Hiya, Meg. Hiya. Here's Betty wanting to talk to ye." She handed Betty the receiver with her hand over the mouthpiece. "Be quick, you've got to get them dressed."

"Aunt Meg! Yes, it's me! Oh, it's wonderful to hear your voice. I wish I'd thought to call. Yes, they are, right here, Margot and Gabi. No, he's not here. I'll write you. How is Aunt Lillian? Her nephew cooked the whole dinner! A goose? Mommy used to make them. No—roast beef. And Robert? I see. And his little girl? No, not so little. Rosie must be what, eleven? Yes. Give my love to everyone. Yes, I'll write. You got the card? Good. Tell Robert I'll write, too. Yes, I understand, bye-bye…oh, the operator cut us off."

Handing the receiver to her mother, Betty said, "We were cut off. Guess the three minutes were up. Why didn't you speak to Meg first, though?"

My throat closed. I couldn't speak.

Betty looked at her mother for a second, her brow furrowed, then began to steer her children to the apartment door.

"Hi, Betty, do you want me to wait for Sam up there with you?" asked Ned.

"That would be nice, Daddy, yes."

The apartment suddenly empty and quiet, Annie continued to sit at the kitchen table, the receiver in her hand. She heard the clicking of the dead line and put it down into the cradle.

A fine tenor's voice drifted in from the living room radio, his voice the perfect messenger for an ancient, sad carol, its words profound. Unexpectedly, Annie was shaken with a sob. Her hand flew to her mouth to stop them, but alone, she gave voice to the sobs, gave over to waves of sobs, the tears dripping onto the black telephone perched on her lap.

JUST US—DECEMBER 1968

BELFAST—PORTSTEWART

*S*tanding behind the seated Albert, Robert kissed the top of his head. He draped his arms around Albert's neck and thought, *He's gone quite bald, poor love. At least he's stopped trying to hide it, cuts it very short.*

Readjusting his reading glasses, Albert asked, "What do you think of quenelles?" He turned the page of the cookbook he was reading.

"I don't. What are they again?"

"You grind fish and—"

"Stop. No," said Robert firmly.

"They're not for you, they're for the aunts' birthday party. *They* love fish. Rosie, too." Albert craned his neck to peer up at Robert. "Me, too."

"Why ask me, then? Go on and make them." Pointing at the open book in front of Albert, he asked, "Elizabeth David?"

"Yes. I'll make your favorite for the main course." Albert looked back down at the book.

"Not from her book you won't. It's all things we can't pronounce and can't even buy here."

"I can pronounce them." Albert exaggerated the movement of his mouth to loudly ask, "PORK ROAST? And a birthday cake for the aunts. It should be a nice weekend. What about your father?"

Robert straightened and faced Albert. "I haven't asked him, yet. I know, I know, I should. If Rosie does come, I'd like her to drive up with us, especially if he comes." Looking up at the kitchen clock, he asked, "You can be here when the man delivers the television this afternoon?"

"Yes, I'll be here. My tutorial's coming here."

Smiling, Robert said, "As long as they don't bring their Petri dishes."

"Of course not. It's a history of science tutorial. We're going to discuss the history of the development of penicillin and whether Alexander Fleming was bonkers. Plus a lot of formulae and drug development science."

"Was he?'

Albert nodded. "Definitely. What do you mean *if* Rosie comes?"

"It's near end of term. She's better things to do—she's twenty-two." He hurried down the hall. "See you later—don't forget I'm taking my dad out for a pint after work."

Patting his pockets to check he had wallet and keys, he heard Albert call down the hall, "If you decide to invite him, make sure he knows when we're picking him up on Friday. Will you be home for dinner?"

"I'll eat something with him for his tea, then tuck him up— one pint and he's out by six."

"Enjoy the fish and chips then."

Robert made a noise like a strangled cough. "Yes, I'll be home for dinner."

He closed the door behind him and walked out into a fine December morning, joining the stream of students, staff and faculty, hurrying down the Stranmillis toward Queen's University campus.

∼

Seated at a Formica table in the noisy, bright orange cafeteria of Ralph's lodge, he asked his son, "You sure you don't want the full meal, Robert? It'd be on me."

Robert shook his head and ate a chip. "You know I don't like fish, Da."

Watching his father eat the fish and chips gave him a pang. The fork shook dangerously as Ralph raised it to his lips and rattled it in under his white mustache—Robert shifted his eyes away.

"Here, George! George, come and meet my son, Bob. Royal Navy he was—served in the North Atlantic." Motioning frantically to another old man to stop his progress, his father's watery blue eyes came to life.

Robert stood and shook the old man's hand. "Hiya, Mr. Graham. Howareya?"

"Oh, fine, fine. 'Bout ye then, Robert?"

"Bob's an electrics engineer at Queen's, did ye know that? And would you look at the size of him? Strong as an ox, he is. Does his Royal Navy exercises every day."

"Alright, D-Da. Mr. Graham knows me." *I've known the man since I was a boy.*

His father's face fell a little, but he recovered and said, "Of course, of course he does. Bob's taking me for a pint at me local after."

George Graham winked and yelled, "That's grand, Ralph. You fellas enjoy yourselves." George moved off, carrying his tray of fish and chips to another table, his tea slopping over the side of the mug, flooding the tray.

"George worked at the market, for years, ran a sweets stall. Remember? When I was a candy salesman? You loved what I brought home in them days." Smiling, his father continued eating, before stopping and frowning. "All gone now. The great candy companies, the markets...even Smithfield's a load of secondhand rubbish."

The racket in the cafeteria made it difficult to have a conversation, even if Robert hadn't found it hard to think of things to say. He shifted in the molded plastic chair and imagined asking the question he'd rehearsed, *So, Da, we're all going up to Port-stewart Friday afternoon. We'll leave at noon. Come with us. Albert's cooking and baking to celebrate Meg's birthday a few weeks ago and Lillian's on Saturday.* But nothing came out of his mouth. *Don't be so petty and mean, it'll be less than three days, a few hours...and hours.*

Robert settled his father in a snug alongside the small, glowing fire grate and waited while the pours settled at the bar of Ralph's local pub.

"Here, Da, get that down your neck," he said, placing a pint of Guinness stout in front of him. Robert sat down on the low stool with a purple velvet cushion across the small wooden table from his father, who sat on the padded bench built like a high-backed pew. "Nice and quiet in here."

Robert always enjoyed the first sip of bitter through the creamy head tasting of nut more than the rest of the pint. He licked the foam off his mustache. Father and son sat together in companionable silence, drinking the heavy, dark stout. Robert's gaze wandered around the dark-paneled interior of the old pub to the incongruous flashing lights of the row of games machines across the room. The setting sun shone down the Lisburn Road, through the stained-glass window of the Red Hand of Ulster, bloodying the floor at their feet.

"Ah, Guinness is good, but I miss the ales made in the big breweries we used to have in Belfast. There's none left! How could Caffrey's go under, I ask you?"

"They were bought out by bigger companies," said Robert.

"Aye, but it wasn't the same. The doctor prescribed auld Caffrey's to your mum when she fell with you, to keep her blood strong, full of iron." He took another sip. "How's Albert?"

Here we go. "Busy with end of semester."

"He's a fine man, a well-respected professor...tall, strapping, is Albert." The old man looked around before continuing, "Listen, Bob, son, Albert is a fine lad and I know he's your best pal, and you and Jo didn't work out, and that's a shame, but you're a young man yet, you could find another woman, settle down. Rosie's grown up now, so she wouldn't mind, I don't think."

Lowering his eyes, Robert took another long draft. This conversation would replay itself as it always did, whether he participated or not.

"I mean you've lived together for years now, you and him, on your own. People might think you're a couple of poofs, you know?" The old man laughed too loudly before succumbing to a coughing fit.

"Have a d-d-d...sip, Da."

Ralph raised the pint glass shakily. They were quiet for a few moments again while sipping their pints. A group of four men came over to the corner opposite the snug, pulled the green baize cover off the dartboard, removed their coats and began their preparations for a match. They were large, beefy men with weathered red faces, their rolled sleeves revealing massive forearms and hands like hams, possibly from having spent their lives in jobs on the docks or in the Royal Ulster Constabulary.

Robert took his tweed cap off, pulled his scarf off and wriggled out of his trench coat. He noticed his father examining his head.

"You've kept your hair, haven't you? Got that from your mum's side—I've been bald since a young man—where you got them curls from, I don't know. Oh, wait, I do. My mum had lovely curly hair and hazel eyes, green in the right light. Hers went salt and pepper early, too. It looks distinguished on ye."

Robert broke into a sweat. He pulled his Queen's college of engineering striped tie down and unbuttoned the top of his shirt.

Plucking from thin air, seemingly, Ralph asked, "How is Meg Preston then? Do you ever hear from her?"

It's now or never. Ask him!

"Yes, and in fact, we're driving up on Friday to celebrate her birthday last month and Lillian's on Saturday. Would you like to come? We'll stay through Sunday afternoon, then drive home."

His father, whose gaze had shifted back to the dart players, asked, "How many of the sisters are left? Lizzie's all right. What about Annie? She's alive?"

He didn't hear me! Thank God!

"I got a Christmas card from Annie's daughter, Betty, last year. Her father died a few years back, but Annie was fine at Christmas. Betty and her girls moved into Annie's apartment."

"Ned's died? That's right, you told me. That's a shame. A nice fella," Ralph's voice dropped, "Catholic, but we got on. She's no husband, Betty? What's happened till him?"

"They're divorced. He remarried."

Ralph's eyebrows shot up but before he could give an opinion, Robert rushed to ask, "How is Lizzie?"

"Ach, she's the same, older, but Tom's crook. She does everything for him, but when I sit with him, he whines and complains. He's not allowed alcohol." He took a deep drink and smacked his lips. "There was no end to the Preston girls years ago—five of 'em." Smiling, he said, "Your mother was the beauty of the lot. Rosie reminds me of her and me own mum, I see her too in Rosie's eyes and hair. She got the curls from you." His father's smile faded. "Well, we all get old, if we've luck. Wish Florrie had."

"Me too," said Robert. They fell into silence until Robert thought to say, "I should stop and visit Lizzie and Tom. I mean to, but I never do. Do their b-boys visit?"

"Not that I've seen. Lizzie says they ring sometimes. If you stop in, for God's sake don't settle—say you're on your way somewhere. That Tom'll drive you mad."

"Here, Da, I bought a new telly—a super one, top of the line. You'll have to come over and watch the football with me."

Ralph's heavily lined face regained a lighter look. "Oh aye?

That would be grand. You always liked your football—got that from me." Frowning again, he added, "I don't like that George Best, though."

"No? He was named European Player of the Year this year, but we don't have to watch a Manchester United match, or Northern Ireland."

"Oh, aye, he's a great player alright, but off the rails as a man. He's an Orangeman, but he hits the bottle, runs around on his wife, so they say. What about the Old Firm? I'm still a Rangers fan. I love watching an Old Firm match. I tune in when one's on. Now here's a funny thing, son—I turn the wee telly on after tea and next thing I know I'm asleep in the chair and the test card is on. The cat curls up on me and keeps me from freezing." The old man laughed before draining his pint. "Your mum used to say, 'Now Ralph, I'm off to me bed and I'll not leave you here to die.' That was before we had telly, but I fell asleep to the wireless, too." His watery eyes glistened.

"Do you not turn the heater on when you sit down?" Gesturing at the empty glass, he asked, "Another?"

"Aye, I do turn it on. No more for me. Gets me waterworks going no end. Have another yourself."

"One stout's enough for me. It's like a meal. Whiskey?"

"Oh, aye! A small one, mind."

It was a mistake to feed him more alcohol, Robert knew, but it gave them something to do and would bring the evening to an early close.

When he returned with the drinks his father was watching the dart match.

"Thanks, Bob. Cheers."

"Cheers, Da." *When did he start calling me Bob?*

Too loudly his father said, "That great fat fella's a good darts player. I can't think of his name, but he's won some big matches. He's famous."

Men crowded around the darts players now, their voices rising, until they blocked Ralph's and Robert's view of the match. Cigarette smoke blew over them like a heavy fog. Beer spilled as elbows were jostled and the yeasty smell mixed with the men's body odor.

Whiskies quickly downed, father and son made their way through the crowded pub to the door and the cold December air.

Slowly, they walked the two blocks to the house where Robert had grown up. Walking downhill on short Rathcool Street, Ralph said, "The people on this street have always kept loads of cats, for as long as we've lived here. I got Charlie from auld Mrs. Thingmabob who lives in that house. Careful you don't trip over one in the dark." They turned into the front garden of the house. "It's dark so early now, but that's December for ye. Pitch black or as good as one end of the day to the other. Ach, I forgot to leave a light on." Ralph fumbled with his key but got the door open. The sound of a mewing cat greeted them.

"Alright, Charlie, I'm home. Mind how you go, Bob, he'll trip you if he can."

Robert reached around the door and flicked the hall light on. The grey tom twirled at their feet shivering with excitement and indignation.

"Alright, alright, I'm coming," said Robert's father, walking back toward the kitchen.

Robert stopped in the parlor and turned on the light. *Neat as a pin.* "Shall I turn the heater on, Dad?"

"Eh? Here you go wee man, a nice bit of sardine for your tea."

Robert reached into the old fireplace grate and turned the heater on. He checked the orange glow of all four bars before turning it off again and walking into the kitchen.

His father stood, watching the cat enjoy the fish. "He's used to being fed at five on the dot. I swear he's a wee clock in his stomach. Tea?" he asked Robert.

Robert's eyes flicked over at the kitchen clock before saying, "Aye. I'll put the kettle on."

"I'm just out the back. Back in a trice."

Filling the kettle at the Belfast sink, he noted his father's neat habits: washed eggcup, plate, mug, and small teapot in the wooden dish dryer. Placing the kettle on the hot hob, he felt the presence of his mother in this familiar space so keenly that tears sprang to his eyes.

The old man came back inside, and Robert quickly wiped his eyes.

"Take your coat and hat off, man—you won't know the good of them later."

After taking his hat and coat off, he pulled a package out of his coat pocket. "I brought those chocolate b-biscuits you like."

"Oh, thanks, son."

"Does Rosie visit you, Da?"

"Aye, she does. Calls it 'popping over' or some such. She doesn't stay long, but she comes regular, a few times a month, maybe twice. Has tea and tells me about her studies, her friends. Chats and laughs. She's a tonic for me, I'll tell you. Although what she's on about half the time, I don't know."

"What do you mean?"

"Says she wants to be a barrister! Well, what can we expect when the mother's a solicitor. No wonder your marriage didn't last. Anyway, Rosie says she wants to be a, what is it? Oh, a civil barrister and help those hurt and jailed at the hands of the police. Sounds like a load of Fenian rubbish, to me. What is she on about?"

"Civil rights b-barrister. She's passionate about civil rights D-Da, and you must admit, the police are free with their truncheons and rubber b-bullets with Catholics, and with throwing them in jail without due process."

His father looked at him with a mouth fallen slack. "Keeping the peace I call it. She calls it 'police brutality' or some such. I change the subject and she comes back to her real self, laughing and smiling. Whatever she thinks now, she'll mature—I'd have hoped you would, too—still, she's a dear soul. She even visits Lizzie and Tom, although how she puts up wi' him, I don't know." His father yawned widely. "You know, I don't think I can keep me eyes open for tea. Sorry. Do you mind? Thanks for the biscuits." He yawned again.

Robert's stomach was rumbling with hunger, "No, Da. You go upstairs and get to bed." Picking up his hat and coat, he asked, "You didn't answer me earlier—we're driving up on Friday to celebrate Meg's birthday. Would you like to come? We'll stay through Sunday, leave after breakfast or early afternoon."

"Oh, aye? Meg's birthday? Two nights? I don't know." Rubbing his mustached upper lip, he asked, "What about Charlie?"

"Well, you could leave him his food for a few meals, or ask Lizzie to feed him, couldn't you?"

"Is Rosie going with ye?"

"She may do…I'm not sure, yet. She may not."

"I see. It's nice you asked, son, but I better stay here with the wee cat."

"Are you sure, Da?"

"Aye, I've me own bed here and I know where everything is. But I'll come over to watch your new telly with you, any time you ask, alright?"

"Of course. I'll find a match next week for us to watch, alright? Take care of yourself now. I'll ring you."

Outside on the front step, he waited until he heard his father lock the door before turning away. He walked a few paces up Rathcool Street, watched by cats squatting in the doorways, turned and saw that the downstairs of his father's house was dark and the upstairs hall lit. When he turned onto the Lisburn Road, he walked quickly before breaking into a run.

Two blocks later he stopped, panting, and walked the rest of the way home.

∾

"How are you back there? Alright?" As they drove northwest, Robert looked in the rear-view mirror to see Rosie squirming among the boxes and packages. "There's twelve cubic feet of storage with the back seat folded down, but when you have a passenger *and* loads of stuff, it's tight. Sorry." Robert watched Rosie in the rear-view mirror. Her green eyes crackled with intelligence and honesty, and often turned a lighter green with humor. Her arms cradled a box, and she blew a stray strand of dark curls out of her eyes. She'd inherited her mother's easy, wide smile. Her skin was a shade lighter than Jo's and lightly freckled in summer. Her build was slim like her mother's, but she was taller. *Like Johnny, her real father.*

Robert would love to see photos of her father's people, but if Rosie had been given any by Johnny, she had never shown him. Jo's family photos had been destroyed in the bombing, except for the three framed portraits her father kept on his office desk.

After a moment of gazing at her, Robert dragged his attention back to the road.

"I'm fine, Pa. It's a good thing Granda stayed home, though. How had you planned on squeezing him in?"

"No room on my lap," said Albert, who squirmed under his box of wines and whiskey.

"He'd have like sitting in the middle of all the flowers, though. Smells like a florist shop in here, one located next to a restaurant," said Robert.

Rosie succeeded in moving a box of casseroles off her lap, pulled open a packet of crisps, took a few and passed the bag up front. Albert reached and took the packet. He crunched on a crisp while holding the bag out for Robert, who shook his head.

"What's new with you?" asked Robert.

Rosie leant forward between the two men and retrieved the crisp packet. "We're gearing up for a larger march—from Belfast to Derry next month. The march on city hall was a wee bit of bust even though there were thousands of us, but it got the People's Democracy formed, so, not such a bust. We're emulating the civil rights march from Selma to Montgomery in Alabama led by Martin Luther King in 1965—like them, we'll continue to march."

"Londonderry? Weren't there many marchers injured in a march there, in October?" asked Albert, frowning.

Robert's eyes met his briefly.

"There were. I saw that look, by the way. During that march, the RUC had a field day, thanks to the Apprentice Boys' counter-march threat. This will be a long march, obviously, but we'll have much better press coverage, too, so whatever they do will be broadcast far and wide. We're trying to get the RUC to accompany us, protect us, and letting the Tele and Irish Times know our route and cover it."

"And you're planning on going to this march?" asked Robert. He exchanged another quick look with Albert.

"Of course! There will be a large law student contingent."

"What does your mother say?"

"Wear comfortable shoes."

"She does not."

Rosie laughed. "No, she does not. But she knows better than to try and stop me. Anyway, she believes the injustices need to be challenged, as much as I do."

"Jo—a republican?" asked Robert.

"I wouldn't go that far, but she's on the side we are, of ending the Special Powers Act finally, and restoring freedom of speech and assembly, fair allocation of jobs and housing, and the one man/one vote, one woman/one vote, although it's never called the latter. I'll work to change that, too. Surely you're for basic justice?"

"Of *course* we are," said Albert. "It's just...in our circle, the religions don't divide us as much, we're all outcasts," he laughed, "but our friends enjoy good jobs, like us. I tend to forget it's very different for others."

"Yes, but the semi-decriminalization of The Sexual Offenses Act in the United Kingdom doesn't even apply to Northern

Ireland. That's something we must tackle also—you two could help."

"I am for decriminalization here, of course—it's always hung over our heads." Robert frowned. "How large is this march to be?"

"I can't give you a number, but we hope there will be lots of us leaving Belfast and if we can keep together, we'll pick up many more marchers along the way to enter Derry City."

"Have you ever walked that many miles, Rosie?"

"Never, but I started training last month. We'll have to walk nearly eighteen miles a day to enter Derry on the fourth day. And I do have comfortable shoes."

Robert hit a pothole hard, which pushed Albert forward, his knees making audible contact with the dash.

"Ow!"

"I told you to stretch your legs out, not up—there's plenty of legroom, even for you. Ah, we're here," said Robert, ignoring Albert's exaggerated look of pain. He toggled the indicator stalk, and the blue 1963 Hillman Imp began to climb the drive up to the cottage car park. Robert braked to a stop smoothly, pulled on the parking brake, and pushed the engine switch off. Jumping out, he pushed his bucket seat forward.

After a moment of moving packages around, Rosie was able to scoot over to the open door and climb out, managing to do so gracefully.

Once out of the car, her shoulder-length dark curls were blown across her face, as her long tweed coat unfurled like a sail. "Whew! What a lovely day! Chilly, but sunny." She tied her baby blue striped law school scarf and buttoned the coat. She leant back into the back seat to collect the box of casseroles.

Albert said, "Ignore her—she's just grateful to be alive. Robert, come and get this box. I'm in agony and can't move. Please!"

"Coming." At the passenger side, he took the wine box off

Albert's lap. Albert unfolded one long leg at a time and pulled himself out with a grunt.

Pressing the small of his back, Albert groaned and stretched.

Robert handed the wine box back to Albert, placed the box of casseroles on top, opened the bonnet and reached in for the overnight bags. "Alright? Let's walk up. I'll come back for the rest."

"Hello!" called Lillian from the top of the steps, clutching her purple heather coat tightly around her. She walked down to meet Robert. "Give me something to carry."

"You're fine," he said.

"You mean fine, but an auld one, is that it? Hello, Rosie. Welcome!"

Smothered by the wrapped bouquets of flowers she carried on top of a box, Rosie issued a muffled, "Hello, Aunt Lillian! No don't take anything—I've it balanced so." Shod in brown suede boots, her feet moved deliberately as she climbed the steep steps by feel.

Lillian called over her shoulder, "Hello, Albert!"

"Aunt."

Lillian stopped at the top and waved them inside. "Come in, come in, quick. The wind is that sharp today. Albert, you didn't have to bring *everything*. I was planning on providing…"

"Yes, I know Aunt, but you're feeding all of us for a couple of days. Plus, I am fond of the wine my wine merchant sells."

"A wine merchant is it now?"

"Aye, off Donegall Place. Received his sommelier credentials in France. William's a very knowledgeable and pleasant fellow."

The group entered the utility room, pink-faced and talking all at once.

"Biscuit, girl! 'Bout ye?" Robert patted the tall, curly-coated dog, excited by the arrival of the guests. "I'm thinking of getting a dog. I need the exercise. Even though I stopped smoking, me wind's still not great."

Lillian said, "Oh, aye? She'd give you that all right. If you live near water, it's a mistake getting a water dog, but Meg fell in love, so. Biscuit will chase anything in and out of the water for hours, and she needs a lot of exercise, so we get a lot...I do. Choose a dog used to the city, a poor stray, like our dear Gordie was." Lillian sighed. "We miss him and dear wee Bobby."

Albert turned and smiled at her.

To Robert's surprise, she teared. She said, "Sorry, it's me birthday tomorrow so I've been thinking of the past all day. Biscuit is a tonic for us, that's sure. Here, hang your coats and come into the warm kitchen. Mind the laundry basket. I've a fresh pot of tea. Oh, before I forget, Jo rang. Holly's mother isn't well, so she's not coming. Jo will arrive this afternoon by train, the Portrush call. I'll run over and fetch her at three."

Robert said, "I'll fetch her. Nothing serious with Holly's mum, I hope? I'm fond of crazy auld Bertha."

Rosie stood hugging herself near the cooker, her arms wrapped around the long raspberry knitted turtleneck she wore over brown woolen trousers.

Lillian said, "A chesty cough, but at her age...the doctor's been. Holly is home barring the door to keep her from going to her dusty auld archives."

"Hello! Hello!" Meg came into the kitchen and went to Robert to kiss him first. "I just gave the fire a good poke. Come sit in the parlor."

Rosie, after kissing Meg's cheek, said, "You look very well, you both do."

"Rosie, dear, hello!" She took the young woman's arm. "Thank you for coming! You look frozen. Come into the parlor where it's lovely and warm."

"There's little heat in that wee car of Robert's. I'll bring the tea things," said Albert. "You go ahead in."

~

In the warm kitchen, Albert chopped and stirred at the cooker, while Lillian cut and arranged flowers in vases and pitchers.

"These are lovely, thank you. So many! A real treat to have flowers this dark time of year."

"Rosie went to St. George's Market for them early this morning. Who's coming to the party tomorrow?"

"So, Jo's on her way. Reverend Horne—Ted, he begs us to call him—but he won't stay past one sherry. David and Niall—they'll come tomorrow in the afternoon—Niall has surgery hours Saturday mornings. Mildred, obviously."

Albert said, "Good—I've prepared for ten at dinner. Did the oysters arrive?"

"Yes! What a treat! Sorry, I meant to thank you. I've left the box in the utility room—there's plenty of ice, I checked. The man who delivered them said he was a friend of Frank's, a Mr. O'Lappin, so I had him in for a cup of tea and we had a nice chat—he told me my nephew had ordered the oysters. How did you contact him?"

"I had the telephone number for their pub in Portrush. That's how they take their fish orders. Was it Billy or Isaac O'Lappin? There's two of them—Tweedledum and Tweedledee. Both were great pals of Frank's, although I think Frank liked Isaac better. Frank thought Billy," Albert's voice turned gruff and his accent country, 'took weak at the first sign of work'."

Lillian laughed. "I do miss Frank."

Albert said, "Do you remember? Isaac took us out on his boat a few times when we were lads? We sailed out of Port Ballintrae to their oyster lines and lobster traps, which Frank made us boys pull up, and we hauled fishing nets, while he and Isaac enjoyed the view. We were completely knackered, as I recall."

Lillian said, "We came to rely on Frank for so much, especially for treats like oysters. We haven't had them since he took sick...he was a great friend to us. Dear Frank." She cut flower stems in silence for a moment. "No, I don't know which O'Lappin he was, but he did give me a telephone number where I can leave a message and order fish, and I will. Do you know how to open oysters? I don't and I remember my poor father slicing his hand open instead. The kitchen was like an abattoir and Mother fluttered about like a frightened chicken. Beryl and I couldn't help but dissolve into giggles. Poor Father."

"Wish I'd had a chance to know my granda longer, later in my life. Especially after my father was killed."

Lillian turned to look at him, but Albert continued to carefully stir the contents of a saucepan.

"I wish that about my mum, too."

Lillian said. "My poor sister. Gone too soon, all of them."

After a moment, he said, "I do know how to open oysters because, of course, Frank taught me that very day on the boat. I buy a few oysters for myself often, but however good, none taste like the ones straight out of the sea. Robert hates them, of course —can't even watch me eat them." He laughed. "Not sure how he'll survive tomorrow night's first two courses."

Rosie walked into the kitchen. "Pa's reading a letter to Meg from Betty—she's planning a trip to Belfast in summer with her children. I gather she has never returned since the family emigrated?"

Albert said, "Really? That *is* news. No, none of them have ever been back. Robert will be pleased if she comes."

"Meg, too," said Lillian.

Rosie said, "Is there something I can do to help with the tea?"

Shaking her head, Lillian said, "Everything's under control. It's just us tonight and I've a stew warming. Mildred's bringing dessert even though I told her not to bother, but she enjoys baking, so."

"Count on me later for clearing up, then. I should go for my walk before it's pitch black." Rosie brightened. "Shall I take the dog?"

Lillian asked, "Oh, aye! She'll love it. Do you mind if I come, too?"

"Not at all, I'd like the company. I'll ask Pa and Meg, too. Albert?"

"I'll stay here," said Albert. "I love puttering in this kitchen on a dark December day—reminds me of my boyhood, toasting loaf ends to hold me till tea, studying at the kitchen table, cozy and safe, even during the war. But take my advice and just go on your walk. If you start asking everyone it will be midnight before you're actually out the door."

"He's right about that, let's just go," said Lillian, looking thoughtful. "I'll just change my shoes."

"You see?" asked Albert, a twinkle in his blue eyes.

"Ach, it's just a wee stop," said Lillian, shaking her head.

Rosie laughed and followed Lillian into the utility room.

Robert came into the kitchen, his coat over his arm. "I'm off to fetch Jo. Alright? Do we need anything?"

"We don't and everything's all right. Mind how you go. The roads may have iced."

"Aye, I will."

He was closing the door behind him when Albert called, "Robert!"

Robert stuck his head back in.

Albert whispered, "Have a talk to Jo about this march of Rosie's."

Robert came back into the kitchen and shut the door behind him. "That's why I'm fetching her, to have her to meself."

"I don't know what I could have said to her...she's twenty-two and brilliant, and she's not wrong about the reasons for the march. I'm worried, of course, but what would you have me do?" asked Jo.

Robert drove the Imp smoothly along the coast road as the soothing dark of a December afternoon descended. At latitude 55.1869°N mid-December daylight shone on the faces of the people of Portstewart for a very short period of each day. The intense, shifting layers of sunset's purple, gold and orange, filling the western sky at the start of their journey, were pressed down to lines across the horizon behind the looming dark inkblot that was Inishowen.

"I'll tell you what *I'm* going to do. I'm going to follow the march. I'll trek all the way to Derry behind her and hope she doesn't spot me. In fact, the Imp and I will go ahead and wait, then drop back—play hopscotch around the march—in case I need to get her out of a bad situation. But you mustn't tell her."

"You don't actually think she won't see you?"

"I'll make sure she doesn't unless I'm needed."

"It's a four-day march, Robert. I should go with you, spell you. And Albert."

"Then I'll have *all* of you to worry about. I know you, remember—you wouldn't be able to keep our existence at the march a secret. Neither would Albert, sticking up above most as he does."

Jo laughed. "Very true. Listen, perhaps it won't be dangerous. Rosie explained that it's a nonsectarian march. The marchers will be Protestant and Catholic, and so will be the areas on the route —they'll be mixed, too. She said the march leaders think the non-sectarianism will be obvious as they march peacefully through Loyalist and Catholic towns and areas. There'll be no provocation."

Shaking his head, Robert said, "That makes no sense. The marchers will be coat-trailing and everyone along the route will know it. Rosie could walk anywhere she wanted with her friends and nobody would notice, unless they wanted them to— and they will want them to notice. Isn't that the point of the thing?"

Jo was silent as she looked around the dark interior of the car. "Possibly because I'm famished but it smells absolutely delicious in here. Something floral, but also potato and onion. May I hope for champ?"

He laughed and said, "You've detected one of the many dishes we drove up. Albert cooked ahead."

"Oh, thank goodness. I'm looking forward to it!"

Robert said, "Listen, I'll look after our girl, don't worry."

"Don't worry? If I didn't trust you so, I'd lock her in the flat on New Year's Eve."

"Things were easier when she was little, weren't they?"

Jo sighed. "Not for me, they weren't."

They drove through lights shining onto the dark road from the houses and hotels lining one side, while on the other side, the seaside, the sky was now night black. The car headlights picked out the white foam of the waves as they entered curves and dips.

Jo said, "Will *you* be all right? Nobody's going to ask which religion you are before cracking your head open. The violence in October was dreadful."

"She won't be wearing a sign either, which wouldn't help through the mix of communities anyway. That's why I'm going." Robert looked over at Jo's profile, so like Rosie's.

Jo ventured, "I have another worry about the girl. Two actually—two worries and news for ye."

"Two worries? What?"

"Most parents wouldn't worry about this, but she does nothing but work. I've seen her interested in neither man nor boy, have you?"

Robert thought for a moment. "There have been a couple of fellas who have been regulars—George and the other one, the handsome one, Iain. They seem like friends, though, not boyfriends. I wonder…does she like girls do you think?"

"I've seen no sign of that either. George and Iain are friends of hers, but there's no romance there. I hope she doesn't take after me and prefer wildly inappropriate older men. It could be the reason we've seen nobody."

Robert shrugged. "She may want a bit of privacy or perhaps she keeps herself to herself. What's the other worry?"

"Perhaps...oh, yes, the other worry. Take warning. Once she hones her already formidable prosecutorial skills, and that won't take long, she will winkle Bletchley out of us. She's taken to cross-examining me about what I did, what you did, what Holly did. Holly will crack—I've warned her as well."

Robert was silent for a moment before he laughed briefly. "You're right, Jo, most parents wouldn't worry about a cheerful, healthy daughter who is loving, takes her beauty with a pinch of salt, a witty and brilliant girl, serious about her studies, and helping the world."

"Put like that, you're right enough." Jo laughed.

"Holly will crack. Not sure you can do much about that. And the news for me?" asked Robert.

"Oh, yes. It's good news. Rosie's legacy from Johnny's estate has come through probate, finally. I'll be her trustee until she's thirty and I've begun weekly lectures on never touching the capital."

"Capital? Is it much then?"

"Aye, I'd say so—nearly 50,000 guineas..."

Robert whistled. "So that's what in pounds?"

"Twenty-five hundred pound more. They'll be tax of course. Solicitors count in guineas, accountants too, and in this case, it also works in Rosie's favor. Enough for her never to have to worry about money, nor her children—*if* she never touches the capital. The money comes with Johnny's house and land in Gloucestershire, a village near Cheltenham called Lower Slaughter..."

"Lower what? Slaughter?" Robert looked at her and laughed.

"When I rang them, I asked the family solicitor in Cheltenham, and he said slaughter in this case is from another word that meant wet land or muddy in Old English. Anyway, I like to imagine an ancient manor house, with lands and forests, however soggy. We've not seen the deed, map, or any photos yet. Anyway, I'm thankful she's such a wise girl. The money will

allow her to practice law as she chooses—to live as she chooses
—and I know she'll put it to good use."

"He never had any children, other than Rosie?"

"Not that the estate lawyers found, and they looked. No issue
besides our girl. His wife and siblings are dead. No nieces, nephews, cousins—no family living—just like me."

"How does she feel about his death? She told me when he
died but didn't say much. And what was his surname? I forget."

"Burford-Cox. John Charles Richard Burford-Cox, according
to the probate papers. She does clam up a wee bit when the
subject of Johnny comes up. She only met him a few times, but
he kept in touch with her, came to see her, even when I didn't
want him to, tried to send money regularly when I was still
struggling. Not that I let him. Had I known how much he was
worth...anyway, I'll give him that much. Of course, you did the
same, you and Albert, with much less of a cushion. She's very
grateful. I'm very grateful."

"You needn't be. She's our daughter."

They drove up the hill, parked in the small car park and sat
still for a moment, facing the warmth of lights blazing in the
cottages above.

Jo said, "Gratitude is a nice quality, I always think, and I'm
grateful that you think of her as your daughter. She is too."

Pulling the emergency brake with a smooth, strong tug,
Robert said, "I love her like a daughter. I couldn't think of her
otherwise. If there's gratitude going, it's that I have her."

PARTY TURN—DECEMBER 1968

PORTSTEWART

ecember 12th broke as a clear day, windless and mild, but as the day wore on, the temperature dropped as a cutting wind rose. At Meg and Lillian's cottage, the day was filled with laughter as old stories were retold, party preparations, drying the dog after walks on the strand, rearranging the parlor, and answering the ringing telephone. David and Niall arrived at two o'clock, just as Holly rang. A little breathlessly down the blower, Holly announced, "Mum's gone to work—I mean, can you even *believe* it? When I went out with our weekly messages she was as good as gold, sitting by the fire and knitting. I returned, not to a seated mother with a chesty cold doing as she was told, but to a note telling me to drive up and go to my party, she'd gone to work. I fairly flew around the flat just now, putting things away and packing. I'm still invited?"

Lillian said, "Of course you are!"

"See you around four, half past, I reckon."

"Holly, mind how you go in that wee MG of yours. The roads are icy up here, especially over the hills and bridges, alright? The gritters don't always get to them in time."

Holly laughed. "My beloved MG's gone. I drive a '67

Humber Super Snipe. It weighs three and a half tons. If I crash, I won't even feel it!"

~

"I could run you home—it's bitter cold, and the wind's worse," said Lillian, standing in the hallway as Reverend Theodore Horne struggled into his overcoat. "It'd be no trouble, Ted."

"Thank you, Lillian. That is kind, but I like a constitutional in the evenings. I find it a contemplative time and I sleep better for it. I've wrapped up warm."

Homburg pulled down, muffler wrapped around the upturned collar of his coat, the reverend pulled on gloves and tested his small torch.

"Goodnight, my dear, and happy birthday! See you at vespers tomorrow."

"Aye. Safe home," said Lillian. He waved from the lighted front path before turning into the darkness, the light of the small torch his savior.

Closing the door on the night's bitter chill, Lillian returned to the crowded parlor, where her mother's dining table and all its leaves and chairs had been arranged. Set and laid with pressed damask napkins and tablecloths, the polished silverware and wine glasses sparkled in the firelight.

A blast of wind down the chimney blew sparks onto the ancient hearthrug. Sitting in one of the armchairs alongside the fireplace, David tamped them with his shoe.

Rubbing her hands together, Lillian said, "The wind's back up. That's the Reverend off home. Told you he wouldn't stay. More sherry anyone? Whiskey?"

Niall said, "Whiskey please. I've been on call most Saturday nights for years, so this is a treat. A grand treat to be here with you on your birthday."

"One finger's worth, Lily, please," said Mildred from the twin chair on the opposite side of the fire.

David held his glass out and laughed, "Large one, please."

Sitting on the ottoman pulled in between the two armchairs at the grate, Holly said, "Same again, please."

"I'm nursing my birthday party whiskey," said Meg. Putting her glass down, she stood and said, "Let me see what they need in the kitchen."

"Yes, alright. We'll check with Albert on timing," said Lillian.

Holly said, "It smells luscious, whatever he's cooking."

After they handed the drinks around, Lillian and Meg left the room for the kitchen.

Mildred said, "Niall, I hate to ask, but would you look at one of my chickens tomorrow? Not to give you a busman's holiday, but our local vet is impossible, said he wouldn't look at poor Gertie's foot, and it looks so sore. The auld man's ninety if he's a minute and won't take on a younger man."

"Not at all, I don't mind. I'll look at them all. Cheers!"

Mildred laughed, "You're in rare spirits tonight, Niall."

Niall waggled his glass a bit. "I'm in spirits, for one thing, and if this isn't a jolly occasion, I don't know what is! Your man the vet is an old fool. He should retire and let younger people take the practice. I'm shifting my practice over to a young couple who completed their practicum with me. They've logged many hours at the surgery and calls to the farms for a year, and now they've taken over the on-call responsibility. I've been called out of bed to freezing barns and yards for long enough. They want to start a family, so I don't know how they'll juggle things then, but they come from large Ballycastle families, so. Anyway, I'll be able to retire entirely, perhaps next year, when I'm sixty-eight."

Mildred said, "Oh! One's a young woman vet then? I've never seen one of them."

Holly said, "We take our cats and dogs to a woman veterinarian. She came over after the war, from Yugoslavia, which is funny since Mum's doctor is a Yugoslavian woman, too. Worked in displaced persons camps until her patients were well enough to emigrate to Sweden and then she was out of a job. She came here and had to redo a lot of her training. She knows how to handle Mum alright, and in several languages. I keep meaning to ask if they know one another, the vet and the doctor, though I don't see why they would."

"How many do you have?" asked Niall.

"What, Yugoslavians?" Holly asked.

"No, cats, dogs," he said, laughing.

She laughed. "Two dachshunds, two cats."

A sharp rap of the brass front door knocker reached them from the hallway.

Looking at one another for a second, David said, "Maybe it's Ted come back? I'll go."

Holly, Mildred and Niall waited in silence in order to hear who was at the door.

"Oh, hello. Em, come in."

A woman's loud, cheery voice rang out. "Sorry to dishturb, but I was looking for Mildred. Make sure she's alright. Is she'ere? It's David, Meg's brother, 'n't it?"

Mildred muttered, "Tsk. For heaven's sake." She rose out of her armchair on the second try and walked into the hallway.

"What is it, Mary?" Mildred snapped.

David walked back into the parlor and made a face. "It's Mary O'Neill," he whispered.

They listened as Mary rattled on about her worry that Mildred wasn't home after dark.

"As you can see, I'm safe and sound, so you can make your way home."

Now Meg's voice reached those in the parlor. "Mary! What...?"

"Meg! I found I'd misshed, missed your birthday so I've brought a wee gift. Nothing much—a fair malt."

Mildred's voice rose. "Mary, I don't know what's got into you lately, but I'll speak my mind—you must stop barging into places uninvited, including my house, and especially when you've had too much to drink."

"I'm sure I'm not *barging* in. Am I Meg? I've only had a wee nip for the cold, so."

Rosie squeezed past the crowd in the hall and made her way into the parlor, smirking. David put his finger up to his lips.

Her voice rising, Meg said, "There was no need to buy me anything."

Lillian's voice joined the group in the hallway. "Whatever is the matter? They can hear you over the road."

"Mary wanted to wish us a happy birthday," said Meg. "As you can see."

"Ush?" asked Mary.

"Mary, please," said Mildred. "You've wished them well, now please go."

"Them?"

Meg said, "I think you should leave now. Please."

"I'll just stay for one drink, then I'm off."

Rosie giggled and whispered, "Where are the others? They must hear the row in the kitchen. I did."

David whispered, "Sure you don't think they're stupid enough to enter the fray with four Irishwomen—one drunk and disorderly, one ragin' and two on the boil? They're in the kitchen listening, same as us."

Niall and Holly laughed loudly, which provided the distraction Mary needed to slip past the gatekeepers and into the parlor.

Her scarf fell on the floor after her entrance. "Oh, hello! Now, David I've met, but...I'm Mary O'Neill." Bottle in one hand, she held her hand out to Niall.

Niall stood, took her hand, and said, "Niall Morrison."

With a little wave, Holly said, "Holly Aarons."

"Hullo, I'm Rosie Bray, Jo and Robert's daughter."

"Niall Morrison? Holly? Robert's daughter? Now I know a Jo Bray, but whoever are you all? What have you got to do with this lot?" Mary waved her free hand dangerously near the wine glasses and candlesticks on the set table.

"I'm Meg's grand-niece, and David's," said Rosie, looking at David nervously. "And Holly's godchild."

"Grand-niece?" Mary shook her head. "That's too complicated. It's lovely and warm in here. Let's have a drink."

Meg squeezed past to face her.

"Meg dear, the room is so crowded with this ridicule, thish ridiculously long table. Why didn't you let me throw the party for you? Remember the lovely dining room at Carstairs? I'm bringing it back to its glory."

"Mary, may I speak to you outside?" asked Meg, stooping to pick Mary's scarf up.

"In this bloody cold?" She belched. "'Scuse me."

"Here, Meg, let me," said Mildred. "Mary, there's something I need to discuss with you. Let's go to my cottage, alright?"

"Alright, in a moment—just a small drink. Would you pour, em, Niall is it?"

Mildred sighed deeply, "Give her a small one, then I'll shift her."

"I *am* right here, Mildred," said Mary, flopping into the armchair Mildred had vacated. Her head wobbled slightly as she smiled at Holly sitting on the ottoman. "You're a fat wee thing, aren't you? Like me. I don't remember when I got fat. Do you? What about that outfit you've on? Terrible."

Holly, munching on a cracker, looked down at her brightly colored, geometrically patterned blouse and grey suit. She brushed crumbs spotted off her chest and trousers.

"I love your blouse, Holly—very *au courant*," said Rosie.

"Thanks, Rosie. I bought it at Sinclair's. Pucci. I like the colors, the design."

Meg looked at Lillian, standing in the doorway, who waved her forward and the two retreated to the kitchen. Upon opening the kitchen door, they were greeted by delicious smells and an excited Biscuit.

Robert stood at the Belfast sink, peeling potatoes. Jo stood at the sideboard, arranging opened oysters and lemon slices in a platter filled with ice. An aproned Albert, his glasses partially fogged, stood at the range. He turned and asked, "What on earth is going on?"

"Mary O'Neill is what. Drinking and settled," said Lillian.

"Is she drunk?" asked Robert.

"And asking for more," said Meg.

Albert said, "Settled, you say? I've got to serve the quenelles in fifteen minutes or they'll congeal." Gesturing toward Jo, he said, "The oysters are ready now and they should be served first."

Jo raised her eyebrows and asked, "Mary O'Neill? Please don't tell her I'm here. I'm still her solicitor. No slanging matches with clients—first rule of the bar."

"That's the first rule of any bar," said Albert.

Robert turned and laughed.

"Rightee-o. Mildred and I will shift her out now." Squaring her shoulders, Lillian left the kitchen, closing the door behind her.

"Your roast smells wonderful," said Meg. "What can I do?"

"As one of the birthday girls, I'd say sit down and relax, but I understand the new visitor has made that impossible. What's she doing here? You never invited her?" asked Robert, shirt-sleeves rolled up over his biceps.

"No, of course not. She's been driving Mildred mad, always popping over uninvited. I imagine that when she found Mildred wasn't home, but our house was full of people, she decided to invite herself. She'd a bottle in her hand, which she claimed was a birthday gift for me, but it was open, and she's two sheets, so."

The door opened and Lillian announced, "Mildred can't shift her. She can't drive home, so we've got to get her up to Mildred's somehow." Hands on hips, she asked, "Well? What to do? We can't let her drink more, that's sure."

Albert shook his head and said, "I'm serving the quenelles in twelve minutes. The oysters should go on the table now with the white wine paired. Sounds like she doesn't need any wine, but will she grab it?"

"Maybe we should give her something to eat?" asked Robert.

"Not sure she could handle oysters or quenelles at this stage of her evening, and that would be a disaster," said Lillian.

Meg said, "I'll help Mildred get her over to her cottage. She can sleep it off there."

Meg walked into the parlor to find Mary holding court. "My guardian, Vincent Carstairs, MBE—well, my actual father he was, and my guardian...why hide it? You all must know, anyway..." After a moment of silence, she turned to Holly and asked, "Where was I?"

"Your father," said Holly, drily.

"Right you are, so."

David's eyebrows were pointed into his hairline.

Meg moved around the table to where Mary sat. "Listen, Mary, let's get you over to Mildred's cottage, shall we?" She put her hand out to help Mary out of the armchair.

"Do you know, Meggie dear? I'm quite peckish. I don't think I've eaten for a while. You couldn't squeeze an old friend in 'round that huge table, could you now?"

Flustered, Meg looked at Mildred.

"No, she cannot and we're going home now," said Mildred. "Right now."

"Aw now, leave off about bloody going, will ye? Now Meggie, conshidering what we once s'were to each other..." Mary's head and hair had fallen forward. She swayed slightly in the chair and the glass in her hand threatened to spill.

David stood and taking Mary's free hand, said, "Let's have a wee one for the road, alright?"

"Aye, alright. Thas the ticket."

David took the bottle and waggled it under her face. "In fact, let's have that drink over the road. I'll pour once we get there." He took her hand again and half pulled her up.

"Alright, alright, I'm coming." She tried to down the contents in her glass, but Meg pulled it out of her hand.

David pulled her upright.

"No need to pull me arm off." Mary belched and swayed dangerously as he led her past Holly and around the table. Meg and Mildred stepped out of their way.

"I'll get me coat," said Mildred.

David put his arm around Mary's shoulders to steady her.

Niall stood and said, "Let me help. I think we've only seconds before she blows."

The men ushered Mary into the hallway and out the door held open by Mildred. "Sit tight, Meggie, we've got her."

"Alright." Meg shut the door, turned, and found Rosie and Holly standing in the parlor doorway. "Come on girls, let's help serve this dinner. I'll not let Mary O'Neill spoil it."

Meg and Lillian sat at opposite ends of the table wearing paper party hats. Meg pulled hers off and said, "I think I'm going to explode, I've eaten so much. But I couldn't stop, it was so delicious, Albert."

"And this cake!" said Lillian, picking up the silver server to pull off a bit of icing.

"You won't let me help wash up, so I'm going to leave you young things and check on my charge," said Mildred, stifling a yawn.

"Young! Ha!" said Lillian.

"To me, you are. Happy birthdays, dear hearts. Thank you for the party, the delicious dinner, all of you."

"Here I'll walk you home, Mildred," said Niall.

"Tosh. There's no need, you sit down and rest yourself," said Mildred.

Niall said, "I've got to walk to our cottage anyway. Long week. Lots to drink."

"I'll come too. I could use a smoke," said David, winking broadly at Meg, who shook her head.

"Oh, now I've broken up the party!" wailed Mildred.

"It's alright, Milly. I don't think any of us are long for this world," said Lillian, stifling a yawn.

Rosie came into the room, the sleeves of her jumper pushed up. "What can I get anyone?"

Albert said, "Come back with water, dear one. Lots of it."

Rosie took the water pitcher off the table and made her way through the milling leave takers at the doorway.

"Aye, goodnight! See you tomorrow." Jo came into the room, pulling down the sleeves of her cardigan. "Well, that should do it. There's little left, just what's draining, and Rosie and Robert waved me off. I must say, Albert, in addition to cooking supremely well you clean up as you go. Most men don't do that, do they?" She looked around the sleepy group at the table.

"You're asking the wrong group," said Holly.

"Yes, I suppose I am. I was seeing a man for a short while who fancied himself a gourmet cook. The first time he cooked for me was at his place and the kitchen was a disaster but he insisted we leave it. The second time was in my kitchen and when he walked away from the disaster, it was the last time I saw him, even though his food was delicious. May I help myself to a nightcap?"

"Of course," said Lillian. "The wee bar is in the desktop, there."

"Thank you. I generally have a small something before turning the lights out. Sends me off like a top."

They listened to the clink of bottles being moved around. "Ah! Drambuie, perfect."

Jo returned to the table with her small glass.

"Did Robert talk to you about the march, Jo?" asked Albert.

"Yes, but you're not going to like it."

Albert said, "What? That he's going on it with her?"

Jo's eyebrows shot up. "How did you know? Has he told you?"

"No, but I know Robert. I'll go too."

"What march?" asked Holly.

Lowering her voice, Jo said, "Quickly, it's a civil rights march of students and activists from Belfast to Derry over four days. But Rosie mustn't hear us discussing it—it's hush-hush. Alright?" Turning back to Albert, Jo continued, "I don't think he'll let you. He refused to let me come with him because of my supposed indiscretion—me! a solicitor— and you since you're taller than most mortals she'd see you. His words."

"I don't see how he can stop me. What do you mean? That he plans to hide from her?" Albert sat up.

Jo raised her voice. "Yes, I…oh, hello, dear."

Rosie stood in the doorway holding a pitcher of water. "Who plans to hide from whom?"

Her mother answered, "Hmmm? Oh, we were talking about avoiding Mary O'Neill tomorrow. I plan to hide, should she stop over again."

"Rosie, be a dear and get me a clean water glass from the kitchen? I used the water glass for my wine," said Albert.

Rosie cocked her head to one side, but said, "Yes, of course."

They listened as the kitchen door opened and closed again.

"I'm usually the one to spill the beans, but not tonight, although all sorts of beans were spilled," said Holly.

Speaking in a low voice, Jo said, "He plans to sort of hopscotch the march in the Imp, take parallel routes to jump ahead, then fall back, and if there's trouble, which he's worried about, he'll scoop her up. He may have learnt subterfuge during the war."

"What? You're never talking about Robert? His thoughts are written on his face," said Holly, laughing.

Jo narrowed her eyes and gave her friend a long look.

"Oh," was all Holly said as she looked down.

Meg and Lillian, sitting next to one another on the sofa, exchanged a look. Lillian shrugged.

"Have I lost the plot again?" asked Albert. In answer to his question, however, Biscuit ran into the room, followed by Rosie with a tray of clean glasses and Robert, rolling his sleeves down.

Robert stood near Jo. "That looks good. What is it?"

"Drambuie, desktop, there," said Jo, pointing.

"May I?"

"Only if you get me one," said Lillian.

He asked, "Anyone else?"

"Water for me, thanks," said Meg.

"Drambuie," said Holly.

"Water," said Albert, raising the pitcher to fill the glasses.

"Rosie?" asked Robert, as he pulled the bottle out of the cupboard.

"No, thanks, Pa. Water for me, too, please. I'm up early tomorrow—still have a few exams left before end of term so I thought I'd get a few hours in swotting. In fact, I think I'll get myself to bed." She drank from the glass handed to her.

"Have you a torch, love?" asked Meg.

"I do. Wonderful meal, wonderful party. Especially Mary O'Neill's party turn."

"I wonder how Mary O'Neill is now?" asked Holly, curling her lip.

"Out like a light I should think," said Lillian.

"Night-night all," said Rosie blowing kisses to everyone.

The older people called their goodnights.

After Rosie closed the parlor door, the group fell into silence, broken by Holly. "Meg, you knew Mary…a long time ago, I think."

"I did. When we were young."

"Was she always…?"

Meg said, "Peculiar? I suppose so, yes."

Holly began to laugh. "Sorry, but did you hear her ask me when she'd got fat? She only said that after calling me a fat wee thing, just like her." Holly wheezed. "Which is only the truth on both ends." Her laughter made the others laugh—all except Meg.

"No, she wasn't fat when we were young, or drunken. It's a shame she's so unhappy," said Meg, frowning.

The laughter in the room stopped abruptly.

"Aye, all the money in the world, to do whatever she likes… travel, all sorts, she could enjoy herself," said Lillian.

Meg said, "We're spoiling the party now, Lily. Time for bed. What about the dog?" Meg pointed at Biscuit, lying on the rug in front of the fire, sound asleep and paws twitching in a dream.

"I'll take her out before we go to bed," said Robert. "Go on then."

"And me, I'm done for," said Albert, who standing, stretched. "Night-night."

"I won't be long," said Robert.

"For heaven's sake, let's sit in the comfortable chairs," said Jo quietly.

The three old friends moved to the armchairs and sofa with their glasses. They sat drinking the spicy amber liquid and staring into the fire. Quietly, Jo said, "Rosie's been asking a lot of questions about the war. Has she asked you lately?"

"Yes," said Robert. "Wanting to know *exactly* what I was doing when I met you two."

"And me," said Holly. "I stick to the sending messages, receiving them, boring, boring, routine line, but she probes very well."

"Aye, she does," said Jo. "She'll be a good barrister."

"Nothing to be done about it. We can't tell her," said Robert.

"Not ever. I hadn't realized what a burden it would be before I had a grown daughter," added Jo.

"Be on your guard, Robert. You know she can twist you 'round," said Holly, holding up a pinky.

He sighed. "Aye, she can that."

"Let's turn ourselves in," said Holly, yawning.

"Biscuit and I will walk you over to the cottage."

He stood and offered Jo a hand up, then Holly.

"God, I'm that stiff. Mary's right about one thing, I am a wee fat thing. Time was I could eat and eat and drink, and never gain an ounce. I might have to take some exercise. God help me."

Jo asked, "Let's start tomorrow and take a long walk on the strand before we go back, alright? I could use the exercise, too."

"And me," said Robert, patting his stomach.

"Ach, you! You look fit, as always," said Holly.

Moving to the hall and the coat stand, Jo said, "Rosie'll want to come. She's in training for the march."

"I should train for it, too," said Robert, winking at Jo.

BURNTOLLET BRIDGE—4
JANUARY 1969

DERRY—BELFAST

*R*obert stopped the car in the road. Driving ahead of the march toward Derry City, he'd arrived at a small bridge over the River Faughan—Burntollet Bridge. A crowd blocked the other end of the bridge, police vans parked straight across, a line of police and civilians carrying long sticks. Above the bridge and lining a ridge, at least one hundred men stood behind a stunted hedgerow and watched him before taking action. The road leading onto the bridge was so narrow, it took many turns of the wheel and four frantic changes of gear to turn the Imp around. As he worked the wheel and gearbox, rocks pelted the top of the Imp, crashed and bounced around the little car.

The civil rights marchers from Belfast were nearing the bridge, he could hear them singing, but they were still out of sight. Back the way he'd come was a pullover carved out of hedgerow. He drove back, pulled into it, parked the Imp and, sweating from his exertions and first flush of fear, urged his brain to calculate the right action to take quickly.

He suddenly felt tired and muddled. His overwhelming thoughts a longing for a decent night's sleep and a hot meal. Tapping his fingers on the steering wheel, he struggled to think what to do, but his thoughts wandered to the previous evening. After ringing Albert from Killaloo, he'd spent his third night in the car, the pubs and hostels on the march route having closed to strangers. With the backseat and passenger bucket seat folded down, the back of the Imp was roomy, but he couldn't lie flat and so slept badly. Before leaving home, he'd kitted the back with a sleeping bag, camp stove and kettle from a mountaineering shop in Belfast. A pillow, towel, bar of soap, toothbrush and paste, and changes of clothing in his old RN kit bag completed his home on wheels. In each town he'd managed to buy food and fill the kettle and bottles with water. In the yards of friendly farmers and empty parking areas, he'd boiled water for tea and a navy wash.

The BP Map of Northern Ireland for motorists was well-creased, as he'd lost the march many times during the course of the three days. Each time the Royal Ulster Constabulary had rerouted the march, Robert had had to scramble to find an alternate route to jump ahead or follow.

While explaining this to Albert from a phone box, he'd heard the now-familiar wracking cough interrupting Albert's worried demands. Stricken with 'flu on Boxing Day, Albert finally admitted how sick he was on New Year's Eve as shivering, he got into bed and lay his burning head down. Now he was convalescing and cranky.

"For God's sake, pull her out of there before something happens and get yourselves home!" Cough, cough, cough. "Sorry."

"Do you have a fever still?"

"I don't think so."

"Has Jo been?"

"Yes, she came this morning and made tea and"—cough, cough, cough—"a boiled egg, toast. Left chesty cough syrup and the Tele. Bless her. No chit-chat, just assessed my condition and got on with it. I've got the last of Holly's soup to heat. I wish I could taste it. I'm fine." Cough, cough, cough, hack. "Ach!"

Shaking himself out of this useless reverie, Robert got out of the car, locked it and hurried toward the head of the march, waving his arms. This was no time for secrecy and continuing to hide from Rosie—the marchers were walking into a trap and he had to warn them. Several young people held a long banner on sticks at the head of the march. Scanning their faces, he found a young man at the front who was not singing "We Shall Overcome," but watching Robert. Robert waved more frantically as he moved toward the young man. Walking backwards in front of him, he explained the trap-like situation ahead on the bridge, pointing, and described the presence of men who lined the ridge. The bridge came into clear view for the marchers. Some of the police officers had moved forward to the marchers' end of the bridge. The young man brushed by Robert and walked toward the most senior-looking officer. Robert followed to listen.

As the older officer solemnly explained that the march would have safe conduct across if they stayed pressed against one side of the road, the marchers behind them stopped singing and walking. The young man was handed a bull horn and he instructed the marchers to press against the righthand side of the road while crossing.

Robert stepped back and to one side of the flow of the march as it started again and began to look for Rosie.

The sound of bottles smashing and ricochet of rocks reached him as the screaming began. Walking into the middle of the part of the march that hadn't reached the bridge, Robert strode into the stream of young people, who continued moving around him and forward.

Unintelligible instructions continued to be issued through a bull horn. The marchers ahead of him stopped and the sounds of the screams intensified.

He stood, waiting for her. Rocks and bottles rang around him, pinging off the metal bridge railings behind him, hitting the humans with dull thuds, followed by piercing screams. Around him, hands and arms were held up to protect heads as marchers passed. Up on the ridge, the men were joined by women and children—he could hear their high-pitched oaths—coming through the gaps in the hedge to hurl objects down on the marchers.

A dark, familiar head was just behind the next row of marchers, moving inexorably forward. He pushed his way toward her.

"Rosie!"

"Pa! What…?"

Grabbing her arm he tried to push her back and off to the side of the road, but the force of the marchers moving forward held them in place.

"Get off the bridge! Get off the bridge!" Robert shouted, his arm around Rosie.

Ahead, people began jumping off the bridge as a phalanx of weapon-bearing civilians moved forward through the crowd. Wielding long sticks and bicycle chains, they began beating the bleeding injured, lying and sitting on the bridge pavement, before turning to those hesitating on the parapets. The River Faughan filled with the splashes of students, waist-high in freezing water stained with blood. The screams under the bridge reverberated. Panicked voices yelling instructions criss-crossed the bowl that was formed by the bridge and road.

Those up on the ridge turned their bottle- and rock-throwing attention to the group trying to flee back the way they'd come. Robert and Rosie were pelted with rocks, thuds barely noticeable in the noise of the melee. Crouching and trying to run, Robert placed his arms over Rosie's head to shield her. "Run! Run!"

He clocked a missile approaching at the extreme limit of his peripheral vision, the vision that had made him a Huff-Duff man, but it was too late. The bottle hit the left side of his face with force, shattering, lodging and cutting. He screamed and fell down, his hands covering his face as the blood poured. As forcefully as he could manage, he yelled, "Run, jump!"

"Get up! Come with me!" Pulling on his coat, she tried to move him but managed a few inches only.

Pain, unlike any he'd experienced, radiated from his head and eye.

Running feet trod on him. Into his own bloody hands, he whimpered, "Help me."

He heard her yell, "Get off him! No! No!"

Something hit his knee with such force, again and again. Relentless. To his own ears, his screams sounded like an animal's, like the screams he'd heard from below deck on the sinking ship his ship had failed to rescue. He curled, knees to chest, but the thing striking him found his kneecap over and over. He dared not take his hands off his face. After the hardest blow, it stopped.

He was moving again, through the roar of the crowd, but not under his own steam. People carried him by the arms, as blood poured from his head. He screamed again as his foot dragged.

Into his right ear, Rosie yelled. "Pa! Is the Imp parked near us? Can you point?" Rosie's face, blurry behind the curtain of his blood.

He could not see well, but he pointed straight ahead. After a few yards, hands rooted in his overcoat pockets for the keys. The back hatch was opened as he was half-carried to the passenger seat. Out of his right eye he saw Rosie get into the driver's seat and switch on the motor. The Imp rocked up and down, again, again, and again. The doors closed and there was quiet except for the girl crying behind him. He closed his right eye and put his head back, one hand trying to hold his left eye in its socket.

He felt Rosie reverse and drive away. "We must get him to hospital, her too. Have you got a handkerchief he could use?"

A deep male voice behind him said, "Here, put that on your eye. It's clean." A cloth was pressed into his free hand. "We've got to continue toward Derry, that's the closest hospital, the Altnagelvin is, as far as I know." The deep voice quavered.

"But how?" asked Rosie.

Behind him, the woman continued to cry.

Blindly, Robert pointed down the road ahead. Coughing, he said, "...a crossing. I..." The taste of metal filled his mouth. He spluttered, "Killaloo."

Deep Voice murmured, "You're safe now." He patted Robert's shoulder.

The girl in the back sobbed. "But the police said we'd be all right."

Another male voice, different from Deep Voice's, said, "Should have known. The bastards."

Something was tugging at him, prodding and pushing. He came up out of a dreamless state, opened his right eye in the dark. A bright light flicked on behind his head and he shut his eye quickly. Two hands, a stab of sharp pain. He opened the right eye again. A woman, a nurse, her white cap winged, hovered. She had a beaky nose, angry black eyes, a significant moustache, and dark, greying eyebrows. A hawk.

Loudly she said, "I've given you something for the pain."

Looking over her shoulder for a moment, she leant down and brought her face too close to his good eye.

He flinched.

Eyes narrowed, her face twisted as she hissed, "You deserved what you got, you and the other Fenian rubbish. Bringing trouble to our town...go back to your Catholic slums in Belfast. You've lost your eye, you know. Tomorrow they'll tell you a specialist can help, but he can't. Your leg's a wreck, too. Good on whoever hit you."

He felt sweat dripping down the sides of his torso.

With that, she pulled away and stood up straight. She fiddled with his drip and turned the light off. On her way past the cast on his right leg, she gave it a nudge, setting off a flash of fire from knee to brain. He cried out, but she continued to walk out of the ward toward a blue light at the end of the corridor.

He blinked but could feel nothing on the left side. Gingerly, he tried to touch his left eye but found instead a large and thick bandage, not his eye, nor most of the side of his face. Only a large, raised bandage.

∿

"Pa, Pa, it's me."

Rosie's voice. Rosie. He opened the right eye and there she was, framed by the daylight streaming through the window. People around them coughed, rustled, moaned.

He tried to say her name, but croaked and put his hand up to screen the light.

"Are you allowed water?"

He had no answer.

"I'll be right back."

Watching her walk away, he wanted to cry out. He closed the eye. She returned immediately. "You're not allowed to swallow, but you can rinse. Here, let me help."

One hand under his head, she lifted gently. A glass was pressed to his parched lips.

"I've got you. Rinse and spit, Pa. That's it." She lowered his head gently back to the pillow.

An unseen woman's voice said, "Mr. Henderson, I'll ask the attending when you can drink and eat. He'll be on his rounds soon. For now, I'm afraid you're allowed nil by mouth."

Fingers gently held his wrist, then "Under your tongue, now," and the cold of glass and metal in his mouth. After a few minutes, "Good. All normal."

Afraid to open his eye, he listened.

Rosie asked, "Is he in pain? Can you give him something for it, please?"

"He's due for injection in half an hour. It will help."

The nurse's voice sounded mild enough, so he opened his eye. A pretty young nursing sister in a different uniform. *Not last night's witch. She'd been a hawk in uniform. Had that even happened?*

The nurse wrote something and then moved away.

Rosie sat down on the bed on his right side. Turning his head, he could see that her coat was covered in dried blood. Following his gaze, she wriggled out of it.

"Sorry, Pa, it's bitterly cold today—I'd no choice but to wear it." She shrugged. "Holly's driving Mum up—they'll be here very soon. She's talked Albert into staying in bed so that he gets well. He was frantic to come, but she prevailed."

"Where…?"

"Where are we? Outside Derry in the Altnagelvin Hospital. It's Sunday, January 5th."

Taking his hands in hers, she leant forward and said, "I am so sorry. This is my fault, my arrogance. The march was stupid, trying to cross the bridge, only a disaster. Not the reasons, but the planning." Tears filled her eyes and she stopped talking. He grasped her hands for a moment, nodded slightly, and closed his eye.

Whispers woke him. Two, three? voices. Speaking over one another and with some urgency, but in whispers.

The whispers stopped.

Robert woke to rocking. He was on board ship, rocking in his bunk, but there was no engine sound. Why were they stopped? It was dangerous not to sail at speed—safest at full speed. At full stop they were sitting ducks for the U-boats. He listened and opened his eyes. It was dark in the bunk deck, the only light a blue one at the far side. Blue light meant what? He'd forgotten. Danger? All's well? U-boat sighted? All hands on deck?

He slept again, but was awakened by singing. Opening his eyes, he saw Jimmy Byrne, perched up on his top bunk, singing.

Jimmy grinned at him. Robert felt very afraid then, because Jimmy Byrne had been killed in action, swept overboard and drowned whilst on a team tying up a captured U-boat. Robert dared not move. Rigid with terror, he watched Jimmy sing the entire song. Jimmy jumped down from the top bunk and came toward him, thumbs in the waist of his bell-bottoms and with a rolling gait, grinning. A devilish grin.

"Ah!" His throat felt like he'd swallowed sand. "Ah!" The scream stuck. He pulled his hands up to cover his face. More pain.

A hand touched him and he jumped as though struck. He opened his right eye in a panic. A nurse stood at his side, her hand took his. He tried to pull away, but her face remained gentle and kind. Not the witch, not the hawk. Her voice low, kind. "Wake now. You're safe now, safe."

"Robert." A woman's voice. A hand on his shoulder, gentle. He opened his eye. Jo's face, soft and worried. "We're here. We've come to fetch you home." She took his hand.

Next to Jo, looking down at him, Rosie appeared. Someone took his other hand. Holly.

"The ambulance men are here now with the gurney. The doctor said that you'd fare better in hospital with specialists, so I've arranged it. We hired a nurse for the journey to Belfast. They'll move you now."

"Wait," he croaked.

"What is it, Pa?"

"Where?"

"Outside Derry City, Pa. But we're taking you home to Belfast. I'll ride in the ambulance with you."

"No. Albert. Where?"

Jo said, "He's down with 'flu still. He was frantic to come, but I told him he needed to stay in bed and get well, for your sake. You'll see him in Belfast."

"'Flu?"

Rosie and Jo looked at one another. Jo frowned.

The ward nurse walked to the foot of his bed with two men pushing a gurney. A nurse in a cloak accompanied them. "This is the patient, Nurse. May I see your paperwork please?" After a few moments, "Everything's in order, then." She took Robert's wrist and looked at her watch. "Mr. Henderson. We're going to move you onto this gurney now, preparatory to your ambulance trip to Belfast. We'll be gentle. Ladies, would you wait in the corridor please?"

"I'll be with you, Pa. We'll just be outside."

The three women stepped away and walked down the corridor. They sat on a straight-backed bench opposite the nursing station.

"He doesn't seem to remember things," said Jo. "Things he should do."

Sitting in between mother and daughter, Holly asked, "He had quite the bang on the head, hadn't he? Concussion is it?"

"Mmmm. Might be. He'll need a lot of mending. A lot of care," said Jo.

"Oh, God, what have I done?" asked Rosie.

"*You* didn't do anything. The mad bastards who hurt him did. Police—meant to protect him—hurt him instead. All because they thought he was Catholic. Don't forget that," said Holly.

"Holly's right, Rosie. You'll need to help your Pa mend. We all will. Focus on that. Anyway, you might have been the one in the hospital bed if he hadn't come to protect you. I'm very grateful to him."

"Yes, of course, Ma. A moment of self-indulgence. Sorry."

Holly patted her hand. "Have you told his father?"

Shaking her head, she said, "I plan to, but I'll tell him in person when I fetch him to the Royal Victoria for visiting hours."

Jo leaned over to touch Rosie's hand and said, "Let's put one foot in front of the other. First thing, get Robert to Belfast and the specialists without further injuring him. As soon as we know how he fared after the journey, tell Ralph."

"He won't be well pleased," said Rosie, quickly wiping a tear from her cheek. "With me or Pa. Me especially."

"Mind, I suspect he'll be so upset about Robert's injuries all the prejudices will come spilling out—I've seen him in action before. He becomes upset and worried about something in Robert's life, he lectures him, Robert pushes back, Ralph says what he's wisely kept unsaid, they explode," said Jo. "It happens, parents fret, but with Ralph, he lets everything fly. But we'll focus on helping Robert heal. Albert will need our help, too."

"How is he feeling, do you know?" asked Rosie.

Jo said, "I talked to him yesterday and his voice still sounds awful. Oh, that reminds me, I said I'd ring him when we're on the way. I'll ask the sister where I might find a call box." Jo rose and walked over to the desk. From the gestures and pointing, it appeared that the phone box was some distance. The nurse looked around before handing Jo the telephone on the desk. Glasses on, Jo dialled the number.

Robert's gurney was pushed past Holly and Rosie toward the elevator.

"I'm off with Pa, Holly. Will you follow us, keep us in view?"

"Tell the driver to wait for us before driving off, then we'll be right behind you. We won't let you out of our sight."

Rosie ran over to the group waiting at the elevator. As she passed, she waved at her mother, who waved in return. The elevator door opened and the large group squeezed inside. The hospital nurse closed the gate behind them and the elevator descended.

On the line with Albert, Jo said, "They're going down in the elevator now. Yes, we'll follow them to Belfast. Do you want me to ring…? I will, don't worry."

Holly was standing next to her when she rang off.

"Thank you so much, Sister. That was kind," said Jo.

The two women hurried down to the main entrance. Jo began to rush through the front door, but Holly stopped her. "I must use the loo before crossing Northern Ireland again. I swear you're a camel, but I'm not."

"No, you're right, unless they stop, we won't. Let's find one. Quickly, now."

Albert sat in the visitor's chair. Robert's head was turned toward him, his one eye trained on Albert's face. "Mr. Davidson suggested we use his own barber. Your lovely beard will have to go for the eye operation. The man even rang him for us. I mean, imagine a surgeon going through all that trouble! The barber will come in about an hour."

Gesturing to his face, Robert asked, "Will it hurt?"

"I shouldn't think so. What? What is it?"

A tear rolled down Robert's exposed cheek. "It's just that everything hurts. I can't bear much more…"

"Oh, my dear." Albert took his hand in his.

Albert looked at his watch. "There's more pain to bear, I'm afraid. Rosie is bringing your father to visit. They'll be here any minute. She'd planned to tell him what happened and what your injuries are, then come here with him. She's a brave girl."

"Is she alright? Not blaming herself?"

"She blames herself, of course. Jo and Holly have talked to her, I have too, but…"

"Alright, I will talk to her, but…will you take him home so we can talk properly?"

"Aye, I'll try." Holding a handkerchief over his mouth, Albert coughed before saying, "Here, let's put your head up a bit."

Albert slowly cranked the bed up a few degrees. "Alright?" Turning, he said, "Oh, here they are."

Ralph, stooped and cap in hand, walked with Rosie, who held his arm. She was as pale as the hospital bedsheets.

Coming up to Robert's bedside, his father said, "Oh, my God! Would ye look at what they've done to my boy?"

"Sit here, Ralph," said Albert.

"What? Oh, you're here. I thought they said family only."

Rosie frowned, but Albert flashed a brilliant smile and said, "Yes, well, I told the nursing sisters we were cousins."

Ralph sniffed and sat down. "You're quick on your feet. How are you, son?"

Robert was working at looking cheerful, Albert could tell, but with half his head swathed in thick bandages and his leg, fresh from an operation, covered by a hoop under the sheet, the task was difficult.

Rosie hovered nervously.

"Alright, Da. They're taking good care of me. Everyone is." Robert reached for Rosie's hand, who took it and perched on the other side of the bed.

"Rosie's told me where ye were and what ye were doing. I could hardly believe me ears. What were you thinking of? To lose an eye and use of your leg? It's beyond me...to take your chances with the likes of them...who was it, Fenian rubbish? You don't know it wasn't one of them who done it, mind." Ralph wiped his mouth with a shaking hand, the few white hairs on his head picked out by the light streaming through the window.

Robert said, "I d-do know. RUC and P-Protestant t-towns..."

Albert spoke firmly. "We don't know that his eye can't be saved and after this operation, we were given to believe that his leg will mend well. It will take time and a lot of physio, possibly another opera..."

Ralph looked up at Albert, his watery blue eyes narrowed. "'We'?"

"Yes, us." Albert gestured to Robert, Rosie, himself, with a circular motion.

"I see. Us. Tell me this—where were you when he was getting beaten to a pulp?"

Albert lost his breezy air and colored. "I was down with 'flu."

Ralph shook his head and sneering, said, "'Flu was it?"

Rosie piped up to say, "I don't think this is helping, Granda."

"What do you know, you stupid wee girl? You're the reason he's lying here now, a wreck!"

"S-stop, D-Da. Now," said Robert.

The nursing sister arrived at the foot of the bed with a rustle. "The patient is to be kept calm and quiet—all my patients require it. I'll have to ask all of you to leave if there's one second more of this carry on."

"That's alright, Sister. I'm leaving," said Ralph, rising.

"D-Da—"

In tears, Rosie said, "Granda, don't!"

Pointing at Albert, Ralph said, "Just so you know, Sister, he's not family to *us*. *He* shouldn't be here, but I see I'm the one not wanted." He shuffled toward the door, banging into a bedside tray stand as he passed the last bed.

"I'll fetch him," said Rosie, standing.

Robert kept her hand in his. "N-no. L-leave him be. He was s-spoiling for a d-donnybrook."

Albert sat down in the vacated chair. "He found it."

"Is this true? The rules are family only," said the nurse, looking flustered.

"N-no, it's n-not t-true. He's family," said Robert.

"Sorry. We'll be calm and quiet," said Rosie.

"Alright, so." The nurse shifted her gaze, pulled the chart off its hook and took it with her.

They watched the starched white form walk away.

Albert braced his hands on his thighs and looked down at his feet. "I nearly said something I shouldn't."

Robert answered, "I'm not so sure you shouldn't, but not with him like that. Not with me like this."

Rosie blinked and asked, "What do you mean? What—which did you mean, about saying something you shouldn't? About you and Pa, or about me not being Pa's actual child?"

Albert walked over to Rosie and put his arm around her shoulder. "I wouldn't do such a thing, certainly not to you, but not even to Ralph. You are Robert's daughter and you've always called me uncle. I feel that way, I hope you do."

"Oh, Uncle Albert, of course I do."

Robert put his hand up to touch her arm, "Don't let his t-temper shake you like this. Please."

She kissed Albert's cheek and leaning down, kissed Robert's forehead over his good eye. "I won't, Pa. I'm just upset."

"It must have been hard, telling Ralph. You were very brave, Rosie," said Albert. "He doesn't make things easy."

Robert said, "N-no. But when there was real trouble, like the b-bombings, he protected us, stayed calm, steady. He made me feel safe. But little things? Especially if he thinks he's been insulted or made a f-figure of f-fun, he flies off the handle, as though he'd the right to lose his mind over every trifle. My mother was the opposite—steady and calm, thoughtful. Strong, except for during the bombing, which makes more sense to me. But he's gotten worse with age—s-starting when we lost her."

Rosie said, "I wish I'd known her."

"And me, but she knew about you, and it m-made her last day very happy. I'm happy I t-told them you were mine, I'm happier it's come true."

"Oh, Pa! You've made me cry again and I've no handkerchief."

Albert reached into his breast pocket and said, "Here. It's clean."

Robert thought about his father, whom he imagined standing like a ghost at the hospital tram call, despondent, this very minute, full of regret, especially about calling his beloved Rosie a "stupid wee girl." Once at home, he'd sit and stare, and swing from self-pity, back to rage and on to the realization that he could have, should have kept his anger to himself. Robert had seen him stew in swings of self-immolation often enough. Picturing his mother's reaction to such an event, he smiled. "Now, Ralph, you know you got yourself twisted in a knot for little reason. Why do you let yourself have a go at people? It's always you who suffers. They roll their eyes and go off for pint. Why not say sorry and have it done with?"

In answer to her question, Ralph, sitting stubbornly still, would puff his lower lip out, just like a toddler, at which point Florrie would look at Robert with a barely suppressed smile until the two of them erupted with laughter, making Ralph so mad he'd stomp out of the house, only to return an hour later with his tail between his legs, a bag of sweets in one hand, flowers in the other. There was no Florrie to help him now.

He'll not let himself apologize and get this blown over. No, he'll suffer because of what he said more than Rosie will, far more than I will, certainly more than Albert ever will. Oh, Da, you silly auld bugger. Robert decided to ring him as soon as the nurse would bring him a telephone.

EVERYTHING WILL BE ALL RIGHT
—WINTER-SPRING 1969

BELFAST

*W*ave after wave: fear, dread, anger, self-pity— every day and especially during the long nights in hospital. Royal Victoria hospital had stopped giving him whatever drug the hospital near Derry had. The Derry drug made him feel awful, but knocked him out. A blessing. Without it, he often was awake feeling several points of pain. The only relaxation he'd had was during the haircut and shave the surgeon's barber had given him that morning.

His nearest and dearest did little to calm him. Scrabbling and tussling with one another as they had. *No, that wasn't fair. It was all Da, not Rosie or Albert.*

The last day of waiting for the eye surgery. Tomorrow morning, he'd be wheeled into the operating room. The afternoon visiting hours began. Other people's visitors walked hesitantly into the ward and then to their person's bedside. Rosie walked in with more confidence, holding Ralph's arm. Ralph, stooped and shuffling a little, walked as though he'd never been on the ward before.

Rosie smiled and said, "I walked over to Granda's house. He'd just rung off with you and wanted to come back with me, so after a quick lunch, here we are!" Eyes wide, her hands flew to her mouth. "Oh my goodness! Your face!"

Looking from one to the other, he saw that somehow they'd made it up, imposter granddaughter and grandfather. Robert didn't know how, exactly, but he was sure Rosie had done all the work.

"Bad?"

"No, no, not at all. You're very handsome, but I've just never seen you without a beard. Not ever."

"You look fine, son, fine. Like yourself when a boy," Ralph added.

The two stood over him peering at his face for more than a few seconds, but they moved back when a woman brought a bowl of soup on a tray and gruffly placed it on the bedstand for him, leaving without a word. Now they sat watching while he slurped, Ralph on his blind side. Nobody spoke.

Dropping the soup spoon down with a clatter, he said, "This is like dishwater."

"Are you hungry, Pa?"

"I thought I was." Robert turned his head. "You're quiet, Da. C-cat got your tongue?" With that, he could have bitten his own tongue.

Ralph shrugged, his watery blue eyes unfocused, his mouth slack.

Pitiful.

Rosie spoke brightly. "Albert says the head of the medical school at Queen's is chuffed to have Mr. Davidson on the faculty. He's an internationally renowned surgeon, apparently."

"Where is he?"

"Mr. Davidson?"

Robert said "No. Albert."

Rosie looked quickly at Ralph before saying, "He has class this afternoon. He'll be back as soon as possible. He did say."

Robert closed his good eye and rested. Rest led to sleep. When he woke, Rosie and his father were gone. Instead, Albert sat in the chair, writing in a notebook propped on a crossed leg, ankle to knee, glasses near the end of his nose.

Albert looked up "Oh, hullo. How are you, old love?"

"Terrible. Banjaxed entirely."

"You look very handsome. Your face, from what I can see, like when we were boys."

"Pain."

"Ah. You're in pain. I'm so sorry."

"Pain, yes. Fear, dread. Anxiety almost worse than on board ship with U-boats underneath."

"Hasn't that nurse given you something for any of it? Shall I fetch her?"

"She says she does, but it doesn't work very well."

"Shall I ring Davidson? I've met him at faculty dinners. He's terribly interested in antibiotic resistance and our research. Unusual in a surgeon, I would have…"

"No. He'll make rounds after visiting hours. He stops to see how I am every evening. I've only a few hours left. He's already told me the eye pain will disappear shortly after the operation."

"But that's wonderful news!" Albert leant closer and asked softly, "What about your eye—the chances of saving it?"

"He said he won't really know until he's operating. T-to be honest, I really d-didn't want to know more, so I d-didn't ask."

Barely audibly, Albert asked, "Didn't you?"

"No. I'm afraid of the answer. I'm afraid, f-full s-stop."

Albert put his notebook and pen on the bed. He put his hand on Robert's arm and whispered, "I'm so sorry. If it makes any difference, I do love you very much. Rosie loves you and I'll throw Ralph in for nothing, and the rest of the family. We'll work to help you mend."

"It does make a difference of course, but…"

"If I could change places with you, I would."

"Would you?"

"A useless hypothetical, but yes, I would."

A nurse came into the ward and rang a little bell, signalling the end of visiting hours.

"I'll be right here when you wake up after the operation. And in the morning, I'll be in the waiting room during the operation. I've cancelled everything."

"Albert?"

"Yes?"

"I love you, too. Very much."

Albert smiled, leant down as though he wanted to whisper something, and kissed Robert on the lips, briefly but firmly.

"Mr. Henderson. Mr. Henderson." Who was calling his father? Why couldn't they be quiet? All he wanted to do was sleep.

A hand resting on his shoulder. Slowly he came drifting up. He didn't want to, it was such a deep sleep, but they'd woken him. He opened one eye, the other would not budge.

A kind face, leaning over him. A young woman, she smiled. "Mr. Henderson, Mr. Davidson will be in to talk to you shortly." A gentle, sibilant accent. County Fermanagh? "Are you awake? Good. Now, I'll raise the head of the bed gently. Would you like some water?"

He croaked, then nodded slightly.

"A wee sip only." A glass straw was put to his lips and he drank.

"Nurse?" a male voice. The nurse melted away as Mr. Davidson's large head swathed in an operating cap hovered overhead. "You've done very well, Mr. Henderson. Very well. You'll have no pain for several hours."

Robert pointed to his eye.

"Yes, no pain in your eye. Mr. Kidd is organizing the pain management and rehabilitation of your leg. We had a chat yesterday. He'll be to see you later today, when you're back on the ward."

Continuing to watch the man closely, Robert whispered, "My eye, is it…?"

"I'm very sorry, but no. We could not save it. We used all of our skills, but it was too damaged."

Mr. Davidson and Robert looked at one another for a few beats.

"We'll talk about all of it tomorrow. I'll let them take you down to recovery now where they'll keep you for a wee while." The man patted his shoulder. "I'll visit your family in the waiting room now, tell them the outcome."

With that, he was gone and Robert was alone again with the nurse. "I'll be with you in the recovery room, Mr. Henderson. Go on and rest, now. Rest." She placed a small kidney-shaped metal pan next to the right side of his head. "If you feel sick, the wee pan's right here. We'll take you down to recovery now."

The gurney hesitated at the ward door while some adjustment was made before proceeding to his bed, the agent of this action unseen. Rosie, Ralph and Albert waited bedside for him. Rosie pale-faced and red-nosed, Ralph seated and trying to bring the glass of water shaking in his hands to his lips successfully, and Albert flushed, tie loosened, top shirt button undone.

Albert smiled at him. Everyone moved back while two porters and a nurse moved him from gurney to bed with a coordinated swoop. He gasped with the pain to his leg. The nurse straightened and made adjustments to his IV drip.

"Post-operative visitors are allowed ten minutes only, I'm sorry." With silent tread, she walked away.

Rosie looked up at Albert.

Ralph said, "Bout ye? Alright? The surgeon said you did well in the surgery, very well indeed, son. I told him, a strong lad like ye…" He patted Robert's chest lightly, cleared his throat and turned his head away.

Albert waited a moment before saying, "Mr. Davidson told us about your eye. He's given you more anaesthetic locally to get you through the next hours. After that, you shouldn't have any pain, he said. How do you feel?"

"I've a headache, but I can't feel anything in my eye."

"I'll find the nurse, ask for paracetamol."

"No, Albert, d-don't g-go."

Albert persisted, "Are you nauseated?"

"No."

Ralph chimed in, "That's a real blessing, eh, lad?"

Rosie stood next to Albert, her eyes cast down.

"Oh, Pa. What *have* I done?" She began to cry, pressing a sodden handkerchief to her pink nose.

Robert reached for her. Albert put his arm around her shoulders.

"You did nothing and I'll be fine, Rosie. I'll be fine."

Taking his hand, she tried to smile.

He squeezed her hand. "You'll see, dear girl, everything will be all right."

Robert sat in a camp chair in the tiny garden behind number 34 St. Ives Gardens, Health and Social Care crutches lying on the grass next to him. Sunshine warmed him, the birds obliged by twittering prettily.

Sleeves rolled up and tie loosened, Albert arrived with a tray and placed it on the small table between the chairs. In his pretend English voice, he said, "Your ale, sir."

"Ah, Jeeves, 'bout time," said Robert, smiling.

Drawing a camp chair up to Robert's, Albert said, "This is nice." He sighed. Pulling his tie off and rolling it up, he said, "Week's end. Friday afternoon in May, end of term in sight, but not near enough for the usual panic of final grades and credits left to tally. Gorgeous."

Taking sips, they sat back.

"Once my leg bends a wee bit more, I'll want to replant this garden. We've let it go and I remember how nice Meg kept it, before the war. I'd like it to look nice for Betty's visit. She may remember it too."

"Plenty of time—she doesn't arrive until early July. To get your leg to bend, you'll have to swim in the pool more often."

"Ach, I hate the idea of swimming, and since me dear auld Da walks me 'round and 'round the blocks or along the Lagan and to the very painful physio sessions, I don't think I need to. By the way, it's cheered him no end—taken ten years off him. I swear he's even standing up straighter. He was thrilled to take me to my appointment with Mr. D-Davidson today. We had a pub lunch after."

"Haven't seen much of Ralph, but when we meet, he's kept a civil tongue in his head."

"I've kept him out of your way, but yes, he's on his b-best behavior."

"May he remain so. But you don't have to plant the garden on your own. Only, digging and dunging Meg's victory garden in Portstewart remains my only experience with gardening, and that was to Frank's instructions."

"And mine. But will you have time? Don't you have hundreds of recommendations and a paper to finish?"

"I've written and sent all the recommendations requested, and we're on our last round of editing the paper, then we'll submit. We'd like to publish this paper in *The Lancet*. I think it's important enough for their review."

Robert shuddered. "Such a painful name—gives me the willies."

"That's because you've experienced the business end of one too much this year. But it's the foremost medical journal in the world. Point is, I'm all yours during the summer vac this year. No courses, no research even—I've asked Marie Morton to run the lab during the vac. She's brilliant and dedicated—thrilled to run the show."

"B-But that's wonderful news about the summer vac! Rosie's graduation is a big enough do, but with Betty's visit!"

"Speaking of which I've rung whatshisname—he'll come next week to paint, and paper indoors. Sorry, I hope he doesn't put you out too much. His son will scrape and paint the doors, and window frames, inside and out."

"If they d-don't do a good job, Ralph will let him know. It will be nice to have the place looking like a b-band box for Betty's visit."

Albert sipped ale and then asked, "I wonder if there's somebody who would plant the garden for us?"

"Well, there's the B-Botanic Gardens down the road. We could ask the fellas working on the grounds if they work for themselves, too. Why not?"

"Brilliant. I'll stop and ask the very next time I see a gardener planting the outdoor displays."

They sat in silence and sipped their ale.

Looking up at the patch of sky that was theirs, Albert asked, "Do you want to talk about it?"

"What?"

"Your appointment this morning—what Davidson told you about the prosthetic."

Robert laughed. "When I asked Rosie to drive me to the prosthetic shop next week, she laughed and asked, 'You're never asking me to go eye ball shopping?'"

Albert laughed. "It's good she's gotten over crying over everything connected to your injuries. Shall I come, too?"

"You're welcome, but you're also color b-blind. She's good with colors. I want it to match my real eye color—it's important the two eyes match, I think."

"I'm only weakly blind for red—an inherited protanomaly from my mother—since you're not a white rabbit, it doesn't affect how I see your eye color. I wonder how it will feel?"

"Explains why you ran around in those terrible p-pink swim trunks. The pro-prosthetic should feel normal. Mr. D-Davidson reminded me that during the surgery he added a p-plastic p-placeholder to keep the socket the correct shape, so it should feel no different. Also, he told me it's possible I'll be able to move it, to follow my real eye's movement at some point. At the fitting, they'll buff it to make it smaller or a different shape, if need be. P-peculiar, isn't it?"

"I'll say, but fascinating. I'll have to quiz him on how your false eye could track your real one. Expensive?"

"All on the Health and Social, so no. Apparently I'm at the head of Northern Ireland's g-glass eye queue."

"Well done, you."

"I thought you meant d-did I want to talk about returning to my job."

"Go on."

"Alright. The leave is much on my m-mind—it's up next month. Six months of full pay ends next month. I'll have to ask for an extension or re-re-re…"

"Resign? Retire?"

Robert shook his head. "I'm too young to take my pension from Queen's or the n-nation, and I wasn't in long enough for a n-navy pension. We can't afford me being on the dole, can we?"

"I can meet our essentials. Do you want to resign?"

"I'm n-not sure. Some of my depth perception may return, but right now, I can't see well enough to handle anything adeptly, let alone anything f-fiddly like circuits. Re-reading and writing are tiring so I don't think I could create a 1-D plan, let alone the circuits themselves."

"You are a wee bit clumsy, which you never were. Give yourself more time. Ask for another six months, that will take you past Betty's visit and allow more than a year of recovery."

"And if they say no? There's a rumor the university administrators are Orangemen. Very d-disapproving of my march participation, so I hear. Do they approve of the ones who did this to me, I wonder?"

Albert took Robert's hand. "Orangemen? Doubtful. Free Masons possibly. But they won't say no—your boss won't. Clarke has always valued your work and he's known you for years, brought you with him back home from Manchester. I don't see that happening. Who told you of the disapproval?"

"That eejit in the lab, the one who calls me B-Bob—Nigel. I should have known better than to believe him. G-God, I can't stand the man."

"Forget the eejit. Are you fit enough to be in an electrical engineering laboratory?"

"No, I'm not fit. No vision on the left, terrible d-depth perception, a crook leg—I'm a liability around equipment. And to think I was a Huff-Duff man...I scored the highest in the peripheral vision and acuity test during training."

Smiling warmly, Albert said, "You're still handsome, if that helps. Although with the beard grown back and the eye patch— the fearsome Blackbeard in our midst!"

"Blackbeard! I loved my book about p-pirates—*The Golden Age of P-Piracy*. I still have it somewhere. Ralph bought it for my ninth birthday. Henry Morgan, 'Captain' Kidd, 'Calico' Jack Rackham, and Edward Teach—B-Blackbeard. He was my favorite—the brute. I was a blood-thirsty wee thing. Anyway, you must admit the left side of my face is b-banjaxed."

"Which is why I sit and sleep on your right." Albert laughed.

"Albert..."

"Sorry, it wasn't funny."

"No, it was, but. Here's the thing—I don't know if I want to go back to my old job, my old work life."

"No? You love your work. Why not?"

"It doesn't seem all that important now. Not as important as what's happening in this country. Working with B-British Tabulating Machine to design computers for Irish Sugar is all very well, but it's not trying to win a war. And after what's happened to me, maybe because of it, I want to be active. I've felt so down, felt such a victim for months. I could do something useful, maybe."

"You've designed some very important computers and elements for critical jobs. I'm sure you could do something else that's very useful, but perhaps not march into gauntlets of vicious loyalists again."

"No, definitely not. I'll ask Rosie if there's anything I *could* do to help."

"I'm sure she's matured enough to realize the very real dangers in this fight."

"She has, but I hope to God she truly understands the harm done to me and the others came from the locals—ordinary men, the local police, even the women and children of that town—not her involvement bringing me to the scene. But also, by the system, because the real damage was done by off-duty RUC at Burntollet Bridge and they've not been prosecuted! And how is it there's no consequence for maiming peaceful protestors? Citizens of Northern Ireland, meant to be protected by them? *They're* the ones protected by the system, that's how!" As Robert sat up with a jerk in the camp chair, the ale in his glass sloshed. He shook the ale off his hand and continued. "How is it that an entire group of citizens are denied *all* their rights, their livelihoods, decent rooves over their heads? A system based on what? Christian technicalities they choose to believe, ones made law by that brute Henry VIII and enforced by that vicious wee daughter of his? It's 1969, not 15...something, not 1690, or even 1920, but nothing's changed! And speaking of which, what about us? When will we see the end of criminalization of homosexuality? It's insane we're still judged as criminals, especially since it was decriminalized in England and Wales two years ago. Who are they to judge how we live our lives? Politicians and judges who pay prostitutes? Who beat their wives? That's the morality you and I are missing? They were happy for me to serve in the Royal Navy on active duty, to have you a leader in medical research, for us to pay our taxes year in and year out..." He stopped abruptly and took a deep breath.

Albert's mouth had fallen open. He clapped. "Good on ye, firebrand! And you said all of that without stuttering once! I agree on all counts. Of course I want laws demanding threat of our arrest repealed, but with regard to that, I think the danger to us will come from all sides, the law, police, loyalists *and* republicans. What can we do about this?"

"The campaigners worked ten years to get it repealed in England. I don't know how Wales got it repealed as well. We could research it, contact those activists."

"I recall that one politician, Berkeley, I think his name was, lost his seat because of his support for repeal. I wonder if that Labour fellow is still in his...I'd need to find his name, can't remember it."

"Of course they had the Archbishop of Canterbury on their side, and the shame from hounding one of the greatest minds B-Britain ever produced to his death."

"Turing?" asked Albert.

Robert looked at him sharply. "Yes, Alan Turing. The s-s-s-s-state m-murdered him—for being homosexual."

"Activists here have their hands full with the government crackdown on Catholics, but anyway, everything is run from Westminster. Why don't we contact the groups who campaigned for rights in England?"

"Who? How?" asked Robert.

"I don't know, but what about Bernadette Devlin? Now she's in Westminster, she must have an office we can ring."

"Good idea. Let's ask Rosie—she knows many activists. Anyway," said Robert, raising his glass, "to being an activist! B-better that than a victim."

HOME AGAIN, HOME AGAIN,
JIGGITY JOG—JULY 1969

NEW YORK—IRELAND

*A*nnie sat at the kitchen table, her legs, feet and lower back feeling the weight of sixty-nine years. The noon news program burbling from the small radio in the corner mostly ignored, but without it, the silence of the empty apartment made her ears ring. Her attention wandered before tuning into the broadcaster's words. "Apollo 11...moon landing." *The moon—why would anyone go to the moon? Waste of money.* Muttering aloud, "If not the moon, all they talk about is Chappaqua, or wherever it happened. Mary Jo Kopeck...nik. Why can't they leave the poor man alone? It was an accident." She got up from the table where so far she'd failed to focus on paying the month's bills and shuffled to the stove to light the gas under the kettle.

At this hour during school term, she'd plan for the girls' return home. Plan a snack for them, listen to their chatter while they ate it—the rare afternoons they came home before dinner—then make dinner for them, served when Betty got home from work. Annie liked living with her daughter and granddaughters. To her, it made more sense to rent the one big duplex apartment than paying two rents, two sets of utilities, and there was plenty of room with the three bedrooms upstairs, the large rooms downstairs.

After Ned died, Annie felt lonely in the apartment, even though Betty and the girls lived just upstairs in the building. True, the girls spent more time with her when they were little, when all it took was Coke and Cheez-It snacks and the television on to keep them in her home. Now the girls were busy with after-school projects and their friends, their mother worked late more often, and Annie's loneliness had seeped back into her life.

Until Ned died, she'd thought of her Belfast childhood home rarely, but during her nights alone, she thought of it often. Growing up in the tiny two up, two down house on Moore's Place, she was never alone. She'd slept in a bed with Lizzie and Meg, two arms' lengths away from the bed where Jinny and Florrie slept. Across the hall were her parents until she was ten, their father sleeping alone in the bed after their mother died. Underneath them all, the three boys slept in the parlor on pallets, rolled up every morning. Privacy didn't exist, nor did quiet, and time in the outside water closet, called the library in their family, was limited to minutes, but in the small bedroom with her sisters, she felt safe and secure.

Annie hated being alone, always had. Alone meant her thirteenth birthday living on the farm with the fiends, Aunt Polly and Uncle Jack Dorans, and not another soul, not even a dog for company. *Good thing there was never a dog, they'd have beaten and starved the poor thing.* Alone meant those two could do as they pleased with her.

The harm Uncle Jack did her was mostly invisible, although he slapped hard sometimes. The evident harm—a bruise on the arm or under the eye—was delivered by Aunt Polly, her father's sister, her flesh and blood. Functioning as their skivvy, Annie ate alone in the kitchen, allowed to serve herself only the cheapest tea and the worst grade butter on her bread and spuds, and very little of any of it. Alone at night in her bed off the kitchen, she trembled, terrified of the black beetles in the pantry and the threat of her uncle, crawling toward her little, hard bed.

To Annie, the farm seemed in the middle of nowhere, although her grandparents, aunts and uncles, Polly's brothers and sisters, lived not even a mile away. Scanning the horizon while feeding the chickens or slopping the pigs, she saw nothing. She might as well have been in the middle of nowhere since those relatives never visited, never checked on her, asked how she was faring—they didn't save her. Nobody did—not her sisters, her brothers, nor her father, not for a year—until finally her father and brothers appeared out of nowhere, saw the state of her and brought her home.

These morbid memories came to her in nightmares while Ned was alive, but rarely. Even with Ned on the night shift, the dog at the foot of the bed and the sleeping children made her feel safe. With the children grown and gone, no husband and no dog with her at night, the memories gnawed at her and kept her from sleeping well. There were no beetles and no uncle, but they may as well have been lying in wait under the bed. When she did sleep, the farm and its misery revisited her in shocking, blood-curdling nightmares.

While she'd managed to talk Betty into moving in with her, Annie wasn't at all sure Betty liked the new living arrangement. The nearly middle-aged Betty moved back into her girlhood bedroom with a silent air of defeat, even though it removed financial strain from her narrow shoulders. There could have been other perks too, as the living arrangement would have allowed her to go out in the evening with co-workers on the spur of the moment, but the reality was she seemed too down for spontaneity—until she'd suddenly announced the plan for all of them to travel to Belfast that summer.

Annie's gaze left the Con Ed electric bill again and lost focus. Her fingers reached into the Social Tea biscuit tin. *Should I have gone to Belfast with them? Did Betty want me to come, really? Or was she happy with the break? Did the girls? What about the ones on the other side? Would they have wanted me to come?* Counting on her fingers, she named who was left in Ireland: *Lizzie and Meg, David, Ralph and Robert, and his daughter, em, what was her name? Lizzie's sons Tom and Will and…*she felt a little dizzy and closed her eyes.

Had they landed in Dublin yet? She looked at the clock on the wall, located next to the framed portrait of JFK. *Yes, Betty said they'd land very early morning their time, late last night ours—they've landed hours since. Were they already in Belfast? Aye, by now they are in Belfast.* The thought that she could be standing in a Belfast street at that very moment hit her. *I could have gone with them. I could have gone back. Ned's gone, but he wouldn't have fought my going. In fact, he'd have told me to go. Why didn't I? I have the fare sitting in the bank.*

The piercing kettle whistle made her jump. She pulled the kettle off the flame and turned the gas off. Tea-making abandoned, she wandered down the hall to the stairs and slowly up to her bedroom. She sat on the bed and leaned forward to switch on the window fan. The purr of the rotating machine was soothing. Lying down, she pulled the summer blanket over her and closed her eyes.

Sleepless, she thought about the day Betty insisted she go with her and the girls to the passport office in Brooklyn's Central Library, Grand Army Plaza. Two weeks before, they'd all trekked to a wedding photographer on Third Avenue for the photos. Betty had said, "Just in case you change your mind, Mommy. You can buy a ticket and just come."

Annie complained, "But I'm not traveling, Betty. I just don't feel up to it."

Betty persisted and brought her mother along to the photographer, promising a lunch and a movie afterward.

Margot agreed with Annie, a rare event. "I'm not going to Belfast either. As soon as school is out, I'll move in with Dad and Nora and have riding lessons every day."

Betty persisted, everyone had their photos taken and a few days later, travelled to the passport office. It was exciting just passing through the library's majestic and ornate Art Deco façade, the gigantic doors. Even Margot was excited about getting her first passport, Ella was thrilled, and of course, having been born in Brooklyn, there was no problem for the girls at the passport office. Annie brought Ned's naturalization papers along, which she'd always thought extended to her and Betty. But there was a bit of a rumpus about citizenship that preceded waiting around in a dreary, airless room on a beautiful day in May while the passport officials conferred.

Betty lost her temper and threatened to wield all sorts of power she didn't have, but it was enough to send the male official flying out of the room. A different official replaced him, a woman, who sat down with them and asked Annie, "How long have you been in this country, Mrs. Wright?"

"The three of us came in 1930—my husband, my daughter and me."

The woman affixed the photos and stamped them.

Annie woke to the whir of the fan in the apartment bedroom. She had no idea what time it was. Light streamed through the gap in the curtains. She looked at the clock, three o'clock, and calculated the date and day of the week. *19 July, 1969. Sunday. No, Saturday.* She realized it had to be Saturday because that morning she'd gone to a Scandinavian delicatessen for a cold dinner and they were never open on a Sunday. Also, she hadn't spent the best part of the morning reading *The Daily News* cover to cover, including all the celebrity photos and puzzles in the Sunday Coloroto section—that she would do tomorrow morning, Sunday morning.

She sat up and slowly got out of bed. "Oh, God, I'm that stiff."

Pulling her dress straight, she returned to the kitchen and made tea before reapplying herself to balancing the checking account and paying bills. A baseball game crawled through its innings on the radio. The sound of a game soothed her, reminding her of Ned, who slept in his armchair through the games on the radio and the TV, but always knew the score when asked.

~

Betty's younger daughter sat between her and Margot on the Aer Lingus flight, JFK New York to Dublin Airport. Margot sat on the aisle, wearing the sleep mask included in the passenger kit, presumably asleep under the eyewear and the blanket, her seat pushed as far back as possible.

The interior lights switched off.

Gabrielle, who had renamed herself Ella partially in reaction to kids calling her Gabby Gabi, finally finished the airline breakfast and asked, "Why didn't Grandma come with us, Mom? She's always talking about Belfast. How she misses the butter and the tea."

"She misses Belfast, it's true, and beyond the butter and the tea. She is a little funny about her relatives. Is that it? I don't know. I did try to talk her into coming with us, made sure she could." Betty drank the rest of the tea in her cup.

"What do you mean, 'funny?'"

"I can't explain it very well, except to say that she sort of… shied away from them. One brother called to say he was in New York and asked could they meet. She said no. Her sisters have written to her since we left, not often but at least every year, but she's rarely responded by writing back or calling, not that I ever saw." Betty shrugged. "She didn't explain about not coming other than to say she didn't feel up to it. I think she'll regret not coming, but I did try."

The Aer Lingus flight attendant arrived at their row to collect the trays and trash. Betty and Ella handed theirs to her over Margot's still form.

The captain's lilting voice came over the speaker to tell them they were minutes away from landing. The flight attendants called for landing preparations as they passed.

Nodding at Margot, Betty said, "Nudge her awake."

Ella shook Margot, who moaned, "What?"

"We're landing."

With some show of reluctance, Margot pulled off the eye mask and blinked. Yawning widely, she pushed the blanket down.

Betty locked her tray in the upright position and pushed the button to spring the back of her seat upright. The plane was descending rapidly, if her inner ear was anything to go by. The Aer Lingus attendants walked down the tilted aisles briskly, steadily. Bright as new pennies in their emerald suits, retouched makeup and French twists, they touched passengers' shoulders to hasten them into landing mode, their soft accents sibilant against the quick roar of the flaps lowering. Betty looked out the window into the clouds. Suddenly, the clouds cleared and there it was: Ireland. Fields appeared out of the mist, hedge rowed and emerald green jostling for space next to hunter, forest, Kelly and moss green spaces. Unmistakably, Ireland.

Oh! Tears sprang to Betty's eyes.

Ella leaned around her to see out the window, her chin on Betty's shoulder. "It's so green!"

Betty kept her glistening eyes on the land below them.

"Oh, wow! Ireland, green? Who knew?" asked Margot and at seventeen, contemptuous of her fifteen-year-old sister, a contempt she often tried on for size with her mother.

Betty felt rather than saw Ella's familiar look of wounded rage as she fought back. "You've never been here, either," she tossed over her shoulder.

"Seatbelts now, girls," said the flight attendant, stopping momentarily on her last trip down the aisle, balancing a tray of crushed cigarette packages, errant tea mugs and drinks glasses.

The girls buckled up. Betty checked hers, even though it had been buckled for hours. A sob threatened to escape her throat. Pressing her lips together she watched the lowered flap on the wing jiggering this way and that as the ground came up to meet them. With a soft thud and a roaring whoosh, they landed on standard runway tarmac, poured over the green land of Ireland.

~

"That restroom was weird," said Margot. "And don't they have elevators in this country? Imagine making people just off an overnight flight drag suitcases up and down stairs!"

Betty turned from studying the bus schedule on the kiosk. Her brown eyes flashing, she said through gritted teeth, "Lower your voice. Lower your voice a lot and from now on." *Why did I make her come? She didn't want to—made that crystal clear and now she'll what, be a complete misery the entire time?*

Margot shrugged.

Ella, looking pleased, asked, "Will they meet us at the train, Mom?"

Margot mumbled, "If we ever get to the train station..."

She wanted to stay with her father, his wife, her horses, and their four kids, so much more fun than us. Made it perfectly clear that was preferable to coming to this country, to meeting my family here—to coming on a long trip with Ella and me. Yes—and that's exactly why I insisted she come.

Betty's hand reached out to touch Ella's arm, noticing that Ella was taller than she was now, taller than her older sister, too. *Good for you.*

"Albert will, I think, but we'll manage in Belfast, don't worry. Listen, let's get a cab to Connolly Station. I don't want to miss the train and the buses don't seem to follow the schedule posted, do they?" She checked her watch again. "There should have been at least two stopped here by now." Stepping forward to the curb, she raised her arm and called, "Taxi!"

~

As the trio left the train and entered the main waiting area of Belfast Central Station, Betty scanned the various individuals and groups standing and waiting. She wasn't sure she'd recognize Albert or that he would know her. She stopped at the first bench to rearrange the luggage in her hands. Margot dropped her bags, sat down and studied her nails. Ella pointed at a man of about Betty's age and asked, "Is that him?" The man paid them no attention.

Betty shook her head, but coming toward them with a big smile, another man caught her attention.

As he approached, she studied the very tall, bald man sporting long sideburns and thick-framed black glasses.

He smiled. "Betty?"

"Albert?"

"Aye!" He bent to kiss her cheek.

She kissed his and stood back to look at him. "You look just the same as the photo Robert sent!"

He laughed. "I do not. He told me he sent one of us from years ago, but you do look the same as yours. I'd have known you anywhere."

"These are my girls, Gabrielle and Margot."

"Hi," said Ella, smiling shyly.

With a nod from her mother, Margot stood and grimaced as she said, "Hello."

"Hello, hello. Shall we go? I've the car on a double yellow line, so. This way, girls. Here, Betty, give me those bags." Betty hurried to fall in with his long strides and the girls chased behind. "Robert wanted to come, but there's no room for all of us. Are you excited to be home?"

Excited? Overwhelmed is more like it. Why did I wait so long?

When they got to the Imp, the Americans seemed shocked by its size. Albert said, "The funny thing about this wee car is that with the back seat down, there's loads of room, so if the girls don't mind kipping in with the luggage? Betty, in the front seat, please—yes, other side. I'll hand the luggage in through the hatch, girls. Hurry, now, we're on a tight schedule."

"Mom, he says 'shedjewel' like you do!" said Ella, giggling.

"Here, Gabrielle, take this case, would you? Sorry. We haven't far to go," said Albert, fairly shoving a suitcase into the back.

After she wrangled the case and Albert got behind the wheel, she said, "My name's Ella."

"What? Oh, Ella, sorry—I'm Albert. Alright, here we go." Albert pulled away and deftly negotiated his way into the stream of traffic on East Bridge Street. "I'm afraid we have to cross my namesake bridge and turn around, but you'll have your first view of the Lagan River. Not your first view, Betty, eh?"

"When she was little we called her Gabi, but she didn't like it. Doesn't like Gabrielle either. She loves Ella Fitzgerald, so the ending, the —elle of Gabrielle—became Ella," explained Betty.

Turning his head a little, he said, "*Do* you love Ella? So do I! We travelled back to Manchester to see her two years ago with her sidemen, *and* with Duke Ellington and his band. What a fantastic concert."

"That must have been super! Mom has all her albums, the ones with Louis…"

"I'm a Doors fan," said Margot, managing to sound bored.

Albert flicked his eyes up to the rear-view mirror and said, "Very good musicians. The organ riff in *Light My Fire*. Excellent stuff."

Margot's perfectly manicured eyebrows shot up.

Betty looked at Albert with admiration. Two minutes and he'd made both girls his.

"It's been a wee while since we were on a train," said Meg, watching the Lough Neagh fly by, the train riding along the shore at lake level, the vibration of the wheels at speed a pleasant thrum for the passengers at this late stage of the journey. Mildred sat across from them, snoozing, Biscuit curled and asleep at their feet.

The door between cars slid open as a passenger navigated his way on the swaying train back to his seat from the bar car. They heard raucous laughter and overly loud, cheery talk from the bar until the door slid shut.

A dark green fountain pen poised over a small red notebook, Lillian said, "Aye, it has that. Tell me again when your appointment with Dr. Boyd is?"

"Tuesday, 4 o'clock. I wonder should I make one with a dentist too—a tooth in the back is achy now and then." She placed her hand on her jaw. "Dr. Boyd will want me to take penicillin before I go. I must tell him."

Writing in the notebook, Lillian said, "I don't think you should unless you're in pain. I think we've got more than enough on this week. Betty's arrival, Rosie's graduation and the party. Anyway, I don't mind the young dentist in Portstewart. Why not go to him? I've said, the new chap's gentle, not like the old monster."

"Alright. I'll ring him when we return." Meg watched Lillian writing her list. "I'll bring the prescription to our chemist when we go home."

Lillian looked up from the notebook and at Meg, her mouth slightly open with concentration. "I've messages down in centre city, too. I need a new pair of walking shoes. There may be a sale at Robb's or that new Marks and Spencer. There was an article about the opening in the Tele."

"Good. I'll buy a hat to wear to the graduation. I'll get my hair done, too." She patted the back of her short, curly hair. "Should I have them dye it? There's little brown left."

"No." Lillian looked down and continued writing in her notebook.

Meg looked out the window again. "Not long now till Belfast." She sighed.

"Alright, if you want to dye your hair, go on then. Isn't an expensive habit? For film stars, not for the likes of us."

"Hmmm. Are you sure you don't mind not going to the graduation ceremony?"

Lillian said, "Mind? No, not at all. Rosie's only got the four tickets. I think she made the right choices, certainly in her father, you, Ralph and Lizzie. Those two would be heartbroken not to go—they helped raise her. Albert said that he, Jo and Holly don't need tickets, teaching at Queen's as they do. Except Jo, none of us is actually related to her, which is funny when I think of us as family. We are her family. Not by blood, but that's less important, if you ask me. Rosie's grateful for your family, and mine, since Jo hasn't any."

"Oh yes? Glad she thinks so." Meg turned to look out the window again. "And it's true, being related by blood doesn't always work very well. Take me and my two living sisters."

Lillian went back to her list, ticking off items before asking, "Do you think the dress I brought for Jo's party at the hotel is nice enough? Fancy enough? I could buy one..."

"If you see one you like better, buy it. Why not? We never spend a penny on clothes any more. Speaking of family, David and Niall plan to stay in the hotel where Jo's holding the party." Lillian returned to her notebook. Meg bit her lip before asking, "I wonder will Betty know me?"

Looking up quickly, Lillian said, "Of course she will! You look the same."

"I do not."

Lillian noticed tears welling in Meg's eyes and took her hand. "Oh, Meggie, nobody on earth looks the same near seventy as when thirty. But you look like your lovely self. Some people age into being unrecognizable. You look the same and you're lovely still. Are you nervous to meet her?"

"I am nervous."

Sitting back and closing the notebook, Lillian waved a hand and said, "She'll be so happy to see you, she will see *you*, not an older woman. Believe me."

"I hope so." Nodding her head toward the sleeping Mildred, Meg whispered, "She's so excited to visit Belfast, she's worn herself to a frazzle."

"And with worry about the chickens."

"Oh, I know, but Frank's auld pal has a wee farm nearby. What's his name, then? The chickens have a chance." Meg laughed.

Lillian smiled. "Jackie. I talked to Mildred while you were overdoing the housework. She says auld Jackie knows how to care for chickens, but will he? His head tends to fall into a pint glass now and then. So she's paying his wife too, to make sure he does, behind his back of course!"

Meg shrugged and said, "It wasn't overdoing. I like to come home to a clean house, but." She looked down the aisle. "Where is the man with the wee cart? I'd love a cup of tea. Here, I'll fetch three cups. Do you want anything to eat?"

Lillian said, "Not for me. How long 'till Central Station?"

Meg looked out the window. "I'd say we have time for tea and the loo. We've just passed Templepatrick. But wake Mildred while I hunt for tea. Oh, never mind, here he comes." Meg waved at the man pushing the cart.

Touching Mildred's knee, Lillian said, "Milly dear, time for tea."

Mildred woke with a loud snort. "Oh, dear me."

The dog stood, shook herself and looked at Lillian with some expectation.

Meg said, "Hang onto her collar, just in case she tries for a bap off the wee cart."

For the second time within an hour, Albert told his prospective passengers that the Imp was larger inside than it looked from the outside. He ushered Mildred to the front as Meg and Lillian arranged themselves and Biscuit in the backseat, returned to its upright position. He shoved their luggage in through the hatchback. They hadn't as much as the last batch of travellers, so it worked.

"Alright, so. We're off!" he announced, pulling away and inserting the Imp into the now heavier traffic flow with more aggression.

When they turned onto the Dublin Road, Mildred, who had been pasted to the window, said, "Oh! Would you look at all the people! Isn't it grand to be home?"

"Here we are! I'll bring the bags in, go ahead. No, really ladies, go in."

Meg entered number 34 first and let the dog run ahead. "Here comes Biscuit," she called. "Mind how you go!" She laughed.

She could hear conversation drifting down the hall from the kitchen, so she walked straight back to the open back door and the garden. Robert was sitting in a camp chair, but when she stepped out, she was surprised to see a woman and two girls seated around the small table. The dog romped over to them.

"Oh, hello. Sorry, I didn't…"

Quietly, the woman she'd thought a stranger, said, "Aunt Meg." The woman stood up. A slight woman of medium height, in her forties, with dark hair, large dark eyes—she was so familiar—very like Robert. *But it's like looking at Florrie's face!*

"Betty."

The women took a step toward one another.

Meg held her hands out. "Betty, my dear." Changing her mind, she opened her arms.

The hug was shy at first and each patted the other's back in preparation to ending the hug. After a moment, the two were still hugging.

"Oh, dear Aunt Meg. I can't believe we're together. I can't believe it," said Betty, in tears.

The girls watched round-eyed as their mother gave herself over to this emotional scene.

Pushing herself back, Betty said, "I'd have known you anywhere."

"Dear wee Betty. Oh my goodness!" Turning, she called, "Lillian!"

Lillian arrived at the open door to the garden and said, "Betty! Wee Betty!"

"Aunt Lillian!"

Lillian enveloped Betty in her arms without hesitation. "We didn't know you'd be here today! This is wonderful! Albert, where are you?"

Albert stood in the doorway, grinning.

"Oh, you two! Thank you for this wonderful surprise. We didn't expect Betty today. We didn't know."

"You really didn't know, Aunt?" asked Albert. "Robert and I had fun hatching the surprise, didn't we?"

"We did. I wasn't sure it would work, but it did, very well, I'd say," said Robert.

"Now, as for these young ladies," asked Meg, wiping her eyes. "Which is Margot and which Gabrielle?"

Wiping her eyes, Betty said, "This is Margaret, after you, called Margot. She has your coloring and your name. And this is Gabrielle, Ella. Their father is blond and blue-eyed, as you can see in Ella. Neither of my children has my coloring."

Lillian and Meg, and the two girls repeated their hellos. There was something about Margot that prevented either of the women hugging her, which prevented them reaching out to Ella, who seemed much warmer.

"They have your looks though, very pretty," said Meg.

Margot stepped back from the trio of women staring at her.

"Shall I call you aunt? What's the dog's name?" asked Ella.

"If you like. That's Biscuit," said Meg.

Ella knelt and scratched Biscuit's ears. "What is she?"

"An Irish Water Spaniel," said Lillian.

"Oh, I've never seen one before."

"Ella's crazy for dogs. They both love animals—dogs, horses…"

Lillian turned and called to Mildred, who hovered in the doorway, "Come out, Milly, and meet everyone. Betty, this is our dear friend and business partner, Mildred Greer. Have you never met one another?" she asked Mildred.

"I don't think so, but goodness, I've heard so much about you, Betty. How do you do?"

"I was a child when we left," Betty shook hands with Mildred. "Hello, it's nice to meet you."

"And you've never been back?" asked Mildred.

"No, it's wonderful to be here."

"I haven't been here much myself during the last, oh, almost thirty years is it? I miss it. It is wonderful being here, I agree."

Albert rubbed his hands together and said, "Now, we've a table booked for lunch at two. Just down the Malone Road, they serve an excellent Sunday lunch. It's a short walk, but I'll drive those of you who prefer it. After lunch, I expect you'd love a wee rest, all of you. Let's get you settled into your rooms. Alright? Girls? You and your mum are up on the third floor, so let's get the bags upstairs. Mildred, you'll be across from us on the second floor. Ella, will you help Mildred with her bag, please."

Ella jumped up and she, Mildred and Albert left the garden. Biscuit took herself off around the garden, sniffing. Betty shot Margot a look before following. Margot sauntered in behind her.

Once up on the third floor, they stowed Ella's and Margot's bags in the bedroom with the large bed. Albert opened the door to what had been a box room before undergoing redecoration into a single bedroom. "I'm told you should recognize this room."

Betty looked around and out the window. "I do. The nursery. My nursery."

Margot stood in the doorway.

Betty turned to Margot, "This was my nursery. When I was born, my parents slept in the room where you're staying. Imagine Grandma walking up and down two flights with an infant, over and over again. Why didn't they live on the second floor, I wonder?"

Albert tried to squeeze past. "I'll get the others settled. Excuse me." He ducked his head and left the room. Ella took his place.

"A nursery? Were you born in this room?" asked Margot.

"Next door. Possibly the same bed. Is it a feather bed?"

Margot made a face and said, "Ew."

They trooped into the larger bedroom next door. Betty pushed down on the mattress. "No, not feathers." She sat on the bed.

Margot went around to the other side and kicking her shoes off, lay down on the bed. "I'm exhausted. Can I just stay here—not go out to lunch?"

Betty said, "No, you may not." *I'm going to have a very large wine at lunch. Possibly two.* "I'm going down to freshen up. Will you be ready to leave when Albert…"

"I suppose so," said Margot, her arm over her eyes.

Ella said, "I'll come down with you, Mom."

Sitting in the garden, Meg asked, "Lillian, I hadn't thought, but will Biscuit be alright alone in a strange house?"

"She's never put a foot wrong in ours, but I don't know, you're right. Let's leave her in the kitchen. Robert, is there still a dog basket in the house?"

Robert said, "There is. I checked when I was thinking of getting a dog, just before my…it's in the pantry, I think." He began to get up.

"I'll go and see," said Lillian, getting up and going into the kitchen.

Meg sat down next to him and said, "The garden looks wonderful, Robert. Thank you for the work you've done. Do you enjoy it?"

"We love it, but truth be told, we didn't plant it. Albert found an auld fellow working at the Botanic Gardens who likes to keep busy with side jobs. He did a nice job and I'm very pleased you like it. I'd remembered yours when I was a child—it was very pleasant. I'm sure Betty remembers it, too."

"I do like it very much. The plants are nicer than the ones we used and the way he blended them, the colors and shapes, they complement one another. You can tell a professional planted it." She continued looking around the garden before turning back to him and asking, "How is your leg? Are you climbing stairs yet?"

"Yes, I am and it's mending well. Stairs are part of the physio, in fact. How about yourself?"

"I'm happy to sleep in the parlor and not climb stairs, if you don't mind us in the parlor? I feel well on my medicine, but stairs are hard. And hills. Otherwise, my breathing is good."

"We sleep on the second floor again now, but we got a fairly comfortable sofa bed for the parlor when I left hospital. It's large enough but we felt the bar, so Albert put a futon on top of the mattress. It's marvelous. You'll be very comfortable."

"A what?"

"Futon. It's a Japanese-style mattress. He has a Japanese graduate student and she sent home to Japan for one, for us— imagine! We couldn't find one here. Really nice of her—he paid for it and the shipping, but still. Go in and look at it, we've set the bed up for you."

"I will." Looking into his eyes, Meg lowered her voice. "Your eye…I don't think I could tell if I didn't know."

"That's what I like to hear. You'll see that it doesn't move like the real one, which is the right one." He pointed.

"Have you pain still?"

"No, not in my eye. None at all. Nor my face, although I did for a wee while, but my leg still gives me the gyp often, especially in the rain. It may always. The knee cap was smashed, so now the leg is fused. Aye, it was a mess."

"Oh, my God, I'm so sorry. How are you feeling now? Alright, within yourself?"

"Sometimes I feel fine, cheerful, like now." Robert looked away. "But sometimes I feel angry or low. Very low." He looked back at Meg. "Very angry."

"Low, yes, even angry. That happened to me when I first became ill. I imagine it's the same sort of feeling, that it's the end. But it isn't and the more you heal, the better you'll feel, within yourself. I had nobody to blame and you do, of course, so it may be different to how you feel."

"That's good to know. I'll try and remember what you've said when the black cloud comes down." Robert smiled.

"And your father, how is he?"

"Not low at all, in fact, never better. He's helped me and that's helped him. Given him purpose and taken ten years off him. They'll be at the lunch, Ralph and Lizzie. "

"And Rosie?"

Looking at his watch, he said, "Oh, aye! Wild horses, she told me to tell you. She's fetching me da and Aunt Lizzie in a cab to the restaurant."

Meg smiled. "She must have a lot to do before her big day?"

"Aye, she's looking for a job and also planning a trip to England, a holiday. Ahead of graduation they've all these parties and receptions at university for the graduates. I'm very happy for her. She's worked very hard."

"What's it like seeing Betty?"

"Oh, grand. She's remarkably like the girl I remember. I think we'll have a good craic." He lowered his voice. "The daughter,

Margot, the older one, she's in some tiresome phase, but wee Ella is a dear. I think we'll have a nice visit. Betty says she tried to get her mum to come, but she didn't."

Meg frowned and shook her head. "I wrote and asked Annie to come, too, but...I don't understand why she didn't. She's on her own now, with Ned gone, and the girls here. So it is." Meg raised her hands for a moment.

"It's near one. Why don't we have a sherry? Albert has a tray set up in the kitchen. No, no, sit where ye are. Part of my therapy." Standing, he grunted softly. "It's a wee bit stiff when I first stand, but I'll bring the drinks. Two ticks." He turned back and lowered his voice, "Meggie, everyone knows not to say anything about Rosie not being...I mean those that know in the first place?"

"The Americans won't learn it from us, so no worries. For our lot, Rosie *is* your daughter."

Meg watched Robert limp into the kitchen. *This garden has seen so many of us over the years, in so many circumstances. When she came back to have her baby, Annie and wee Betty sat out here with Jinny and me. Poor Jinny breathed her last here. David and Martin came through it to the back door in the middle of a bombing. And now it's lovely again, and we're together, here. When I think of it, it's a miracle.*

WELCOME HOME, MISSUS
—JULY 1969

NEW YORK—IRELAND

*A*nnie hung up the phone, picked up her key and left the apartment. Letting the door close behind her, she took the elevator to the top floor of the apartment house. She only had to knock once before the door was opened.

"Mrs. Wright, come in," said the beautiful young woman holding the door open.

"I didn't want to bother you on your day off, Miss Howes, but I know you are an air hostess, so…"

"Nancy, please. Come in and sit down."

"Annie. Thank you."

When seated, Nancy asked, "How can I help?"

"The thing is, my daughter and granddaughters have gone to Northern Ireland to visit my family. In Belfast?"

"Oh! And you didn't want to go with them?"

"That's just it. I didn't…I thought I didn't, but I do, now. Is there a way I can fly over there, as soon as possible?"

"Well, you need a current passport and I'm afraid that takes time." Nancy frowned.

"I have one! Betty insisted I get one when she and the girls got theirs, just in case."

Her face brightened. "That was smart. Let's see. A ticket will be expensive, very expensive, but sure, there is a way. I'm on the London route tomorrow, in fact. I'll get you on that flight and then to a connector in London, London to Belfast, yes? Or, let me think, a direct on Aer Lingus to Dublin? Or my airline and then London to Dublin? We'll see which is faster, or which I can swing, OK?"

"Yes."

"It's twelve hours to London, so you may miss a connection, but it will be a local server under BOAC and they fly out frequently. I'll have to check on Aer Lingus. Anyway, you'll be in Belfast in two or three days, our time. Does that suit you?"

"It does! I can't thank you enough."

Nancy stood and said, "Right. I fly out tomorrow evening. I'm leaving for the airport at four o'clock sharp, tomorrow afternoon. Meet me in the lobby"

"Four o'clock. I'll be there. Oh, how do I pay for the ticket? I mean…"

"Have you got a credit card?"

"No. I've an A&S card, does that…?"

"No. OK, you'll have to go to an American Express office and buy traveller's checks to pay the fare and cover your expenses. I'm sure there are other offices, but the one I know is in Manhattan, in the Pan Am building. I fly for Pan Am." She looked at her watch. "You know what? I have to go into Manhattan, to the Pan Am building today, to sign something for work. Come with me and we'll get the checks and buy your ticket at the same time. I know some of the agents." She checked her watch. "Can you be ready by two?"

"Yes."

She walked behind Annie to the door. "Annie, it's going to be very expensive. Are you able? At least one thousand dollars for the fare and then you'll need money for your trip. You'll have to get a bank check to pay for the traveller's checks before we go into Manhattan. Can you get to your bank and back before two? Is it nearby?"

"Third Avenue at 85th, and..." Annie gulped audibly. "I can manage it."

In the open doorway, Annie turned. "What can I do to thank you?"

"My roommates' flights land tomorrow and at least one will be home for a few days. You could get that plumber to come and fix the leaky toilet and all the faucets. They're driving us crazy."

"That new plumber's a lig. We're not the supers anymore, I mean, since Ned...and since the new owner, he's hired a service. I have his number. I'll call him now."

"Oh, nobody's told the tenants about a new owner, have they? What happened to Mr. Wood?"

"The man was over 100 when he died last year. The son owns the house now. He's supposed to send a notice to the tenants, but."

"OK, gosh, sounds like the rents will go up. Thanks for calling the plumber." Nancy counted on her fingers. "Two more things, Annie. One, pack light. Two, wait until you see my plane. You're in for a treat!" She winked.

"Sit here. We'll serve cocktails in a minute. What would you like?" Nancy, wearing perfectly applied makeup and dressed in her blue tailored suit and white gloves, smiled at Annie.

"Cocktails? I don't...orange juice?" *Whyever did I order that? The acid!*

"I'll be back in a second."

Through the meal service, Nancy attended to Annie. She sliced the tenderloin seat side, served the potatoes and carrots, and poured a glass of red wine. Annie's head was in a whirl, but she enjoyed the food and after drinking the wine, fell asleep, exhausted from days of indecision, fretting about her decision, and running around to the bank, the American Express office, and the ticket agent.

~

"Annie. Annie."

Annie opened her eyes and looked up at Nancy. "We're serving breakfast. You slept well."

Annie looked down at the blanket someone had put over her.

"Goodness, I did. I must use the, em…"

"Yes. That way. Coffee or tea?"

"Oh, tea, yes. Tea would be lovely." Struggling to stand, Nancy helped lever her up. Embarrassed, Annie thanked her again.

Annie made her way up the wide aisle, past sleeping passengers, some of the ladies with their hats on. Ahead was a twisting staircase. An air hostess came down expertly holding a large, silver coffee pot. A different air hostess smiled at her and pointed to the bathroom door.

Braced against the movement of the plane in the tiny washroom, she'd used the toothbrush and paste in the passenger kit, washed her hands and face with the fragrant soap, combed her hair, and used a little of the cologne on offer.

Refreshed, she'd regained her seat. Nancy served what she called the full English breakfast. Finding that she was inexplicably hungry, Annie ate the entire meal and drank a pot of tea.

"Would you like anything else?" Nancy asked.

"Oh, I couldn't eat a gooseberry, thank you. The bacon was lovely, the tea, too."

"Good. Now, after we land, wait for me at the Pan Am desk just inside where they'll route you after Customs. If they try to move you through, tell them you're flying out again, not leaving the airport, OK? Be firm. I'll be as quick as I can and then we'll find your connection."

~

Nancy didn't keep Annie waiting long and then she hurried them to the BOAC desk.

"Hi, Fi. This lady's my neighbor and she needs the next connecting flight to Belfast. What have you got?"

"Hello, Nance. Up for a drink later?" The Englishwoman behind the desk looked at her ledger and then up at the departures sign. "A Vickers Viscount is taking off in three-quarters of an hour. Terminal 2."

"Cheers. One ticket and return, one she can change, OK? And absolutely to the drink later—see you at The Blackbird. What's the best way to get to Terminal 2?"

After a mad dash, Nancy handed Annie over to the BOAC desk for the flight to Belfast.

"Well, you made it! Enjoy your reunion. See you on the flight back to New York," said Nancy, as she propelled Annie onto the tarmac for the next flight.

Annie was so exhausted and overwhelmed that she forgot to thank the young woman.

Relieved to be rid of the noise of the prop plane and the turbulence of the flight, Annie asked the customs officer, "Excuse me, Mister, but where am I?"

"Belfast International, Aldergrove, Antrim."

"Aldergrove? That's not Belfast. How do I get to Belfast?"

Stamping her passport, he said, "Bus. Ulsterbus to the train station here, then train to Belfast Central. Round the corner, down the stairs to the bus. Welcome home, Missus. Next!"

As the train pulled into Belfast, it passed the back of the Guinness brewery. Annie had begun to cry earlier in the trip, a handkerchief pressed hard to her lips beginning in Dunmurry, but now she pulled herself together as the number of tracks increased and crisscrossed, and the train slowed entering the yard. She was there—she was home.

The cabman pulled to the curb, opened the door for her, and put her suitcase on the sidewalk, all from the ease of the driver's seat. She had to pay him with a five-pound note, since she'd only been able to make the exchange at Aldergrove airport for large bills. Breaking a tenner for a pot of tea and a bap with butter on the train, the cartman had been less than pleased with her.

The cabman also grumbled, but made the change less the generous tip she suggested.

Not five minutes here and I've had two donnybrooks.

She stared up at Number 34 St. Ives Gardens. Knocking on the front door, she waited. She thought it was half five or six o'clock in the afternoon, but she never could wear a watch, so she didn't know. Looking around, she continued to wait. Nothing. She stepped back, looked up at the windows, then walked around to the back garden and the kitchen door. Placing her case down on a stone step at the back door and draping her bombazine coat on top, she looked through the glass and knocked. A dog jumped up at her on the other side of the glass so suddenly that she jumped back, crying "Oh!"

Liver-colored and mop-headed, its pink tongue lolling out of a smiling canine mouth, the dog continued to stand on its hind legs to watch Annie. Hand on chest, she said, "You're pleased with yourself, giving me a fright."

Trying the latch, she found it unlocked. She opened the door and squeezed in, closing it quickly. "Hullo? Hullo?" A few seconds later, she said, "Nobody home, eh? Well, I know where the loo is, thank God."

Coming out of the loo, Annie said to the dog, "Now, where's your lead? Where the dogs' leads always hung?" Indeed, the lead was on the hook by the door. She took the lead in her hand, straightened and turned with a gasp. The kitchen, her kitchen, snapped into focus. The copper pots hung where she'd hung them. Somebody polished them, somebody used them. Two rocking chairs bookended the fireplace. The table was hers, but not the chairs. She pulled a chair out and sat down, breathless. The sink, the windows and door, the range—scrubbed and painted, but all the same. The young woman, the young Annie, the newlywed who'd moved into this house, her mother-in-law's, had made it her own, but too soon she'd been pulled out of it, out of her city and her country.

Annie tried to steady her breathing as she looked around, tears blurring her vision.

The dog brought her back, sitting at her feet, smiling and wagging a rat thin tail.

"I'm sorry, wee fella. Didn't mean to tease." She attached the lead, stood stiffly and took the dog back out into the garden with her. "In case you have to go, with all the excitement."

Walking the dog around the small perimeter, Annie admired the shrubs and flowers, then sat down in a chair, the handle of the dog's lead around her wrist.

"I see, you're a wee lass. I'll sit meself down." Petting the dog who sat at her side, Annie asked, "Where *is* everyone?"

The thought of a walk to Great Northern Street was unappealing, but she could leave the suitcase inside and walk over. If Lizzie wasn't home, Ralph might be.

She removed her hat and stuck it with the hatpin. It joined her handbag on her lap. *The smell of Belfast!* A touch of salt and iron from the sea air wafting over the houses, the flowers in the garden, something else…she could not disentangle the smell of the place from the silver light, which was so different to the sky in America. *In the old days, it was the seven smells of Belfast…fish and flowers in the big markets, the soap factories… cattle yard and the slaughterhouse, gasworks, sloblands at low tides…not all so nice.*

Her eyelids felt so heavy, her weariness so complete that she gave into temptation and closed her eyes. *South Belfast, always so quiet, I can hear the birds in the trees and little else…*

~

The dog yipped and pulled Annie awake with a start.

"Oh!" she said, her heart racing.

The dog leapt, yanking her arm. Annie looked up. A woman leaned over her with a benign but questioning look in her dark blue eyes. A tall woman wearing a nice dress, her silver hair piled up on her head.

"Alright, Biscuit, sit. Hullo? May I help?"

Annie wiped her eyes and focused. She knew this woman. "Lillian?"

"Down, Biscuit. Sit. Aye, I am, but sorry I don't...oh! Annie?" Lillian's mouth fell open a little. "*Annie!* You came! Oh! they *will* be pleased."

Annie tried to stand up and Lillian helped her. "The door was open. I thought the wee dog might need..."

"I only came back to get more film and check on the dog, but I see you've taken care of her. We must hurry. Wait 'till they see you!" Shepherding Annie and the dog, Lillian picked up the case and coat, and brought them inside.

Lillian charged around the kitchen opening and closing drawers. "Robert said the film was in a drawer..."

"Listen, I'm off to use the loo, freshen up, alright?"

"What? Oh, sorry, of course. It's...well, you know where."

Annie picked up her case and carried it to the bathroom. After a lightning-fast bird bath, she changed her under things, stockings and dress, combed her hair and brushed her teeth. Panting from the effort, she looked in the mirror. *If this trip doesn't kill me...*

When she emerged, she found Lillian sitting at the kitchen table.

"Better?"

"I've travelled for days to get here, so aye, much better."

"I'm so sorry to rush you, but I must. It's only over the road, so..."

"What is?"

"The hotel. The hotel where the party is being held. Alright now, Biscuit, be a good girl. Found the film," she said, holding up a few boxes.

"A party? But I'm not dressed for a party."

"You look fine. Come on then." Once in the back alley, Lillian linked her arm in Annie's and marched her forward. "A wee walk to Eglantine, not far, you'll remember, so."

Once through the main doors of the long stretch of brick Victorian hotel façade, Lillian steered Annie past the front desk on one side and the bar entrance on the other. They passed through several lounge areas, wing chairs occupied by chatting guests, and entered a ballroom. Eight large dining tables, elegantly set for eight, occupied the middle of the room. On one side barmen handled a brisk business, on the stage at the front, a piano, music stands and chairs awaited musicians. Fifty or so people milled near the bar, several of them wearing long red academic gowns.

Lillian was relentless in pulling Annie along past the empty tables and into the crowd until they stopped at a table occupied by several middle-aged and elderly people. Lillian's eyes met Meg's and she gestured to the woman at her side. Puzzled, Meg threw a questioning look at Lillian, but only for a split second.

"You've come! Look! Lizzie, look, it's *Annie! It's Annie!*"

An old woman turned her head to follow Meg's pointing hand. Her eyes brightened and her hand flew to her mouth. "My God!"

Struggling to stand and move around the table, Annie's sisters moved to her and enveloped her. The three women stood in a huddle. Meg's head came up first. "Where's David? David!"

"I'll find him," said Lillian, moving quickly.

A minute later, David joined the group. "My God, it *is* Annie! I thought Lillian was pulling me leg. Annie!" He hugged his sister and Annie sobbed into his tweed jacket. She looked up at his face, an old man's, but David's. Close clipped white beard, white hair, but behind the spectacles, those eyes—David's.

Annie could feel the crowd growing around them now, looking at them, talking about them. She turned to see Ella running over, "Grandma! Mommy! It's Grandma!" Behind her, Betty walked to Annie's side and said, "I thought you'd come. I hoped you'd come."

"Could I sit down?" asked Annie. "And could I have a handkerchief?"

Betty took her mother's arm, kissed her cheek and brought her to the table.

Pressing his handkerchief into her hand, Albert said, "I'm Albert, Albert MacKinley, Lillian's nephew."

Annie nodded, unable to speak.

"Here, Annie, in between us now," said Meg.

Annie was sat next to an old man. Bald and blue-eyed, he smiled warmly. "Do you not know me, Annie?"

Her mind reshuffled his face for a moment into a young face. "Ralph! How are ye?"

"Still bald. And you, lass, 'bout ye? Wait 'till you meet me granddaughter. I've met yours. Bonny lasses." Motioning, he called, "Here, Robert!"

A man with curly salt and pepper beard and hair, and wearing a red tie smiled down at her. He bent to kiss her. "It's Robert, Aunt Annie."

"So it is!"

"And here's my girl, the reason we're here." He pulled a tall young woman forward. Radiantly beautiful, green-eyed and one of the young people dressed in a red academic gown with salmon silk trim, Robert introduced her. "Rosie, here's your Grandaunt Annie. From New York."

Rosie stuck her hand out and smiling, she nodded her head and said, "Welcome, Grandaunt Annie from New York. Very pleased to have you here. I've graduated from law school, just this afternoon!"

Tongue-tied and shy in front of this vision of a girl, Annie could only smile and say, "Congratulations."

Albert pushed through the crowd around the table. "Right now, make way for the champagne!"

Behind him, the waitstaff carried bottles in coolers and a large tray of glasses.

"Alright now, charge your glasses, everyone," called Albert. "Robert?"

Robert nodded and waited while glasses were handed around and filled with champagne. Annie did not recognize many standing around the table, but in the middle of them, a smiling Margot raised her glass to Annie.

Robert looked around the group and asked, "Alright? Yes, well, f-first, to our d-darling girl, Rosie...wait, where is J-jo? J-jo? Sorry, wee bit nervous."

A middle-aged woman came and stood next to Robert. Beautifully dressed and attractive, she beamed at Rosie, who kissed her.

"C-congratulations, Rosamund Holly...wait." Everyone laughed. "Where *is* Holly?"

"Here, Robert," a hand went up from the third row of party guests.

"Come forward, Hols," beckoned Robert. "Your mum's not here?"

A small, middle-aged woman made her way forward after the crowd parted. "Aye, she is, sitting at the table over there."

Albert, standing farther back now, called, "Robert, do get on."

The crowd laughed.

"R-right." He took a deep breath and let it out. The group around him tittered. "First, before you feel death creeping on ye, we've g-grand food, endless d-drink, singing and dancing later, so hang on." He took another breath and spoke more quickly. "Alright. I talked to Rosie about what I should say today and we agreed I must first thank and congratulate those here today as much as her, all of whom have helped her through life in one way or another, we agreed that we should ackn...ackn, *thank* everyone, near or far." He peered at the scrap of paper in his hand. "So, b-beginning with those who spent every day getting Rosie to where she is, apart from Rosie herself, we have her mum, Jo, my da, Ralph, her Grandaunt Lizzie, and godparents, Uncle Albert and Aunt Holly, and em," He turned to look, "And in the back, Holly's mum Bertha. Wee Rosie was babysat in a law office, a museum or two and in your homes—a well-travelled bairn, a well-educated wee thing, even before school, thanks to this family. There aren't the words, t-truly, but I know Rosie will find good ones later. Thank you and c-congratulations to you— she did it! C-congratulations to Rosamund Holly Henderson-Bray, Doctor of Law!"

Robert raised his glass and the crowd cheered, "Cheers!" and "To Rosie!".

Albert yelled, "And you, Robert! You forgot yourself."

There was more laughter as Robert smiled. "In all honesty, I did less than the rest of ye, so. Alright, now, I should have mentioned them b-before, sorry, b-but also with us we have Rosie's G-Grandaunts Meg and Lillian, M-Mildred, and Granduncles David and Niall. She spent her summers up on the coast with all of them, and they helped her grow and become the wonderful young woman she is—cheers!" He raised his glass and they drank a toast. "We've Grandaunt Annie here, by some miracle, and C-cousins Betty, Ella, and Margot, all the way from America. So this is for them, cheers!" Robert called "Cheers!" a second time to the laughing crowd.

He took a long sip while waiting for the laughter to die down. "But also a moment for those lost to us, those who c-couldn't be here with us, many who missed Rosie entirely." He stopped to take another deep breath and looking straight at Ralph, said, "So, to my dear mum Florrie." Turning to Jo, he said, "To Rosie's Bray grandparents and her uncle Ronald, lost in action. We remember Albert's p-parents and all the others not with us today—Jinny, Ned and Tom." He raised his glass to Mildred, "To Frank, an uncle to our Rosie, one who taught her to fish, shoot, and other things I shouldn't mention—alright, let's call it the art of b-bartering."

Rosie put her hand on Robert's shoulder and said, "A skill all barristers rely upon!"

Robert kissed Rosie's cheek before taking a moment to himself. He put the slip of paper in his pocket and began to speak again, "After all we've been through—the leaving, the D-Depression, the wars, the loss—those of us still alive, those in one piece, present company excluded..." Robert paused again long enough to hear Albert's hearty laugh, accompanied by Jo's. "We're all here! We're all here, in this room in B-Belfast, together, and isn't that a miracle? Isn't it? So charge your glasses." He stopped to watch the wine being poured. "Alright? Here's to us and the next generations. May we never part for long, ever again. Life is too precious and listen, if you didn't know it before now, you'll well know it today—we love one another. To the future!"

Annie sipped her tea. "This tea is grand."

"Titanic tea," said Lizzie. "Sets you up, aye."

"How is it being here, in this kitchen again?" asked Meg, holding her teacup with two hands.

Annie looked down. "It's like, it's like," her voice cracked.

"Like you never left?"

Annie hesitated before saying, "No. It's better."

Meg reached and put her hand gently on Annie's arm. "It's like that for me, too. Number 34 St. Ives Garden's a special wee house, and I'm so pleased it's still in the family."

Lizzie yawned broadly. "I've to get home to me bed. This house must be full up. You'll have to come home with me, Annie."

"The place is full to the rafters, I'm afraid. I'll call ye a wee cab, shall I?" Meg got up, moved over to the phone on the sideboard and pulled the telephone book open. "Now, where are my glasses? Where's me handbag? Ah—right in front of me face."

"Aye, a cab'll be grand. There's plenty of room in my house. Ye'll come home with me, Annie," said Lizzie. "You'll not catch a wink jammed together. It's not like when we were slender wee girls, you know. Except for you, Meggie. You never gain an ounce."

"Ha! That's a lie," said Meg, glasses on and flipping through the telephone book.

Annie pulled her arms off the table and looked from one sister to the other. "Tomorrow, could we spend the day together, walk over to Moore's Place. See the old place?"

Lizzie said, "It's not there."

"What's not there?"

"Moore's Place. They knocked down the wee houses and built some modern thing that covers the whole street, there's no street there now."

"No Moore's Place?" said Annie, looking pale.

Meg turned back to the table and looked over her glasses at Annie, "Aye, we'll spend time together tomorrow. Just us and we'll fetch David, too, eh? We'll walk down the Sandy Row. A wee dander. You'd like that, wouldn't you? Roseland Place is still there, the house where we all were born, and Aunt Jane's wee house."

Annie smiled and said, "A wee dander with you in Belfast? Aye, I'd love it."

THE END

ABOUT THE AUTHOR

Constance Emmett was born in Brooklyn, New York, where her mother's family landed after leaving Belfast, Northern Ireland. Her debut novel, *Heroine of Her Own Life*, set in Northern Ireland, was published in 2019. *Everything Will Be All Right* is the second novel in the *Finding Their Way Home* series. She lives in a hill town in Western Massachusetts with her wife and their wee dog.

To learn more about Constance Emmett and discover more Next Chapter authors, visit our website at www.nextchapter.pub.

ACKNOWLEDGMENTS

Deepest gratitude to the generations now passed of my mother's Northern Irish family and the inspiration provided by the stories of their complex lives and times. Knowledge of the lives and actions of the men and women whose World War II service at Bletchley Park was secret, and those of the men and women serving in the Royal Navy in other roles was provided by: the BBC's History of World War II; Bletchley Park Museum archives; Sinclair McKay's *The Secret Life of Bletchley Park*, and Dermot Turing's *The Codebreakers of Bletchley Park*. Thanks to the authors of the following resources for the history of Northern Ireland: *Ireland in the 20th Century*, by Tim Pat Coogan; *Nell*, by Nell McCafferty; *A History of Ulster*, by Jonathan Bardon; the RTÉ Archives and The Irish Times. Much gratitude for the inspiration provided by "Everything Will Be All Right," by the late Ulster poet Derek Mahon—a poem that offers the perfect mixture of irony and comfort to readers mired in trouble. My deepest appreciation and gratitude go to my wife, Suzy Q Groden, who, in addition to her many other accomplishments and talents, is a skilled, creative and patient editor. Finally, a note to acknowledge the centenary of the partition of Ireland in 1921, and the cleaving of history and generations that act wrought, and still brings to bear.

Everything Will Be All Right
ISBN: 978-4-82412-269-8

Published by
Next Chapter
1-60-20 Minami-Otsuka
170-0005 Toshima-Ku, Tokyo
+818035793528

7th January 2022

CPSIA information can be obtained
at www.ICGtesting.com
Printed in the USA
LVHW011750260122
709316LV00001B/1

9 784824 122698